I wear my sunglasses at night
So I can, so I can
Watch you weave then breathe your story lines
And I wear my sunglasses at night
So I can, so I can
Keep track of the visions in my eyes

—— COREY HART, "SUNGLASSES AT NIGHT"

(1984)

Chapter One

The air around my mother's face glows white as she starts to die. It's a sparkling white that sucks her in, a lonely white because I know I'm the only one who can see it. I've seen colour around people all my life, but never white. This white seems more permanent than flashes of orange or strokes of pink. This white fills in the space inches above my mother's head in every direction, blinding me, covering her up like she's not there at all. I squint to try and dim it but it shines stronger through my eyelashes, humming its way into my skull.

It hardly hurts anymore, she says then, though her lips don't move and no sound comes out. I'm glad to hear inside her head, but I don't know if she's telling the truth. For the last six months I've been startled by snippets of what other people are thinking — doctors, teachers, strangers — I can't tell if the words are real or if I'm making them up, but when they come from my mother I listen harder. Her thoughts are the only ones I really want to hear, especially now.

I pull the hospital blanket up. Underneath, her arms have weakened and the iciness I felt yesterday in her hands has moved into the room around us. The nurses notice only the temperature from her fever, her matted hair, and the dirt under her nails when she pulls at the skin on her sunken face.

My mother's eyelids flutter open and closed with each gasping breath she takes. When they are open, she seems to be looking past the white light to something only she can see. When they are closed, I feel the invisible part of her pulling away, snapping imaginary strings connecting her to the sky.

I adjust the plant beside my mother's bed, the one with the yellow flowers matching her skin. One nurse said it would be better on the windowsill, but when she stopped coming around I moved it to the bedside table, close enough so it could almost touch my mother's face if she rolled the right way. And now, it almost does. I wish its tiny green fingers would spread and reach out to her, comfort her with the garden smell from its soft faces.

I tell her then that she can go, and I force myself to smile even though I don't mean it. I run my fingertip over the collar of her mint-green hospital gown and then look at the ceiling, wondering if she's up there yet, watching me.

I reach into my denim purse, hanging by a string near the belt loops of my shorts, and pull out the envelope creased in half, coated in the incense she was burning when she wrote it.

"Read this out loud at the very end," she had said. I unfold the single white paper inside, one folded rectangle turns into eight and in the middle, her handwriting. I can only manage a whisper that shakes: "Death is as sure for that which is born, as birth is for that which is dead. Therefore grieve not for what is inevitable."

I wonder: how can these words help me now? Does she really think I can believe something she copied from a book? Or was she just trying to make herself feel better when she wrote this out?

Tears choke the back of my throat and flood my vision. I hear what sounds like my mother's final thought, again from inside her head. *None of it is real*, she says. And then she disappears. She disappears and takes my sister with her. And there's nothing more I need to do to try to save them.

My heart folds itself into a hundred tiny parts, folds until I wonder if it's still there. I clench my teeth and feel tears pushing to get out. But I hold on.

My father comes in right away, like he knows the instant it's safe to return, the moment he will no longer have to see her looking at him. He stands on the far side of the room and says my name, his tie hanging loose around his neck like a weary businessman's. I look at him and nod. He hangs his head so that his hair, dark with grey bits, completely hides his eyes.

———

Later, when they are covering her up, I tell my father, "She hated the hospital."

"I know, Maya." He rubs his jaw, then smoothes his hand up over his forehead and through his hair.

"She shouldn't have been here."

"But they might have been able to save them." He stares into open air.

"Did you even want to save her?"

"There was nothing I could do. It was too early, you know that."

"I meant Mother."

"You knew this was coming, Maya," he says, leaving a second of thick silence. "I guess we should go now." He looks at the floor and taps his right arm on the leg of his black pants, which have become creased from sitting in a hunched over position.

Cold air hits my cheek and I wonder: can Father feel it too?

I put the white piece of paper I have been clutching back into my purse and zip it up, catching a strand of my hair in the zipper, black hair inside a metal mouth. It stings when I yank it out.

My father's shiny shoes squeak on the floor as I follow him down the stairs at the end of the hallway, through the front lobby and out the entrance doors. On the other side, the August sun attacks my eyes. I suck in humid air and cough when I release it.

A news reporter, cameraman, and a small crowd of women wait in the parking lot of the hospital. They have signs that say, "Prayer Can Save a Life," "Tragedy of 1985," and "Marigold, You Are Divine." When we walk by, a woman thrusts a microphone close to my father's lips.

"Mr. Devine, can you give us a quick update on your wife's condition?"

"My wife's condition . . ." he holds me behind him with his arm, ". . . has deteriorated to the point of expiration."

Then he grabs my wrist and pushes us past the lady, bumping her with the side of his body. Someone behind us starts to cry and I turn to look at her: large hips, permed hair, bouncing shoulders. "Be strong, dear!" she shouts out to me. "You have two angels watching over you now!" I don't turn back as we stagger across the concrete. I don't want to tell her the truth, that I'm not sure if Mother ever did enough nice things to become an angel.

When we are seated in my father's car, and the leather seats have attached themselves to my thin legs, he speaks. "I was glad they let you stay in there by yourself. Those damn nurses didn't think you were old enough, but I told them you were a hell of a lot more mature than any eleven-year-old I knew." He reaches out to touch the top of my hand, but then pulls away.

"It was fine," I answer without looking at him. "I'm almost twelve." He turns the key in the ignition and the engine sputters, then stops.

"Fucking piece of shit," my father says and I shoot him a stare that fills the entire inside of the car. "Sorry," he says. I glimpse the colour swirling around his head, brownish and muddy like a river after a storm. He has no idea what he is in the middle of.

He tries to start the car again and this time it goes, winding up to spew cool air into my face from a vent on the dash.

We say nothing, express nothing.

As we drive home, I concentrate on the world through the glass of the window. Trees, buildings, cars, all a blur to me — Saskatoon has never seemed so big. When we drive over the river, I look down into the water at a person in a silver boat. Is he waving at me? Or is he just sitting there, alone, waiting for something to happen?

Emerald Crescent looks the same as when my mother lived there, houses lined up behind green lawns, fathers starting mowers and whackers, cats laid out on the sunny sidewalk. A couple of kids run through a sprinkler in the grass, screeching each time the water sprays the naked parts of their bodies. Their mother sits on the front step, smiling at the rainbows growing in the mist above their heads.

When we reach our house, the windows from my bedroom look like eyes and the door, a closed mouth. We fill the empty driveway and get out; two car doors slam. No one greets us.

"We're not taking it down," I tell my father.

"What?"

"The teepee. It's staying there. Maybe forever." I'm surprised to be feeling sentimental about the stained pieces of tarp holding in the stinky space where my mother gave up on her life.

"Fine, Maya. Whatever you want."

I have not won the argument — teepee or not, my mother is not coming back. And this man I call my father, this man fumbling with the lock on the front door of my house, makes me feel like I have just been orphaned.

"You must be hungry," he says in the kitchen, taking a box of Kraft Dinner out of the cupboard and shaking it in the air. Its rattle scrapes against my backbone, causing me to wince in irritation.

"I don't want that!" I snap at him. "I'll just eat grapes." I look down at the bowl of shrivelled green grapes on the counter, the ones we tried to get my mother to eat days earlier. The ones she touched before she refused them. I pop the grapes into my mouth, ingesting my mother's fingerprints one by one, squirting tartness between my teeth.

"I'm going to sleep for a while then," my father says, throwing the box on the counter and whipping his tie out of his collar. "We'll talk later." His voice shakes a bit when he says it. He hobbles away from me and up the stairs, a defeated man, leaving me with nothing but the smell of his aftershave — cedar and citrus. I wrinkle my face until it fades. I wonder then if it was true what Mother said before she went, that she didn't deserve him. And if he meant what he said back, that he wasn't a very good husband.

My mother's leather mules are staggered on the floor beside my feet. We wanted her to wear them after we dragged her in from the backyard but she insisted on going barefoot. I reach down and hold one in my arms like a baby, running my finger along the side. A shoe without a home. Misplaced. I stick my nose in and breathe the last few steps my mother must have taken as a whole person. I put my hand inside and point the toe to look at me. "Sorry you will be without a foot from now on," I say. "I promise to wear you as often as possible." I nod the mule on my hand and drop it to the ground. I slip my bare toes into both shoes, oversized for my feet, and stomp my way upstairs in my father's invisible footsteps.

I land with bare knees on the pink carpeting of my bedroom and open the white chest in the corner. Inside are my old toys, the stuff Father brought back from extended business trips, the stuff I packed away the day the doctor told us Mother was sick.

I see the scary doll first. The one Father bought for me in Toronto, the one he said looked just like me. I don't think this doll looks like me at all. She stares up at me with her glazed yellow eyes, much creepier than mine, and her stiff black hair. Aunt Leah called her the "Devil Doll" once. I toss her aside to see what else I've kept underneath.

Picking up each toy and placing it on the carpet around me, I repeat the following words: "At least I still have my hairstyle Barbie, at least I still have my Strawberry Shortcake, at least I still have My Little Pony, at least I still have a family of Pound Puppies, at least I still have my Rubik's Cube, at least I still have my 3,000-piece *Mona Lisa* puzzle."

But none of this stuff means anything without my mother. Will I ever have a family again? Be happy? I feel my mouth start to sweat and my eyes grow itchy with sadness.

I imagine that each Barbie, each doll, each glittering pony is reaching out to console me, catching my tears in their little hands, their faces morphing into sympathetic smiles.

Because I'm crying, I almost don't see her standing there. My mother. Like a faded picture in the corner of my eye looking down at me from inside the closet, my hanging clothes creating fabric hair around her see-through head.

And in her open palm she holds my baby sister, small like a Christmas orange, hugging her legs into her tiny chest.

Chapter Two

Aunt Leah dangles her glasses in front of my face, spectacles that line her cheekbones and turn darker when she's in the sun. "Wear these," she says, "so no one will see you crying." She leans towards me and winks, her fuzzy hair dropping in around her face, the sharp corners of her front teeth peeking out from under her lips.

I'm not crying, but wonder why it would matter if someone saw me if I did. She was my mother after all.

The glasses find the bridge of my nose anyway and through the lenses I see a new version of the world. Magnified images drag in and out, screaming the strength of Aunt Leah's prescription. My temples buzz and my eyes beg to be released, but after a minute, they settle and make out what appears to be around me. My mother's oak coffin. My father licking his lips. Rain growing in dark clouds. Cut tulips wilting in a spotlight of sun. Somewhere, someone burns a fire.

The fifteen people around the grave have a combined mass of grey circling their heads, spongy grey that wanes and lifts with their heavy breath. I can hear their inner voices, some asking why, some wishing they had brought an umbrella, some worrying about what will happen to me and my father. And then Trudie Roughen, the woman who called herself my mother's best friend during the last six months of her life, steps out in her sticky red lips, hair-sprayed bangs, and floral sundress. She makes my mother sound like a pair of shoes she once owned.

"Marigold made me feel comfortable and eased much of the pain I was feeling," she says. "She had such a gift. She helped me see things in a different way. It is comforting to know that she is finally free from all her suffering." She steps back slowly, into the line beside her son, Elijah, with slicked back hair and a suit jacket that's too tight. He is looking down and playing with the fraying Velcro on his digital watch. I want to go over to him. I want to thank him for the bees, but I know I can't. I try not to stare at him, but I can feel him there like he's ten feet tall.

If I close my eyes behind these darkened glasses, will I disappear?

Mrs. Roughen has decided to move away from Saskatoon. I don't want her to take Elijah with her, but she is. They are going to live in Toronto now that Mrs. Roughen is finally divorcing Mr. Roughen. To think how she lectured my mother on how to make a good marriage, and now she is divorcing and my mother is heading into the ground. I panic when I remember they are putting my mother in the earth. I never wanted that. Invisible ants race up my spine and chase each other around the base of my neck, burning a hole. I imagine myself racing from my spot beside my father and throwing myself onto the coffin we picked out, scraping at the lip with my fingernails until the wood grows thin enough to push through, climbing in and lying beside her, kissing her face, stroking her earlobes, and wrapping each stiff arm around me.

People start to walk away. They are lowering the box into the earth, without me in it. There are some things that even tinted specs cannot hide. Softly, to try and block out the sobs and whimpers from those around me, I start to sing a song I learned last year in grade five: "My eyes are blind, I cannot see, I have not brought my specs with me."

My father, standing on my right, is the only one who can hear me singing. He jabs me in the ribs with his elbow, lightly, telling me to be quiet.

But I don't stop, I can't. "My eyes are dim, I cannot see, I have not brought my specs with me."

"Maya, I'm serious, cut it out," he says.

I finish so only I can hear, "I haaaaavvvve noottt brought . . . my specs . . . with . . . me."

I turn twelve on the day after my mother's funeral, which takes a lot of the fun out of having a birthday. My father still carts a cake home from the IGA that has "Happy Birthday, Maya" written in red in the middle, but there is no singing. My father's younger sister, Aunt Leah, age twenty-one, is here to help us again, so she cuts three pieces of cake and puts them each on white saucers for us. She licks her fingers after each piece drops to the plate and my father gives her a disgusted look. Then, my father, my Aunt Leah, and I hold our forks and look down at the chocolate clumps in silence.

In September I go back to school. On the second day, I count the flattened plops of chewing gum on the step out behind the school. I do it to appear to be content and to keep myself busy throughout recess. After I have finished counting them — twelve, like my age — I begin to categorize them in my mind. Four pink (most likely strawberry), three blue (blueberry or blue raspberry), and the other five black from the weight and dirt of people's sneakers.

"Maya, when you pretend to look busy, you just look like more of a loser." It's Jackie — friend turned enemy.

"Piss off," I say to her in my straightest, most disinterested voice.

She walks towards me with one hand on her bony hip. Her white blouse has been tied in a knot and her belly button peaks out at me. Her denim skirt hangs on by what seems like only a few threads, exposing the white of her legs. Her penny loafers scrape on the cement as she moves closer.

"What's the matter, Maya, got no friends this year? Maybe you should try attending class sometime." I take this as a shot at my mother's illness.

"Jackie," I say, letting my mouth gape open after her name falls out. "Unless you want me to tell your new friends how you wet your sleeping bag at my house last year, piss off like I told you the first time."

From Jackie's mouth, "Go to hell!" and from inside her head, *Did anyone just hear her say that?* She turns her head to monitor the backs of what I like to call her "Superstar Gang" — her new friends, three girls with bangs teased four inches off their foreheads and neon scarves tied around their ponytails.

At first I thought that hearing what people were thinking was the only good thing that came out of my mother's sickness. But now, I would give up this strangeness for just a glimpse of my mother. And not her ghost from the closet, either. I mean the real thing.

I've been hearing things off and on in short snippets. Not all the time, and not when I try to. The voices usually sneak up on me while I am reading *People Magazine* in line at the grocery store, or riding my bike past a flock of old ladies. And some of the things I hear have gotten monotonous, annoying even, like listening to a song you hate played over and over. I don't mind hearing about why my father hates his boss, or how Aunt Leah wished her thighs were less lumpy, but with school back on, I could do without listening to Mr. Wigman debate whether or not to shave his back. I just want to concentrate on science class.

"You just keep your mouth shut, Maya," Jackie yells. She walks back to meet her gang. She was never this loud when we walked home together last year. I used to think she was clever and elegant, which is a great mix, especially for a girl.

"See ya, Jackie," I say, mainly to spite her, as if pretending we were friends again would be the biggest insult she received all week. I return my attention to the chewing gum and think about scraping it off with my banana clip before the bell rings.

My father makes me come home after school to an empty house. He gave me my own key to let myself in because he works most nights until around 8:00. Sometimes I like having the house to myself but sometimes I get lonely. I spend a lot of time trying on

13

my mother's clothes and reading her books, especially the *Bhagavad Gita*, which I have gotten as good as her at pretending I understand. When I read the fancy words that make no sense, I feel like I am having a conversation with my mother because she herself was a fancy word that made no sense. As I read, I smell her aromatherapy bottles, the ones meant to heal her, and dab the scents in my hair. The girl who brought them to Mother told me that it takes something like five pounds of plant material to make one drop of these oils, which makes them precious enough to wrap in a towel and keep in the top drawer of my dresser. Sandalwood to help me think, lavender if I can't sleep, orange to be happy. I wear the orange one a lot but try not to waste it. I know my father won't buy more when these run out.

My father works as a senior agent for Shining Star Talent Agency across the river, where he is in charge of finding "gigs" for actresses with blond hair, white teeth, and large breasts. He gets TV shows, fashion shows, and fancy trips to Toronto for beautiful-looking people hidden from everyone out in Saskatchewan. Sometimes they travel from Manitoba to see him, if they have something special. He says that as well as having a certain look, they have to be able to act. But I know what it takes to make it in Hollywood, or Toronto for that matter.

When my father comes home from the office, he has talked himself out. I once heard him think that he was sick of blathering on all day and I guess that's why he has nothing left for me but grunts and weak smiles. We sit across from each other at the table while he eats the takeout dinner he brought home with him. I usually save some of his leftovers for my own dinner the next day. Sometimes I can tell that he's trying. He asks me how school was, I tell him fine, he says what did you learn, I say not much, and then we stare at each other some more. These are occasions when I can't hear a word from inside his head, and I want to more than anything.

One day after work, my father tells me that he thinks I would be perfect for a shampoo commercial he is casting. "What with your shiny hair and gorgeous canary eyes, you will light up the screen."

I have never thought my hair was gorgeous. When I try to run my fingers through it, they get stuck. But I guess with the right shampoo it could be better?

"What would I have to do?" I ask him.

"Well, we'd have to audition you first. And then if you get it, I would come with you for the shoot."

"The shoot?" I say.

"Yes, when they film the commercial."

"Oh, okay. I guess." I am not sure about my father's plans to combine office and home life, but am comforted by his attempt. And maybe he's right; maybe I would look good on the screen. If nothing else I can pretend to be beautiful.

I have to take a day off school to go to the audition, which I know will please Jackie and her "Gang," forever on the lookout for ammunition. Jackie hears me tell Mr. Wigman that I will be absent tomorrow and that my father has written a note.

"Got a hot date?" Jackie shouts from the back of the room. Giggles spread throughout the classroom.

"For your information, I have an audition," I say and realize that everyone in the class has stopped reading their math textbook to listen. "I am going to be in a commercial."

15

"What are they selling? Dog food?" Jackie barks back.

"Ladies, that's enough," Mr. Wigman interjects. "Jackie, leave Maya alone." Mr. Wigman pats me on the arm and signs my note to take to the office. I feel the combined gaze of everyone in the class on the back of my head as I turn to leave.

Before going to the audition, my father and I stop at his office to pick up forms and a school picture of me that he had blown up on the computer. "Your headshot," he proclaims, shoving it inside a manila envelope. The woman who gave it to him concerns me the most. Long black hair that touches my father's arm when she hands him the photo, almond-shaped eyes that were not born in Saskatoon, that's for sure, and a curvy figure wrapped in a black dress and surrounded by yellow light that weaves itself up and down inches from her body. She introduces herself as Consuela, only my father calls her Connie. She looks like a flamenco dancer, but younger than any I have seen on television.

"It's wonderful to finally meet you, Maya," Connie says when my father leaves the room for paper clips. She sounds like the tall guy in the white suit on *Fantasy Island*. "Your father talks about you all the time." I nod and look at the sleeve of my striped shirt. The cuff seems to have moved further up my arm since I last wore it. "You know, your father is a pretty important guy. He has achieved a lot — the other agents learn much from him. He works hard so you can have everything you need."

"I know," I say. Then Connie smoothes her finger over her bottom lip and puts her hand on my back.

"I am so sorry about your mother, Maya," she says, pronouncing every one of her syllables with distinct beats. For a second I remember what it's like to have a woman comfort me — anyone, for that matter — and submit myself to her pretend niceness by nodding again. My bottom lip protrudes and tears prick the insides of my eyeballs.

My father returns with my paperwork fastened together. He's developed a résumé for me that includes my age, height, weight, hair colour, and eye colour. When we leave, he thanks Connie by looking straight into her eyes and smiling, something he must save for the office.

The audition passes quickly and is far less glamorous than I would have expected. My father talks to a lady with a clipboard and she lets me into the room before any of the other girls waiting. Inside the room, two men with matching grey hair and warm red light shooting out around their faces sit behind a table. They ask me how old I am and where I go to school and that kind of stuff. Mostly they just want to look at me. And then they make me read something off a piece of paper. "Shinesse helps me be the girl that everyone notices." I say this straight-faced while scooping hair off my forehead like they told me, and they thank me for my time, to which I respond, "No problem. I like to take the day off school."

My father and I go to McDonald's for lunch. I eat a Happy Meal while he sucks Coke up a straw and moves around in his seat. "So you think it went well then?" he asks me for the tenth time since we left the audition.

"I don't know. What is 'well'?" I say, peeling the pickles off my hamburger and throwing them to the corner of my tray.

"You're not going to eat those?" he asks.

"Why should I?"

"I don't know, I just thought . . ."

"What does Connie do at your work?"

"Connie? Oh, she's an agent, just like me. Only she's just out of school, so she doesn't have a lot of clients yet. We're working with her."

"I bet you are." I fling a pickle slice onto the floor.

"Pick that up!" he says, crossing his arms, and I do.

It takes the Shinesse shampoo company two weeks to contact my father about my audition. He calls me right after he hears the news. It is a quarter to seven in the evening and I am at home inhaling patchouli essential oil from a tissue, rubbing my fingers over my mother's green healing stone, and watching *Jeopardy!* Martha Pronk from Mississippi has just answered two questions from the category "Not as It Appears."

ANSWER: *The appearance of a sheet of water in a desert or on a hot road caused by the refraction of light by heated air.*

QUESTION: *What is a mirage?*

and

ANSWER: *False contractions experienced after the third month of pregnancy but before labour.*

QUESTION: *What are Braxton Hicks?*

"You weren't their first choice," my father says through the receiver. "But the girl they picked first has come down with a case of head lice, which of course makes it difficult."

"So I was second choice?"

"They offered you the job. You got it, kid." My father announces this like I just won a shopping spree at the Saskatoon Centre, but for me it's only good for another day away from school.

Chapter Three

Dr. Peacock, with his bald head and beady eyes, sat across a desk from my mother, my father, and me. His teeth were clenched and his lips puckered while he scanned the papers.

Test results.

He was sucking on a cough drop, which clunked against his teeth as he moved it back and forth and wafted cherry menthol in our direction. Every few seconds he would either cough or inhale phlegm from his nose into his throat and swallow it down with a gulp.

It was March of 1985 and I was eleven years old.

Just when I was about to say that a sick doctor was not what my mother needed, I heard three simple words, thoughts from the inside of his head: *She's a goner.*

I looked up to see the doctor's face, his lips still glued together, silver stethoscope hugging his neck, still interpreting my mother's file.

He had yet to open his mouth to speak.

My heart slapped me from inside, my fingers numbed, and my shoulders rose up. I wanted to run away. I had grown used to seeing colours around people, but that was the first time I had heard what someone was thinking. I didn't know where the words came from or why I was the one to hear them. Were these words what they meant to say? Maybe what they were afraid to say?

So as it happened, I knew before anyone else in my family that my mother was dying. But I let Dr. Peacock tell them. It was easier on me that way.

"Mrs. Devine," he said, looking at my mother.

"Marigold. Please call me Marigold."

"Marigold. We have the results of your biopsy and it's not good."

"Everything can be good if you alter your perception," my mother said. Her insincere optimism caused my father to roll his eyes and throw his chin up towards the ceiling. I reached out and grabbed my mother's soft fingers but she turned her head away, sending me the scent of her lavender shampoo.

"It's a good thing you decided to come see me," Dr. Peacock said.

"The bleeding didn't seem normal," my father said and my mother looked at the floor.

Straight-faced, the doctor told us, "It's cancer." What is it about those words? Three syllables that can put a stop to everything you once thought true. Take your life and turn it inside out, into a dream world. "Stage four cervical." The doctor didn't blink when he said it. He looked straight at my mother's forehead with an unwavering gaze while my father shifted in his seat. "Now, we'll have to do a series of scans to figure out how much it's spread."

My mother closed her eyes.

"It could already be in your liver and maybe other organs." My mother stood up and walked towards the light at the window, shuffling her sandals over the polished floor. "It will be your choice to do radiation, which will only slow things down a bit." A fluorescent bulb hummed at us from the ceiling. Then, from inside the doctor's head, *This never gets easier*. And then, *Maybe I'll have chicken noodle soup for lunch. Yeah, that's it, chicken noodle.*

—————————

The first time they met, my mother spilled an entire foam cup of hot chocolate on my father's ski jacket — or so it goes when my father tells the story. In her version, he was the one to spill on her, black coffee that covered her Hudson's Bay parka and dripped onto her suede boots. When I imagine that moment — one of them wet, one of them apologizing — I picture a gigantic bubble encasing them both, secluding them, protecting them as they once were.

What I do know is that they were nineteen when they met. And that they were both students at Trent University in Peterborough. My father was studying marketing, and my mother, English literature. I've heard my father say he never understood my mother's love of British Romantic fiction, but because he was trying to "woo her," he tried to listen when she nattered on about it.

Around age seven, I found an old copy of Jane Austen's *Pride and Prejudice* in a box in the basement. The dog-eared pages were covered in highlights and scratchy notes in the margins explaining important passages. The first line of chapter one was still glowing from pink highlighter: *It is a truth universally acknowledged, that a single man in possession of a good fortune, must be in want of a wife.*

"Is this yours?" I asked my mother.

"It was, at one time," she said without flinching, "when I was still in university." She was folding bathroom towels, straight from the dryer, still hot and radiating Downy softener.

"How come you never read it anymore?"

She looked at me with sad eyes, collapsed a towel to her chest and wrapped her arms around it. "Maya," she said. "People change. Things happen that change them and there is nothing you can do about it."

I don't know a lot about my parents' courtship. Only that they walked around attached to each other like spider monkeys (my Aunt Leah told me that) and that my father only had eyes for my mother. I also know that my father was the only one of them to finish university. And that she broke his heart before he married her.

There's a picture my father keeps in the top drawer of his desk: he in a black graduation gown and flat hat with matching expression, and she, looking so much smaller than him, meeker. Her strawberry-tinted locks shelter the baby version of me in her arms. Black tufts of hair sprout from the top of my head. Her eyes rest on dark circles. Both of them look at the sky in opposite directions. Or maybe at other people walking by in the crowd?

Shortly after my mother died, I spent hours looking at this photo. Hoping if I concentrated hard enough, I could get my mother to smile. And maybe, just maybe, reach over and hold my father's hand.

On the day we found out about her cancer, my father had tears in his eyes on the way home from the hospital. Round tears that wouldn't fall, perched on the edges of his bottom lids (I could see them in the rearview mirror). As he drove, turned corners, stopped at stop signs, eased on the brake, he stroked the steering wheel with his hands and muttered like he was angry with an invisible person sitting on the dashboard. "I can't understand how this could be happening, to you of all people. Things were finally starting to get better, normal . . . We were a family . . . What did we ever do to deserve this?" At the time, I thought it was my mother he was angry with, but I know now that you can't really blame someone for getting cancer — even if she may have wished it on herself.

My mother didn't say anything to him when he talked. She must have known she could never find an answer to his questions. She just looked out the window, with one hand's fingertips perched on her chapped lips.

———————

My father always made enough money so that my mother didn't need to do anything except look after me. I went with her everywhere and even when they asked, she was not interested in get-togethers with the other stay-at-home mothers on our street. She was committed to her eternal quest to busy herself. She made lists: what to buy, where to go, what to say, what to wear. She made lists of what lists to make when we got home. I would carry them for her in my pockets, but she never looked at them again.

When I was six, we started visiting a Hindu temple in the

afternoons, usually on the days she had yelled at Father for something like forgetting to take the garbage to the curb, or leaving a tea bag in the sink. The temple was a strange place for a part-Irish woman to bring her daughter. Saskatoon had a population of about two hundred Hindu families. Prairie Hindus. They had taken over an old church to hold prayer service, and though Mother and I were without religion, they always let us in when we arrived. Dark-skinned men nodded and touched our shoulders in greeting, woman wrapped in saris pointed to where our shoes should go.

My mother said that with my black hair and olive skin, I almost looked like I belonged with them. This puzzled me, but the promise of a big family was tempting, even back then, and especially since I knew only a few relatives aside from my mother and father: my father's sister, Leah, and his parents who flew out from Prince Edward Island once when I was five. Their faces, though warm and smiling, had stayed blurry in my mind.

In the large room of the Hindu temple called the nata-mandir, Mother and I would kneel down in our sock feet. Incense burned from long sticks and short cones, tracing squiggles of smoke through the air. Cloths of red, white, and gold covered the walls, along with pictures of men with elephant noses and ladies with too many arms sitting on flowers. And at the front was an altar, blessed food, and bottles of milk. Old ladies grabbed the bottles with their boney knuckles to sprinkle the pictures, entranced in their worship.

In this temple my mother prayed, her head bobbing like she was reliving her past, trying to wipe out stagnant guilt. She went away for a while when she prayed, swaying forward and back, chanting words to herself. Afraid she might cause herself to disappear from

so much concentration, I stayed by the door with the other children. We danced to scratchy Hindi songs from a ghetto blaster, twirling, swinging our arms through sandalwood air that stuck in our clothes.

Each time we left the temple, Mother stayed quiet for a long time. I agreed not to tell Father where we had been. She didn't have to tell me he wouldn't understand.

I didn't go to school until grade three. Mother home-schooled me the best she could. Part of this schooling included visiting the local library to listen to speeches with titles like "Making a Fortune by Age Thirty," "Overcoming Anxiety," "Growing the Perfect Garden," or "The A–Z of Filing Your Tax Return." Instead of listening, I watched the colours dancing around the bodies of the speakers — red, orange, sometimes green, rarely blue — coating the air, spinning, whirling, popping like flashbulbs. I reached for my mother only when the colour was black and sturdy, clinging in a solid mass around the head and shoulders of the speaker (like the guy who once presented on "How to Make a Million Dollars Without Working"). Though she starkly told me I was imagining things when I told her what I saw, she tried her best to console me, nodding and patting my hand without looking away from the person at the podium. She always acted this way when I told her about the colours, and her denials were almost enough to convince me it wasn't real. Almost enough, but not quite.

Library speeches gave way to yoga classes and walks on nature trails, petting stray dogs and collecting flowers to display in vases on our kitchen table. Sometimes, on Tuesday evenings, my mother snuck us into the local AA meeting, telling the tall and mustached organizer that she was trying to admit her problems and that my support was

the only thing that could help her do it. The first time she said this, the man nodded his pointy chin and stroked her gently on the arm. When we sat down in the circle I saw I was the only child there, but it didn't really matter. The alcoholics fascinated me with their stuttering voices and interesting twitches. My mother listened intently when they talked about the people they had hurt, the lies they had told, and the messes they had made of their lives. She even stood up once herself. I was nine and sipping orange water out of a spongy cup, feeling my eyelids numbing with sleepiness, when she got up, stood in the centre of the circle with her shoulders back, and said in a loud voice, "My name is Marigold Devine and I am an alcoholic."

When she spoke, heads turned to look at me sitting just outside the circle. With their heads cocked to the side, the alcoholics sent me looks that mixed sympathy with relief — like I had just lost my first tooth and the blood was tripping down my chin. I smiled back at them without showing teeth and slumped down in my chair.

My mother never drank, but she told me she envied those who could forgive themselves for their mistakes. I was almost ten when I realized that drinking too much was actually a bad thing. I met my friend Jackie's alcoholic father in the kitchen, and with the reek of his breath and the madness in his eyes, I knew almost immediately.

The thing I hated doing the most with my mother was standing on street corners and handing out flyers she had made. This usually happened after she and Father had a fight, or she had cried after dinner for no reason at all. The flyers she made, about the size of postcards, were copied on every colour and had drawings of rainbows, lotus flowers, or smiles that my mother had sketched. Along the outsides or in the middle, my mother would write quotes from

the *Bhagavad Gita*, her favourite book, a Hindu epic poem. It was part of the *Mahabharata* written thousands of years ago in India. She said she chose the parts she thought could help others, but I think now that they were the parts that made her seem like a better person for having chosen them, lines like "That which is can never cease to be; that which is not will not exist," and "Abandoning desires which shake the mind — finds in his soul full comfort for his soul."

I don't know if she believed the words or understood them, but she tried hard to pretend she did. When she put the papers in my hands, I would squint my eyes until the sentences were too fuzzy to read.

Our flyers confused people. Often they just stared blankly or refused to take one, especially if it was winter and a hand removed from pocket risked instant frostbite, but when they talked to us it was the worst. The conversation usually went something like this:

To my mother: "What are you doing?"

My mother: "Spreading a message of reaching God's love through the wise words of the *Bhagavad Gita*."

[Pointing at me]: "And why is she with you?"

"My daughter is equally committed to a simple and self-aware existence. I think it is important that children be brought up in an environment of simplicity and surrender in order to find their authentic selves."

I would study my feet, rolling my loafers or boots up on their sides, trying to fly out of my body.

And then they told us how they really felt with something like, "You are a freak and a child abuser."

I couldn't understand what they meant by freak, or child abuser

for that matter. At that time in my life, I beheld my mother with the eyes of an ant staring at the sun. Everywhere I looked, she was all I could see. And as far as I could tell, no child was being abused, especially not me.

My father represented a pebble in my mother's smoothly oiled wheel of forward motion. He talked to us very little, but sometimes, if he had a good day at work, he would sit me on his knee when he returned home and bump his leg up and down so I bounced. He said his knee was a horse and he was taking me on a big adventure where I was in charge of where we went. I choose to fly past camels in dusty deserts, jump off waterfalls, and stroll down the streets of Paris. He never argued with my choice of destination, he just smiled and said, "Well, Missy, I think that can be arranged." My mother was never part of these journeys. She watched us from the other room as she read from one of her books, her face expressing a look of cautious concern. Though I loved my knee rides, they were rare, especially as I grew older and too big for him to bounce. "How about you just explain your adventure to me," he would say then. After a while we didn't travel together at all.

My mother encouraged him to work as much as possible, telling him that I needed new clothes and that it would only get worse from here. The way she looked down when she passed him in the hallway and stayed busy in the kitchen until just after he left in the morning made me think that she preferred him out of the house anyway. My father appeased her by working long days and nights, calling home before bed to say he wouldn't be making it for dinner. He worked to provide for my mother, but most of the time my mother was too busy to notice.

And then there were her other times. When her spirit got sucked down into the ground and buried with her own hands. When she strayed even further from the essence of the inspirational messages she handed out. When she was asked by those around her, "What are we going to do about your lousy mood?" During those times, her silent meditations seemed to be conjuring spells that would make both my father and me disappear.

———

After her scans, the doctor told her the cancer had already spread to her liver and pancreas. He said she had between six months and a year to live.

I believe now that people will create their lives based on what you tell them. If you tell a kid he is stupid from when he is really young, well, when the time comes to prove himself on a test in school, his thoughts about being stupid will be just about all he can remember. Such is the case with Mother. My mother lacked faith in herself, unless someone reminded her she should have it. If that doctor had told her that she had cancer but chances were good she would last another sixty-four years on earth, she probably would have.

Chapter Four

"I think people choose to be sad," Aunt Leah said to me as I pulled my mother's clean underwear from the dryer. It was March Break, about a week after Mother's diagnosis. I said nothing then, but over the years I've thought of many comebacks that would have shut her up, including, "Well, why don't you choose to go home" and "Just like you choose to be ugly?"

Instead, I stuck out my bottom lip and nodded as she squatted beside me over her thick calves. Her short hair had recently been permed and hair-sprayed and her eyelids were coated with blue shadow. By then it was no big deal for me to see colour around people and that day, Aunt Leah's was orange. Citrus swirls of light danced around her head and bounced off her shoulders as she insisted on continuing, "At some point, you have to make a choice: do I get out of bed today or do I stay in and feel sorry for myself? If you choose not to get up, there must be something you are getting out of it." I just stared at her. "I mean, it must be satisfying some part of you." I looked away and she said, "I hope you will always make the right choice, Maya."

"I'll try," I said, tilting my head and rolling my eyes. I carried the laundry basket on my bony hip to the kitchen, then dumped the clothes onto the table to fold.

My grandmother had flown Leah in from PEI for an extended weekend. They probably remembered how my father complained about taking time off work the last time Mother wouldn't get out of bed. And since my grandparents couldn't make the trip by car or plane because of my grandfather's heart condition and my grandmother's allegiance to him, they could never be there themselves. Aunt Leah was often around to help us out when my mother had periods of sadness. But this time was different. This time everyone knew that her sadness was permanent.

My aunt's twenty-year-old mentality meant she felt a duty to lecture me with her own faulty revelations. She was also trying to decide whether to go to university the following fall — which seems so petty now in light of the news we had just received.

I worked hard while my mother slept, which I secretly resented, especially after considering the idea that people can make a choice not to be sad if they want to badly enough. I was starting to think that my mother didn't have much of an idea at all of what she wanted to do next, and that's why she stayed in bed hoping everything would go away.

When the dishes were done and the cobwebs had been dusted off my mother's bud vases, I sat on the floor of the living room and flipped through her books. I had taken out some of her old novels from university: *The Mysteries of Udolpho* by Ann Radcliffe, *A Simple Story* by Elizabeth Inchbald, Mary Wollstonecraft's *Maria; Or, the Wrongs of Woman*, and the copy of *Pride and Prejudice* by Jane Austen. Each one had my mother's neat handwriting in the top right corner of the first page, her old name traced out in faded pencil: *Marigold McCann*. Together the books represented random snippets of who she was, a blueprint of her life that I would turn to for comfort throughout my own.

"What'cha reading?" Leah asked that afternoon while more laundry was churning.

"Nothing," I said. A lie, of course.

"Mind if I listen to some music?" She plunked her ghetto blaster down on the shag carpet in front of me. Before I could answer she had turned it on. A synthesized rock beat rose from the metal box, and a male voice began to punch out words through what sounded like puckered lips. I was instantly transfixed by the sound of him.

I wear my sunglasses at night, so I can, so I can . . .

"It's Corey Hart," she said as the music played. I nodded. Something fresh bubbled up inside me.

While she's deceiving me

She cuts my security

Has she got control of me . . .

"He's good!" I said, putting down the book. "Where did you get this?"

"At the music store. Duh!" she said, moving her padded hips.

"You've never heard of Corey Hart? Where have you been, under a rock?" I bobbed my head slightly to the music, which made Aunt Leah laugh. "The kid has some taste after all," she said, clearing a path through the books on the floor and grabbing me by both hands to dance.

"I have style," I said, swivelling my hips and flipping my hair upside down quickly to give it body.

"Nice moves, kid," Aunt Leah said. "Take a look at the tape, he's totally hot!" She handed me the cover, which I took and peered at. I danced beside her, a stiff, awkward sort of dance, with the picture of Corey in my hand and my butt swaying provocatively. I danced to a song I had never heard. For a moment, I forgot to remember what I needed to do to be happy and instead I just was.

That is, until she screamed.

My mother, from the top of the stairs. It sounded like rusty nails and scratched on my spine.

"Shut up down there!" The words melded together in a high pitched cry that stunned me. I turned my head to see her leaning on the banister beside the top step. She was naked from the waist down except for her underwear, and her tangled hair hung loose around her face, the long slant of her nose creating the impression of a witch on the prowl. Like the other times, it was apparent that the sweetness I tried to find in her was gone entirely, that she had been tossed into an evil pit that would take her weeks to climb out of.

"Sorry, Mother," I said. Aunt Leah shrank down onto the couch and pressed stop on the tape player. She had the look on her face of being stuck between two fat ladies on the bus, and we sat in silence for almost ten minutes after.

When we felt it was safe to move again, I continued reading my mother's books and Aunt Leah skimmed through a Dalhousie University course calendar. She rarely stopped to read any of the course descriptions but instead seemed to be studying the posed pictures of students around campus (I could see them over her shoulder). Each fake student beamed at the camera, looking like they might lose consciousness at any moment, high on the fumes from their new textbooks. Though these pictures were meant to motivate prospective students, Aunt Leah's face remained somber.

When I think back on her reading that calendar, it makes me wish her parents had sent her to university. It wasn't fair that just because she was her parents' afterthought they didn't support her financially like they did my father. I don't think that school is necessary for everyone, but I could tell that day that deep down she wanted nothing more than to be one of the shiny students on those pages.

My father returned from work by seven, a deluxe pizza greasing through the box onto his white shirt. He let the front door shut slowly so the click would not wake my mother or inform her of his presence. He knew it was simpler if he just stayed out of my mother's way entirely, which is why he may have been working that day, a Saturday. He transmitted his messages to her through me.

"Maya, take these slices up to your mother," he said, lifting two pieces from the box onto a white plate. "No matter how she tries to convince you, tell her she has to eat. Her body needs the strength to try and fight this."

"Okay," I said, taking the plate. I liked to think that my father had a plan that was so intricate he didn't take the time to explain it to me.

"Leah, would you mind pouring some fruit punch for Marigold?"

"Sure, Steve," Leah said, hopping off the countertop. We worked together like we were part of a complicated sting, the goal being to appease my mother and make her seem well again.

As I passed my father with the plate and fruit punch balancing on an oak tray laid across my arms, he put his hand on my head.

"Hang in there, Maya." I smiled at him for saying it. It reminded me that my real mother was not missing, only hidden behind some sort of mysterious monster who was sure to leave if we ignored him. Or fed him pizza.

Step to step I balanced the tray, held my breath, and told my own stomach to stop punching me from inside. There was no time to be hungry.

"Mother?" I said from outside the door. "I'm coming in now." I opened the door and was smacked by the smell of sweat and moisture. My stomach tightened with nausea at the odour. I had smelled it before and as much as I wanted to help her then, I couldn't get over the thought circling in my head, that my mother was choosing this. That if she cared about me at all, she would choose to get up, try to get well and be my mother again.

"Maya? Maya is that you?" I could tell from the crackle in her voice that she had been crying. "Maya, I am sorry to do this to you — you deserve better than this."

"I just want you to be happy again," I said. I felt my way through the dark, put the tray down on her bedside table, and swallowed down tears loitering in my throat.

"I know," she said. Red swam around her head, intensified by the black air. Red interspersed with green streaks, a tortured mosaic emanating above her. Swirling, diving, festering. I would have thought the confused colours were a masterpiece if I hadn't seen them before. "I promise I will make it up to you, Maya," she said as I handed her a slice of pizza. She sat up a bit and as my eyes adjusted I could see that she was wearing the top she wore to the temple: purple cotton with tiny lilies, scooped neckline, and a small bow on the collar. Her bare legs scissored out from the ruffled sheets.

"Let's open the drapes a little."

"Maybe tomorrow," she said quietly, which gave me hope, but then her voice got louder and more accusing. "What are you looking at?"

She could see me following the colour above her head in the dark.

"Nothing."

"Keep your mind in reality, Maya. Look at me!"

"I'm looking at you."

"Good. Now leave, please."

In the kitchen later, Aunt Leah and I nibbled on pizza crust while my father tried to repair a broken burner on the stovetop.

"Must be tough, eh, kid?" Aunt Leah asked, pepperoni stuck between the tiny gap in her two front teeth.

"What must be tough?"

"Living with her."

"No, actually, it's not hard at all. It's very easy because she's my mother and I love her." I stormed to the other side of the kitchen with my arms crossed at the elbows. Without turning my head, I delivered the final jab, "Don't you know that people do the best they can?!" The words had originally been from my mother's mouth, on a day she had called my father an asshole for missing her dinner of shepherd's pie. The day my father had just sighed, closed his eyes for a minute, and taken a chug of milk right out of the carton before going upstairs to sleep. She told me then that she had only reacted the best she knew how at that particular moment. And as Leah and I sat in the kitchen that day and my mother rotted away in her darkness, she was doing it again.

That night, when I heard my mom's sniffles from her darkened bedroom, I stole Leah's cassette and dreamed about what it would be like to have Corey Hart as my own boyfriend. I studied the curves of his face with a flashlight under my sheets and wrote out the details of our entire wedding on a piece of foolscap:

Outside ceremony so we can smell cedar and grass.

Small gathering of close friends and family.

No veil, only flowers in my hair.

Bare feet.

I would relegate Aunt Leah to helping the caterers in the kitchen. My father would walk me down a grassy aisle with rose petals, and Corey would be waiting at the end with shiny skin, professionally greased hair, and a black pair of sunglasses — the kind where you can't see the person's eyes. I wouldn't need to see his eyes because I would know they were beaming with love for me.

You've got it made with the guy in shades, oh no.

And my mother, my mother would sit in the front row, wearing a flowing white gown, with the sun tickling the smile spread across her tranquil face.

Chapter Five

A pimple blisters on the side of my father's chin. Its presence is a mystery. Maybe it grew from the stress of taking a day off work, or the unexpected October heat. Either way it shouldn't be there, not on a man his age. Don't adults ever outgrow those things? To distract myself I rest my head on the car window frame and watch as the side of the road flies by in a blur. Now that we are out of the city, I can see for miles. Or kilometres, which Mr. Wigman has told my class is more Canadian. Jagged green machines spin to create circles of hay that dot the fields like gifts waiting to be opened. The road ahead of us extends so straight I could nod off from the monotony.

Even though he won't go to the office today, my father still wears his brown pinstriped suit. He uses one hand to drive and in the other hand he grips a coffee mug, covered with a plastic lid so nothing spills out onto our laps. I breathe twice as fast to inhale the French roast wafting out of his cup. The engine pings with each rotation of the car's wheels, but if my father hears the sputtering he pretends not to notice. I try to tune in to his thoughts and am met with a steel wall, cold and unwelcoming, shutting me out with no mercy. It should be different because I'm his daughter.

"Have a nap if you want to," my father says. The digital clock on the maroon dashboard between us says 7:45 a.m. and I have just watched the sun blossom out of the shiny fields of wheat around us.

"I'm not tired," I say. I prefer to watch nothing as we speed along. Watching nothing gives me relief.

My shampoo commercial shoot is to start at 9 a.m. We travel the prairie highway on route from Saskatoon to Regina. My hair, matted from sleep, drapes over my headrest. It's greasy — the opposite of glamorous — and I pull at it. I did not wash it this morning, partly because of time and partly not to affect what they do to it when I arrive.

"Don't worry, they will prepare you," my father says.

"Prepare me for what?" I say, snapping my head to look at him.

"Your hair. They will get your hair ready."

"I'm not worried," I say. I put my chin in the air and lean back against the head rest.

The car radio provides the soundtrack for the silence between my father and me: Tina Turner, "Private Dancer"; Cindy Lauper, "Time after Time"; The Buggles, "Video Killed the Radio Star"; and at 8:15 a.m., my secret voice of encouragement, Corey Hart, "Never Surrender." He croons and I melt. I instantly vow never to do it, surrender that is.

"Mind if I change it?" My father asks.

And when the night is cold and dark.
You can see, you can see light.
"Wait until this is over." I intercept his hand.
'Cause no one can take away your right
To fight and to never surrender.

Corey's voice reminds me of what my father would sound like if he sang, deep and rocky, the vibration seeping through my pores and into my cells. When the song is over, my father flips the dial. Soon, brass horns and flutes fill the space around us while my eyes dart back to my father's pimple friend. Then it happens. I hear a small air bubble pop from under my father's pants. In horror I realize that I am smelling my father's fart.

"What was that?!" I say as I roll down my window.

"Oh, excuse me," he says, his faced flushed with a red that extends outwards past his skin. For a moment I can see him as a little boy. Chasing butterflies in a field, begging for ice cream, crying when he didn't get his way. My father clears his throat to recover. "You just concentrate on yourself, Maya. Acting in a commercial is a lot of work. Who knows if you can even do it."

"It's not that hard, I'm sure."

"You just wait and see." I pull the lever on the side of my seat and swing backward to try and escape him.

The woman who is supposed to meet us outside the door of the studio, Velma Cawshanks, is not there when we arrive, so we stand beside a black bolted door with the sun stabbing our eyes. When she finally pushes open the door out from the inside, her necklace beads clink around her neck and add music to everything she says.

"Maya and Steven, I presume," she says, reaching out her hand from under her clipboard so my father can shake it. "I'm so sorry, guys. I flew in from Vancouver last night and I must still be in their time zone." Her laugh pierces holes in my eardrums, high and cackling. I nod and smile to make her feel good.

"That's no problem," says my father. "We were just enjoying the weather."

"It is beautiful for October, isn't it? I'm Vel, by the way. Come on in!" She pulls the door open, and I feel like Dorothy being let into the Emerald City. Only the inside of the studio is not green (not even the so-called Green Room, which is peach) and no one is happy or singing. They do want to make me over, only not with an extra layer of hay like they did for the scarecrow, or a polish of my armour like they did for the Tin Man. *Nip, nip here, tuck, tuck there.* They focus instead on my hair.

Vel leaves with my father to show him the set and I am brought into a makeup room with a blond-haired woman named Jennifer. If you ask a fake person how they are, they will always say "wonderful," which of course is what Jennifer says when I say, "I'm fine, and you?" Only she stretches it out so the "o" takes four times as long as it should have and the "I" is capped off by a forced smile.

"Mia, together we are going to make your hair look amazing! Are you ready?" She flips a bunch of my hair into the air.

"It's Maya, thanks."

"Let's see where we should start. With the mixture I think."

"What mixture?"

"You'll see." She leaves the room and comes back with a paintbrush stuck into a clear plastic cup. The cup appears to be full of egg yolks and brown and black streaks and something gritty. "This is my own magical hair tonic."

"It smells," I say, sniffing.

"No matter, we'll wash it out after." She dips the paintbrush into the cup and starts to brush the substance onto my hair. Every few strokes a piece of the goo drops off her brush and onto my bare neck, leaving slime on my skin. *Watch it*, I warn her in my head, but I can hear that she is only concerned with the size of her new boyfriend's muscles. She thinks, *I know they say that size doesn't matter. He works out pretty hard at Gold's. That should be enough. But maybe size does matter. Am I the only one who actually thinks it doesn't?*

I make the mistake of telling her out loud that she should lighten up and stop being so superficial.

"What?" She looks at me with concern and I feel embarrassed for having responded to her inner worries. "How old are you?" she asks me.

"Twelve."

"Have you got a boyfriend?"

"No, not really." *And when the night is cold and dark.*

"Just you wait. With this hair and your creamy skin, you'll get all caught up soon enough. Your mom and dad will be chasing the boys away with a stick."

"My mother is dead."

"Oh, sorry." I can tell she means it.

"And if she was alive, she would never hit anyone with a stick."

"You are a terribly serious child," she says, dragging me to a sink for a rinse.

43

After the concoction comes an old-fashioned shampooing. Only I am surprised to see that she doesn't return with a blue bottle of Shinesse shampoo, but with a white bottle, one of those fancy salon kinds.

"What are you doing?" I ask as she shakes the bottle.

"Putting shampoo on your hair," she says with one eyebrow raised. "You'll see, this will make it look really nice."

"But it's not Shinesse?"

"You're darn tootin' it's not Shinesse," she says.

"I refuse. That's false advertising."

"With all due respect, young lady, it is not in your capacity to refuse." She squirts the shampoo into her palm.

"It's not?"

"'Fraid not, missy. You've signed up for this, and now you're ours to do with what we like . . . so to speak." She laughs like a bimbo. I don't say anything, slumping down in my waxy black chair that reclines into the sink while she slaps on the shampoo and lathers me. She leans me back to rinse and water spurts draw tiny circles on my scalp.

When I see my father again, my hair has been blow-dried, curled, moussed, arranged, hair-sprayed, and set. He has a bloody crater on his chin where his zit used to be. (He must have popped it in the bathroom — yuck!) He's still chatting with Velma, who stands beside him and seems to be moving closer and closer to him as they talk. She even reaches out to touch his arm every few sentences. I squint my eyes and build up a flirt-proof barrier around his body that is clear and deflects any attempt to connect with my father. She pulls her eyebrows up and sways back when I have completed it. It's not that I don't want him to make friends, I just wish that he would do it with me first.

They have put me in a tube top, neon pink, which Velma says is "sassy," but I know it looks just plain weird over my mosquito-bump boobs. Stardom is not worth this. I wonder what Mother would say if she saw me. I think she would tell me to take it off. To stop acting like such a hussy. She'd probably tell me I needed to meditate to get some authentic direction in my life.

I baby-step my way out into the studio, afraid to move and shake a single hair loose from its position. I am awed by the bright lights and how everyone looks like they have something really important to do. I wedge myself between my father with his see-through barrier and Velma who annoys me, like a yapping poodle, until I notice she is wearing a band on her left hand's ring finger.

"Stand over here, Maya," Velma sings out to me. My father only nods and grins. I feel like a show dog, being groomed, dragged around and now poked and jabbed once I am in position. "Your feet should point to the left, look over your right shoulder, two strands of hair in the front, two on the side, the rest on the back. Bring out this dimple here . . ." Velma's finger pokes into my cheek. "That's it, smile." When I am balanced into position, they expect me to remember my lines — the words I studied during the last week, at home and on the steps behind the school when no one was looking. I speak my lines even though I don't believe what I'm saying.

"Shinesse transforms my hair into a bodacious masterpiece," I look into the singular eye of the camera. The red light is on. There was no practice run.

"More energy!" Velma throws her arms up like she is praying

for a miracle, but in her mind she says a swear word I have never heard out loud, and the dark blue around her slim body turns thin and murky.

"Shinesse transforms my hair into a bodacious masterpiece!" I say louder but what I really want to do is put my hair in a ponytail and leave. Instead, I repeat just under my lips something I used to hear Mother say when she was having trouble making it through the day: *I can be okay, even through this.*

"Maya, I need to see more enthusiasm from you. You love the softness of your hair, you love Shinesse, you love life!"

I can be okay, even through this.

The pressure of the moment leaves a dull hum in my head, intensified by the lights pointing at me like a collection of vengeful suns.

I feel like a fraud.

"Shinesse transforms my hair into a bodacious masterpiece," I say again, this time my lips have started to close down over my teeth and invisible strings have lifted my shoulders.

"Maya, you're going downhill here, maybe you need a break?" Then my father's voice from the black void beyond the lights: "C'mon, Maya, concentrate. This is going to be great."

"Shinesse transforms . . ." The inside of my mouth starts to sweat and bubbles jump in my throat. "My hair . . ." I can feel a hundred faces staring at me from the dark. ". . . into . . ." The black from behind the camera closes in on me, wrapping me up and taking me over from my feet, legs, stomach, heart (beating fast), shoulders, and then it explodes — I fold in half while chunky throw-up spews from my mouth, jerking me in waves until finally with my feet soaked and my hair crusty, it pukes itself out. I smear the gook off my lips and look up into the camera.

"I can be okay, even through this," I say out loud into the silent black space.

———

According to my father, the "takes" before I got sick weren't nearly as bad as Velma had made them out to be, and a week later he returns home with the news that they have decided to use the second one, where I screamed the lines.

"The company just doesn't have the money to do another shoot."

"Sorry," I say from the kitchen table slurping a milkshake I made with vanilla ice cream, chocolate sauce, and the syrup from a jar of maraschino cherries.

"It wasn't your fault, Maya," my father says and for once I feel like his mind is thinking the same thing, though I can't hear. "You can't help getting sick."

The first time I see myself on TV comes while I'm stretched out in front of our twelve-inch black-and-white during a *Three's Company* commercial break. The girl's voice, which sounds nothing like my own, knocks me from a daydream about flying over pointy evergreens. "Shinesse transforms my hair into a bodacious master-piece," says the miniature version of me, squatting inside the black box. It surprises me to hear that the girl, made only of colour and light, seems to be telling the truth. It makes me sad to think I may be the only one who will know she doesn't mean it. And that with a flick of the TV's off button, she will disappear.

Chapter Six

Jackie snaps the elastic stirrups on the bottom of her turquoise stretch pants. Mr. Wigman has left the classroom and everyone sits cross-legged, forming a human circle in the empty space created when we pushed the desks out of the way. It's time for music period. Once a week we are forced to endure a campfire singsong without the burning logs or wilderness. Mr. Wigman's guitar rests its strings up against the cream cinderblock wall where he left it when he ran out. Jackie has enlisted two of her "Superstar Gang" — the rest are in Mrs. Lewis's class — in a competition to see who can create the snobbiest face and deliver it to me across the circle, where I sit with Brian Bellamy on one side of me and slimy Willy Hisscock on the other. Since the other girls aren't really trying, so far Jackie is the winner. Her straw-coloured hair and pinched lips hold control over most of the other students.

"Shinesse shampoo makes me look like an ugly dogface," Jackie cracks. Every student looks at me and spits out chuckles, guffaws, giggles that end in hiccups, and smiles that want to explode.

"Very smart, Jackie, you're hired," I stab back and hear hesitant laughter from the group.

"Shinesse shampoo makes my eyes look like piss-balls." Brain Bellamy adds this without warning. He's not smiling or laughing. I am stunned. From his thoughts I hear, *Jackie was right, she is kind of a nerd. I don't know what I was thinking. No one will like me if I'm nice to her. Is it mean, though? Considering her mom died.*

It was only yesterday I thought I caught Brain looking at me as I combed my hair in front of my locker, five to the left from his own. I decided then I would go out with him on a date if he asked. I don't respond to his comment about the shampoo. Jackie doubles herself over in response to Brian's comment. She has a crush on him, I know it. She coughs out her laughs through her nose, making her sound like a pig (fitting).

"Brian, that is the funniest thing I have heard all month," she says finally, flopping her hand at him. He grins with one side of his mouth and plays with a loose thread along the bottom of his sweat-shirt.

Willy Hisscock has taken off his socks, tied them in a ball, and is hitting Doreen Parchewski on the shoulder.

"Grody!" she screams. "Get this barf bag away from me!" Jackie's laughing continues.

"What's so funny?" Mr. Wigman says returning to the room, grabbing his guitar and squatting, knees spread to either side, in the one spot in the circle that used to be vacant.

"Nothing," Jackie responds, leftover chuckles still rocking her stomach.

"Willy touched me with his socks!" Doreen says.

"Willy, put your socks back on your feet," Mr. Wigman says settling his guitar in his lap.

"I was just saying how lucky we are to have a celebrity in our class," Jackie says. She looks at me. I tilt my head and wave my eyelashes in sarcastic thanks.

"Yes, we are very proud of you, Maya," Mr. Wigman says pointing the neck of his guitar in my direction. His tiny fingers are already positioned for the first cord of the camp song he is going to make us sing. "Why, the first time I saw it, I couldn't believe my eyes." He winks at me, wraps his leather guitar strap around his slight shoulders, and brings a hand through his spiky hair that looks soft enough to fall asleep in. I close my eyes and pretend that Corey Hart is the one playing the guitar.

The commercial has aired for one week, and by now, everyone in my class has seen it. Me on camera, pretending to be beautiful while puke gurgles in my stomach — *what was my father thinking?* I am plotting my revenge when Mr. Wigman begins to sing.

"Hang down your head, Tom Dooooley, hang down your head and cry, hang down your head, Tom Dooooley, poor boy you're bound to die." At first no one sings except for Mr. Wigman, who remains oblivious to any significance of the word "die" in the song. An awkwardness hangs over the circle — everyone in the class knows about my mother. They saw it on the news.

Jackie doesn't care. She sings every word and continues to glare at me. *That'll teach her for throwing banana bread in my face*, I hear her think. *I was only trying to be nice to her because her crazy mother was sick. I was being a good person. Was she trying to say I wasn't a good person? To hell with her.*

I look her way and let out an exhausted sigh. Why do people always think it's about them? I stare at the spot between her eyes until her whole face seems to be swallowed by a yellow light. "Stop it," she mouths, like she can feel it.

"Met her on a mountain, and there I took her life. Met her on a mountain, and stabbed her with my knife." A few more kids have started singing. We've sung this one before, in another music class last year. Before.

"This time tomorrow, reckon where I'll be. Down in some lonesome valley hangin' from a white oak treeee." As Mr. Wigman takes in more air for the chorus, she says it, straight to my face. Her mouth opens wide so that the words form shapes that float into the split second silence. She says it for no good reason at all: "Your mother was a psycho."

Time as I know it stops and I can no longer hear any singing. From my seat, I fly across the circle, screaming, "You witch!" and land on top of Jackie with my nails digging into her cheeks.

"Get her off me!" Jackie shrieks. Mr. Wigman stops strumming the guitar and the circle collapses, all twenty-five of my classmates reacting by tackling me. I struggle with them, grabbing fists full of hair and shirt collars. "Get her off me!" I hear again and then I am pinned — two hands on my shoulders and another two hands holding my feet.

"Maya, for Pete's sake." Brian Bellamy has my shoulders.

"Okay, everyone, it's all right. We've got it under control. Sit back down," says Mr. Wigman, only I can't sit because I am lying on my back. Even when Brian and the people holding my feet step back, I remain motionless. I can hear Jackie crying.

"She just freaked," she says through her tears. I bring my hand to my nose and see the blood. My eye socket feels like it is inflating.

"Maya, get up and let's get you to the nurse." I look to see Mr. Wigman standing over me, his pointy chin almost touching his long neck. He looks disappointed. I sit up and feel a weakness in my hands and feet, like little cries that don't know how to make it to the surface. "You're bleeding, Maya, take a Kleenex." I reach out to take the wad of white that Mr. Wigman has fished from his pocket. No one is laughing, only staring. The cries in my body start to get louder, and soon they are at my lips, escaping in sobs. "There's no need to cry about it, Maya. You're okay, you just got a little upset is all." Mr. Wigman takes my arm and pulls me up so I stand on my feet. "I'm sure you're just feeling under pressure with all that has gone on in your life. Come with me." I take a step closer to him and share in the soft lime-coloured light that makes him up. "Jackie, go to the washroom and put some cold water on your face," he says, and for the first time since I pounced, I see Jackie's face. A strand of her blond hair has come loose from her ponytail, her cheeks are streaked with tears and red scratches, raised like welts.

"You're crazy too, I don't know how we were ever friends." She says this as she walks by me and for a moment I think, she may be right. *Crazy. Maya, you're crazy*, I think, and the words seem to be driving me there.

They leave me alone in the nurse's office for a couple minutes, with my head tilted back to stop the bleeding and a blue gel cold pack on my eye. Who knew that shampoo could cause so many problems? What would my mother say? I can't even think of anything. All the things she actually said are jamming up my head, "You may not believe this, Maya, but it's almost a relief to know how you're going to die. If it wasn't for you, I'd almost be ready to go."

If it wasn't for me. If it wasn't for me.

Am I a cause of suffering? Did Mother deserve it? Why isn't she here to help me now? She left me all alone. I almost hate her.

"How's that eye doing?" the nurse, a chubby woman I have never seen before, asks when she returns.

"Fine, I guess," I say, lifting the cold pack.

"You're gonna have a shiner, that's for sure!" she says, laughing.

"So what?" I am tired of being laughed at today. She tells me that I will be okay and should go back to class — if I feel up to it. Instead, I meet Mr. Wigman in the hall. His arms are crossed so that his hands grab at his elbows, creasing his white dress shirt.

"All done?" he says.

"I guess so. Do I have to go back in there?"

"It's up to you. Jackie went home for the rest of the day. What do you feel like doing?"

"Digging a hole and going to live in it for the rest of my life," I say to him.

"It would be so dark down there."

"I would bring a flashlight or something."

"Bet it feels pretty dark up here these days too," Mr. Wigman says, and I suddenly feel itchy all over my body.

"I guess."

"I'm sorry about your mother, Maya."

"Why? Did you give her cancer?"

"No." The bell buzzes to signal the end of class.

Of course not, I think. *She gave it to herself.*

I decide not to go back to class, only they won't let me go home until my father comes in to meet with Mr. Wigman and talk about what they now refer to as "The Incident." By the time my father arrives, called from his office on account of what they must have told him was some sort of emergency, my eye has swelled as far as it is going to go and is starting its way back down. Blood swims to the spot like a magnet.

"Maya, my God! Are you in pain?" my father asks at first sight of me. He wears a blue suit with tiny lines and a thin, red paisley tie.

"You should see the other girl," Mr. Wigman says, and I am not sure if he is joking because, really, Jackie looks fine. Those scratches weren't deep enough to turn into anything. Mr. Wigman coughs into his fist. "Thanks for coming, Mr. Devine."

"Nobody punched me," I tell my father. "Must have been an elbow or something when they were trying to get me off her."

"I have to say, Mr. Wigman, this is very unlike Maya."

Mr. Wigman answers my father like I have spread my body with a mysterious substance that turns me invisible.

"I don't think she has quite been herself lately. Some of the girls were bugging her about the shampoo commercial."

"They're just jealous," my father says. "She beat out a lot of other girls for that spot." I see that droplets of sweat are growing along my father's hairline.

From inside Mr. Wigman's head: *Is this guy pushing her too much?* And I feel thankful to have Mr. Wigman sticking up for me — even if he's only thinking it.

"She had it coming," I say into empty space. "Jackie. She made a crack about Mother. She said she was a psycho." My father scrapes at his bottom lip with his upper teeth while Mr. Wigman looks towards the black and white clock above the door.

The next words are my father's. "If you'll excuse me, I need to call the office. I forgot to tell them something important."

"Of course, Mr. Devine. You can use my phone." Mr. Wigman pushes a black rotary phone towards my father, who dials and waits for the pick-up.

"Connie, hi. I'm still at the school. I forgot to tell you that the contracts we were looking at this afternoon need to be faxed back to the client. By five if possible. Call you later." The click my father makes when hanging up the phone seems to last for a full minute. A click that ends something and begins something else. A click that covers up.

"So Maya, what were you saying? She made a comment about your mother?" Mr. Wigman seems to be the only one who wants to talk about it.

"Never mind," I say to them both.

"Mr. Wigman," my father's voice turns deeper, like when he talks business or tells the door-to-door salesman that he is not interested in a set of encyclopedias that will "show him the world." "You will surely be able to understand the difficult circumstances that Maya and I have recently found ourselves in as a result of my wife's passing."

"From what I've heard, she was a wonderful lady," Mr. Wigman says politely. "Why else would so many have been drawn to her in her final days?"

"Yes, well." My father's turn to pretend he has a cough. "We miss her, but I can assure you that Maya has all the support she needs. Today was merely a hiccup in her recovery. I will deal with this at home."

"We are only concerned about her well-being, Mr. Devine."

"I realize that. But she is fine." Again, I have faded from view for both of them. Like I now hover on the ceiling and my body has wilted to the ground, not to be seen by anyone. I am looking down at their straight bodies, engulfed in swirls of maroon and tangerine.

Outside the school my father makes another phone call on the pay phone in the parking lot — Connie again — while I wait with my back leaning against the tailgate of his car. I watch his head bobbing as he yaks into the phone. He talks so quickly I can almost see the syllables dropping from his mouth. If I wasn't busy holding an icepack on my eye socket, I could catch and collect them into my school bag and carry his words around with me everywhere.

Even though she is only a lady he works with, Connie makes him happy. I can tell by the way his eyebrows raise when he talks to her, even over the phone, and how he rubs his hand down the side of his pants. My mother never made him do those things. With her, his eyebrows sometimes rose up, but for different reasons.

With my mother gone, it has become quiet enough for me to

hear the whispers and murmurings running over my own thoughts. They tell me things to do, like a kindly old teacher with wrinkled palms and a fuzzy sweater. Then, other times they turn on me and tell me I should be ashamed — that I don't fit in. Like a bully, they ask me to repeat after them, "I, Maya Devine, am not good enough to be in this classroom, in this family, in this city, in this commercial, in this world."

I think about this as I wait for my father to finish with Connie.

Heather Hickle, a girl I have seen in the library during lunch, walks up to where we stand. My father still spits into the black phone that carries bits of other people's lunches in its small holes, and I wait with my face hidden behind the icepack. Beside her sidles up Chauncey Mercer, the only black kid in our school — skinny, frail, with an afro that covers more space than his own face. They are both in the other seventh grade class, with Mrs. Lewis.

"Did it hurt'cha?" Heather asks me.

"What do you think?" I say lifting the pack to show my puffy eye.

"I heard she clocked you good!" Chauncey says, raising his tiny fist towards the sky, his eyes growing wide so that his brown pupils seem small compared to the white parts.

"No one clocked anyone," I say, putting the pack back in place and wincing again as the ice pinches at my wound. "We just had a disagreement that got out of hand is all." I act diplomatic despite the parts inside me that are still smoldering.

"We just wanted to tell you that we support you. That Jackie is a b-i-t-c-h," Heather says, tugging at a strand of her sandy brown hair. Her face is pale and even more so beside Chauncey.

"Heather and I want to know if you want to eat subs with us tomorrow, to celebrate."

"Celebrate what?" I ask. My father has hung up the phone and is walking towards us.

"That you stood up to her. She thinks she owns this school," Heather says.

"And we all know that the school board owns the school, not snobby bitches," Chauncey adds in a nerdy but brave way, for him anyway.

"Maya, I'm ready. Now let's get you home and talk about this," my father tells me when he reaches us. "You'll excuse us?" he says to Heather and Chauncey, and I know that his businessman suit and slicked hair has intimidated them.

"Sorry . . . we didn't know. . . ." Chauncey says through the spit that has formed in front of his teeth.

"He's my father," I say, getting into the car. "See you tomorrow," which is weird to say because I haven't even really seen them today, or any other day before this. Wherever they were isolating themselves. must have been really different from where I was.

As we drive away, I turn to see their salt and pepper faces getting smaller and smaller.

Chapter Seven

My mother refused all treatment for her cancer. She said she didn't need radiation or drugs. She said it was too late for her anyway.

She even told some people she needed her strength to look after me. The real reason, as I see it now, was that she had made a secret decision to give up on her life. Destiny had given her a way to escape what she had created for herself. And nothing my father or I could say could make her change her mind.

A few weeks after we all sat in the doctor's office, I walked in on her in the bathroom with my father's electric razor in her hand and a mushroom-coloured towel wrapped around her shoulders. "You can watch if you want," she said to me when I saw her. I turned away, but then back. She put her hand on my bare arm then, her fingertips making five indents in my skin.

"I know this might be hard for you, Maya, to watch me lose my hair." Did she mean it? "But I really have this strong sense that I don't need it anymore."

I nodded like a puppet, even though I was screaming and swearing at her from inside my head, and sat on the toilet while she separated the hair on her head into sections in preparation for the slaughter. And with the razor buzzing in her hand and into the air, she began the cutback. Each long ringlet, confronted at the root and removed, until her head was a patchwork of leftover beauty that she then trimmed all down to bald. Zip, zip, zip — and soon, her hair lay abandoned on the floor around her like auburn snow. She ran her hand over the new stubble as if trying to decode a secret message in Braille.

When I had all her hair scooped into the bag, I reached in and combed my hands through it. Each strand was reaching up to me, trying to hold on for one last chance, but instead I turned on them all, knotted the ends of the bag, and put it outside on the back deck. When I got back inside, my father was standing looking at my mother. I only saw the back of him. The bluish light around my mother's head was fuzzier and moving faster than I had seen it before. It made me dizzy to follow it. I noticed then that my father's head was lowered and his suit-jacketed shoulders seemed to be shaking a bit.

"You have made a big mistake, Marigold," my father said to her bald head. "This was totally unnecessary — you look ridiculous. Why would you do this to yourself?"

I wondered why she would do it too and what the neighbours, especially Mrs. Roughen, would say when they saw.

"I had to, Steven," she said. "You wouldn't understand."

Then she ran to her bedroom and my father shouted out, "What have you got left now?" and went outside without turning around to face me.

Her hair was not the only thing my mother felt she had to give up. She told us she didn't want to let cancer take anything away from her. So she was going to give it away instead.

"I am going to live in the backyard for the rest of the time," she announced one Saturday afternoon in April. Jackie and I were playing in the kitchen sink. We were trying to float her little sister's mermaid doll. I was teaching her that mermaids didn't float, but in fact, they lived under the ocean.

"But how would they ever breathe under there?" Jackie said to me, the cuffs of her shirt soaked with water.

"They breathe because they believe they can breathe." And then my mother walked in and made her announcement. My father was standing behind her, eyes rolled back like he was looking at the ceiling.

"I need some space to stay focused on what's happening. This is a lot for a person to go through. I don't need to be inside anymore." When she said this, I felt my temples start to tighten and my fingers fold into fists.

"What do you mean you're going to live outside?" I asked her.

"I bought an old teepee off of this man who sits in front of the Drug Mart on First Avenue. You father is going to help me set in up in the backyard."

From Jackie's head then, and only the second time I had heard someone's thoughts, *And I thought my mom was embarrassing. Maya's mom is a weirdo.*

"Be quiet, Jackie!" I said and snapped my head to look at her. She was concentrating on combing the mermaid's aqua hair with a plastic comb.

"I didn't say anything, Maya," she said prissily, faking innocence.

At that moment, a ball of resentment, anger, and overall misery at the situation began to shake itself loose in my throat.

"What the hell is wrong with you!?" I screamed despite my desire to keep it inside.

"Excuse me?" my mother responded, her bald head cocked to one side and her lips pushed up towards her nose. "Where did that language come from, young lady?"

"You think this isn't hard enough for me without you acting like a freak in front of my friends?!"

I wish now that I hadn't said those words, as they appeared to hurt my mother, annoy my father, and help Jackie fully grasp how truly bizarre the situation was.

"Maya, take that back," my father said.

"No."

I ran upstairs to my room, slammed the door, and sobbed uncontrollably into a waiting pillow.

Pounding up the stairs two at a time, I had heard my mother speak again. "In case you didn't notice, Steven, I raised her to be a strong girl. She'll get through this." I don't know what Jackie was doing then. I felt bad for just leaving her with them, but there was no way I was going back out there.

After what seemed like a couple of hours, I emerged from my hole of self-pity with a hatred for my mother still swelling inside me. Jackie was gone but had left the sink full of mermaid water.

I put both my hands in and spun them around to make two whirl-pools that didn't touch. Then I pulled the plug to drain the water. It sputtered and spat on its way down, and I wondered if there was anything alive being pulled down.

Evening light filtered through the kitchen window from the backyard. I followed it with my eyes and saw them. My father, on his hands and knees, fitting together thin wooden poles and my mother unfolding what looked like dirty grey tarps and smoothing them down on the grass. They didn't notice me watching them — as though they were inside an aquarium, with me observing them. All I learned was that teepees are difficult to assemble, and some events made no sense at all.

My mother took the single mattress off my box spring for her out-side bed, because it took up less space than a double. And to replace it, Father brought the queen-size bed from the guest room into my bedroom. As far as we knew, Aunt Leah (or anyone else) was not coming to stay any time soon. I liked my new big bed. I could stretch out from side to side if I wanted to and not just from top to bottom. And I never rolled off if I tossed and turned too much. I found it difficult to concentrate on sleep knowing my bald mother was dying by herself in the yard on my old single mattress with no box spring. (Father had propped it up against my bedroom wall.) Was a teepee tarp enough to keep the chill out? Couldn't the mos-quitoes get through the holes? The bugs were starting to get bad out there. These sorts of thoughts led to sleepless nights for me, which made me tired at school the next day. I didn't mind though, because to walk around sleepy was almost like I wasn't anywhere at all.

Jackie and I didn't talk much at school anymore. I think my family scared her off. I think she thought I had become a bit too weird to associate with — especially with the next year being grade seven. I didn't talk much to anyone. I concentrated most of the day on deciding whether I would sit with my mother when I got home or pretend she didn't exist.

"Don't you get lonely out here?" I asked her one night after deciding she needed me with her.

"You are never lonely when you have yourself," she said with a pout to her lips, and I wanted to yell at her, "What about me, you freak! You have me. And your husband?" But she was my mother, my protector, the one who raised me. And she was sick, which made it even harder to say what I really felt.

"I'll keep visiting you, Mother," I said. "You don't have to sit out here all alone."

She put her hand on my shoulder to say thank you. She was weakening, which was probably as much to do with her diet as preparing for the end. She ate mostly saltine crackers, and sometimes I brought her bowls of boiled vegetables — carrots, spinach, and broccoli — when she asked for them. Her arms were turning small like twigs and the bones in her cheeks growing pointier. When it was time for her to sip water from a blue plastic cup, her hand rose to her mouth in a slow motion that seemed to follow her everywhere.

Aside from the single mattress, my mother had one wooden chair that used to belong to our old dining room set, a TV stand she bought my father at a garage sale, and a scratchy wool mat she rested her feet on. The prairie sun and the moisture created from spring rain meant that she had to keep the hanging door of her teepee flap open instead of tied tight, but even this didn't help with the suffocating heat. She wore only a white tank top with no bra and an elephant-print skirt that reached her knees.

She had one more thing beside her bed: two red milk crates that I had stolen from outside the cafeteria at Holy Cross High School and brought home for her to make a bookshelf. And on the bookshelf she put her copy of the *Bhagavad Gita*, cones of incense, her water cup, and a copy of the Bible — which her mother had given her right before I was born. It looked new and straight, like it had hardly been opened.

"I've figured it out, Maya," she said. "They wrote the Bible only to keep people in line by scaring them with punishment. God is such a villain in there." She pointed to the black book. "It's like he's ready to condemn anyone who makes the tiniest mistake."

"Is it true we get punished for doing the wrong thing?" I asked her.

"If we do, I can see why he did this to me."

Maybe she was mad at God. Or my grandmother, whom I had never met, for trying to make her read the Bible.

I remember hearing a phone call made by my father once when I had returned back to the house to sleep (sometimes I would curl up beside my mother on the single bed in the teepee, but on this particular night the howling wind had been keeping me awake). My father's end of the conversation went like this: "Eleanor, we can't forgive what you tried to do, but I'm willing to put that aside now. She's your daughter and she needs you. She's sick." He paused to listen and

I clung to the wall around the corner. "I'm sorry you feel that way. She would have been happy to get a visit from you." Stale air. "I know that your pension isn't enough for a plane ticket. Forget it."

My father hung up the phone without saying the words that would have made any mother run to be with her child: "She's not going to make it." I still don't know why he hung on to those words. Maybe he didn't want to say them himself. Or maybe he was scared my grandmother would actually come.

The next afternoon after that call, a plant arrived at our front door. It had waxy flat leaves and small white flowers that were wound up too tight to bloom. Around the green pot it came in was a pink ribbon, too thin to be satin, too coarse to be worth keeping. I took it out to my mother, but not before I peeled open the tiny envelope. On the card, with the words "Get Well" in the corner surrounded by a border of hearts, were six words written in all capitals (probably by an attentive floral shop worker): "Sorry to hear you are ill," and underneath, the word "Mother." My mother took the plant and read the card without smiling. She told me to put it on the grass outside the teepee, "So the sun can get at it better," which I did. It stayed there for almost a week, until one morning I arrived to see the neighbour's German Shepherd, Tonto, ripping its leaves from the broken pot.

Though she may have wished he would have, my father didn't forget about my mother when she was out there — how could he with her teepee so obtrusive and only a few metres behind the house?

"Stinks in here" would usually be the first thing he'd say when he'd come in after work and sit down on the cracked wooden chair across from where my mother lounged on her mattress. In a low voice, low like approaching thunder, he would ask her how she was and if she needed anything.

She usually said no, she did not need anything from him. Except sometimes, she would ask for more saltines, which he would bring her. He would light a stick of her incense to cover the smell inside the teepee. Mother had stopped using deodorant or bathing much. I guess she didn't see a point to it anymore. And she was going inside to the bathroom a lot, and spending a long time in there, which probably didn't help the aroma coming off her body.

My mother spent most of the day lying down, resting. She said her back ached. Her lips were dry and when she smiled sometimes at my father, they stretched over her teeth like an animal skin drying in the sun.

To be polite, Mother asked Father about his job. She usually did this without looking at him. He would tell her how he thinks he found the next Heather Locklear, and that she wants him to represent her. Mother would say, "That's nice," and he would tell her how hard he was working to make sure that I had a good future, how important it was for him to move up the corporate ladder at the office. But from inside his head I once heard the truth: *I honestly don't give a shit about this job. Not with Mari like this. Who's going to look after Maya?*

Yeah, I thought, *who's going to look after me?* But I couldn't ask him out loud: he would know what I heard.

This mind-reading business was getting tricky.

When my father ran out of things to say, he would reach out and hold one of each of our hands, just until they became sweaty, and then go back into the house to take off his suit.

Chapter Eight

In May she wrapped a bedsheet around her body — queen-size with tiny flowers barely pink and blue. It used to be on her bed inside the house. She laid it flopped over her shoulder, down a bit and around her waist. I watched her put it on the first time. After taking off her clothes and before wrapping the sheet around her, she stood naked in front of me, her nipples hard with the dampness of the teepee, her pubic hair dark and matted between her legs. I tried not to stare, but my mother's nakedness never became comfortable for me.

"Put these in the garbage, Maya. No use for them anymore." She handed me her clothes: a white tank top, a black T-shirt, and a pair of white jogging pants my father used to wear when he ran around the block.

I did as she said and when I returned to her shelter, she was wrapping the sheet around herself. I still wonder: had my father been the one to fetch it from the linen closet and deliver it to her?

"Yes, this will do just fine," she said with the sheet in place, but I had my doubts. The faded pattern on the thin fabric made her look like a tacky monk. And who wore a sheet anyway?

She stopped wearing shoes around that month as well. She ventured into the house to use the toilet in her bare feet, her toes fitting between the green blades on the way, moist from the dew left at sunrise or golden dry from the afternoon sun.

"Do you want your shoes, Mari?" my father had asked more than once, and she always responded in the same way.

"I like the feel of the grass on my feet, Steven. Do you have a problem with that?"

Maybe she was just over wearing shoes by that point.

My father spent most of his time engrossed in his work, or in the TV, or in the scary headlines that he studied from the daily paper.

"Maya, can you believe that banana-chin Mulroney is actually our prime minister?" he would say as he read, trying to suck me in to a political world that seemed more like made-up stories to me. "Look out, Canada, with this guy."

Instead of worrying about politics, I occupied myself by combing through my own thoughts. It was hard to see through them. I thought about things that an eleven-year-old shouldn't have to, like: Where will my mother go when she dies? Will my father cry? Will he take down the teepee or will he let me move my own pillows and blankets out there to be close to her?

Mother never answered my questions. Not directly. Instead, she would point me to some random passage in the *Bhagavad Gita*.

While I held the slim book in my hands, she would nod in a knowing way with her lips tucked in.

"Maya, things will take care of themselves. At least you're not Arjuna. You could be facing a battle with all your friends and family members. Krishna helped him out, and it all turned out okay."

I've since learned that in the further episodes of the *Mahabharata*, Arjuna and his entire family get killed because Krishna convinced him to fight, but at the time I agreed with her. I supposed it could be worse.

That night I dreamed that I was Arjuna, on a golden chariot heading out to fight against my own family — brothers and sisters I never had. Around me, the girls from school, Mr. Wigman, my father, all shouting at me and telling me to get down, that it was dangerous up there. But I heard the booming voice in my ear and kept riding, waking up before I hit anything frightening.

A Sunday morning. My father awoke to see it first. He came into my room. I remember looking up to see him standing over me like an ancient oak.

"Maya, I need your help outside. It's your mother's teepee." Wrinkles traced out from the corners of his eyes, creating a maze in his skin. I followed him into the yard to see the paint — red, bold, and thick on the outside of my mother's teepee.

"Freak Inside," written in a childish way that made me think it must have been some kids on the street. Egg yolk dripped from the letters like yellow blood, oozing its way down to the grass and settling around broken white eggshells. The door flap was ripped as well, like someone was trying to get in and gave up halfway.

"We can sew that back in place," my father said, pointing to the flap, his voice hovering in the still air before dropping to the ground. He ran his open palm across the words, so that they smeared into a red blob. He only spoke one word: "Insensitive."

Inside the teepee, my mother still slept.

When she woke up, we didn't tell her what had happened. Instead my father occupied her in conversation about the weather and the bills and his boss. My mother nodded and tried to smile while he spoke. I scrubbed the red blob and egg yolks with soapy water from a green bucket until I thought my arm would detach, and I looked through the ripped entrance every few minutes to check on them. He held my mother's hand and cradled her head with his bicep. She seemed comfortable — that is, assuming she knew where she was at all (it took her a while to get moving in the mornings). Eventually she had to go inside to use the toilet. By then, I was almost finished scrubbing and hid the bucket and rags behind a bush when she walked by.

"Good morning, Mother." She nodded weakly and hobbled past me. I don't think she even noticed the rip in the door. And if she did, she had passed the point of caring.

Jackie came over because I asked her to. By that afternoon, I was longing to escape to some sort of fantasy world that we created — a play we wrote and acted ourselves, a dance we created to something off of Michael Jackson's *Thriller* album. Only when she arrived, Jackie didn't want to play with me. She wanted only to sit in the backyard and talk about my mother.

"Why does she stay in there?"

"She likes it."

"Why?"

"She's going to die."

"Are you sad?"

"I don't know."

"Are you afraid she will haunt you?"

"No."

"How do you know for sure, though?"

"I don't."

"Does she ever come out?"

"Sometimes."

"For what?"

"To get food and go to the washroom."

"What does she eat?"

"Crackers, fruit, water."

"Can I see her?"

"No."

"What is that red blob on the outside?"

Jackie's blond pigtails curled into small balls at the ends. Her cheeks were white like milk with red splotches in the middle. Her nose was perpetually wrinkled in curiosity.

We met in grade four, when our teacher assigned us as partners for a project on the first moon landing. Then, when Jackie asked me to come shopping at a flea market with her mother, I agreed. Her mother even bought me a pair of earrings, small silver peace signs with pink borders, for my recently pierced ears. Her mother, at that time, still had some of her leftovers from her hippie days in the late '60s — leather sandals, the flower she sometimes tucked behind her ear, the hugs she doled out like tissue. But as Jackie and I went from grade four to five, her mother decided to return to work as an insurance broker and most of her whimsical qualities disappeared. By the time we reached grade six she wore mostly lady-suits and was making a good business selling people back-up plans on their own deaths.

I had grown tired of all Jackie's questions about my mother, realizing I had appeased her at first simply out of fear of losing my only friend. But I didn't want to talk about my mother anymore, so I asked Jackie to leave.

"But I don't want to go yet, I have another question," she said. I could hear her taking mental notes in her head: *Stays in teepee because she is dying. Only comes in to use bathroom and prepare food. Maya doesn't know if she's sad.*

"Go home, Jackie. Now."

Her round face dropped in surprise. "I told you, I don't want—" I stood up and pulled her by the forearm towards the front door. "Owwww, that hurt!" she screamed.

"I don't want to talk about it anymore, and I don't want to talk to you."

Kicking Jackie out was the only retaliation I could find for her intruding into my mother's situation. I hadn't yet figured out how to get back at the people who peered over the fence, stopped my father to question him in the driveway, or those who had painted the teepee.

Jackie went to the door and slipped on her pink jelly shoes that had been waiting on the tile floor.

"You'll regret this, Maya," she said as she left. "You lost your one chance to be friends with me." I only shrugged and closed the door behind her when she stomped off.

The afternoon that Jackie and I spent in my backyard, after my mother was vandalized, was the last one we spent together as friends. But shortly before dinnertime on that day, I met Elijah Roughen, thirteen-year-old son of Trudie Roughen who lived at two Emerald Crescent, right down the street from us. Even before my mother was sick, Mrs. Roughen had showed interest in my mother. There was a time, when I was around nine, that Mrs. Roughen had picked my mother up and they had gone to a craft show out by the river. My mother had returned with a macramé teapot cozy in the seven chakra colours and a mini dreamweaver for me to hang in my bedroom window — to catch nightmares, she had said.

Mrs. Roughen, she had told me, had bought only a knitted cover for the Kleenex box in her bathroom. "That Trudie is a strange woman," she said, "but I guess it's nice to get out."

Mother was the one to tell me about Elijah, two years older than me. And how he was shy, but sensible (Mrs. Roughen's words), and had many part-time activities that had earned him distinction, awards even — first place ribbon for horse jumping and all his swimming badges (yellow to white). This had all happened a few years ago, but lately, Mrs. Roughen worried about her son. He had turned coarser, gotten some new friends, stopped many of his activities. Mrs. Roughen hoped that with the right attention, he could still be salvaged. Mother warned me that Mrs. Roughen was hoping for me to be a good influence on Elijah, because I seemed quiet, studious, and square.

"You got her fooled, eh?" my mother said (as a joke, I think). "You're a firecracker, my dear." She looked down when she said it, like somehow, she only hoped.

Jackie had just left when Mrs. Roughen knocked on our door.

"Hello, Maya," she sang when I opened the door. Blue eye shadow coated her eyelids and her thin eyebrows were plucked to within an inch of their lives. "I am here to talk with your mother. Now, I know that she is ill and that her new lifestyle alienates her a bit from myself and the rest of the ladies in the neighborhood, but nevertheless, I thought I should stop by." When Mrs. Roughen said "lifestyle," she created quotes on each side of her head with four of her manicured fingers, and her left eye seemed to wink. I tried to hear her thoughts but was met with a fuzzy wall of static.

"I hope you don't mind I brought my son, Elijah." Mrs. Roughen came through the door then and kicked off her heeled sandals. Elijah followed, his chin dropped in embarrassment, cradling a pineapple upside-down cake in his arms. His appearance contradicted itself. Although he wore a black Duran Duran T-shirt with a rip at the collar and a black leather wristband, and his dark hair peaked into tiny spikes on top of his head, every inch of him was thoroughly groomed — teeth gleaming white, no crust in the corners of his eyes, shiny skin that I could almost see myself in. He had wonderful eyes — brown and inviting. Nestled behind the brown was the soul of a kid who had seen stuff. He puffed his cheeks in a fake smile.

"Where should I put this?" he asked me.

"The kitchen, I guess." I was unrehearsed at that sort of etiquette. He followed me into the kitchen. His mother peeked through the kitchen window at the teepee.

"So that's it, is it?" said Mrs. Roughen, pointing. "Your mother is out there?"

"Yes." I had grown tired of all the questioning.

"And she never comes in?"

"Sometimes." I felt like I was repeating myself.

"Can I go out there?" She said this slowly, stretching out each vowel and consonant like she was painting them across a canvas.

"Let me tell her first." I left both Elijah and Mrs. Roughen alone in the kitchen and ran out to my mother, who was sitting cross-legged on her mattress, eyes closed, sheet draped tightly over her shoulder.

"Mother?" I interrupted her. She opened her eyes slowly. "There is someone her to see you. Mrs. Roughen."

"Why?" she asked, dropping her eyelids closed.

I shrugged.

"Tell her to come around, I guess."

Mrs. Roughen inched round the side of the teepee and mimed a knock on the door flap.

"Come in, Trudie" was my mother's response. Her voice came out even and smooth with an invisible period at the end of her sentence. Mrs. Roughen ducked into my mother's air, in one complete swoop.

While she was inside, I stayed in the yard with Elijah. He dropped to the grass, lying back on his elbows and crossing his ripped jeans at the ankle. I could see his knees through the holes. I pushed my lips together and sat cross-legged beside him, my fingers interlaced in my lap. I watched the yellow light pulsing like tiny spotlights out from his chest. *I can't believe I let her drag me here*, I heard him think. I could feel his emotions drift through my mind like a bubbling stream: hunger, boredom, frustration, and finally, an image of a male face with a handlebar moustache.

"My parents are splitting up," he said like an axe through a log. "At least, I'm pretty sure they are. My dad screwed some other chick." I flinched and thought how weird the sentence sounded coming out of his perfect Chicklet teeth. Open sky above us began to cloud over while I thought of what to say next. "Have you ever done it?" he asked. I grimaced. "Of course not, you're probably too young anyway."

"I'm only eleven," I added in my defense. All I knew about sex at that time was what I had learned earlier in the year from a boring film at school about the menstrual cycle.

"Have you kissed someone at least?"

"Yes." I studied the grass with intensity to avoid facing my lie.

"Hmm," he snorted. "So you're a virgin then, eh?"

"I guess."

"Let's go in the shed."

"What?"

"I want to show you something."

Going into the shed with a boy I had just met seemed extremely appealing then. It could have been an escape, a refuge. Maybe what awaited me inside my father's shed was more brilliant than a dying mother in a teepee? Maybe just for a moment I could be normal again — an adventurous, risk-taking version of the normal me.

So I followed Elijah into the shed. He slapped the door shut behind us and we were left in only medium darkness, thanks to one small plastic-covered window letting a thin stream of light through. I backed up and stumbled over the foot of my father's wheelbarrow (I had never seen him use it), and Elijah reached out his hand to touch the hoes, rakes, and shovels that hung from the ceiling. The smells of damp chipboard, grass clippings, and grease created a comforting bubble around the both of us. Then Elijah squeezed out a small box from the waistband of his pants — red, DuMaurier, half empty when he opened it.

"Want one?" he offered, pulling out a thin stick and placing it between his lips.

"No thanks." I was let down by the cigarette, as if I was expecting a fancy lizard in a jar. He lit it with a match from his pocket, inhaled with a smacking sound and blew smoke into the air between us.

"My mom was pretty pissed when she found out about my dad." His voice cracked on the word "dad." "She threw her makeup bag at the wall in the bedroom and everything went flying: lipsticks, eye shadows, bottles of skin-coloured crap — it totally covered the white paint on the walls."

"That's too bad," I said.

"She cracked one of her mirrors, which is supposed to be bad luck, but she didn't seem to care much." I knew Elijah was only thirteen, but he seemed to be aging in front of me as he spoke, grey hairs sprouting at his temples, wrinkles spreading out on his cheeks, the skin sagging under his chin. "It was the girl's gym teacher from the school where he teaches. Maybe they did the nasty in the utility closet or some shit like that." The walls of the shed felt like they were shrinking around us. My armpits grew wet and the thoughts in my head grew louder and more threatening.

She's cute — this from inside his head, though I didn't ask to hear it.

"Come here," he said out loud, but instead he took two steps towards me. I replied with one tiny step in his direction.

"I know you are too much of a browner to smoke yourself, but if you lean forward, I'll blow some of it into your mouth."

"After you have inhaled it?"

"No, just from my mouth. No biggie." His response sounded logical and I complied, leaning into him so that I could smell the seaside freshness of his underarm deodorant — the first time I had smelled a "man" close-up. And somehow at that moment, Elijah Roughen morphed into a flesh and bones version of the secret love who had followed me around since I first heard him sing, Corey Hart, finally here to rescue me from the chaos of my mother's illness.

"You're here," I said with words that hovered before disappearing, but I still have no idea if Elijah said anything back. He probably just smirked and nodded, giving high fives to his ego. The dim room filled with light and I floated above the shed and back beside Corey in one swoop. And then again, and up and down so that the sky fell into my father's shed, and my father's shed floated into the sky. I squinted my eyes so that I hardly noticed when Corey filled my mouth with the gritty smoke, and it swam into my nose, my ears, my eyes.

And then he filled my mouth with something else from his face — slimy, wet, spongy, sticking me — I stuck out my tongue to meet it. My Corey, my saviour, my future.

Knuckles fell on the outside of the shed, creating a hollow echo.

"Oh, shit," said Elijah.

"Maya, are you in there?" my father said from the other side. "Open

up!" He knocked again, and I saw that Elijah had moved our old barbeque in front of the door and that it shook as my father pounded. I
felt deceived and scowled at Elijah for it. I turned around and banged
my head on a hanging lawnmower. Pain shot through my body.

"I'm here!" I said as tears sprang to my eyes. "Let me out of
here!" I grabbed the dusty barbeque, toppled it onto its side and
whacked open the door with my fingertips. There stood my father,
stunned-face, in baggy jeans and an orange tie-dyed T-shirt, the one
he wore for yardwork.

"Jesus Christ, Maya. What's going on? Who's this?"

"Elijah Roughen, sir. Trudie Roughen's son. She's in there with
your wife right now." Elijah held out his hand, but instead of taking
it, my father said, "Were you two smoking in there?"

"Yes sir, Mr. Devine. But only me. I can assure you that your
daughter is still very innocent." Elijah had stamped out his cigarette
on the floor of the shed and it still smoked when my father went
inside. "Next time use an ashtray," he told Elijah and then to me,
while poking his head out the door, "Maya, your dinner is ready. Go
inside and splash cold water on your face." He had no other words
for us — outside or inside.

When I got back from a dinner of burnt fish sticks and creamed
corn from a can, Elijah was still waiting for his mother on the back
deck, his feet up on a chair and his hands folded behind his head.

"I need a ride home," he told me matter-of-factly as I passed him.

Mrs. Roughen came out of the teepee then. Around her head
was a strange sort of light, violet and red sprinting around together,
like she didn't know what to feel. She asked me if she could use the
bathroom inside.

I nodded.

Then, she walked by me, silently, but I heard inside her head. And like that, I knew what was going on, what had happened. Why she wanted Mother as her friend.

I think it all came down to this: she was comforted by the fact that someone's life was more dreadful than her own.

And though my mother had never encouraged any of my supernatural abilities, I decided that this time I was going to tell her what I had heard — for her own good.

What I learned after that was that sometimes split-second decisions can change a lot of things.

Mother was on the bed with her knees hugged up to her chest, and she was looking out into nothing and biting the inside of her mouth like she had had enough of it all.

Maybe I wanted to impress her.

"Mrs. Roughen tried to kill herself last night," I said. "On account of her husband breaking up with her because of some floozy in gym shorts." I took a deep breath and continued. "She took a whole handful of blue pills with milk, but at the last minute she puked them all up into the sink."

"What makes you say she tried to kill herself, Maya?" She looked surprised, more than I expected.

"She is relieved today that she didn't do it. She thinks that in the light of day, things look better. She's glad for what she does have. She could be dying, like you."

"Did Elijah tell you that, Maya?" My mother's dark-circled eyes were wide open, like she was trying to see inside my head.

"I heard her think it."

Mother just stared at me, unflinching. "Maya, I've told you, don't pay attention to that stuff. It's not who you are."

"But it's real, Mother."

"I know, Maya." She was too weak to disagree with me as she usually did. She put her hand on mine.

Mrs. Roughen came back in fussing with her hair and blotting her freshly painted lips.

"As I was saying, Mari, you're going to get through all this just fine—"

My mother interrupted her. "Trudie, promise me you won't hurt yourself, okay? Nothing stupid, no man is worth it."

"Excuse me, Mari?" I think they had both forgotten I was there.

"I know about the pills, Trudie," she said with a sigh, dropping her ear to her shoulder.

"But how? I mean, why would you say something like that?" Mrs. Roughen began pacing around the teepee, like she was trying to walk off the awkwardness.

"Just don't do it, Trudie. I know what it feels like to get jerked around by someone who you thought could be the one for you. Trust me, you can go on without him."

"Mari, how could you know about this?" Tears had flooded her eyes, purple spirals of light had swirled out from her head.

"Just try to pretend the whole thing never happened. Really."

Mrs. Roughen's face had dropped in shock; her chin was practically resting on her collar bone.

"Mari, I don't know how you know all this. But I have to say, at the risk of making this all about me, that this is exactly what I need in my life right now."

"You need what in your life, Trudie?"

"You have a gift. A gift that points to something more. Something bigger than this earth. Something to believe in."

"I just wanted to tell you, Trudie. That's it. It's nothing more."

"You are so brave, Mari," she said, stroking my mother's bare shoulder. "Could it be you already know what is in store for you? You've seen it, haven't you?"

"Trudie, I don't know what you're—"

"Mari, please. Can you tell me more? I want to know exactly what life has in store for me."

I looked at my mother, waiting for her to brush it off, or maybe even to tell the truth, but she didn't. Instead, she took a long, slow breath, dragged her tongue across her teeth, and said, "You'll meet someone, Trudie. A new boyfriend, with dark hair and broad shoulders, younger than you. You'll be so happy together." My mother looked to the left. She was making it all up.

That night, after Mrs. Roughen left, I refused to stay outside with my mother. She knew why. So, after Father had finished scrubbing the red mark off the side of the teepee, he went in to be with her. I opened the back door real late and thought I heard them laughing. He stayed there all night, and even until morning. It was the only time I remember him sleeping out there, and thinking back, I am pretty sure that was the night it happened.

That must have been the night the baby was made.

Chapter Nine

My father, or Steve, as Connie from his office calls him, has a tattoo over his heart. I sometimes wonder if Connie has seen it, especially now that Mother is gone. Maybe he has hidden it from her as he has hidden it from me my whole life. I have only seen it a few times.

When I was around seven, my mother told me the story of how he got it. We were waiting to hand out flyers in front of the public school I would have attended if I had not been home-schooled, when she told me how he had made the tattoo himself. He had taken some black ink out of a pen, looked into the mirror shirtless, and with one of his mother's sewing needles, trapped black ink under his skin by pushing the pin in and out. She didn't mention how much it hurt him, but I'm sure it must have. I'd have been done after the first prick.

He got it before they were married and before I was born.

When she told me about it, she had a look of regret, like maybe she wished he hadn't done it.

His tattoo says "Mari," my mother's nickname. Maybe he had intended to create her entire name, "Marigold," but had got tired at the "i." It's hard to say with my father. Regardless, from then on my mother's nickname made its home on my father's chest. "Mari" in black, shaky letters. "Mari," darker in some spots and spread out along a crooked line.

The first time I saw it, I was five and my father had taken me swimming in the outdoor pool at the end of Lakeview Street. We had to get out of the house that day — Mother was sad in bed for the first time I can remember.

"Why do you have that there?" I said, pointing when he removed his shirt. This made a wrinkled lady look too and crinkle her nose in distaste.

"'Mari' is short for your mother's name," he told me as he slid into the chlorinated pool and bent his knees so that his tattoo dropped under the waterline. That's all he wanted to say about it.

After that, I would try to catch glimpses of the "Mari" tattoo whenever I could. When I caught him changing his shirt I would look right at the spot. When he wore white thin T-shirts, I would squint to try to make out the outline, as if my mother herself was trapped under there.

At the age of eight I vowed to get a tattoo myself, as soon as I was old enough to take the bus downtown.

As far as I am concerned, my father is careless. Getting ready for school, I whip around the corner into the bathroom to find him standing there. Two beats provide me with an unobstructed viewing of his "Mari" tattoo, black on his wet skin. I try not to look at anything else.

"Shut the door!" my father screams.

"Lock the door next time," I mutter, closing it myself without turning the knob.

From behind the closed door: "What did you say?!" It opens again with the kick of a heel. My father, with a towel wrapped around his waist, tosses a stick of deodorant into the sink and comes after me.

"Don't talk back to me, Maya, I'm sick of it!" He grabs me in the hall by my pyjama top, taking a handful of fleece into his fist, and pushes me to the ground. Gravity stuns me quiet. My father trips to his knees and I wonder if he is going to pounce on me. Instead, he covers his face with his fingers. His bare back curves and his shoulders start to rock.

"I'm sorry for talking back," I say curling myself into the carpet, into an indestructible ball, protecting myself from the mucky air mixing itself up around my father's head. When he speaks, I can tell that his nose has filled up, and when he looks up I can see that his eyes are swelling red. *It's not your fault. It's never been your fault*, I hear him think, but out loud he says nothing, only pats me on the head, stands, and turns to go back into the bathroom. I feel as though a hurricane has switched direction at the last second, saving my home from being destroyed.

To apologize for throwing me, my father takes me to his office to photocopy parts of my body. I choose to do my face first, while he stands guard at the door of the copy room. Balancing on a stool, I press my nose onto the cool glass and push the lid into my head with my right hand. The machine squishes my body like I am the meat in a Xerox sandwich. I push the green button with my free hand. Light travels across my face, bringing heat with it. Through my eyelids, my eyeballs fill with white and my head and my body. I disappear into a hot, bright world. And it seems more real than what is supposed to be. I press the button again, repeating the flash. Does it hurt? Not really. I hear my face slide out on paper, for as many times as I have pressed "start."

"I told you, not your face," my father says, hanging over me, pulling me back. "You're going to fry your brain. Do your hands instead."

I take his advice and place my palm flat on the glass, crunching the lid over my knuckles. He presses the green button for me three times. Soon I wave at myself from the out tray. I pick up the pages and study the black and white image of my hand. The tiny lines form a triangle that traps empty space within it. I imagine living there with what Aunt Leah told me was my lifeline, stretching halfway across my hand. Not long enough to shelter me, I hear a repeat of Aunt Leah's words — "It's short, but it may just mean you will reinvent yourself."

"Wanna do your butt?" my father asks, laughing.

"No, thanks." I flip past my hand picture and see the one of my face: me — only squished, like I am trying to get in, or out.

"Are you done then?"

"Yes, thanks."

We go back into my father's office. Connie's there. And just like most days I'm there, she runs over to him like he's a magnet.

Green. Green. Green. I can hardly see her because of all the green around her face and body.

"Steve, Steve," she says. "There you are. I need you, hon." She puts her hand on the small of his back, which makes him smile.

"Uh, yes, hi Connie." My father seems unsettled. "I will come and sign that contract in a moment."

Connie licks her lips and picks at her bangs, trying to tease them up with her index finger and thumb. She stares at him, to me, and back. Finally she speaks. "Right, the contract that needs signing. That's why I need you, exactly." She winks at my father and walks past him, the curves of her bottom shifting back and forth under her black dress. To my surprise, I hear her thinking, *Mi corazón, mi corazón, mi corazón. Tell her, Steve.*

"Tell me what?" I yell at her without deciding to.

"Huh?" she turns back and blurts out, contorting her face into something ugly.

"Maya, stop it," my father says and I say sorry. (I've got to watch that.) "I'll catch up with you later, Connie. I've got to take Maya back to school."

At school I discover that I have missed the morning class, mathematics, which suits me fine. Kids are already milling in the hallways before lunch, which is where I meet Chauncey and Heather.

"Maya, hi!" Chauncey says through his nose, scraping a pimple off his chin. "Did you hear that Jackie isn't here again today? That's almost seven days away from school. What a baby."

"I heard her mom is keeping her away because she's scared of her getting hurt again," Heather adds.

"It was her own fault," I say, pleased to have new comrades. "She has to learn to keep her trap shut about my mother." They grow silent then, but Heather adds that her own mother attended my mother's funeral, that she had also come to pray for her near the end. This is not something I want to dwell on, so I ask them what they are doing for lunch.

We eat our sandwiches in the lunchroom together (I made mine myself). Chauncey drops some "sloppy" from his Sloppy Joe on his blue button-up. Heather eats only one small corner of her bun and I eat mine down heartily, like this was my last supper.

By Christmas time, Connie is spending at least one night a week sleeping with my father in my mother's bed. I pretend not to hear her as she quietly knocks on the front door after I'm asleep and my father lets her in. I hear them talking, followed by silence in which I lie awake in bed listening, tracing the outline of my father's "Mari" tattoo in my mind's eye, and watching crimson streaks of light from my own body shoot around me in the dark.

Chapter Ten

Father and I have our first Christmas without Mother there to pack the ripped-open wrapping paper into green garbage bags. In fact, there are no real presents at all. On Christmas morning, without a tree, my father gives me a gift certificate for ballet lessons (like I'll ever use them), and I give him four Mars bars wrapped in newspaper topped with a Christmas bow I found on the street.

Neither of us can really be bothered this year, especially when only half of our family is left.

After Christmas, in the days leading up to New Year's Eve, Father tells me that he is taking a business trip to San Francisco with Connie from his office. That's what he says. And inside his head he is saying, *I should be able to do this. I can get on with my life. It's not a sin to need a little physical pleasure.* Yuck, is all I can think, but I say he can go, that it's fine.

He wants me to stay at our neighbour Mrs. Pretty's house, which I flatly refuse.

"I'm not going anywhere. She'll make me sit on her flowered couch and listen to her play the piano."

"Maya, please," he says, which doesn't help his case. I know Mrs. Pretty will want me to talk with her about Mother's "passing," which is something I don't want to do right now, especially with her.

He says that he knows that Mrs. Pretty and her annoying cocker spaniel are not the ideal New Year's Eve dates, but that I am still only twelve and it is his responsibility to look after me.

"Why don't you stay home then?"

"Maya, it's for work. You know I have no choice."

"Sure."

"You'll go over then?"

I nod yes. But as soon as my father has loaded his suitcase into his car and driven away, I call Mrs. Pretty to say he decided not to go.

"I'm glad, Maya," she says. "He should be putting you first, anyway."

"Yes, he should," I say.

"You have yourself a happy New Year, Maya."

I hang up the phone.

New Year's Eve is lonely and silent. Without my father, the walls of our house seem to be growing out, like a balloon expanding as it fills with my hot breath. In the middle I sit very still, a scared animal, trying not to be discovered.

The New Year has arrived — 1986. My father is still not home from his trip, though he said he would be back on New Year's Day.

He hasn't called me. I don't know whether to be furious or

worried. I tried calling the number for the hotel, but I only got a lot of ringing and an automated voice — "Room 1111, leave message after the tone."

I did not leave a message. But the phone rings after I hang up.

"Father?" I say into the phone, like I'm some sort of lost little girl in the mall.

"No, Maya. This is Mrs. Pretty."

"Oh. Hi."

"I don't appreciate you playing games with me, young lady. I just got a call from your father. He wanted to tell you that he's going to be a few days late coming home, but of course you're not here, are you?"

"Sorry."

"You're lucky this time. I told him you were in the shower, but I think he was wise to me. I think the best thing for you to do is pack your bag and come over here right away. We can pretend this little lie of yours never happened."

"I don't need your charity."

"It's not charity." Her voice sounds softer, like she's trying to soothe me with her words. "Just come over, please."

"No, thank you. My aunt is coming over."

This is the first time I have ever hung up the phone on somebody. Then I lock the front door and watch *Dynasty* on the living room couch with my mother's comforter wrapped around me.

I spend the weekend heating up cans of beans baked on the stovetop and nibbling on a loaf of Wonder Bread piece by piece. And now, with the Sunday sun dropping down behind our back fence, I wonder if maybe he's not coming back at all.

Floors creak when I breathe, clocks tick like they are telling me something. There must be a mouse zigzagging across the hall floor because I hear tiny footsteps. I sleep in my mother and father's bed. One tiny me that can't possibly take up the whole space of the mattress.

And tomorrow morning I have to go back to school. I have already laid out my clothes for the day on my bed: red stockings, a plaid skirt, and a white blouse which I ironed myself and spread out neatly so that no teachers would think I looked uncared for. But the night is so long, the clock only seems to change numbers once an hour or so. Cars are going by outside; they don't know I am inside, alone.

I have put my mother's aromatherapy bottles up on the night-stand, just the special ones, calming ones — lavender, patchouli, orange. They are lined up like tiny soldiers and I am sniffing them one by one. Each fragrance bursts out of the bottle and into the darkness when I suck it up my nose. My brown tape player has a handle so I can carry it, and I have put it on the floor beside the bed. Inside is the *Boy in the Box* tape I bought with Aunt Leah shortly after the funeral. When I think I need to hear a man's voice, I turn on Corey Hart.

> *So if you're lost and on your own*
> *You can never surrender*
> *And if your path won't lead you home*
> *You can never surrender*

I can pretend I still have two parents, even though I don't. A lot of things appear to be real even though they aren't underneath — television shows, for example, the man from that movie *Tootsie* who pretends to be a lady, waxy fruit in a bowl, clouds that look like animals,

Mrs. Roughen's blond hair, bacon bits from a jar, the feeling that thunder is hitting the top of your house. It's become windy outside, and I worry that the windows in my parents' bedroom will break through, though I'm not sure why because they never have before.

When morning comes, I slide red tights up each of my pale legs, pull my hair into a ponytail, and brush my teeth with much more than a pea-sized drop of toothpaste. I'm under my winter jacket, scarf, and wool hat, but the January sun still paints my nose, mocking me — *what do you think you're doing? People are going to find out you're all alone.* I keep going, turning to lock the door behind me and reaching a foot out to drop myself down the front steps. My body cuts through the air — arms swinging, head looking up, backpack sturdy on my back, lips pursed together.

"Why are you so dressed up today?" Brian says to me, and I can feel my face flush hot. But then, "I think you forgot to brush your hair, though." I run my fingers through the knotted hair of my ponytail.

"Mind your own business!" I blast out to him as I slide into my seat.

"Maybe you are trying to go out with one of the greasy museum workers at Boomtown!"

I scowl at this and then remember it is field trip day. "I forgot, today is the day we go to Boomtown," I say mostly to myself but Brian hears.

"No duh!" he replies.

"Shut up." My father signed the approval form before Christmas holidays — when he was still here.

Even though I have been to the Western Development Museum

tons of times and feel like we have outgrown it, the trip does let the grade seven classes be merged, which means I can spend the day with Chauncey and Heather.

They greet me beside the bus. Chauncey with his arm in the air, waving, and Heather with her head cocked playfully, smiling.

"We thought we could sit together!" Chauncey says. His words seem to get trapped in bubbles that float from his mouth. "Bitch Jackie is not coming!"

Heather links her arm in mine and pulls me onto the bus. Her attention makes me feel like I am the only one who has been chosen, ever.

The brochure they hand me at the door says, "Welcome to Boomtown, a prairie main street depicting life in 1910. A step into Boomtown is a step back in time."

"Hey, aren't you that kid from the shampoo commercial?" — this from the lady behind the counter as we enter. I feel red cover my face again, and I give her a smile with no teeth.

"Yes, she's famous!" Chauncey yells out to her as we pass through the metal turnstile. He pats me on my head, which makes me laugh. "You can have her autograph, but you'll have to pass it by me first. I'm her manager."

"Who says you get to be her manager?" Heather says.

"Because I'm a guy, that's why. People will take me more seriously."

"Yeah, right! And you are barely a guy even."

"What did you say?"

We are standing at the end of the Boomtown main street: Chauncey, Heather and I. The fake houses that we couldn't wait to explore in the third and fourth grades are waiting before us like aging celebrities. I look up to the sky, to the place above our heads, above the wooden buildings that say things like "Harness Shop" and "Feed Stable" — and I see the black ceiling. Crossbeams cut through the sky with huge floodlights creating suns. Chauncey and Heather are still fighting over who gets to be my manager.

"Do you think I'm not manly enough to be someone's manager, Heather?"

"I never said that." Heather's body seems to be shrinking, her bones getting smaller around. I can hear from inside that she is sorry, either that or I am getting the sense.

"Well, why don't you just screw off." Chauncey takes off by himself through this inside town. A town set up to be real, to be outside, to be home to people going about their lives, going to school, going to the general store, going to jail. But the people we see are only mannequins, and they're not fooling anybody.

The teachers herd us into a circle like we're cattle, and we set out down the boarded sidewalks together — all except Chauncey, who has disappeared. The boards create a hollow echo under our feet when we walk, making us want to stamp harder. Heather and I do.

"Girls, please," says Mr. Wigman, who is looking through a pile of notes and pamphlets. We all follow him inside one of the houses, but all forty of us cannot fit inside and they realize then that we will have to take two different paths around the town. Heather and I stay with Mr. Wigman, leaning over the rope barriers of every exhibit.

"Now, this is an example of a typical home in 1910," Mr. Wigman says. "You can see that the table is set for dinner, which would probably have included something like bread and different meats." He isn't looking at his notes anymore and no one is really listening to him, which makes me feel bad.

"What's that?" I yell out, pointing.

"Good question, Maya. Why, that looks like some sort of pump. They must have used it to pump water into the house."

"They didn't have taps?" says Brian Bellamy and I want to yell out, "Of course they didn't have taps, and of course that is a pump to bring in water — I just asked to make Mr. Wigman feel better!"

We move from building to building. "This is the general store, look at all the different remedies." Then, "This is the police station. Who would like to sit inside the cell while I close the door?" Heather is too scared, but I'm not. The cell makes me feel safe, black bars holding me in.

"These are the stables, where they used to keep the horses. Just look at the heavy leather saddles on the wall, so intricate, eh?" Still no one is listening, but we all nod anyway.

When we reach the fake schoolhouse, the one-room classroom from the 1900s, we find Chauncey. He has hopped over the rope barrier and wedged himself into one of the small desks. His cheeks are puffy, almost like he has been crying. He has a tiny blackboard in his hand and is drawing on it with a piece of chalk. Mr. Wigman pretends to see only the blackboard.

"See class, that is what they call a slate. In class you would write on that instead of paper, using chalk instead of a pencil."

I can't decide what is stranger, Mr. Wigman explaining things that we have seen every year since grade three (there are not that many different places to take field trips in Saskatoon) or Chauncey, stuck inside a tiny desk, pretending to be a student in 1910.

"Chauncey, what are you doing in there?" asks Heather.

"Just sitting. I'm sick of all this."

Heather lifts her small jean leg over the rope and goes over to grab Chauncey by the arm. "C'mon, Chaunce, everyone is looking."

"Who cares if they look?" Chauncey concentrates on his slate; he has drawn a sun on a straight-line horizon.

"Let's move on!" Mr. Wigman says interrupting them. "You have free time from here on. We'll meet back at the bus at three."

The grade sevens file out of the classroom, except for Heather, Chauncey, and me.

"Take back what you said, Heather," Chauncey says.

"Okay, I take it back."

"But do you mean it?"

"Yes."

"Really?"

"Totally."

"C'mon, guys," I say. "It's not worth fighting over who can be my manager. I'm not exactly planning on doing anymore commercials."

"But what if your dad finds you some?"

My dad? My father. The fact that he is still away and may never be coming back swings at my forehead and hits. I had forgotten for a bit. The dusty air of the old building feels instantly foreign within my nostrils. Strange. Unfamiliar. Like I am riding a time machine that only stops briefly in each place and takes away my memories when leaving for each new destination. Where am I now? Where is my father? Why would they make this fake town inside instead of outside?

"Maya, are you okay?" Heather asks. Chauncey has gotten

up from the desk and they have both slid under the rope and are standing in front of me.

"Do you ever wonder what is really real?" I say. They both shake their heads no. I can't tell them about my father. Not until I know for sure what's happening — and what I'm going to do about it. Thinking about it too much gives me secret tears that I refuse to let loose.

By the gift shop there is a lady sleeping in a rocking chair. An old-fashioned lady made of paper or something. Her eyes are closed halfway and her head tilts towards the sky like she is trying to see while she naps on the porch. Like she is watching. Like she has no idea when it will be time to truly relax.

He comes back after all. Father. On Wednesday, and he's carrying a pizza box when he walks through the door, only he's holding it sideways under his arm instead of in the flat of his palm like he's supposed to.

"There you are," he says when he sees me. He's tan. And he's wearing a white linen shirt under his parka — I can see it poking out around his neck.

"Where else would I be, really?" I'm not looking at him when I say this but at the ceiling, at a tiny spot that needs repainting.

"At Mrs. Pretty's!" he says, louder this time. There are red sparks springing out around his face. I have no idea what he is thinking, his voice is too loud. "I left you specific instructions, Maya. You were directed to go to Mrs. Pretty's house." He's got a little vein pulsing on his temple like it might explode.

"Well, I didn't go! Don't pretend you care about me anymore. Not as much as Connie — dogface."

"Maya, don't say that about Connie. You like her, don't you?" It's like he's begging when he says this.

"Just forget it. I hate you."

"You don't mean it," he says as I go up the stairs. "After all I've done for you." But I don't come down.

My father eats the entire pizza himself and doesn't talk to me for the rest of the night. Before I fall asleep, I decide it's me who is not talking to him. I'm giving him the silent treatment. And if I could stop myself from hearing his stupid thoughts, I wouldn't have to deal with him at all.

Chapter Eleven

It's a miracle that an egg was even released at this stage of the game. This is what I heard my father think, and that's how I knew it was true. My mother never wanted to acknowledge the pregnancy, though. Maybe she was pretending herself that it wasn't real — like her own thoughts had some sort of power over how things really were. I hated her for not caring about the baby. That here was this tiny thing growing inside her, and she couldn't even bother to try and get healthy again.

Mrs. Roughen returned to our house several times in the weeks that followed her first visit. She didn't bring Elijah, which I was kind of glad about. Each time, she wanted more information from my mother about her future, which my mother made up, using it as a chance to say everything on her mind.

"Trudie, you have to stop being such a fake ass," she told her, to which Mrs. Roughen only nodded like a jackhammer. "You need to shift your attention off of superficial things like your makeup and handbags. Your demise will come from your own ego."

This wasn't true at all. If my mother really could read Mrs. Roughen's mind, she would know that all she thought about was her estranged husband, her son, and her hatred of herself.

Mrs. Roughen stopped wearing makeup entirely and instead let her wrinkles leave the house unfilled and her eyelids, unpainted.

It infuriated me that my mother was wasting her time with this game when she had more important things to worry about. Soon Mrs. Roughen started bringing other ladies she knew to talk with my mother: Mrs. Parchewski, Mrs. Bell, Mrs. Pretty — one by one they all traipsed in through my front door, removed their shoes, and followed Mrs. Roughen out to my mother's teepee. Sometimes they would suck in their lips and shake their heads at me when they passed, thinking, *Poor, poor girl, she's going to have to live without a mother*.

When I saw these ladies, I would go up to my room to read Archie comics, simple tales of Betty and Veronica chasing a red-headed guy, while Jughead laughs about it. I had no interest in anything these ladies were thinking or what my mother was saying to them. But I did see from my bedroom window that they usually emerged hours later with tear marks on their faces and tissues wadded up in their fists.

I had entered a sort of dream world. Some mornings I would wake up and for the first instant I would forget what was going on. "Time for another day," I would think in the seconds before I remembered. Until it slapped me in the face. My mother would soon be gone and I would be left alone with my father and maybe a baby to look after.

A week into the last month of school I saw Elijah in the hallway for the first time since the shed. He didn't acknowledge me, not really. He only tipped his flat chin down slightly when I passed, and I looked the other way. Right behind him, dressed in cut-off jean shorts and a shirt that showed her belly button, was Jackie. Her lips shone with pink gloss and she had her thin arm linked with Diane's. Diane — her new best friend. Jackie and Diane only smirked at me as they walked past, but I heard what Jackie whispered.

"I know her mom is dying and all, but it doesn't mean I have to like her." I stopped and turned, clutching my books to my chest.

"If you have something to say, why don't you say it to my face," I said this like Joan Collins would say it on *Dynasty*, loud with a hint of superiority.

"I have nothing to say to you," Jackie said without turning back. She said it not to be cruel but as a statement, like she was saying, "I have finished my dinner."

"Stop being such a bitch!" A male voice — Elijah. Elijah talking to Jackie, not me. Jackie's face flushed when she saw that a boy in grade eight had spoken to her.

"Let's just take a moment and think about who the real bitch is here," she said.

"Why don't you leave her the fuck alone?" Elijah was wearing a different Duran Duran T-shirt, and he had combed out his spikes into one mess of brown on top of his head.

"Gladly," said Jackie. "I don't want anything to do with her, to tell you the truth." Beside her, Diane was frozen, probably worried about what kind of social suicide she had gotten herself into by taking Jackie on as a friend. They took long, proud steps away from Elijah together, their arms interlaced.

"What a bunch of losers," Elijah said to me when they had turned the corner. He smiled, then winked at me, and I watched as he turned sharply and disappeared into the boys' washroom.

Besides the times that Jackie and I exchanged subtle jabs in the hallway, I didn't really talk to anyone at school when I was there. Why bother, really?

My only conversations were with my mother at home in the evenings when the "ladies" weren't over and she convinced me to sit with her instead. And so we would sit. I would tell her about my days at school, and she would tell me about how her joints seemed to be stiffening up, her saliva drying up. And that would make me feel sorry for her despite all the things she said and did. She was my mother. Sometimes she would stroke my hair, like when I was little.

We didn't talk about the baby.

Occasionally, if I was in the right mood, I lit candles for her. It seemed like a positive thing to do, to see the light from the flame reflecting around us, creating shadows of my mother and me. My favourite times were when it rained. Water pounded the canvas of the teepee like an army coming to protect us. It came in waves, gathering intensity and then diminishing like it had a plan all along. I learned then the power that liquid had to create a symphony that smelled like grass and flowers and all the goodness of the earth rolled into one breath.

My father brought it for her — the pregnancy test. He left it on the back of the toilet, waiting for one of the few times in the day she went inside the house to relieve herself. I saw it there. I even picked up the box and spun it around, holding it with fingers on each side. Pregnancy, accuracy, hold in urine stream, wait for results.

"Put that down!" my father yelled when he saw me holding it.

"What is it for?"

"That, my dear, is none of your business. And you should not concern yourself with something that is none of your business. Put it back and leave."

"But I have to go."

"Yes, get out."

"No, I have to use the toilet."

"Use it and get to school. You're going to be late."

"Already am." I said shutting the door.

I didn't go to school that day. When I heard my father's car drive away, I sat in my room waiting for my mother to come in. I pulled the bathroom door open when she was still tying up her sheet.

"Well?" I asked her.

"Well what, Maya?"

"What does it say? The test."

"It's negative, of course." And with that I knew that it was positive. Her body was making a baby. I knew, because after she told me it was negative, I heard for the first time, as clear as if she had spoken it, a thought from my mother's head: *Another baby. Shit. Another mistake.*

I bit my lip.

"Let's get you back out to the teepee," I said putting my small hand on her arm and feeling the bones jut out from her elbow. Were new bones growing? Or were they the same old bones sticking out more. She pushed me away and inched by me with her elbows buried in her hands.

That night I dreamed about having a sister. She had red curly hair and cheeks that puffed out when she laughed. In the dream, my sister and I sat in a garden. I was the age I was, eleven, and she seemed to be about five, only she was small enough to fit in the palm of my hand. She was resting on the fleshy part of my thumb and we were looking at a white flower growing out of a pile of rocks. I reached out to pick the flower, but she stopped me.

"Be gentle," she squeaked as the petals fell. "If you grab it, you won't have any flower left."

Then she began to cry — huge tears that created a thin stream in front of her in the grass. And her face began to change. Her skin turned from ivory to rotting and began to fall off, until she was just a tiny skeleton on my open hand. A skeleton that started to crackle and crumble until it turned to ash and the wind blew it away. Then it was me that was crying, in the dream and in the bed where I slept.

"Maya, Maya." My father shook me by the shoulder, bringing me back to what was; I looked at him and chose to close my eyes again. I learned the next day that I had let out a scream that even my mother had heard from the backyard. I told them I dreamed that I was late for school and when I finally got there everyone was dead.

It took me two full days to realize it: when my mother died, my baby sister might go with her. I decided that since my mother was pretending she didn't exist, it was up to me to try to help them both. I didn't want to lose a mother, or a sister. Maybe this would be what would inspire my mother to hang on.

I went to the library at school and cracked open dusty health books looking only for one answer — how long does a baby have to be inside before it can live outside? I found what I needed in a blue copy of the *Reader's Digest Family Health Guide and Medical Encyclopedia*. Under "pregnancy" it read:

"The condition of having a baby developing inside the body. Normally, pregnancy begins with the implantation of a fertilized egg cell on the inside wall of the uterus and ends, after about 280 days, with the birth of an infant. Given special care, survival is possible if the baby is born anytime after about twenty-eight weeks of pregnancy."

I knew that twenty-eight weeks meant seven months and that my mother might not make it that long, if there was any truth to what the doctor had told us. My younger sister didn't stand a chance.

When I got home that night, I wanted to yell at her to get to a hospital, take some drugs, start taking care of herself, for frig's sake. Start caring about something!

Instead, I wimped out and asked her to promise she would never leave me.

"I don't want to leave you, Maya."

"Are you sure?" I crossed my arms across my chest.

"Yes, Maya, you are my daughter. I will try to stay here." She was sticking out her bottom lip just a little when she said it and wringing her hands like she had a secret.

But I knew the truth as well as I knew the pattern of blue veins in the folds of my own arms.

Mother spent more time sleeping in the mornings, her tiny knees pulled up to her gaunt chest. She rocked back and forth like a baby in her own mother's arms. Eventually, when Mrs. Roughen came to the door, Mother would say she was too weak to see her. Once my father and I were eating salads with my mother in her teepee, balancing our plates on our knees, when my mother clutched her belly with both hands and arched her back.

"Your mother's going to be sick, take her outside," my father said and I tried to remember the moment he started talking about her like she wasn't there. Like her tiny body was thinning into a memory — a memory that used to be his wife. I grabbed her by her arm (my fingers could touch round) and tugged. She cried, "Ouch!" and I winced. Did I want to prove that she could still feel?

She tiptoed on her knees until she reached the grass outside, where she leaned over and emptied her stomach into the green blades. Father and I looked right through one another. I crinkled my face and attempted to jump inside his head — the more I tried, the louder the silence buzzed between us. Instead, I scanned the teepee and spotted a laminated card face up on the small table beside the bed — a faded picture of Jesus on the cross, his hands and heart dripping with blood — had someone brought it for her? And on the floor, a small fern with tiny vines and peaked leaves, wet from watering, trying to reach out and kiss the ground. Beside the chair where my father sat, a tub of Vaseline which my mother had been spreading on her dry lips, trying to bring the moisture back.

"Mother, are you all right?" I asked.

"Just fine," and she came back in with a fake smile, like she thought she was fooling us. But that night she told us to leave her at seven, because she needed time to think. And I knew she was upset because thinking was the exact thing you should do to feel more miserable.

In my bedroom I plotted a way to keep my younger sister alive. I imagined it was as simple as planting her in the garden and watching her come up with the carrots and zucchini. Or mixing up the parts of her in a petri dish and keeping it under my bed until she sprouted.

Then I remembered — Corey Hart. A rock star like him, with number one hits, with his picture in the paper and interviews on TV, would be able to help me find a way to save my mother and sister. It was worth a shot. I took a blank pad of lined foolscap out of my desk drawer and began to carve the words with a sharpened pencil:

Dear Mr. Hart:

I have looked up to you for a long time (many months) and I know that because of your good singing voice and engaging personality, you will be able to help me with a problem I am having.

My mother is due to have my baby sister in about nine months. I'm sure you can understand how nice it will be to have a sister because you have four siblings yourself. (I read it in my father's copy of the Saskatoon Sun.*) There is one small problem. The doctor told my mother that she is going to die and I think it might happen before the baby can be born. Please help me, Corey. I need to find a way to help my mother live and my baby sister keep growing.*

I was thinking maybe you could raise money at your concert, and then we could hire the best doctors in Canada to find a way to do it. I think that might work but if you have other ideas, I would take them into consideration.

With sincerity,

Maya Devine

Age 11

Saskatoon, Saskatchewan.

I signed my name in flowing circles to the bottom of the page, tucked the note into an envelope, wrote "Corey Hart, Montreal, Quebec" on the outside, and dropped it into the mailbox at the end of the street.

Chapter Twelve

Cancer ate my mother from the inside out. And at the same time, it ate my baby sister. This is how I used to think about it when it was happening.

Long hours were spent between my mother and father when they were deciding what to do about my mother's pregnancy. At least I think they were deciding. But sometimes, I would peek through the plastic window of the teepee and see them there together. My father stroking her hair, and she with her eyelids glued open in a shocked stare. Like she was made of wax. Wax that was melting.

I never heard back from Corey Hart, although I imagined a million times how his eyes would have looked when he read my letter: soft, sympathetic, caring. Maybe he wanted to help, but didn't know how — which I could understand because the problem itself was big enough to stump anyone.

At the time when my mother was refusing to see anyone, Mrs. Roughen showed up at the front door.

"Oh, dear. I just wanted to bring your mother some chocolate mousse cake that I made. Don't worry, I brought my own plates and silverware" was what Mrs. Roughen told me at the door. "Is there any chance that I could bring it out to her?"

"You can try, Mrs. Roughen. But she hasn't been feeling well."

I led Mrs. Roughen through the house and onto our back lawn.

"Elijah told me he saw you at school." She was clutching a Tupperware container, two paper plates, and plastic forks and had a camera dangling from her wrist. "Perhaps someday you two could be friends. He's a wonderful boy."

"We're just so different," I told her.

"How do you mean, Maya?" She looked hurt.

I remembered the shed, but said, "It's just that I'm in grade six and he's in grade eight. When you're my age, that's years apart."

She laughed like she was pushing it out and trying to show only what a joyful and good-humoured person she was. She laughed too long to be true.

We stood outside the door of the teepee. I could hear my mother breathing and moaning from the inside: *Pain, pain, why, make it stop. Fuck it all.*

"You can go in. But I am going to come with you this time."

"Oh, but I brought only two plates."

"I don't need any cake."

"All right then."

She followed me into the teepee. Dark space even though it was day. Air that had been hanging instead of circulating, air that wanted to get out. My mother was curled on her cot with her hands resting on the soft part of her stomach.

"Marigold? Marigold, it's me, Trudie."

Waxy stare from the bed.

"Marigold, I brought you some chocolate mousse cake. I thought we could eat it. It's been so long since we got together, and I wanted to let you know how good I've been doing about the separation. I really have started to see what you said, that I need to start paying attention to the more important parts of life — like Elijah, for example."

She put the plates down beside my mother on the bed and started to spoon out chocolate mousse from the Tupperware container. My mother remained stoic, like a trapped bird in a cage who has flapped its wings against every side and sees no way to be free.

I don't say anything. Mrs. Roughen did all the talking and eating. She bit brown off the end of her plastic fork while maroon pulsated around her puffy hairdo.

"Mari, I have to tell you, this mousse cake is wonderful. I can understand if you don't feel like eating it. Why, your body must be going through such a battle right now. I know how you must be feeling."

"No, you don't." A cold and stiff version of my mother's voice.

"What did you say?"

"She said, 'No, you don't,' Mrs. Roughen. You don't know how she is feeling."

"I suppose you're right, Maya. I could never know unless I myself was feeling it. Which I'm not, but Lord knows I have had my own trials lately. What with the separation from Mr. Roughen and Elijah's issues. Don't get me wrong, he's a smart and handsome young man, you can attest to that, Maya, but there is something troubling him. I can feel it more and more. We talk less and less."

Neither my mother nor I responded. So Mrs. Roughen picked up the camera that had been dangling on her wrist.

"Mari, I was wondering if you would mind if Maya took a picture of the two of us?"

Three of them, I thought.

"I would like to have a photo to remember you by. To keep in a frame on my piano so that when people come over—"

"Am I your dying friend, Trudie?" My mother again.

"Excuse me, Marigold?"

"Do you like to have me here, wasting away, so that you can come visit me when you are feeling low or bring your friends to see me, like some sort of lonely zoo lion?"

"No, of course not." But I could tell Mrs. Roughen was frazzled. Caught off guard.

"I think you do. I think that you are so busy trying to create some sort of perfect picture of yourself. Your son, your marriage, your home, and now you have added me to the list. Your poor fading friend who you visit when it suits you, who you show off to publicize your compassionate nature." Mother sat up then and pulled her shoulder blades back.

"Mari, I can assure you that you are mistaken. Why are you being so cruel to me?" Mrs. Roughen's eyes had filled with tears and mine had as well. I wished they would all just be quiet.

"Get out, Trudie."

"Pardon me?"

"Get out!" Mother screamed the words the second time she said them and at the same time, she hurled her plate of mousse cake across the teepee so that it squashed against the far wall and created a chocolate stain as it dripped to the ground.

"Why, Mari? Why are you saying these things? I thought we were friends."

"I guess you were wrong."

"Mother, stop it," I blurted out without being able to stop myself.

"Maya, you leave me alone too. Things are too complicated."

"Grow up, Mother!"

"Leave me alone!" She gritted her teeth together and squinted her eyes. I wondered then if this was what death was like. Anger, terror, frustration. Horrible like we all imagined. Was my mother already dead? Had something terrible and evil taken over her body to usher her out?

Mrs. Roughen and I went back into the house. She was dabbing mascara tears with a white Kleenex and in her mind, she was cursing my mother for making her feel like a fool.

When my father got home I told him Mother was dead. This made him run to the backyard, wringing his hands.

"She's not dead," he called up to me later. "She's just sad." Still, he slept inside the house that night and left her out there alone.

For four days after, she did nothing but rock herself on the floor. Pathetic, really.

I decided to go back to school on the fifth day. The principal and the staff in the administrative office were understanding, looking at me with cocked heads and smiles that hid their lips. "There's only one more week of school," they said, reassuring me. "You can stay home with your mother if you like."

But I sat through final classes. No one around me, not even my teacher Mrs. Baby, had a face, only a smooth white mask where a face should be. Mrs. Baby's voice came out like music from a radio when the dial is just off a station, hollow and fuzzy. I learned nothing, and in a flash, school was finished.

"So your mom went off on my mom, eh?" This voice came from behind a tree. A tree that for a minute I thought was a person, a person with leaves for hair, talking to me with green branches for lips. Elijah came around so I could see him. I was walking home from the school on the last day, past the trees that lined the corner of the schoolyard.

"It's not your mother's fault."

"I was hoping it was. It's cool to give my mom a talking to. God knows she's always on my back." Elijah was wearing a black bracelet that snapped closed and had shiny studs lining the edges. His lips were wet like they were leaking something and his brown eyes grabbed me and pulled me into their warmth. The skin on his face stretched out smooth and white, like I would slip on it if I was small enough.

"She's having a baby," I said, which wasn't exactly true because she would probably never have it.

"Brutal," he said back to me, which made me wonder why I told him in the first place. "I guess that kid is doomed either way."

"It's probably going to be a girl and no, she's probably not going to get to grow long enough to live. Unless there is some sort of miracle." My legs started to weaken until I was on my bare knees. I flopped forward, feeling my nose in the dirt.

"Hey, what's happening to you?"

"If I needed you to, would you help me commit suicide?" My voice rose up muffled.

"Suicide?"

"Yes, do you know the best way to do it? Have you heard?"

"Whoa, girl, I am not going to kill you. Smarten up."

"You don't have to do it to me. I was just wondering, if I was to decide to do it, which is the best way to do it? What would hurt the least?"

"If it was me, I would put the car on in the garage, with the windows down a little."

"My father would never let me drive his car. I wouldn't even know how to turn it on." My lips were kissing the dust then and I could taste each speck, dirty and grimy on the tip of my tongue.

"I guess pills then, if you can get them." He put his palm on the back of my head, like I have seen my father do to my mother. Through his palm came a luscious band of energy that filled me up, made me whole again. I was buzzing with light. "You are not going to do anything to yourself though. I won't let you."

I pushed myself up to my knees and then reached out to hug him, because I could, because he was the only one there. No tears fell, only the darkness inside my body that was falling back into the earth. He was kneeling on his acid wash jeans.

"Ohhhhh, lovers. Watch out for her, she has cooties!" Destiny had put Jackie in our path again at that moment. In ours.

"Screw off, moron!"

Jackie skulked at Elijah's outburst and I began to giggle, spitting dirt from my mouth, my shoulders dancing on their own.

"You okay?" he said.

"I will be. Thanks."

"Catch ya later then." Elijah stood over me. I could barely see him because of the green light swirling across his body. He disappeared back behind the trees. My only comfort then were pine cones and branches reaching down to where I sat on the ground, but never getting close enough to touch.

My mother's screaming episodes started getting more frequent as she travelled through what my father called "her down time." She yelled at me because the water I brought her was too warm, she called my father an idiot three times in one afternoon. I worried about what my baby sister was thinking, from inside. Did she think my mother was crazy? Did her ears hurt? Did she want to get out?

During this time, early July, she moved back into the house, saying she was too weak to be outside anymore. Instead, she wrapped herself in her red duvet with the suns and moons on it, and slept days away like they didn't exist for her anymore. I checked on her teepee at least once a day. Swept the tarp on the floor clean of the dirt I just brought in on my shoes, dusted the empty table, added a wildflower to the bud vase Mrs. Roughen had brought, made sure that no squirrels had curled up on her cot.

Thinking back, I'm not sure why I did all that cleaning. It's not like she noticed, or cared, or like I wanted her to either. I just thought it was important, with the summer weather, to keep things moving inside. I would not listen when my father suggested we take the teepee down. I yelled at him, saying, "Mother was right, you are an idiot!" But later on, I crept into the kitchen where he sat at the table and asked him if she would ever be back.

He told me, that yes, she may have a bit of life left in her yet. That we just had to be patient.

Chapter Thirteen

Our silence continues for most of a week. My father is the one to break it, although I already know what he's going to say because I've been listening to him plan it in his head.

We are in the kitchen. I'm scrubbing a plate, but not like I really mean to get it clean. I'm just trying to focus on something else while he makes his after-dinner coffee.

"I would like Connie to live here with us."

I don't say anything, still.

"I know it seems sudden, but I guess you are old enough to know that we are in a relationship with each other now. It's gotten serious, and well, I think we need to make the next step."

I can hardly hear what my father is saying on account of his jumbled up thoughts pounding out from his head to mine. *God, I'm such a wimp, fucking loser, tell her, don't ask her.* I have to close my eyes just to hear his actual words.

"What about Mother?" I answer finally. He looks confused, as if to say, *She's dead remember?* "So you can't even mourn her death for a year before getting some other woman?"

"Maya . . ." He looks like he is thinking about how to answer. His mind is silent and there is red light weaving its way around his head and across his heart. "You know I cared for your mother." Hair has fallen onto his forehead, and he's continually brushing it away with his fingertips — like a woman would.

"You have some way of showing it, really."

"This has nothing to do with your mother."

He leaves to go upstairs before I can tell him again that there is no way I will let that bitch live in our house. He leaves a trail of yellow behind him that cascades down his back and brushes the floor before disappearing.

The next evening she is there. Connie. Sitting at our dinner table with her sinister raven hair, her perked up boobs, and her bangs teased towards the ceiling. She holds her cutlery like she's trying to show off her manicured nails. My father has cooked dinner — fish and peas and French fries browned in the oven. I eat, but I am not saying anything about it — or anything at all.

"So, how was school today, Maya?" my father asks me, like there is no strange woman sitting at our table mashing up tiny vegetables with pinched lips.

I only glare at him as my answer.

Then from inside Connie: *God and Jesus this is uncomfortable. This food tastes terrible.*

"Did you learn anything new or whatever?" my father asks in a final attempt. I decide it's time to talk.

"Why don't you just tell him you don't like the food?" I say. Connie looks horrified, her penciled eyebrows up near her hairline. "You can totally tell anyway by the way you're eating it."

"You don't like it, honey?" (My father to Connie.)

"Steven, she's just making trouble is all. It's wonderful." She slowly lowers her cleavage onto the table (gross) and strokes my father's arm with her long red nails. He seems satisfied.

When Father is getting the vanilla ice cream, Connie turns to glare at me. *Just like her lunatic mother*, she thinks.

Screw you, I mouth to her and leave the table.

Connie does not come back for another dinner. Instead, my father starts spending most of the evenings at her apartment downtown. He sends a babysitter over for the first little while — this teenage girl named Katie, who talks constantly about her boyfriend, Dan, and how he's going to join the military next September. Katie stays from after school to bedtime. We eat dinner together. Eventually, I get bored of her and one day tell her that my father has changed his mind — that he doesn't want her to come anymore. She agrees without much convincing, takes the money he's left on the dining room table, and leaves early.

I start coming home to an empty house. I eat alone. Father usually gets home when I'm in bed, but I always turn over towards the wall when he peeks into my room. I can hear him thinking — he doesn't like what he's doing, but he's doing it anyway. I keep the money he's left for Katie in a secret spot under my mattress.

By spring, Father has realized that Katie isn't coming anymore (she called him once to see if he wanted her help again), but he still starts staying overnight at Connie's most nights. He checks in every few days, for new clothes and to grab the bills and such. If I'm watching TV, he will sit with me while I ignore him. If I'm not home, or in my room with the door shut, he will leave money on the table. Once he even left a note: "You'll be thirteen soon, which is probably old enough to stay by yourself sometimes. Call me at work if you need anything."

I don't call, but I'm starting to need him again. I sometimes wish I could forget it all, forgive him for dishonouring a woman who needed him so much . . . who almost had a new baby girl for him. I wish I could forgive that. Forgive him for moving on with such a tramp.

It's lonely at home when it's empty. I am hearing my mother's moans through this house — they are stuck in the walls. And her complaints and criticisms are hanging down from the ceiling, smothering me while I sleep. I wonder — do angry people go to heaven?

I hear my father in the night too — his voice clouds my dreams. He's confused and worried — manic almost — and he's going over everything many times, wondering how to make things good between us. He has started to love Connie.

I've been turning Corey Hart up really loud while I try to sleep, to drown everything out.

When I go out
I can see the world from inside
Without a doubt
I can shake my head and scream and shout
Because I can't take it no more
I can't stand it no more

Who's laughin' at me?

Through the night

But even Corey Hart and his deep lyrics aren't helping.

I turn thirteen alone. No cake. No candles. Chauncey and Heather are both at summer camp near Lake Blackstrap. I use twenty-five cents to buy a Twinkie from the corner store and suck the cream out slowly before I eat the rest of it. On this day, a Tuesday, sunny sky, small wisps of clouds, no wind, something arrives in the mailbox. It's a birthday card from my Grandma and Grandpa Devine in PEI. There is a flower on the front, with a butterfly, and a little blond girl who looks about four or something. She's wearing a white bonnet and she's smiling. I open it up and the bills fall out onto the ground . . . *To a wonderful Granddaughter. Happy Birthday.* And in my grandmother's shaky handwriting on the inside flap:

Maya, we wanted to wish you a happy day. You must be missing your mother terribly. We are thinking about you, and though we couldn't be at the funeral (on account of your grandfather's heart), we were there in spirit. I hope you and your dad are doing well. I've been trying to call but no one is picking up. Please tell your dad to call me soon . . . I'm getting a tad bit worried. May you receive all the blessings of the world on this beautiful day.

Grandma and Grandpa Devine

It's been so long since I even saw my father's parents, I don't even know if I would recognize them. Why don't they come get me instead of sending money?

I take the bus to McDonald's and order a McChicken, fries, and a large Coke. I stuff ketchup and salt packages in my pocket when I leave to stock up at home. And I buy groceries: TV dinners, canned beans, hotdog wieners, Kraft Dinner, a tub of margarine, spaghetti, chocolate spread, a package of pencil crayons, birthday candles, candy pink nail polish, apples.

For the rest of the summer, I watch television mostly: *Donahue*, *Diff'rent Strokes*, *Facts of Life*, *Gimme a Break!* and *Family Ties*. I watch these shows over and over, around and around. I watch television until my eyes start to hurt and my head starts to pound. Until the static starts to eat me.

One of the nights at 2 a.m., I go to the bathroom to get an Aspirin, except I forget to turn on the light and just stare into the blackness of my reflection, wondering if it's true what they say: that if I turn around three times saying "Bloody Mary" I will see the horrible and bloody face of an old hag. Isn't that how it goes? Instead, as my eyes adjust, I begin to see my own face, round and small in the tall mirror, with my long, dark hair now falling down to past my shoulders. And soon, a rainbow of brilliant purple-blue light fans out around my head, fluttering like it's protecting me, guiding me. I feel warm all over, and safe, safe like I haven't felt at all since Father started staying at Connie's. Since Mother died. I am safe here inside this brilliant light. It is all that I am, and it's enough.

I wake up in the morning on the bathroom floor — the only light is coming in through the window, from that thing called the sun.

———————

On September 1st, one week before school is supposed to start again, someone knocks on my front door. I am cleaning the toilet with yellow gloves that stretch on and a pail of sudsy water. I peel off the gloves, throw them into the bathtub and go to the door.

It's Jackie knocking.

"What are you doing here?" I say to her. I haven't seen her since school ended.

"I heard a rumour that your father's car is never here anymore, so I wanted to see if it's true that you're living alone." She wears white shorts that are way too high on her thighs. Her knees are scratched up.

"Of course I don't live here alone."

"I'll call the police."

"I told you. I'm not."

"Let me see then."

"See what?"

"The inside of the house." We are staring directly into each other's eyes. She is pinching hers so they are almost shut.

"Let's see inside." A new voice has come up behind her. Vanessa Wychuck. And beside her, Sherry Riptella. Two more sets of small tight shorts. She's brought her gang.

"Screw off, I'm not letting you in here," I tell them. For a moment I think I hear Elijah's voice too; from Toronto he says, "Piss off, leave her alone."

"What's that on your neck, Maya?" Jackie wines. "A hickey?"

"No, she's too much of a prude to have a hickey," Vanessa says. I try to look down and she brings her closed fist up under my chin.

"Ouch!" I yell, pronouncing the word like it has several syllables.

"What a baby," Vanessa says.

"She deserved it," Sherry adds.

"I'm warning you guys, get lost. My father is just upstairs and when he sees you there is going to be trouble."

"Why isn't his car in the driveway then?" (Jackie.)

"It's in the shop. The brakes gave out."

"I don't believe you."

"Take your chances then, Tacky, go upstairs. But I have to warn you, he gets angry when people interrupt him when he is working." Jackie grits her teeth together, Vanessa and Sherry look at their fingernails. "See his running shoes are right there. He's here I tell you."

"You are such a bitch, Maya."

"Thank you, Jackie — and yourself as well."

"We'll be back. I still think you are here alone." Jackie says this after she has decided to leave.

Then they each turn their jelly shoes around and walk away. But something has changed. Jackie heard a rumour. Someone started a rumour. Someone knows my father has left me.

Summer ends and grade eight begins. I go to school. I go again and again. I hang out with Chauncey and Heather at recess but I make sure to put on my happy face . . . the one I keep hidden in the back of the closet when I'm at home. Days begin to appear between my father's visits. He starts to leave me more money instead of food in the fridge. I get tired of lugging grocery bags home on the bus and trying to cook stuff. I start to feel hungry all the time. No one suspects anything.

———————

Halloween arrives and I'm delighted by what it could mean for me. Halloween candy, apples, popcorn balls, tiny sweets that soothe my tongue — easy ways to stay fed. All I need to do is find something to dress up as. I decide to go out as a mother, but not my own:

pearls from my mother's jewellery box, a pink button-up sweater I found in the chest at the end of her bed, red lipstick borrowed from Heather, my long grey skirt with the scratchy fabric I wore in the choir. I wrap my hair into a tight bun and stick in straight bobby pins I found in the bathroom drawer. I grab a pillow case and head out the door alone, dropping down the front steps like I'm happy to be going. I feel like a grown-up for the first time; an adult in grown-up clothes, with lipstick that changes my smile.

I told Heather and Chauncey I wasn't going. It would look too suspicious: taking extra candy, staying out late to try and pick up extras. Plus, I needed to get past my neighborhood, not stay around here where everyone knows me and my father. I didn't need to answer any more questions about my mother's illness, or my father's.

I decide to take the bus across the river. Clutching my sack, I am one of many made-up faces: Cabbage Patch Kids, pumpkins that light up, punk rockers with neon hair and fluorescent hair bands. Most of them are in groups of friends, travelling to the rich neighborhoods. Some of them have their parents with them, hands on shoulders steadying them. I get off the bus near downtown and start to visit doors belonging to big and fancy houses. After each opened door comes something like this:

Me: "Trick or treat."

Them: "Well, what have we got here?"

Me: "I'm dressed up as a mother."

Them: "Hmmm, a mother you say (grabbing chins with thumbs and middle fingers), yes, yes, I guess you do look like somebody's mother, maybe the Beaver's mother (laughing), you know, June Cleaver?"

Me: "I know."

And candy drops into my bag. Unlike the other children beside me, I am not disappointed when nuts or raisins are dropped into my sac instead of chocolate or chips — the perfect late-night snacks. I know that I have to start thinking realistically.

I keep trick-or-treating until 10:00, when the streets are dark and the other children have disappeared into their cozy houses. The chill riding in the air all afternoon has picked up and I have to wrap myself up with the scarf I kept hidden in the bottom of my bag all evening. The air turns frosty thick and snowflakes start to fall as I ring the doorbell for what I have decided will be my final house of the evening. A short man with a round belly shoves open the door. I can see his chest hairs under his white T-shirt, his hair is slicked back, his jeans are too tight.

"What have we here?" he says through his nose.

"I'm a lady," I say. The explanations are starting to make me tired.

"And a beautiful lady you are," he says, running his fingers up and down his thighs over and over. The inside of this man's house smells like tuna, and turpentine, the kind my father used to clean his paint brushes when he stained our deck. "Exotic-looking specimen. Are your parents from the East?"

"Do you have anything to give out?" I say impatiently, wishing my father was waiting at the sidewalk like he used to do when I was little.

"You better believe I do," the man says. "Come in first, though." He reaches out to grab the corner of my pink sweater between his chubby fingers. I swat him away, annoyed, but he does it again, pinching his mouth like he's on a mission.

I panic. I feel my mother standing beside me, stiff, with her arms out to protect me.

I pull my arm back and aim to punch him in the chest like I've seen on *The A-Team*. I miss and get him in the chin instead.

"Screw off, buddy!" I scream, and his head flies back.

"You little whore!" he yells after me as I run away. I look back briefly to see him rubbing his jaw, the colour in the air around his face is confused and undecided.

At the bus stop I start to cry. Holding my large sack of candy that sits like a pregnant belly in my lap, I wish I had someone to take me home. When the bus arrives, my arms have relaxed to the point where I can hardly move them enough to carry the sack. My arms are asleep.

"You really brought it home," the bus driver says as I get on and drop the coins in his slot. "Heading back over the river?"

I nod. He smiles. He has white teeth and kind eyes.

Back in my empty house, with walls like mirrors looking back at me, I dump my bag onto the living room floor and start sorting it out.

"Gosh, can you believe all the Tootsie Rolls?" I say to no one, like I'm making small talk to recover after a hard day. "And Cracker Jacks, wow, people are not this generous around here. And full-size chocolate bars even."

I create families of goodies on the carpet and start to order them by nutritional content: apples, popcorn, raisins, and pumpkins seeds lead to Dubble Bubble gum, small cardboard Chiclets boxes, and Twizzlers in plastic wrappers. I peel one open and hold a pink Twizzler between my teeth.

The phone rings, and in my sugar high, I forget that I'm not answering it.

It's Grandmother Devine.

"Hello, Maya," she says with a soft but shaky voice. "I'm so glad to have gotten you. Happy Halloween. How have you been holding up?"

"Fine," I say back.

"But it must be so hard, dear. Death has a way of pulling the life out of all of us. I know that Leah was quite choked up when she got back from the funeral. I'm sorry that your grandfather and I couldn't be there. You know his bad heart — air travel is out of the question, and I can't bear to leave him."

"Yes, I remember. How is Aunt Leah?"

"She's escaped to Toronto. Starting a crazy life, on the street for all we know. We pray for her. Can I please talk to your father?"

"He's sick."

"What sort of sickness, dear?"

"He has laryngitis. He can't talk."

"Not at all?"

"No, not at all. He can listen though, I'll get him." I pretended to be my father listening while she talked.

"Steven, dear — Steven, is that you?" I grunt. "Steven, I wanted to let you know that your father and I are thinking of you. Gosh, it must be hard without Mari. We want you to know that you can reach out to us if you want to. Remember, Steven, you did the right thing, the respectable thing, staying with her and Maya. Maybe this will be just the kind of fresh start you needed. The fresh start that you were cheated out of."

"He's gone now," I say. "He had to go throw up."

"That's a shame. Tell him to call us when he is feeling better."

"I will."

"And you take care."

I grunt.

"Goodbye, dear."

I hated my grandmother for saying those things, especially when I hardly even remember what her face looks like.

Father comes over the morning after Halloween — when I'm at school. I know because two of my Tootsie rolls are missing and he's left more money on the table and taken the credit card and phone bills I lined up on the counter.

He's also left another note:

Maya, things get so difficult in life, but like it or not, you're still my daughter. I am so proud of you for being so responsible and looking after the house when I'm gone. I am going to make sure this works out. I hope we can start talking again soon — I really do. I'm at a loss for what to do next.

His handwriting is messy and frantic. He must have run out of room on the paper, because he has left no signature at the bottom of the page.

Chapter Fourteen

Prairie winter arrives in November to hurl its strength. Frozen eyelashes, breath that freezes in my throat, ground slippery under my feet, boots out of the closet, warm meals of vegetarian chili from cans I buy, turning up the knob for the furnace at night. The walk to school is longer because I am taking smaller steps to stay in the heat of my body. Underneath my ratty cotton candy parka, my bones are starting to stick out in strange places: from my hips, below my neck, on the tips of my shoulders, maybe even my chin, which is hidden behind the blue scarf my father used to wear. I don't feel much like eating lately.

My house is getting big and lonely. Sometimes, I admit, I want my father back in it. He only stops by now when I'm at school, or when I'm asleep — I hear him poking around at things in the night. Sometimes he opens the door to my room and I pretend to be sleeping so he will go. He leaves money and sometimes a bag of groceries on the dining room table as usual.

Two different days at school I decide I need him back and call him at work from the pay phone out front. Both times I get his machine: "This is Steven Devine, your call is important to me."

I don't leave a message.

There are other times when I just want to leave, so that my father doesn't have to worry about me at all. He can sell the house and pretend that none of this even existed — that my mother was never sick out back.

I have a secret plan to escape and fly to Montreal next summer. I've started saving money to buy a plane ticket, but it means I can't spend much of the money he gives me. I try skipping lunch at school, but I'm usually so hungry that I give in and buy fries with Chauncey and Heather.

I know it's going to cost a lot to fly away anywhere, so I decide to hold a yard sale.

"In November?" Heather says when I tell her. "There are three foot snow drifts already, people will be freezing."

"Okay, garage sale," I say. "My father is away on business. I want to earn some extra money before he gets back and finds out."

"For what?" Chauncey asks.

"Stuff."

"Like new clothes and makeup and things?" Heather says.

"Maybe a vacation. In the summer."

"What will you sell?" Chauncey asks.

"My mother's old jewellery, her clothes . . ."

"Won't you miss that stuff?" Heather says.

"I'll keep the important stuff."

"It's kind of creepy though," Chauncey adds. "To know that someone is walking around in your mother's clothes."

"She didn't wear any of it when she was sick. She mostly wore a sheet."

"Oh yeah." And from her head: *I remember from television. Mom thought she was crazy.*

"Heather, I am going to pretend you didn't say that."

"Say what?"

I put the garage sale sign at the end of my driveway. It is a piece of cardboard nailed to a piece of wood I found in my father's workshop. I wedge it into the snow. On the day of the sale I pile on layers of clothing — sweaters, ski pants, wool socks — and sit on a lawn chair in our garage, my boots resting on the concrete floor. I have taken all my mother's jewellery out of her cabinet: her pearls, a broach with a lady's profile on it, a gold chain that links with a heart, a silver chain. I've laid it all out on a small patio table with a sign that says, "Let's negotiate." I had to look up the word "negotiate" in the dictionary to make sure I got it right but am pretty sure it will help me get more money.

I am not worried about getting rid of the jewellery; my mother hardly wore it and I think most of it was given to her by my grandmother when she was younger — family heirlooms maybe. My mother was not the jewellery type, and if my grandmother had gotten to know her better, maybe she would have known that.

My mother's clothes — blouses, skirts, slacks — are hung up around the garage on metal hangers. Their presence gives me the distinct sense that my mother is watching me, maybe even standing around me. Other than that, I put a few of my father's old suits up for sale, and some of his ties that had fallen to the bottom of his closet.

Heather is the first to knock on the closed garage door. She wears a one-piece ski suit that does up in the centre with a fat zipper, her head is hidden under a toque, and she carries a thermos and a blue box under her arm.

"I brought hot chocolate!" she says when I open the door. "And a Trivial Pursuit game my dad bought my mom as a present. She never plays it, so I thought we could have a game before we sell it."

"Thanks, Heather." The cold air whips against the garage door as I slide it closed again, scraping metal as I go.

"Maya, this is so cool that you get to stay alone when your father is out of town. I can't even imagine my mom giving me this kind of freedom. You really do have it all." Her tiny body is leaning up against the patio table and I think how small and delicate she looks, like she could freeze or fall over if put in the right circumstances.

Chauncey is next to arrive. "Maya, I really don't know how much business you're going to get, what with the cold temperature and all. A yard sale in November? Really?"

"It's important, okay?" I say. "I need the extra money."

He nods and the three of us sit down to play Trivial Pursuit. A small space heater chugs out warmth from its place by the wall beside us and we cover our hands with our mittens to keep warm. After we have chosen our colours — me orange, Heather pink, and Chauncey blue, Heather rolls the dice and lands on the pink square.

Chauncey reads the card: "Heather, who was the first singer to put three consecutive releases on the top of the British charts?"

"How should I know?"

"Just think about it, Heath."

"The Beatles."

"That's a group, not a person."

"Elton John."

"No."

"David Bowie."

"No."

"I give up."

"You suck at this game, Heather. You really do."

"Just give me the answer, Chauncey."

"Elvis Presley." Chauncey puts the card back into the blue box.

"Who knew?"

"Maya, your turn to roll." I pick up the dice while still looking at the garage door. I move forward four spaces and land on a green box. Heather reads: "What colour was the rain that fell on Hiroshima for two hours after the bombing?"

"Black," I say.

"How did you know?"

"Lucky guess."

A knock on the garage door.

"The people are here!" Heather says in a loud voice. I grab the rope attached to the door and slide it upwards. There in front of me, in a heavy parka and Eskimo jacket with fur trim, are Mrs. Bell and Mrs. Parchewski, two of the women who used to come with Mrs. Roughen to visit with my mother in her teepee.

"Maya," Mrs. Bell says. "We saw your sign outside and thought we would come to say hello. How have you been?"

"Fine, thank you."

"And your father?"

"He's out of town on business."

"I see. Well, let's take a look." She rubs her boots across the cement of the garage floor until she peers over the table of merchandise. Mrs. Parchewski follows, saying nothing. "Looks like you have some of your mother's things here."

"Yes."

"Her chains? A brooch. And some of her old dresses."

"Make me an offer."

"Maya, don't you want to keep these things? To remember your mother."

"I remember her just fine."

"But these things were a part of her."

"She never wore them. I asked my father and he said it would be all right to get rid of them."

"I see." Mrs. Bell holds an old teacup in her hands, while Mrs. Parchewski is taking off her scarf to fasten a pearl necklace around her neck. "I guess it doesn't hurt to look then," Mrs. Bell says. "You know how we felt about your mother." And from Mrs. Bell's mind: *Mari never really did anything for me.* I sigh and look at the ceiling while they sift through everything with their chubby fingers. Picking things up, dropping them, trying on, comparing, running their palms over smooth fabric. Over their white faces, huge blobs of cherry light are forming, opening and closing like giant hands, interweaving with each other, momentarily blocking out their sympathetic grins.

Heather pours hot chocolate into the lid of her thermos and starts to sip. Chauncey shakes the plastic bag of Trivial Pursuit pies.

They buy most of it: two chains, the pearl necklace, three old dresses and a pair of dress pumps, the teacup, a pair of red leg warmers.

"How about one hundred?" I say to them.

"Maya dear, don't you think that is a bit outrageous? We'll give you fifty dollars."

"This is expensive stuff. Nothing under one hundred."

Mrs. Bell pulls four twenties from her wallet and Mrs. Parchewski hands me a twenty dollar bill from her pocket. They put everything into purses, under their jackets, and over their arms. I open the door to let them out.

"Maya, good job!" Heather says when they are gone. "You totally negotiated like an expert."

"You have to do what you have to do," I say.

"What are you going to do with the money?" Chauncey asks.

"Buy stuff I need, I guess." I think about warm dinners, lunches from the cafeteria, and maybe a new pair of winter boots.

"Yeah, like the new Corey Hart record," Heather says. "We know you love him."

"Not even!" I say. "Other stuff."

The garage door goes up and down three more times with people from my street. By the end of the day, almost all of my mother's stuff is gone, as well as my father's snowblower and his power drill, which I let go for $50 each — he'll never miss them. Altogether, I have made $325. When Chauncey and Heather are gone, I put all the money inside my pillowcase and fall asleep on it. The garage is empty again, and even more of my mother is gone. I dream that my skin is melting off, leaving me nothing but muscle and bones. And that I take all my skin, pack it into baggies, and sell it at a road-side stand to unsuspecting people who think it is chicken. My sleep passes like a choppy collection of false starts, never letting up, never letting me relax.

————————

Soon, I start feeling dizzy and stop going to school. First one day, then another. My house begins to feel like a safe place — the only place where I can hide myself. On day five away, I lie on my mother and father's bed looking up at a white ceiling that occasionally drops to graze the top of my face. The sun goes down and soon Chauncey and Heather are outside the window of my parents' bedroom. I hear stones being thrown against the glass and their voices, tiny and far away, calling my name.

"Maya, are you in there? Maya, come down," they say in unison. I stand up and throw myself against the window, using the crank by my waist to open it.

"I'm here," I say, my eyes half closed by the pain in my forehead.

"Why weren't you at school?" Chauncey asks, holding his dark arm out like he is carrying a tray of hors d'oeuvres.

"I'm sick," I say weakly. "I need to sleep."

"Let us up," Heather says. "We want to talk with you about something. People are talking about you."

"I can't right now. I'm too dizzy. I need to sleep."

Chauncey: "Maya, are you alone in there?"

"I might be alone for now."

"What?" they both say.

"We don't understand," says Heather. "Come down now!"

"I'm closing this window up now. It's so cold in here. Bye, bye now." I fall to the floor. I hear them pounding on the front door with their fists. They are trying to break the lock. They are trying to open the front windows. They are trying to get in. But soon, the silence returns.

The walls of my house are melting. Shrinking and dripping like candle wax. The TV set in my parents' bedroom is shrivelling up and taking the dresser with it. Falling into nothing. The floor is getting smaller but I am still at the centre of it. Lamps are tipping onto the floor and then burning up into themselves. The second floor of my house is lowering me down to the earth, until nothing is left around me. Nothing but dark earth and grass, and the tree that used to be outside my bedroom window, now reaching down to cover me.

I lie on my back looking up at the stars. I think I see the Big Dipper, carved out on top of the dark sky. I close my eyes and feel the sun come out behind my eyelids. Blue sky being overtaken by clouds heavy with rain, rain that lands on my face, coating me with wet. A grumble of thunder, then nothing but sky again. A faded moon I can see in the light. Heaven?

I can smell the skin behind my mother's ear when I hug her, sweet like a puppy's paws.

The air above is getting closer, like a fog coming down. My body is sinking into the earth, back in. Back into nothing. The worms slither over me now, wrapping me up like a present. They are comforting, not gross like I would have expected. I turn my head from inside the dirt and see my mother's face, lifeless, pale, bony, eyes open, lips parted. I scream and the earth fills my mouth. And then, only open space and a brightness that engulfs me.

I land back in my house. My whole house as it was. In my parent's bed with the sheets wrapped around me like I'm a suffocating baby. I open my eyes to my name being spoken.

"Maya." A man's voice. My father's voice.

"Maya." My name being sung this time, from downstairs. My name from my mother's warm lips. "Maya, we're down here! We're back."

I sit up and open my eyes, moving my numb body to the edge of the bed. There are no sounds from outside, only silence and my feet pounding on the carpet, and down the stairs, to find them standing in front of the door. Side by side, my parents, with smiles, holding hands, with pitying eyes. I stand in front of them and they stroke my hair and my face.

"Maya, it was all a dream. It's all over," my father says. "You shouldn't have believed we would let that happen to you."

"I was all alone," I say to them and my mother tells me to "shooosh," that it's all okay now. We can make it through this all together. That it never happened. They are hugging me, with my mother on the bottom layer and my father on the top. I can't feel their arms around me and then they start to go right through me, like I am made up of nothing. They are hugging me, but I am not really there. Then they vanish too.

"It's all about different levels," a voice says from behind me. I sob and turn.

"They're gone," I say to him. It's Elijah, smiling, casual, relaxed, dressed in white, which he would never wear.

"What if you are the one who's gone?"

"I would never leave, Elijah. You know that."

"I guess you're right." And we both start to laugh, chuckles that send us to the floor, giggles that rise and fall like waves. Then, poof.

I'm awake for real. My nose is leaking onto my cheeks. What day is it? How long have I been sleeping? A few days perhaps? I'm hungry. Every muscle holding my skeleton together feels like it has been stretched out and shoved back into place. My temples are burning, aching. My jaw wedged closed, I struggle to open it. I think I have been crying because my eyes are crusted up. It must be night time because the air outside the window is black and cold. I drag myself into the washroom, hike up my nightgown, and sit on the toilet to release the pee I have been holding — a long steady stream that goes on for almost a minute. I shiver at the end of it.

I hobble back to my parents' bedroom and open my mother's closet to find a sweater. The closet is almost empty because I have sold most things. There is one sweatshirt folded and placed up top, a green one. It has the word "Trent" written on the front of it. It reminds me that my parents were both going to university there when they met. Maybe she was wearing this when they first kissed — when they fell in love. The thought of it makes me smile, despite my sickness.

I pick the sweatshirt up by the shoulder and put my head through the neck hole, sliding my arms into each of its sleeves. That's when I notice it. There is a small picnic basket on the shelf near the back. Was it always there? Why am I only seeing it now?

I pull it down, rest it on the floor and open the lid. Inside the picnic basket is a blue plaid blanket folded up, just a thin one for sitting on, I imagine. But I lift it up and underneath there are several thin metal bracelets with dangling butterflies, and a small black notebook. I run my palm over all these things and feel a jolt. I slide the bracelets over my fingers and shake my arm so they dance. I pick up the notebook. My mother's name is written on the front cover along with the words "Privacy Please." I smooth my thumbs over the cover and inhale deeply.

I open the notebook and begin to read the words my mother had written.

Chapter Fifteen

October 18, 1972

I saw him again today. He sat beside me by the river — me reading *Pride and Prejudice*, him only looking out onto the water. I must have been staring, something about his eyes — dark and calm. And the way his raven hair falls to his shoulders. He looked tired as he sat there, with sandalled feet tucked up under him and his loose clothing fluttering a bit with the wind. He looked lonely. I slid closer, towards him on the bench.

And that's when he told me his name — Amar Ghosh. He looked down to my feet and up to my boobs. And then I told him mine, Marigold, I said. Marigold McCann.

After a while of me reading and him sitting, he walked away without saying anything else. Now I'm wondering, who is this strange guy besides his name? He's older that's for sure, maybe even thirty. It's been two years since I've noticed any man besides Steven. Two years since I've come up for air. Shit.

This guy is so unlike anyone I've ever met that I thought I'd keep a record of when I see him — almost like he won't be real otherwise. I don't know what it means. It's not like I'm leading up to something. I'm not. I know how good I have it with Steven — and that can be enough, for now anyway.

October 23, 1972

Went to the park today to find Amar — under a tree, cross-legged like Gandhi — with a bunch of WASP kids sitting at a picnic table, eating lunch and pointing. And laughing.

Shut the hell up! I yelled at them, though I regretted it afterwards. He didn't flinch. I sat in the grass nearby. I wasn't trying to come on to him or anything. Besides, I told Steven to meet me there. I had to get out of the house, away from Mother and her I-expect-to-see-you-at-church-this-Sunday bullshit. So I was only waiting for Steven in the grass, and reading.

Steven greeted me by kissing me on the top of my head and rubbing his hands over the back of my neck. So gentle, but I jumped.

Do you have to sneak up on me like that? I said to him, real mean like. I regret that too, because he didn't get angry, only dropped to the grass, stretched his corduroy legs out in front of him, and used his straight arms as a backrest.

Who's that freak? he asked when he saw Amar.

I don't know, I said and I was telling the truth. I don't know who he is and I also don't know he's a freak.

He looks a little out of place, don't you think? Steven said.

147

He seems all right. I myself was freaking inside, hoping Amar didn't decide to talk to me at that moment.

We might as well get going then, honey.

Steven and I stood up. Amar didn't move — but I saw him turn his head and glare at us when we walked away (a good sign!). There's something about this guy. He could definitely be a model if he tried . . . in the Sears catalogue at least. He's got an electricity about him that none of the other guys around here have.

October 31, 1972

It's snowing outside. I feel sorry for the kids out tonight, in their pirate costumes and such, dragging themselves from house to house. Idiots. Mother is knocking on my bedroom door, telling me Steven is on the phone. Take a message, I have just told her, because I have to get this stuff down. She thinks it's important I take his call. How the hell could she know that? She needs to find her own man to take some of the pressure off.

What I have to write is this: this afternoon I had a proper conversation with Amar. Nothing profound, but we could probably now be considered acquaintances. He was in the same spot, under the tree, wearing the same baggy pants and striped shirt, with beads hanging round his neck and flopping against his muscular chest. I had on my suede jacket, the one with the fake fur around the collar, tickling my chin, making me sweat around the neck.

I asked him if he taught at Trent or something, and he said no, he wasn't a part of the university or even from Peterborough. Oh I see, I said, continuing to leaf through the *Elements of Style* in my hands and raising my eyebrows to fake interesting passages. So why are you here then?

He said he just liked sitting among the students, around those who were searching for answers to questions.

Of course, I said, like I knew what he meant.

I'm in town to see my mother, he continued. She lives out of town, past Douro, in a cabin on the river. But she's sick, so I go visit her at St. Joseph's.

Bummer, I said. What is she sick with?

She had a brain aneurism last week, he told me.

I'm sorry, I said. (I wanted to walk away then, but I stayed.) It must be hard for you?

I don't really want to talk about it right now, if you don't mind. He was stroking his own arm and looking into my lap.

Gosh, sorry.

He spread his fingers and combed them through his long hair, and then smoothed down a faint mustache with his pointer and thumb.

I freaked out then, like what if he was some sort of assassin, plotting to poison me with a graciously offered herbal tea? Or stab me with a pocket knife? I said goodbye and ran home, like some sort of chicken shit. Found Mother saying the rosary in the living room when I got here, by herself, with the drapes drawn, with not even the television on. She's so lame.

I just want to stay in my room all night, even though it's Halloween. I hear the knocks at the door downstairs, but I'll let Mother hand out the candy apples and popcorn balls she made. I'll let her talk to Steven. I just want to disappear.

November 5, 1972

It's November and he hasn't been under the tree. Besides, the wind off the water makes it too cold for anyone to stand out there.

So I went to the hospital to look for him.

I know it sounds ridiculous, especially since I had class, but I couldn't stop myself from going. I wanted to see him again, plus, I couldn't think of anything else to snap me out of this depression.

I hate hospitals. Fuck do I ever hate hospitals, sickness all over the damn place. Funny how I went there to try and perk myself up. I generally try to avoid the smell of death when I can.

I walked up and down every floor. Saw babies sleeping in windows, kids screaming for their mothers, old people gasping for breath. Yuck. Finally I asked a nurse if someone had a brain aneurysm, where would they be? She said probably in intensive care, but that I wouldn't be allowed in unless I was a family member. I said (kind of rudely) that I was a family member and could she please direct me to the goddamn room. She looked stunned when I told her that, like I had just burped up a pumpkin or something.

I found him sitting on a blue plastic chair in a waiting room. Outside the part I couldn't get into.

Hello, I said and he looked up, surprised. How is your mother?

She's gone, he said.

They moved her?

No. (He looked annoyed with me.) She passed away this morning if you must know. His words had a sort of evil snap to them, but his eyes looked intriguing and handsome when he said it.

The door opened and they wheeled a stretcher out. A stretcher with a body on it, covered by a white sheet.

Is that her? He shook his head no. At the sight of the random dead body, I felt like I wanted to make the sign of the cross, but didn't. He bowed his head and stood up. I walked to the elevator with him.

Sorry about your loss, I said and he nodded again.

He turned his face towards me: Can I buy you a cup of coffee? His teeth danced bright against his toasted skin, he tucked a piece of his hair behind his ear and ran his thin finger over the string of beads around his neck.

Thanks, but I can't. I'm here to see a friend. She fell down and broke her arm.

Sorry to hear that.

Oh well, I said and he actually laughed, a gruff laugh, like the years had attached themselves to his voice.

You can call me, though, I said as the elevator door opened. If you need someone to talk to about your mother.

That's very nice of you.

He held the elevator with his sandalled foot while I ran to the desk and scribbled my number on a pink slip that said "While You Were Out" on the top. He took it between his palms and bowed.

Namaste, he said and winked at me as the elevator door closed.

The knocks at my door have finally stopped and my mother's bedroom light has gone out.

November 12, 1972

He hasn't called, which makes sense considering he must be almost ten years older than me. And he's a different race, not that it should matter. I have a few Chinese friends from my classes — that's something.

But I thought he would call.

I don't really know why I want to hear from him. Or what I would do afterwards. It's just that his energy invites me in. I think I have what you call sexual infatuation. That, or we were destined to be together forever (laugh, laugh).

Steven has stopped calling too. He wrote me a letter, which he slid between the front door and the screen. In it he said: *I don't know what's going on with you, but I'm going to give you the space you need, because I love you.*

My mother opened the letter before giving it to me, and handed me the page with an "I told you so" kind of look on her face.

He's a wonderful boy, she said. You would be lucky to have a man like that as your husband.

Just give me the paper, Mother. I grabbed it out of her hand. Just because she's desperate since Father died, doesn't mean I have to become all needy too. It's not my fault he smoked until his lungs gave out.

November 19, 1972

Saw Steven on campus today. I tried to be nice because well, he looked so goddamn pathetic. Jesus Christ. You'd think I was the only girl who ever let him feel her up.

November 21, 1972

I can hardly write this, my fingers won't stop twitching.

He just called.

Mother said, There's some man on the phone for you (I told her later it was my professor), and I picked up the receiver in the living room to hear his voice.

Hello, Marigold.

Amar?

Are you surprised?

How's your mother?

She died, Marigold. You know that.

I'm sorry, I meant to say, how are you dealing with the loss of your mother? (Oh Christ, I thought. Man, I was nervous.)

As well as can be expected, I guess. Things change.

Yes, they do I guess, I said. Then nothing but breathing, for almost a minute. And then him: Some people are uncomfortable with silence, not me.

No?

Silence is invigorating. Especially between two people.

I guess.

How old are you, Marigold? His voice came out chalky but soothing.

Twenty-five. (I lied.)

Would you like to get together sometime?

Yes.

Just to talk.

Yeah.

I hope you don't find it weird of me to ask. It's just that I don't know many people around here. And now with my mother gone, no one.

I said, yes.

Great then, we could meet tomorrow. Around 5:00, at Trent, on that same bench by the river?

Okay.

So now I am wondering what I've done. And why? And the worse part is I told Steven I would study with him tomorrow afternoon — a kind of reconciliation. I'll have to tell him I'm sick. I think I might be. I just keep thinking about tomorrow, that's the best part.

November 22, 1972

I could hardly wait to write in this book today. God, I hope Mother doesn't find it. I'll hide it under the mattress, she'll never look there.

We had a picnic.

Yes, you heard me right. In November, a picnic! He brought the basket, packed with bread, salami, and garlic pickles. He had a thermos with gin and tonic in it. Can you believe it — gin and tonic! The wind was blowing a bit, but we sat behind a tree to shield ourselves.

I'm sorry, he said. I had no idea it was going to be so chilly. (It's November, I thought. Of course it's chilly.) I hope this is okay, Marigold.

It's fine, I said and he stared at me. He had pulled his hair back in a ponytail and his chest hairs were peeking out from under his V-neck sweater. (I'm embarrassed to say, but I wanted to lick them.) I wore my paisley shirt underneath my suede jacket. My hair down. And blue eye shadow.

We were not sure what to say at first — *fuck, fuck, fuck* is what I was saying inside my head as I scrunched up my toes in my platforms (totally impractical shoes of course — so like me). He asked me if I thought they should have cancelled the Olympics after what happened to all those people in Germany. I said that I didn't really follow sports, but they probably should have — that the organizers were all a bunch of idiots.

He responded by saying that things weren't always as they seemed.

I guess, I shrugged. (Who cares though, really?)

How are your studies going? he asked.

Pretty good, I guess. I'm taking English.

Ah, good for you. My mother studied English as well. And I took some courses when I was in university — I never graduated though, it wasn't for me. He spoke without opening his mouth very wide, which was strange but somehow relaxing. And during one of the pauses, he reached his arm up and placed it on the ground behind my back, and kind of stroked my shoulder with his finger.

What do you do, Amar? I was trying to ignore him, and kind of hoping no one walked by.

Nothing right now. (Oh great, I thought.) I'm been up from Toronto, staying with my mother. She had been living up here for a few years. His eyes were getting teary, and he took his arm away from behind my back, which was a bit of a relief.

Right, I said, nodding like an artsy type at a dinner party.

I'm staying in the cabin where she was living before she died. You should visit sometime. Though lacking in amenities, it's a cool place to find your centre.

I can imagine, I said, though I really couldn't. What about your father?

He went back to India when my parents split up. My mother's from Peterborough, so she came here. The cabin used to belong to her parents — they're gone now as well.

So you're half Canadian then? (A stupid thing to say now that I've thought about it.)

Yes, my father came from India to teach and met my mother in Toronto, where I grew up.

Then the wind pushed over the thermos on top of the loaf of bread we were breaking off with our fingers. He only laughed and commented, Ah the wind, he makes himself known.

Who says the wind is a man? I said.

You make a good point, Marigold, you do. (A pause.) You have beautiful hair, you know that? Like fall leaves. And a beautiful colour around you — crimson streaks like a sunset.

What can a girl say to that — oh thank you, I know I'm gorgeous in every way (laugh)!

I don't know if I will see Amar again. After lunch, he asked me if I would like to get to know each other a bit better by meeting again. He leaned forward a bit when he said it. I turned my head away and sighed, my cheeks stinging red. Why would he ever take a girl like me seriously? Should I let him?

Amar gave me the picnic basket to keep before he walked away. (I've hidden it in the back of my closet.) He touched the top of my hand when he handed it to me, and his fingertips sent up a jolt reaching all corners of my body at once. Every corner.

I should be studying right now. I have a mid-term tomorrow — Canadian Literature — essay questions covering three different texts: *Sunshine Sketches of a Little Town, Who Has Seen the Wind,* and

Roughing it in the Bush. How can I bring narratives together that don't seem to match at all? That's what I need to figure out.

I am staring at a spot of chipped paint beside my bed and wondering where he is right now. Where he is and what he's thinking.

Chapter Sixteen

After days in her bedroom — sleeping, reading the *Bhagavad Gita*, and basically staring at the backs of her hands in a darkened room — my mother appeared in the kitchen. "How's this for magic!" she said manically, reaching her frail arms towards the ceiling. She was dressed in her tank top, with no bra, and denim shorts. "What's the date?"

I told her it was July 17th and she cocked her head towards me and swung it back and forth. "Guess I should try to get up for a while. How has the weather been?"

"Mainly sunny to partly cloudy, 31 degrees, ten percent chance of rain," my father said, reading from his newspaper but not looking up at her.

"Fuck," she said in a shrill voice that popped and startled me. Father looked up at her with a grimace.

"Sorry, I meant to say, wow, still hot. Maya, you and me are going to the market, for groceries and razors. I need to shave this head down again. Then I guess I'll move back out to the teepee."

"I've kept it clean for you," I said to her. "I swept it every day."

"Go get your market purse, we have vegetables to buy." She was trying at least. She was giving life one more shot.

I jumped up then and ran up to my bedroom. On the way back down, I heard her talking to my father.

"Steven, I'm just trying to say that I'm sorry. I should never have acted that way." My father was chewing on the end of a pencil and spitting tiny bits onto the table. When she saw me she added, "Maya, I was just telling your father that I am going to do all I can to last as long as I can. A positive attitude can go a long way."

"Jesus, Mari, enough with the inspirational quotes. Soon you'll be giving out pamphlets again. They're just words, you know."

"I beg to differ," said my mother, and we headed towards the door. On the way across the threshold she tripped and had to wait a few moments to recover from what she called "dizzy stars." While we waited, she bent down and whispered in my ear, "Sometimes you fall off of life, but you get back on."

I wanted to give her the benefit of the doubt, be on her side, let her cry on my shoulder — every cliché I could think of, I wanted to give it to her. I reached up and held her hand as we headed off through the door.

We stopped at the Roughens' house before the market. We went right up the cement steps, knocked on the door, waited. Mrs. Roughen opened the door in a huff.

"Marigold, you're up."

"Trudie, I'm here to apologize." I was still holding my mother's hand while she spoke. "I was not very nice to you, and I really do feel bad about it." My mother's white tank top was a bit yellow, and it was drooping down around the neck. The hair on her head looked like red moss on the north side of a tree. And around her, a grey murkiness seemed like it didn't want to let her go.

"Mari, don't worry, come in." Mrs. Roughen's wrinkled mouth had shaped itself into a grotesque pout. We walk through the door.

Mrs. Roughen's house was decorated entirely in bright colours. An orange couch with yellow cushions and a coffee table made entirely of glass. Blood-red curtains with tiny stars blocked out any light from the street. Our bare toes stuck to hardwood floor. The air smelled of cinnamon, another red, but not like something was baking in the oven, more like a candle had been lit. My mother walked in and sat herself down on the orange couch before Mrs. Roughen had time to suggest it.

"Of course, sit, sit," Mrs. Roughen said. Her hair was now dyed the colour of a clean fire engine and she had started wearing makeup again, blue eye shadow covered her lids and her burgundy lips matched the air around her body. Air that I tried to avoid.

"Trudie, as I was saying, as you can understand, I have been going through a hard patch and, well, I let it take me over. It became way too real to me, and I know it isn't. At least soon it won't be."

"Mari, don't you talk like that, you need to have faith."

"And I do have faith, really." A pause. We sat, the three of us, not speaking. I looked at my mother, from my mother to Mrs. Roughen. Which is when I heard it. With all the commotion at my house and with my mother's sadness, I had not heard anything extra for a while. But I heard what Mrs. Roughen was thinking then, and it made me mad.

"That dirty creep!" I yelled out.

"What?" from Mrs. Roughen and my mother.

"He told you . . ."

"Told me what, dear, and who?"

"Elijah, he told you about the baby."

Mrs. Roughen stood up then and started to wring her hands like she was washing them, obsessively. "Oh Mari, I'm sorry."

My mother closed her eyes then and puckered her lips as if she was trying to keep something out, keep something from arising in her. She looked out the window.

"I don't know what you're talking about."

"That you're going to have a baby, Mother! Elijah told Mrs. Roughen that you are going to have a baby."

"And where would Elijah have gotten such a colourful idea?"

"I'm sorry, but Maya told Elijah and Elijah told me." I put my index fingers inside my mouth and bit down.

"I think that Maya and I should go now."

"Mari, please don't go. I can help you through this like you helped me. We can talk about it; we can pray about it. Jesus has the power to help you last long enough. You can deliver the baby."

"Jesus," my mother said. "Has nothing to do with anything." She grabbed me by the hand, and walked us back to the door. "I know you just want to help, Trudie, and I can't blame you for that," she said with a long sigh that seemed to empty out all the air she had. "Why don't you come by in a few days."

Mrs. Roughen nodded and bit her fist, something that I thought they only did in movies like *Sixteen Candles* and *The Breakfast Club*, and always to try to be funny.

At the vegetable market, my mother threw up in front of the carrots and across from the field tomatoes. I couldn't decide if it was her sickness tossing up her stomach or my sister getting comfortable. Her puke was orange and white with only a few small chunks (the banana she ate for breakfast) and it created an abstract blob on the wet cement floor. We both stood staring down at it for a while, until my mother mentioned how it kind of looked like my father. By that time, the scent had reached my nose and was fighting to get in.

"It stinks," I said.

"Imagine how bad it smells on the inside of us."

"Not too bad for a baby though, right?"

"Babies can't smell yet," she said. My mother smiled then, stretching her cheeks up over her facial bones. It made me think that she had changed her mind — that she was going to try to let the baby grow. I knew that deciding to try could get you halfway there.

"Clean up, produce aisle!" a voice shouted out over the intercom.

"Let's get out of here," she said and we curled our fingers around shiny tomato skins, dropped them in our basket and headed for the front of the store.

In the check-out line I saw him. His picture, between an action shot of Cyndi Lauper and and a photo of Boy George peeking up from under a black hat, his face full of makeup. Corey Hart. His picture on the front of the paper. The headline read: "Musicians Make Waves." You don't have to believe in signs from the universe to notice them when they are blaring out at you. And to me, that was a sign. Some way, somehow, Corey had found a way to be there for me. And he, along with my mother and my baby sister, were here to stay. I could almost see his paper lips start to move then: *Just a little more time is all we're askin' for. 'Cause just a little more time could open closin' doors . . .*

He understood what I was going through — which was enough to make anyone feel better.

Later, I pulled a sharp razor across the skin on my mother's scalp, severing the hairs that had grown. I had to use two or three razors, spraying the cream and going over and over the same spots. She was tired by the time we were finished and was slumping on the toilet. I brought her out to her teepee and she handed me the *Bhagavad Gita* before she sat down. I knew the drill. I held the book and she called out random numbers.

"Page twenty-seven," she said and I read.

"Be not over-glad attaining joy, and be not over-sad encountering grief, but, stayed on Brahma, still constant let each abide! The sage whose soul holds off from other contacts, in himself finds bliss."

Mother closed her eyes and nodded like it was written for her. I think now she was probably trying to hide her own confusion.

"Mother," I asked. "How did you even learn about this strange book?"

"A wise person taught me about it."

"A man from India?"

"Yes, India."

"Did he buy you this copy?" I held up the tattered collection of pages in my hand.

"He gave it to me, yes."

"Can I meet him?"

"Not now, Maya."

"How did you meet?"

"The winds guided us together, that's all."

In my dreams that night, I looked in the yellow eyes of a giant tiger. Shiny mane of fur that shimmered in the light from somewhere, teeth that made me imagine the colour of my own blood, and the taste. I turned to run, through tall blades of grass, my feet coming down into the dirt. "Roooooaarrr," from the tiger and I ran faster. It started to rain and the raindrops turned into people, tiny people cheering me on, telling me to speed up, telling me not to give up. I ran straight into the chest of a man. Turned around to see that the tiger was gone. Vanished, like he never existed in the first place. And the man's arms were long, and they wrapped around me. Creamy skin that matched my own. Strong arms that welcomed me home.

Two days later, Mrs. Roughen came by the house, only she wasn't alone. She had a lady with a microphone and a man with a video camera with her.

They came right in after my father opened the door.

"Steven, delightful to see you," Mrs. Roughen said, teasing up her bangs nervously with her right hand. "You don't mind if we visit with Mari in the backyard . . . I believe she's expecting me."

It was not true. None of us were expecting her, especially not with a news crew. It left me wondering why, and my father, with his mouth dropped opened, thinking: *Why won't this woman just go away? Fucking bitch.*

Mrs. Roughen plowed her way past us before my father and I could stop her. Within seconds, she, the woman with the microphone, and the man with the video camera were standing outside the teepee. Mrs. Roughen tentatively peeled back the flap to find my mother.

I stood briefly on the backyard deck. The humid summer air was awash in colour — colours emanated from everywhere . . . from the people who were there, pestering my mother, from my mother perhaps. They seemed to be mingling to create a bizarre dark-coloured rainbow — plum, canary, pumpkin — the rainbow dipped and flowed, as if to signal an ominous but key moment in my mother's story. I doubted whether any of the people connected to these colours actually gave a crap about my mother.

By the time my father and I got out to the teepee, the lady was already speaking into her microphone while the man with the video camera taped her.

"We're here outside the teepee of Marigold Devine, a Saskatoon resident who in the face of terminal cancer has bravely decided to forgo all treatment and spend her final days in a state of meditation in the backyard of her home."

"Ahh, geez, will you please stop it," my father said, at which point Mrs. Roughen popped out of the teepee to silence him.

"Shhhhh, Steven, it's fine, really. Mari is all right with this. It's going to help everyone involved."

"Trudie, you really make me sick." My father gave up too easily. He went back into the house, leaving me alone with all that. Though I didn't see it at the time, it would have been pretty hard for an eleven-year-old kid to make sure her mother wasn't exploited. I wanted to though — really.

The scene inside the teepee: The lady with the microphone standing over my mother, who was in her bed, sitting up with her hands folded in her lap, lips puckered, mustard light around her face, moaning in her head. Mrs. Roughen, standing by the door of the teepee like she's on lookout, smiling with her head cocked, thinking about how incredibly proud she was to be helping my mother, and wondering what people will think of her for trying to do it. The man holding the camera wearing a white T-shirt and scratching his armpit.

"Now, Marigold, we know this must be a hard time for you, with all you're going through. What gets you through it all?"

My mother winced, annoyed by the hungry lion that had pounced on her while she was sleeping and seemingly unsure herself about how she ended up in this situation.

"I guess I just do the best I can," she said, but apparently they were looking for something more inspirational.

The lady with the microphone kept fishing: "We've heard that you also hold a very special skill, a psychic ESP ability, if you will. Has this helped give you strength in any respect?"

Mother was stunned — I could hear her heart pounding loudly from inside her head, its shocked beat seemed to fill the air around us. Her lips parted. The light from on top of the camera created a glare against the tarp walls. I bit my lip and fiddled with the strings that tied back the door. What was happening? And why? My resentment for my mother — and now for Mrs. Roughen and this microphone lady — bubbled low in my stomach, threatening to explode.

Finally, my mother opened her mouth and instead of denying

that she had any supernatural gift, she said: "Yes, I have been blessed with a little extra when it comes to my senses. I can see and hear things others can't. And I suppose I just really know what others need in their lives."

My mother glanced at me straight-faced, and I raised my eyebrows at her.

"Can you give us an example of these abilities, Marigold?"

"I can see people's auras."

"Auras? Really!" the lady with the microphone said, amazed. "And how am I looking today, in the aura department?" She was mocking her. Her aura was ruby red with darker parts closer to her body.

"You have a nice bright green energy right now." Mother was mocking her back. "You should get out and work in your garden when you get home. You need some time to de-stress from all the work you've been doing."

"That's true," the lady with the microphone said. "How did you know I've been under stress?"

"Just a feeling."

Give me a break, I thought.

I didn't want to hear any more of this conversation. But for some reason, I couldn't will my legs to move. Then, things turned more serious.

"And Marigold, I have also heard that you have received some other, joyful news recently — that you are expecting a child." There was no emotion from my mother's face, but Mrs. Roughen covered her mouth like she was trying to hold in a wail. "Would you like to send out any message to doctors or other professionals who may have advice on how best to protect your unborn child?"

"Get out" was what my mother said to that question. "Leave, now. This whole thing is stupid." My mother started swatting the microphone with her lean fingers — feebly but with determination. But the lady holding the microphone resisted. A fight ensued, which I am embarrassed to recount here because Mother really lost it — screaming, kicking, and squirming like a toddler pulling a tantrum.

As I escorted the news people and a shocked Mrs. Roughen to the front door, it was hard to tell that I was the daughter and she was supposed to have been the mother.

Father shouted, "Good riddance!" from the kitchen when I shut the door behind them.

Luckily, my mother's fit was not included in the footage on the Saskatoon News at 5 that evening. They only showed her wise and smirking, sitting up on the bed in her teepee, telling the lady with the microphone the colour of her aura, and another shot of her inadvertently rubbing her belly and looking down, as a voice-over stated that Marigold Devine was "desperate to find a way to save her unborn child, and would welcome prayers and any support that could be offered. And that in exchange, she may even be able to offer you a psychic view into your future (fake laugh)."

Some people never leave you — they get stuck in your psyche. This was how a lot of people felt about seeing my mother on TV that night — and how I've always felt about her.

Yes, this woman, this Marigold Devine — mother, sufferer, mystic, hero — needed us all. And we all needed to believe that she would be okay.

Chapter Seventeen

My father smashed the television set. The one that had shown us the news interview with Mother. I found the set the next morning after we watched. It was lying on its side in a pathetic heap. Its screen was cracked, antennas bent, knobs missing. Father pretended he didn't notice it.

For the next day he paced. Around the house from one room to the next, murmuring things that I couldn't hear, inside or out.

"We should sue," he said at breakfast the following morning when Mother was out sitting in the teepee alone and I was gobbling down cereal so I could get back to her.

"Sue who?"

"The evening news," my father said, shaking his head so fast he seemed to have two noses and four eyeballs.

"I have to get back out there," I said, dropping my empty bowl in the sink with a ceramic clang.

"Wait, take this out to her," he said as he grabbed a banana from the fruit bowl on the table and placed it in my hands.

"Why isn't she talking anymore?" I asked him.

"Your guess is as good as mine, Maya."

"I don't like it."

I left him alone, leaning against the counter, his left hand rubbing those straight white indents on his forehead.

By the afternoon that day it had started. The people: at the front door, looking over the back fence from the yard behind, trying to peek back from between houses.

The visitors were everywhere, trying to catch a glimpse of my mother. They were like people who turn their heads to catch a glimpse of a gory car crash. Or maybe those who turn their cars around to try to help. Either way, they wanted to be a part of my mother's tragedy. And of course see if maybe she had some sort of psychic insights about their lives.

They carried things with them when they came: blankets, hand-knit sweaters, plastic bags, coffee cakes, bottles of wine, baby booties. Sometimes they left the stuff on the front porch, like bouquets of flowers, but mostly they waited out front, waited for my father to open the front door, which he refused to do.

All afternoon the crowd gathered outside the house. I watched from between the front blinds. By 4:30, there was a circle of women holding hands and humming prayers with their eyes half-shut. Someone had a sign that said: "Save a life. Save an unborn child."

I tried to spend most of my time in the teepee with my mother, who was only staring and starting to shake a bit. My father was out there too. He came out after he dead-bolted the front door and moved the dining room buffet in front of the entrance to block it.

My father held my mother's hand. The three of us were silent, until I spoke.

"Maybe they can help her?"

"Help her do what, Maya?" my father asked with a sigh.

"Get her better. Find a way to save the baby."

"There's no way, Maya." He had tears then. "It's just a waiting game now."

"Maybe I could carry the baby?"

My father would not respond to my suggestion. He was annoyed by my foolish idea that the baby could be taken from my mother and injected into my own stomach. Little did he know, I wasn't stupid enough to believe that we could actually do it — I was just trying to be creative.

By nightfall they had candles. Woman were singing and praying in large groups. One woman with hectic curls flying out from her face was throwing herself around in a patch of dirt on the front lawn screaming, "Please, Jesus!" over and over, on her knees with her arms waving above her head.

I watched it all through the corner of the front window. And when the news crew arrived and started interviewing people, I saw that too. Father didn't see any of it. He forbade me to open the door and stayed out in the backyard with Mother.

In the morning, Mrs. Roughen lowered herself over the back fence while I was eating breakfast, tearing her skirt as she fell. I ran from the back door to see her.

"Maya, you didn't answer your phone!"

"It's unhooked," I said, like she was the reason we did it.

"Where's your father?"

"Still sleeping." The people in the crowd out front had settled into pup tents for the night and were yet to wake.

"Maya, I have to talk to your mother."

"She's not talking. To anyone."

"Just let me see her then."

I rolled my eyes and moved towards the teepee. We walked in together.

Mother had laid herself back on the bed. A sour milk and armpit smell hung in the air around her, and there was grey and black pulsing weakly around her face.

"Marigold, it's me, Trudie."

No response.

"Marigold, I'm sorry about what happened. I'm only trying to help you, you and the baby. . . ."

Nothing from Mother.

"I told you, she's not talking anymore."

"Has she taken some sort of vow of silence?" Mrs. Roughen asked, smoothing her hair down on the side of her face and adjusting her purple leather belt, which had shifted in her climb over the fence.

"Don't know," I said.

"We need to get her cleaned up," she said, shifting back her dangling bracelets to pull my mother up. "Has she eaten?"

"Yogurt and a banana yesterday. She had a few crackers this morning. And I have been using a crazy straw to help give her water."

"Let's get her into the bath."

We carried her into the house, Mrs. Roughen with her arms under Mother's armpits and me carrying her feet, then slid off her clothes and laid her down naked in the bathtub. From the window in the bathroom I could hear the visitors stirring. Someone was singing "Turn, turn, turn," and small groups of voices were loudly praying things to Jesus. While Mrs. Roughen washed her hair and soaped up my mother's frail body, I took a peek through the small window above the sink: about forty of them had returned this morning. The cameras were gone, but the rest of them were still clutching gifts in their arms. A tall, thin woman with blond hair approached our front door.

"Should I answer it?"

"Not yet, Maya. Let's get her clean and back in bed. Then, we can let them visit with her."

"But Father won't like it. Plus, I don't think she wants to see anyone now."

"We have to, Maya, the story has been on the news. People want to help, that's all. We should let them have that."

But Mrs. Roughen's thoughts told me something different. She was thinking about herself — if she looked pretty enough, how she might get interviewed on the news herself, how people might care what she had to say, that she might even meet a new husband out of the whole thing (she didn't want to be too hopeful in case she got disappointed, but maybe).

"I want nothing to do with this!" I screamed, and sat on the floor.

Mrs. Roughen dressed Mother in a robe from her closet, a shiny pink one that zipped up at the front and had a lace collar. Mother only mumbled and looked annoyed while she did it. Her limbs hung heavy like she had already died and her sounds were only little bits of trapped air escaping.

I did have to help carry her back out to the teepee, because I knew that's where she wanted to be.

We got her back into bed, sitting up with her hands crossed in her lap. Mrs. Roughen spread a sheet over her legs and tied back the teepee windows to let air through, August air rich with hot asphalt and lawn clippings.

It was eleven in the morning. My father was still in bed.

I still did not want Mother to be visited. To be exploited.

"They may have ideas about how to help," Mrs. Roughen said, trying to convince me. Which did make sense, I guess.

Eventually, I helped her push the buffet out of the way of the door. It squeaked on the hardwood. "For all we know, they could help make a miracle happen." She squeezed my hand. Her fingers were moist and slippery.

She had me there. I wanted to help. I wanted my mother back. I wanted to start being a kid again, and a big sister. To have my family.

Mrs. Roughen decided to let them in one at a time, and in pairs if they were related.

"Please remove your shoes, walk straight through the house, through the back door, and you can visit her in the teepee in the backyard. Donations are appreciated. You have ten minutes. Maya will show you where."

"Thank you," said the first girl, with a pained smile. She was about twenty-five, wearing a short jean skirt, black T-shirt, and a yellow bandana to hold back her long hair. She held a tiny velvet bag by a string.

The girl had purple around her that radiated out from her head and shoulders like heat on a highway.

"This way," Mrs. Roughen said, walking towards the back door.

"Thank you," the girl said again. I closed the front door and locked it. And I didn't let the girl see my mother alone. I followed her out back to the teepee, and watched with all the suspicion an eleven-year-old girl could muster.

The girl squatted beside my mother's bed. My mother sat up staring, her hands still folded in her lap.

"She's not talking today," I said. "It's sort of a vow of silence kind of thing."

"It's okay," the girl said and turned towards my mother. "Mrs. Devine, my name is Alisha. I wanted to give you something that I think could help you." She opened her tiny velvet bag and took out two eye-sized rocks, one white, one green, turned my mother's hand around and dropped them in her palm. "These are quartz and malachite. They will help you heal your blockages and in your healing."

"How can they do that?" I said.

"By emitting vibrations that will align her again with the divine light energy," Alisha said, folding my mother's fingers over the stones.

175

"And that will help her get better, save the baby?"

"If she believes in it," Alisha said, looking back at me stoically, her blue eyes reaching out to light up the pale air in the teepee.

My mother threw the rocks with one quick snap across the teepee.

I followed the path of the stones, knelt down, and picked them up.

"Thanks," I said to Alisha, and she put her arm on my shoulder.

Next, my father's voice erupted from the house like thunder on a still evening: "Trudie, what the hell?!"

"I think you should go now," I said to Alisha. "My father is awake." She gave my mother a sideways pitying glance and followed me back into the house.

My father stood in only his underwear, the pudgy parts of his belly sticking out, his "Mari" tattoo swimming in his chest hair. Mrs. Roughen stood across from him in the entrance to the house.

"Thank you for letting me visit your wife, Mr. Devine," Alisha said slipping into her shoes, her voice remaining calm.

"Get out" was all he said in return.

"Don't be mean!" I shouted. "She gave mother something really cool!"

"Maya, shut up." He swung his arm to push me onto the first step leading upstairs. At the same time, Alisha opened the front door to leave and Mrs. Roughen came into the foyer: "Steven, I know you're upset, but listen . . ."

The door opened again.

My father was knocked to the floor by the crowd of people pushing their way into the house. He knocked his head on the banister I was clutching.

All the visitors pushed through the door: limping old ladies, bouncy fat women, a Native man with feathers around his head.

"Slowly," Mrs. Roughen said. "You'll all get a chance to bring your good wishes to Marigold." She was rushing them along, pushing them into the backyard before my father came to.

A cameraman came through the door and began to film my father, lying on his back with his arms hurled out to the sides.

"Stop taking pictures of him!" I said, pulling the man's arm. A woman stood in front of my father and spoke into a microphone: "I'm at Marigold Devine's home, where a dangerous mob has stormed the house and attacked Marigold Devine's husband, leaving him unconscious. Stacey Nixon reporting."

The cameraman leaned down towards my father's face and I kicked him in the shin.

"Ouch! You little brat," he said.

"C'mon, Roger, enough of the naked guy. Let's get into the backyard."

They hurried off and then it was just my father and me left. I ran into the kitchen and put ice cubes in a paper towel and put it on my father's forehead. He opened his eyes with the cold.

"Maya," he said, dazed, his mouth formed into a scared grimace. "What happened? Where's your mother?"

"She's in the backyard, with everybody else."

"Is she okay?" he blinked and took a breath, like he didn't quite know what was going on. For a second, he was hidden in a cool grey light that stuck to him.

"I think so. Mrs. Roughen's out there."

"I can't believe she let these people in here."

"Maybe they can help?"

"Yeah, they can help themselves to a lawsuit," he said. "And Trudie Roughen too." I helped him up to his feet and he went back up to his bedroom for some shorts and a T-shirt. We went into the backyard together.

People were lined up single-file in front of the entrance to the teepee, a line that curved like a snake around the yard, reaching to the back fence. The camera crew was set up on our back porch. The anchorwoman combed her hair nearby. The Native man was chanting words I didn't know beside the teepee. Chanting and stamping his white moccasins on the grass so that the hanging bits of feather danced in the air. As he chanted, he pushed out smoke from a small bowl, filling the air with a sweet kind of plant. He had red lines painted on his face and a circle of yellow and green around his body.

"Jesus Christ," my father said. "What is this, some sort of freak show?"

Apparently, they thought that the "freak" was inside. One by one they would poke their heads into the teepee with their lips pursed and their eyebrows raised in anticipation. I could hear their thoughts, each overlapping onto the next: *It smells in here. What am I going to say? Is she contagious? Is she decent? Is she nuts?*

Mrs. Roughen was the one to let them in when it was their turn. She stood at the entrance to the teepee like she was the gate-keeper of my mother. "Just wait a minute please, honey," she said when I tried to pass her.

"Trudie, let her in, now," my father said, a blue vein throbbing on his forehead.

"Sorry, Steven. Sure, yeah, go in, Maya. Just make it fast." But

Mrs. Roughen's inside thoughts told another story. From inside her head, I heard her call my father a self-absorbed asshole, a snag in the whole operation. I didn't know then what kind of operation she meant, but I hoped it was a kind of surgery that my mother was going to have.

"Hey, I was next!" someone shouted out, and Mrs. Roughen told them that they'd all get their turn to help save the baby through their prayers and good wishes.

My mother was sitting up in bed with her arms crossed. She was surrounded by three women and an older man who stood back by the window. One of the women, short, curly brown hair, glasses, and wide hips, was holding a shoebox filled with tiny bottles. Another taller woman was talking: "Mrs. Devine, the healing properties of essential aromatherapy oils are amazing if you just give them a chance," she said while the third woman, thin, huge hoop earrings, neon bow in her ponytail, held one of the bottles in front of her nose. Mother gave a feeble "and so" look by hiding her lips inside her mouth.

"Just take a deep sniff. It's jasmine and peppermint. This'll give you the boost you need to fight the cancer and save your baby's life."

"Sniff, Mother, sniff," I said, running to the bed.

"Stay back, please," the woman with hoops told me. "You'll upset one of the bottles."

"Time's up!" Mrs. Roughen shouted from outside the teepee.

"We'll just leave these here," the wide-hipped woman said, putting the box of oils on the chair beside the bed. The older man who had been watching nodded his head and walked with the woman out of the door.

I reached down to hold my mother's hand, warm fingers with her pulse tingling everywhere. She looked down at me and pulled her hand from mine. A tear gathered and slipped over her cheekbone.

I told all the people to leave, that she'd had enough. And one of them opened the flap so they could get out, letting in the voices and thoughts that had been creating a hum from outside the teepee.

I looked at Mother softly. "It's okay, Mother. We'll figure out a way to save the baby." I was trying my best to be supportive — as much as a young girl could be of her own mother. But she had other demons circulating under her tightly stretched skin.

"There is no fucking baby!" she yelled.

"Stop it, Mother," I said. "You know there is. Why would you say that?"

"Because there is no baby," she moaned. "I made it all up — so deal with it."

"I know you're lying. So stop."

Then — and I hate to disrespect my mother's memory by adding this part — she slapped me. Hard. Across the cheek. And then she laid back on the bed.

Chapter Eighteen

Many hours have passed but I haven't fallen asleep. I only rest my eyes a bit by looking up from the page and out into the darkness of night. The wind badgers me to stop reading my mother's journal. "It's not private now that she's dead!" I scream towards the window from the bed — the words pound through my head and my stomach gallops around in my abdomen.

That's when I hear the knock from downstairs.

I swallow hard.

I cover my head with the duvet on my parents' bed. Sweat forms on my forehead. I breathe in and out like an ocean battering the sand.

Another knock from downstairs, pushier this time. A knock that screams, "I know you're in there!" I look at the clock, it's 2 a.m. Someone fumbles with the lock. My heart. A barrage of thoughts, overlapping, fighting for attention: *What day is it? What's wrong with me? My mother and an East Indian man? Is it true? Did Father know?*

Who is downstairs?

A lot of thinking but I still don't move from the bed. I wrap the duvet around my face. Then I hear her voice, from out the window, louder than the knock that came through the house: "Maya, are you in there? Maya, it's Leah!"

"Aunt Leah?" The words are so quiet enough that only I can hear them. "Aunt Leah, I'm in here." No louder that time, but more determined. I wipe my fingers across my sweaty forehead and suddenly long for the warm feeling that family brings.

I reach the front door in my socked feet and nightgown. The floor spins under my feet, the ceiling dips and circles above me. I turn the knob.

"Maya!" It's Aunt Leah, dressed in a black overcoat that reaches the floor, her eyes tired but frantic. She's not wearing glasses and she has pink eye shadow covering each lid. Sparks of orange and yellow are bouncing off her dark hair and reflecting into the night.

I fall to her feet.

Soon I am lying on the couch in the living room and Aunt Leah is holding my hand and kneeling beside me on the carpet. A facecloth is wet with ice and on my forehead. I open my eyes to look at her: "What are you doing here?" It is strange to be talking to someone from my family, face to face.

"Your father sent me, Maya — well, your grandmother made

the final decision for me to come." Her voice is stern but friendly and it invades my ears like a poker waking up the fire. "You know how she and your grandfather won't fly. They would rather die in a ten-car pile up than buckle themselves into a jetliner seat." She blows out air and looks up at the ceiling for a moment. "Myself, I had to take the red-eye because it's cheaper."

"But . . . why?" I sip water from a purple cup that Leah holds up to my lips.

"Maya, your dad called Grandma. He doesn't know what to do anymore. He feels that he's lost you."

I shake my head and the tears come.

"Do you know where he is now, Maya?"

My words swim out like a prayer: "He's not really living here much anymore."

"For how long?" She seems less surprised than I thought she'd be.

"He's been around, but I've been looking after myself for the most part. I haven't seen him much in the past week."

"Maya, you don't deserve this, babe. I'm here to help, okay?"

"I'm just fine," I say. "I've been managing just fine. I like having the house to myself." I arch my back to sit up but lie back with the dizziness.

"I knew it." She is standing now and pacing the living room in her Doc Martens, which make rubber clunks on the floor. In her head she is cursing my father, screaming inside. "What is he trying to prove?" she finally says out loud.

"Do you think he's coming back?"

She kneels back down beside me. "Maya, I'm sorry, we don't know. He didn't say he wasn't living here when he called, he just said he wanted someone to come get you. That it was all too much for him."

"Does this have to do with Connie?"

"That woman he's seeing? I don't know, Maya, really."

"What do we do now?"

"I'm going to take you home with me. You can't stay here by yourself anymore."

"I can't?"

"You'll come with me to Toronto until your father figures things out."

She takes me to the hospital, to Emergency, where I flirt with sleep for three hours on a stretcher in a hallway. Aunt Leah stands over me, holding my hand, stroking my forehead, making trips back and forth to the vending machine for Humpty Dumpty chips (she's had three bags so far) and Colt Cola. I can't eat. The room revolves around me and the molecules that make up my body seem to be spreading apart until there is nothing left of me. At the beginning of the fourth hour, when Aunt Leah has taken off her trench coat and stands over me in a pink tie-dyed T-shirt and a pair of jeans that start exactly at her waist and stick tight to her legs all the way down, she speaks to me in a monotone: "Hang in there, kiddo, you can do this. At least you're not alone in a teepee." She laughs, but I don't.

I fall back asleep not knowing for sure if I have even woken up.

Awake for sure now because I have to pee. It stings me from the inside.

"Leah, I have to go to the bathroom."

"Okay, My." (She has started shortening my name and I hate it.) She holds her arm out so I can lift myself out of the hospital bed. I shuffle my socks across the shiny floor, with her following behind with my IV bag. She hands it over to me and waits outside the door when I go.

"I think I can manage this myself," I yell at her through the door. I am not sure where my bitterness has come from, but sense that maybe it should be aimed at my father.

"Okay, My," she says. "Be careful not to drop your arm or else blood will start coming up the tube."

I only have the flu. At least that's what the doctors think. I am replacing my fluids. Aunt Leah has told them that my father is on vacation and she is babysitting. All I need is one night in hospital to be observed and get fluids.

At night, Leah goes back to my house and I sleep alone in the green room, with a tube coming out of the top of my hand feeding me a continual drink. There are two other beds in the room, empty beds. The nurse only checks on me every few hours, but I have a button to press if I need someone.

Is this how Mother felt when we left her here? Was she more frightened?

The room is dark except for lights over the other beds. Dark enough to sleep, but I can't. I wish I had remembered to bring the journal. I want to finish it. I want to hear what happened with my mother and Amar. I don't hate her for it.

Scratching.

Something is scratching at the window, trying to get in. It couldn't be a prairie dog — we're on the sixth floor.

More scratching and some banging, like a huge branch is hitting the window (but the trees don't grow this high).

The television up by the ceiling flips on. (I hadn't even noticed it until now.) Static with no sound, but inside my head: *I'm here, I'm here, I'm here.*

I flop onto my left side, close my eyes, and escape into the darkness on the underside of my eyelids.

———————

"What do you want to eat?" Aunt Leah is looking into an empty fridge. "Looks like all I have to offer you are ketchup, olives — well, mostly pimentos — and a rotten cucumber."

"I'm not really hungry yet."

"You gotta eat something, My. The doctor wouldn't have let you out if he knew you weren't going to eat."

"Pimentos then."

"I'll go to the market and pick up a few things. We've got to eat for the next few days."

"So what did he say when you told him what happened to me?" I ask. She had called my father at work that morning.

"He was worried. Upset. He didn't know you had been feeling sick. He wanted to come over, but I told him no. That you just needed space for now, that I would look after you."

"It's not working out, me and him."

"That's why I'm taking you to Toronto."

"Why not Grandma and Grandpa?"

"They're getting older. They are finally enjoying things by the ocean. They don't need a kid there messing it all up."

"How about my other grandmother then?"

Leah makes her lips into a small rose and looks away from me. She speaks without opening her mouth.

"Not gonna happen, sweetie. That lady is a bit too stuck in her ways I think. And a bit batty, don't you think?"

"I've only met her once, when she visited Mother."

"It'll be great staying with me, you'll see. Just until things calm down with your father, and he comes to his senses. I know you're thirteen and all, but he can't just leave you here all the time to look after yourself."

"What about my friends? I have two friends, Heather and Chauncey."

"I can take you to say goodbye to them if you want?"

"Maybe."

"My, think positive, okay? Did you know that positive thoughts create happy lives?"

"Please stop calling me that."

"What?"

"My name is Maya."

———

When she leaves for the store, I run back up to my parents' room and pull out my mother's journal. I had stuck it between the mattress and the box spring. I hold it in my hand for a minute, not sure

I even want to know what more it has to tell me. I read from where I left off.

November 25, 1972

I've told Steven I'd go to dinner with him tomorrow night at Roland's. I had to. He has become so damn suspicious, even though he doesn't know exactly about what. And can never know.

I haven't heard from Amar. Isn't it always the way? Haven't heard and I guess maybe it is for the best. I mean, what was I thinking? Older, Indian, a little bit strange. They should have me committed for even considering it.

The secret is that I still do — think about him, that is. And they are not always the purest of thoughts, if you catch my drift!

So, I'm having dinner with Steven at Roland's. Classy. I'll have to wear nylons. He's picking me up in his father's Plymouth Valiant. I'm preparing myself for a lot of ass-kissing if I ever want our relationship to be how it was. Do I? He's mad at me. Especially since I cancelled our study date to go on the picnic with Amar. He'll get over it though. He always does.

Mother is giddy beyond recognition because I'm going out with Steven again. Spaz. If she paid attention at all she'd see that I'm not even that excited about it myself.

———————

"I'm home!" It's Aunt Leah from downstairs. Boy, she's quick. She must have just gone to the convenience store up the street.

"I'm up here, hold on, I'm coming down." I stuff the notebook back between the mattress and kick the picnic basket from the corner of the room and into the closet.

Leah is spreading out cans of beans, a loaf of white bread, and vegetable soup on the counter.

"I know that you and your mother didn't eat much meat. So I tried to keep it veggie as much as possible. She slaps two black Mars bars on the wooden cutting board making a hallow clunk. "And a little treat for us never hurt."

She has taken my tape player and put it on the counter. She presses the PLAY button on my radio, and he starts singing.

Just a little uncertainty can bring you down
And nobody wants to know you now
And nobody wants to show you how

His voice makes me think about how stupid I was to believe that he would be able to help save Mother. How stupid I was to even send the letter.

"Shut it off!" I run across the room and lunge at the stop button. "I don't want to listen to him anymore." Though I have never had an ex-boyfriend, or even a boyfriend for that matter if you don't count Elijah, I'm certain that the way I feel about Corey Hart now is how it would feel after breaking up with someone. My juicy longing has turned into disappointment.

"Easy, Maya. Just trying to lighten the mood." She turns on the radio to a classical music station. The notes of stretching violins and harps fill my head while we wait for the toast to burn.

Later, someone comes to the door. Aunt Leah opens up wearing a white tank top without a bra — you can see her dark nipples, but she doesn't seem to care. It's two in the afternoon and I am on the couch watching a *Facts of Life* rerun.

"May I help you?" Aunt Leah licks peanut butter from her fingertips.

"Yes, I would like to speak with Steven Devine." It's a woman's voice, small and shaky.

"And who may I ask, are you?"

"My name is Mrs. Clifton. I am a secretary at Lakeview Public School."

"Oh." I hear high heels click on the tile inside the door, and a clump when the door shuts.

"A student has reported to our principal that Maya Devine has been living at home alone, and because she hasn't been in school for the last few weeks, I volunteered to come see if everything was okay."

"Everything is fine, Mrs. Clifton. I'm her aunt and I'm here, aren't I?"

I can hear Mrs. Clifton's thoughts, even from the living room. She's nervous. She doesn't feel comfortable standing up to a beefy girl like Aunt Leah, or pushing this issue. *I wish I could just stay behind the desk*, is what she thinks. *I should not put up with Herbert's abuse anymore. I'm not his slave girl.*

"Has something been keeping Maya from school?"

"Well, yes, Mrs. Clifton, a few things as a matter of fact." (I am still on the couch, now with a blanket over my face.) "She's been sick with a terrible flu that has left her bed-ridden and, well, if you must know, her father has passed away."

"Oh gosh, I am so sorry to hear that." Mrs. Clifton now sounds nervous on the outside, and I can see berry red light from her body, fanning out from the hallway.

"Yes, she's been orphaned and if you don't mind, we certainly don't need to be bothered right now. Maya is moving across country to live with her grandparents. She will not be coming back to school with you."

"I see." Mrs. Clifton's voice is even quieter than before, like the last bit of air from a deflated balloon. "Thank you for telling me. Sorry, I didn't get your name?"

"Penelope, Penelope Wishing. It's my married name."

"Well, okay, Penelope. I guess I can go now. Now that I know everything is okay."

"It is in fact, very okay. Bye-bye."

The heels click out and the door shuts. Aunt Leah comes and sits on the brown chair beside me in the living room.

"Aunt Leah, it's not true what you said, is it? About Father being dead? And me going to live with my grandparents?"

"No, that's not true."

"Good. Because I'd rather live with you."

She smiles and tugs at the frizzy ends of her straggly hair.

————————

Though Aunt Leah says it's weird, I use the picnic basket as a carry-on bag. I put the notebook and the letter on the bottom and pack some underwear, a shirt, and pair of jeans on top of it. I wear my acid wash jacket and slide my mother's butterfly bracelets on my wrist. In a small suitcase that Aunt Leah found under the stairs, I place my mother's copy of the *Gita*, my Corey Hart tape (just in case I reconsider), three of my mother's aromatherapy bottles (sandalwood, patchouli, and lavender), two sweaters that used to hang in her closet, rolled up into soft balls, and some more of my own clothes. I put her journal in the inside pocket of my jacket.

"I can't believe she lived in here," Aunt Leah says when I find her in the backyard. She is standing inside my mother's teepee, running her hands over the tarp walls.

"It wasn't that bad, really."

"I suppose it helped her find some sort of peace within herself. Lord knows that woman needed it."

"I guess."

"It was crazy what happened near the end, with everyone coming here and stuff. I even read an article about it in the *Toronto Star* when I first got there."

I nod.

"Hey, gemstones!" Aunt Leah reaches to the two jagged stones on the bed where my mother's pillows used to be.

"They are quartz and malachite," I say, grabbing them from her and putting one in each of my pockets. "For healing and protection."

"What are those things on your wrist?" She crinkles her eyebrows like I'm keeping a secret.

"Bracelets."

"Where did you get them?"

"The flea market with my friend Heather."

"I guess we better call a cab. Our flight is at six o'clock."

When the cab is waiting on the street and I have loaded my picnic basket into the trunk, I hear a voice from behind me.

"Maya! Where are you going?" It is Chauncey. I turn around and smile when I see him.

"I'm going to live in Toronto, Chauncey, with my Aunt Leah." Leah sticks her hand out from the back seat and waves.

"Really, the big city? Hogtown?"

"Yup. Tell Jackie good riddance."

"I will."

"Cool."

"Heather wants you to know she is sorry."

"For what?"

"For telling the school about you being home alone." I don't say anything. "Don't be mad, Maya, she was just worried about you."

I force my lips to move, "I know." I move to get into the car.

"Maya?"

"What?" I stop with one leg lifted into the back seat.

"Don't become a pretentious city snob, okay? (In his mind he is saying, *I wish she wasn't going*, which feels good.)

"I'll try not to." I bounce into my seat. Door slams and we drive away from my house, from the teepee, from my mother's ghost, from my father. Through the black lines of the back windshield, Chauncey gets smaller and smaller until he becomes nothing.

Our plane rises up over golden fields of wheat, silos, skinny streams — my first time in the sky. I'm not going to Montreal as I planned, but I am going somewhere. Away.

"This is totally awesome," I say to Aunt Leah.

"I knew you'd like it." She is reading the in-flight magazine and doesn't look up.

We zoom up until the clouds engulf us, bumping up until we reach the eternal space. Sun warms up the egg-shaped window.

"Maya, I forgot to tell you, I saw your shampoo commercial the other night after *Let's Make a Deal*. Great stuff. You really convinced me that you gave a shit about what your hair looks like, and that you have the potential of feeling bodacious." She laughs through her nose.

I raise my hand to quiet her and use my finger to brush my bangs from my forehead.

"What's that notebook?" She points to my lap where it sits for safe-keeping.

"It's just something I wrote," I say as she looks back at her magazine.

Out my window, the sky shines blue above the clouds — every space packed tight with spirit. Why didn't anyone tell me such a place exists? I let out my air, the smooth stones are jabbing me from my pockets. I take them out and put them on the tiny table that flips down from the back of the seat in front of me. I look down at my lap and open the notebook to where I left off.

Chapter Nineteen

November 27, 1972

 Christ, where do I start. Shit, shit, shit.

 I didn't go out to Roland's with Steven. I wanted to, I planned to. I got ready to. But on the way out the door I was abducted. I like to say abducted because it sounds much more glamorous, like that little girl who was stolen from the 7-Eleven in the States. Truth is, it wasn't like that at all. I chose to go. My hair swept off my face, a shirt a little tighter than Mother would allow, nylons, and foundation covering the bags under my eyes. I chose to go with him, I did. I can't blame anyone else but myself really. It happened like this:

 I was coming out the front door of my house. I thought I would meet Steven on the street when he came, just to get Mother out of my hair for a few minutes. To prepare myself to make it all up to him and get on with where we were (ho hum). When there he was, coming up the front walk from the street.

Don't you look beautiful tonight, he said.

Amar.

Hello, Marigold. I'm sorry I haven't called.

That's okay.

I was away for a few days, and then resting.

I see.

I was looking out towards the street, where Steven would be pulling up in the Valiant. Amar was looking straight at me. He had a heavier jacket on finally, sheepskin, and blue jeans with desert boots. The same old beads around his neck.

I was hoping to take you out again, he said pointing to the red and white Volkswagen van parked across the street, in front of a fire hydrant.

Were you? I pretended to be disinterested as well as I could.

Are you available now?

I have a date. (I said this with a straight face. God, I really am proud of how I was able to say this, like I hadn't been thinking of him at all.)

Can you cancel?

This took me by surprise. I mean, I wasn't expecting it after six days with no word from him. My first instinct was to tell him, Hell no, I can't cancel — I already did it once and look at the trouble I am in with my boyfriend. But I didn't say that. How could I? He was clean shaven this time, no mustache at all and his skin smooth like it was inviting your hand. If anyone else asked me to cancel my plans on such short notice, why, I would probably sock 'em one.

But him. The fact that he had the courage to ask made it all that more enticing to say yes. Imagine. Saying yes to such a request. Taking off with some Indian man when I was supposed to be fixing things with my boyfriend. Imagine. Making things worse instead?

The inside of his van smelled like mildew, but was extremely clean. Dashboard and seats were polished with something, and the carpet under my feet had not a speck on it. When he shut my door and walked around to the other side, I popped his glove compartment: map of Ontario, half eaten bag of chips, napkins, long stick of something (incense?). I snapped it shut when he got into his seat. (I just wanted to know what was inside him.)

It took him three tries to start the engine — sputtering and spitting until it took. I was glad when it did because having Steven pull up and seeing me in Amar's car would not have been something I could have taken at that moment.

He stuck a tape into the tape deck while we drove. Some sort of weird music he said was a sitar (an Indian version of a guitar as he explained without me asking). And when we got to his cabin — out of town, on the highway, off onto a dirt road, into the forest — I still couldn't believe I had gone. Me. A strange man's cabin. Steven at my house waiting for me. They were probably worried by now.

I didn't care. I was alive, more so than ever.

I told you it wasn't much to look at, he said, opening the front door. The cabin was hidden behind a huge rock on a dirt road off the highway, buried among cedars, backing onto Indian River. The banks were covered with a thin blanket of snow. Snow that hadn't yet fallen in downtown Peterborough. Not at all this season.

It's just fine, I said. We walked in and he shut the door.

There wasn't much furniture inside, not much of anything. A simple plaid couch, a small coffee table with ashes on it, a half-empty glass sitting on a counter, scattered books.

My mother wasn't here long, he said. She didn't have much of a chance to fix the place up.

Must be nice to have your own place, I started to say (getting only the first two words out, must be, but stopped when I realized how immature that sounded). Instead, I asked him what he was going to do with the place now. Do you think you'll stay?

Do you think I should? He reached for my hand and cupped his fingers around it. His palm was rough on the top part but squishy, soft even in the centre.

You should do whatever you want to do, I said taking my hand back to throw my coat across the back of the couch. I sat down, looked up at him, into his brown eyes, his pupils large and round.

Marigold, you have the most beautiful aura around you tonight, he said to me, and I blushed.

Whatever, I said back.

No really, blues and greens, fantastic.

I don't know what you're talking about, Amar.

It's just that sometimes, the most beautiful part of a person is that part that no one can see or hear. The part that no one even believes is there.

He stared to light candles, candles he pulled from drawers and closets and from behind curtains. Candles that he lit and placed mainly on the coffee table in front of me, and on the kitchen counter behind our heads. Soon our skin glowed the same colour in the soft light.

What's that book? I asked him. It was sitting on the edge of the coffee table, dog-eared, thin, black and orange cover.

The *Bhagavad Gita*, he said. Have you ever read it?

I shook my head.

'Tis a shame that no one in the West is interested. Within it are the keys, Marigold.

Keys to what?

To happiness, to living a happy, perfect life.

So why aren't you living one then? I said, flipping through its pages. That old book smell tickled my nose.

Marigold, he said. It's complicated here in the halls of illusion. It's hard to live the truth even though you know it's there. (I have to admit now that his religious gobbledygoop was making me have second thoughts about being there, but I went along with it.)

Ah, you have doubts. I can hear that, Marigold. But it's a life-style you have to embrace, and once you do, fuck, ecstasy is yours.

Is that why you hang out cross-legged under trees and stuff? I said.

There are other ways to get there. As he said this, he sat on the couch beside me, his thin thighs lining up against mine, touching. He put his upside down fist in front of me and opened his fingers. Lying on his palm were two small pieces of paper. Two small squares.

Put it on your tongue, he said. And though I think I knew where it would lead me (devil's work as my mother would say) and though it was not something I have done before, I did as he asked.

I took one of the small squares and placed it on my tongue. It dissolved like nothing. He did the same. And we waited.

Mother is knocking at my bedroom door. Get lost, I just yelled at her. Her knocks and whines are still pounding through my mind. Get lost, I yell again even though she is probably back in her bedroom by now. She's wants to talk about it, of course. I want her to leave me alone.

It took a while before we felt anything. Amar was quiet. He seemed to be thinking about something, maybe his mother? I pulled at my nylons as we waited, watching them spring back onto my legs. His words grew increasingly incoherent. It's useless attachment, he said. That's what keeps us trapped in this delusion that our mind creates, keeps us trapped behind this veil.

His gaze grew softer as he spoke.

We're deluded! he said, more and more space finding its way between his words. We are so bound to this material world and this mortal physical existence. It makes me sick, Marigold, it does.

I wasn't really listening to him, just nodding while the room seemed to be lighting up, candles growing brighter and brighter.

You can't let your emotions toss you around, Marigold. You can't. Your supreme self is more than that.

Supreme self? I muttered.

He lit a cigarette with a lighter he found on the floor and puffed out clouds of smoke into the room, leaning back beside me on the couch.

Yes, Marigold. Surrender! Surrender! Surrender! Have you ever heard of karma? It keeps going. The attachment keeps going if you don't . . . choose . . . differently. It you don't stop it. Fuck the depression and sadness.

His words came out slower by then, each syllable taking an eternity. He was looking down at the dirty floor and his eyes seemed to be getting wetter. When he started talking again and swept his hand through the air, I swear to God, there was colour that followed it. Red, pink, blue, sweeping past our faces, hovering before disappearing again, absorbing. I reached out to grab the colour streaks and he laughed at me, pushing my hand down.

I think I screamed when I saw it (can't remember the last time anything made me scream). His face when he turned around to look at me, to hold my arm down. His features, flat forehead, round eyeballs, pointy nose, melting down into nothing, like a candle that disappears with a flame.

You're melting! I yelled at him. The top of his head wasn't there anymore, just his thin lips smiling and laughing. And his finger pointing at me as it too started to dissolve. He grabbed my arm, hard, with his other hand and held me down on the couch.

Stop it! I shoved him and ran to the door. I ran right through the door (I think?) out into the yard behind the house, and down to the river, screaming. I just wanted to get away. I felt like he was stripping layers of skin off my body or something. I had to get out of there, but there was nowhere to run to. My feet were bare in the snow and I collapsed into it. I looked behind me then to see my own footprints, rising up into the air and landing on top of me.

He followed me out. His head was whole again. He was no longer laughing.

My footprints, I said. My footprints are all over me.

He took his hands and ran them down my shoulders, then

across my chest, then his hands across my face, so I could smell him inside the lines of his palms. And I let him. I felt stuck in place, like a boulder buried deep in the earth.

Does that help? he asked. Are the footprints gone?

Yes. I said. Thank you. I was crying then, only a little.

His hands were on my wrists then, wrapping round and pushing me back into the snow. Back onto my spine. Snow coming down around us. My footprints gone because he made it so. He loosened his grip on my wrists and started to open my arms up and back, slowly in the snow.

Snow angels, he said. And it sounded like he said, Go and tell, which really made no sense, but I started making angels myself in the snow, with my arms and feet and laughing as the black sky filled my head and stars dotted my eyes.

He lay down beside me on the ground. Moving his own arms and feet in and out, until we were both laughing.

His angel wing landed on my breast.

I undid the buttons of my blouse and placed his fingers on either side of my nipple.

He flipped from his back to his side to his stomach, landing on top of me. Open blouse, snow falling, stones from the ground in my back, mildew smell from the car, smoke from burned candles on his chest hair.

His hands worked their way up the sides of my body, over my hips, across my stomach, up to my ears. Then they went down again, down the front, under my skirt, staying there the longest, circling fingers that dipped themselves in, wetness that appeared from nowhere.

What was I doing?

He took me there in the snow, trees around us clapping and cheering, the snow angels we made floating above us, smiling serenely. That which I hadn't let any man touch, I let him take last night.

And now, I want to remember every detail.

I got home at 6:00 this morning. He drove me, but we didn't speak much. He said goodbye with a quick peck on my lips. I couldn't find the words to ask what he was thinking.

Mother was waiting in the kitchen when I came in, asleep at a kitchen chair, the telephone in front of her.

I'm back, I said as one word. And she started crying, moaning about fear of losing me, and how worried Steven was, and how they were going to call the police if I wasn't home by 7:00.

I'm a big girl now, was all I said. You can stop worrying about me.

I pushed her away and went to my bedroom. I slept five hours, and now I am awake. It's almost noon. The phone has been ringing. I am not opening the door.

I can't believe I let him go without asking him. How will I know?

I think I might be in love. Maybe, you never know. He sees me like no one else does and it's not just because of what we took, or what we did. Amar. Amar. Amar.

I'm going back. I am going to take my mother's car keys off the table, and drive out there. Back to the cabin.

I can't wait any longer.

I need to know if we have found something special.

November 27, 1972 (later)

I drove all the way out there, in Mother's car, without her

knowing. It was almost 3:00 by the time I got there (because of the time it took me to find my nerve).

He was gone. The cabin locked up. As far as I could see there was nothing inside, except for the couch and tables. No candles, no books, nothing and nobody. His van was not in the driveway. I felt foolish. The wind whistled in my ear, mocking me.

When I reached home, Mother was holding a thick white envelope. Mari, we need to talk about this, she said when I tried to grab it. She moved her hand. Mari, this was dropped off to me by a very scary looking man.

Just give it to me, Mother.

He was an East Indian man. What is going on? Why do you know an Indian man? Is this where you were last night?

I pushed my mother's hand into the side of the refrigerator and grabbed the envelope from her fingers, telling her again to just give it to me. She did.

I took the envelope up to my room and opened the part that had already been torn (and read no doubt).

On the outside it said my name: Marigold McCann.

And inside, on the slab of white paper torn from the back of a book, a note:

Dear Marigold:

Thank you for sharing yourself with me last night, it meant a lot. I'm afraid though that I woke this afternoon having experienced a sudden but distinct shift in priorities and have decided I must now go to India to live with my father.

It's not your fault. It's important that we both take time to cultivate our souls and work to transcend maya.

Try not to be upset, but instead remember what the Bhagavad Gita *tells us, "The soul that with a strong and constant calm takes sorrow and takes joy indifferently."*

I hope you will wear these to remember me by . . .

Amar Gosh.

P.S. Please enjoy the book as well — never stop searching!

As I move my hand to write this, three thin wire bracelets, red, blue, and gold, with tiny silver butterflies dangling, encircle my wrists. These are the Indian bracelets that he left with the letter. And I've got his copy of the *Bhagavad Gita*, like a last love letter. But what the hell? He's just left me, after that? I want to punch him and kiss him all in one. My heart is skipping on the same beat like my old Beatles records, and my exhale is caught in my throat.

Chapter Twenty

My father called the police. He called the police to try to get all the people out of the yard, but when the cops arrived, they only got in the line to pay their respects to my mother — a line that had not moved because I refused to let anyone in.

Most of the people Mrs. Roughen had let into the backyard were still clutching the things that were meant to help Mother. And I think also holding on to the hope that maybe she could predict their future, or at the very least help them feel better about their own predicaments.

Some just wanted to see the freak in the teepee — and they brought cameras.

There had been another news story about all the people who were showing up, which did nothing but convince more people in the city that it might be a good and noble idea to stop by. It became the cool thing to do. Like watching *Miami Vice*. Or trying to solve a Rubik's Cube. Only my mother could never be solved, and I didn't want her to be watched by anyone.

"Just be patient," Mrs. Roughen instructed everyone, including the Native man who was chanting and pacing around the teepee, wafting sage out of a seashell. "Marigold needs some time to rest. She will see you all as soon as she wakes up."

Father pushed through the door of the teepee and I jumped, like he was someone else.

"Well, the goddamn police are here, but they're not doing anything. They're just standing out there talking to Trudie and smelling the goddamn bottles of perfume."

"They are supposed to be helping her," I said.

"Mari, maybe we should take you to the hospital or something. Just to get away from this madness?"

My mother shook her head from side to side. Her eyes were full. She still wasn't talking much, which I kind of liked. A quiet Mother was like a little kitten. You could hold her and pet her and she never told you what to do or started screaming about anything.

"She doesn't want to go to the hospital," I said for her. "She wants to stay here. She wants the people to leave." He sat down with us on the bed and put the palm of his hand on my mother's stomach.

"Maybe the doctors could do something, Mari?" She shook her head again, grabbed his hand and threw it off.

"Stop it!" I yelled at him.

"I'm just trying to do what's best for your mother, Maya."

From outside the teepee: "Yoo-hoo, anyone in there? It's Trudie! Can I come in?"

"Stay the hell out of here, Trudie," said my father. "And take the rest of those idiots with you."

"Officer Martin wants to know if everyone is okay. We heard yelling."

"We're fine." My father's voice was stern and threatening — a tight package that could explode at any second. "Leave us alone."

And then another voice, of a woman: "Um . . . well, if you think it's okay, Trudie. I'm just wondering . . . if Marigold might have any idea where my teenage son is. You see, he's been missing."

"Fuck off!" my father yelled. "She has no idea about your son."

Silence in the yard. A somberness returned.

Time passed. Inside the teepee, my father and I said nothing. And my mother stayed in the silent space she had been for the last few days, only opening her mouth to sip water or chew on crushed strawberries or grapes. Voices still hummed their way through the walls of the teepee.

Trudie stood guard outside the door, politely refusing anyone who came and asked if my mother was rested enough yet, and when it would be time for him or her to pay their respects. Pay their respects? She wasn't even dead yet. The Native man left when he ran out of purifying sage. I heard Mrs. Roughen say goodbye to him like an old friend, "See you tomorrow, Howahkan!"

Dinner came and people started barbequing on my father's old grill that hadn't been fired up in years. My mother pulled the blanket over her head to block the smells of flesh burning, like maybe it was her own. My father paced angrily.

I said a secret prayer inside my head: *If you just make everyone*

leave us alone, and make my mother start talking again, I promise to never
again act like a child.

And then the bees came.

Bees, in the yard, hundreds of them. And they were angry.
Angry bees are the worst kind. Just ask Elijah. He was the one that
made them that way. We heard Mrs. Roughen's voice before we
heard what was going on: "Elijah, Christ, what are you doing?"

I peeked my head out the door flap of the teepee. Elijah was
standing in the centre of the yard dressed in a full-length mechanic
suit and a screened-in bug hat. Through the mesh I saw his lips were
pulled into a serene smile. He had work gloves on his hands, and
between them, he was shaking what looked like a grey paper ball.
And out they were coming — bees — creating a violent hum in the
air, looking for revenge.

What happened next was like a scene in a horror film: old
ladies dropped casseroles, covering their faces with their hands,
screaming in terror and running from the yard; muscular men in
tank tops swatted bees from their shoulders and winced at the stings
as they hopped fences; a teenager covered her face with her arm
and shrieked as she fiddled with the latch on our gate. Hot dogs and
potato salad flew to the grass when the bees attacked. Bags were
dropped, file folders of photocopied information created paper
angels flying through the air. Mrs. Roughen tried to run towards her
son but stopped when she saw their tiny wings and yellow backs.
She too ran from the yard.

"Stay in there, Maya!" Elijah shouted out to me then and I closed
the flap.

"What the hell is going on out there?" my father asked, taking a step towards me. All I could say was "bees."

When the buzzing and screaming stopped, only Elijah was left in the yard. My father went out to talk to him, shielding his face just in case. "What are you trying to prove, kid?"

"They're all gone aren't they?" Elijah said. "Doesn't that help you?"

I flung open the flap and screamed: "You had no right to do that! You could have hurt people! What if my mother got stung?"

"She didn't, did she?" Elijah asked, his mouth dropping in defeat.

"No, but you could have hurt her. I hate you!" I said this even though I didn't hate him. I hated the part of the situation for which he had played no part. I hated my mother's cancer and because I couldn't tell the cancer I hated it, I told him. "I hate you. I hate you. I hate you!"

"Sorry for trying to help!" Elijah said as he marched towards the side gate, throwing the empty nest to the ground.

"You did a good thing," my father said to Elijah as he left. "A bit crazy, but effective." Then he turned to me in the teepee. "Maya, you were kind of hard on him, don't you think?"

I was almost crying then, the tears growing on the insides of my mouth and threatening to come out. I couldn't get the sound of bees buzzing out of my head. I sat next to my mother on the bed and listened to her laboured breathing.

By sunset, things were almost back to normal. My mother started talking again. She asked me for a piece of bread with peanut butter and if I could bring in her *Bhagavad Gita* from the house. I did both and sat on the floor while she read and ate. Sometimes the words she read would fill the room through her weak voice: "What must be done, and what must not be done. What should be feared, and what should not be feared. What binds and emancipates the soul."

She was back to her nonsense — reciting things almost like a crazy woman would, but I was just happy to have her to myself again. "Mother, why would Elijah make those bees try to sting everyone?"

"He was chasing them away, Maya."

"Yeah, but what if you got hurt?"

"Nothing could hurt me anymore," she said. "You should apologize to Elijah for yelling at him. He gave us this." She pointed to the empty room, sighing, and I could smell her peanut butter breath.

"You're right. Maybe I should thank him for it."

"He likes you, Maya. In his weird little way, he likes you." She laid her head back down on bed, and held her book up with her straight arms. "New growths upspringing to that happier sky — which they who reach shall have no day to die."

"Stop reading that," I said.

"It's just a matter of time now, Maya," she told me, and I shook my head and covered my ears.

"When it happens, remember that my soul will be free."

"But I need you," I said. She smiled sadly.

"Maya, I'm sorry that I slapped you the other day. It was wrong and I wanted you to know that."

"That's okay."

"Now, can you get me a paper, pen, and envelope from the house?" I went and got it for her. Father was hunched over the kitchen table reading papers.

"What's wrong?" he asked.

"She wants paper. She wants to write something down." I slid open a kitchen drawer and rifled my hands around.

"Make her eat something," he said.

"Why don't you go in yourself?" I asked and he told me that he was taking a break. I wondered when that became an option.

When I got back outside, she was sniffing aromatherapy oil from one of the bottles lined up on her desk. She had an incense cone burning and the healing stones tucked into both her palms.

"Is it helping?" She shrugged and took the paper and pen from my hand. She used slow strokes to carve out something on the page, something from her book. Then she folded the paper down as small as she could, put it in the envelope and handed it to me.

"I want you to read this out loud at the very end." Her quartz stone fell from her hand and created a hollow plunk off the leg of the chair. I picked it up, feeling her delicate warmth on my fingers and handed it back to her.

"I will read it, Mother," I said to appease her. And I heard her desperate sobs from inside her head.

Chapter Twenty-One

Aunt Leah and I take a taxi from the Pearson Airport into the city, speeding on cement highways with only a pale yellow line for protection from those going the other way. Lined up along the road, tall, square buildings reflect sunshine from their mirrored windows and the occasional tree struggles to grow through the roadside dust.

"Try to get some sleep if you want," she says to me, leaning her round face against the window frame.

"I'm okay." I want to stay awake. I breathe in air through my mouth and get a throat full of gas fumes from the cracked window. The dark-skinned driver exits at Keele Street and we drive south, through a maze of closely lined houses and decrepit storefront signs for things like hair weaves, fresh fish, and Fine Ladies Fashions. We zoom past sidewalks crowded with people who all seem to be trying get places, fast — people with torn jeans and acid wash jackets, black ladies with high heels, men with moustaches and beards that drop down past their chins, mothers pushing shopping carts and dragging young children by the hand. All kinds.

By the time we reach Aunt Leah's apartment building, I have had it. The adrenaline from the flight, and reading my mother's journal, has sapped the energy from me. We have to get the cab to pull into the alley behind the building so we can unload our stuff (just the picnic basket for me, plus my other suitcase that Aunt Leah carries with her own backpack); there are too many cars flying by out front to do it there. I can even hear a streetcar rattling by as I swing open my door and step out. November is warmer in this giant city. No snow on the ground. I can't see my breath when I breathe. Just like a cool September day in Saskatoon. It's like I've gone back in time.

We struggle up one dusty flight of stairs into the plain hallway that holds the brown door that belongs to Aunt Leah.

I stand clutching my picnic basket while Aunt Leah fumbles with the lock.

"Usually sticks a bit, but I'll get it eventually." Her shoulder-length hair is pulled back with a black elastic and she has rolled up the sleeves of her jacket.

The hallway is narrow, suffocating. Cooking smells float out of the cracks under each door and mix in the air around us: curry, fried beef, burnt toast, rotten lettuce.

"Got it!" Leah says, pushing the door open with her hip. "This is it."

The first thing that hits me is the thick heat, plugging up my nostrils. The rooms of the apartment sit in a long row: kitchen to our left, dining room leads to the living room, past a bathroom to two tiny bedrooms. Each room is painted a different colour: red kitchen, orange dining room, yellow living room, green bathroom, blue for the first bedroom, a darker shade of blue for the final bedroom.

"They're painted the colours of the Chakra centres," Aunt Leah says. "Cool, eh? We needed another room for violet so I just made violet curtains." She walks to the living room window and grabs a purple piece of fabric draped in front.

I shrug and put my basket and paper bag on the floor by the midnight blue couch.

Footsteps from the darker blue bedroom, and a tiny woman walks barefoot across the hardwood towards us, tentatively.

"Buffy! We're back." The woman, who is wearing plastic glasses, square and dark and blocked at the sides, smiles and raises one thin arm in the air to wave. She must be under five feet tall (much shorter than me, I think I'm almost five-six) and her arms jut out of her shoulders like twigs. I know I could clasp my fingers around one of her biceps if I tried. She is wearing a tank top and running shorts with a stripe down the side. Her legs are dotted with bruises and red splotches. Around her ankle is a black tattoo with the words *I see with my heart*. (I have to tilt my head to see the word "heart" because it is written on the back of her ankle.) Her red hair is pulled back with a scrunchie and the skin on her face seems translucent, like you can see blue blood flowing through veins.

"Maya, this is my roommate, Buffy."

"Hi Maya," Buffy says and extends her fingers so they hang in the air near my face. I reach out to grab them.

"Hi."

"Maya will be staying with us while her father gets himself sorted out."

"Nice," Buffy says. Her head is turned towards the living room window, which looks out at a brick wall.

"Why is it so hot in here?"

"Something's wonky with the AC in this building," Buffy says. "You'll get used to it, just have to dress skimpy." Buffy and Aunt Leah laugh together as Aunt Leah removes her jacket, polka dot blouse, and pants and throws them both on the floor. She sits down in only her underwear and bra.

"This is the best thing about having a blind roommate," Aunt Leah says. "You can walk around naked all the time."

They laugh again together. Aunt Leah's giggles fade out before Buffy's.

"Leah, you kill me!" Buffy says, tracing her fingertips on the wall as she walks into the kitchen.

When Buffy is fiddling with things in the sink, Aunt Leah looks at me. "So kid, I'm afraid you'll have to take the couch." She rubs her hands over the velvet beside her naked thigh. "It's actually quite comfortable once you're used to not stretching out too much."

I swallow, heat, and feel my eyes filling up.

"Hey kid, what's wrong?" She pulls me down beside her.

"Nothing. It's just that I miss stuff."

"What kind of stuff?"

"My house, my friends, Mother, Father."

"You can't focus on that right now, Maya. It will only make you sad." She tucks a strand of my dark hair behind my ear. "Besides, you only just got here."

"Toronto smells," I say.

"I'll give you that. Toronto does smell in some places, but I promise you that there are a lot of perfectly fragrant places to visit, and we're going to find them all, right?"

"Okay."

"You'll see, it'll be great."

"Aunt Leah, can I ask you something?"

"Sure."

"Did you ever hear anything about my mother and an Indian man?"

"No, of course not. What are you talking about?" She stands up.

"Before she married Father, about her getting together with him and having . . . sex." I whisper the word "sex" because I think it is one of the first times I have said it out loud. I wouldn't even know the word at all if it wasn't for Mother and the seminar she took me to at the library when I was seven: "Putting the Lust Back in Your Sex Life."

"Maya, I have no idea what you are talking about." Aunt Leah looks back and forth several times turning her head. "I don't know where you would have gotten such a crazy idea, and really, I don't think you should be talking that way about your mother. I mean, she's only been gone a year. Let her rest in peace. She deserves that."

"Sorry I asked."

"And yuck, as if your mother would degrade herself with some sort of sordid affair and have sex with someone she didn't even love."

Aunt Leah barks out a fake cough, stands up, and jerks like she's stretching a kink from her neck. I watch her go back into the light blue bedroom, thinking for some reason how strange it is that I've never known her to have a boyfriend of her own — except Corey Hart, if he counts — and from what I can hear from inside her head, she could probably use a nice boy around to call her beautiful once in a while.

———————

Later we eat dinner together, Aunt Leah, Buffy, and I, at a round card table with a plastic red-checkered tablecloth. The purple around Buffy's head seems to be mixing with the red around Aunt Leah's, but I wonder whether they are both just reflections from the walls and curtains.

Buffy was the one to cook, which I find amazing because she can't even see which temperature the stove is at, or which is even the right knob.

Buffy made spaghetti with marinara sauce, which we all slurp up. Specs of red sauce land on Buffy's black glasses as she inhales the strings of pasta. Finally, Aunt Leah speaks: "Buffy used to be a Corey Hart fan too. Tell her, Buffy."

"He's got a gorgeous voice, don't you think, Maya?"

"We had a bit of a falling out," I say.

"My tastes have changed, too. I'm more into Madonna now . . . and Whitney Houston. I like country and western as well, even though it's supposedly this incredibly uncool thing. Loretta Lynn, Patsy Cline, Dolly Parton — they got the emotion, man. Love it!" As she talks, Buffy's head tilts towards the ceiling and her fork flings mushroom bits around the table.

"Buffy is a photography student," Aunt Leah says and I look at her as if to say, "How?"

"I know what you're thinking, Maya," Buffy says. "How on earth does a blind girl take photography? I don't blame you for thinking that, because if I didn't know it could be done, I probably would wonder myself. Lord knows I doubted the idea at first. But who am I to mess with my inner voice?"

"How *do* you do it?" I say, my words slipping out slowly. She howls with high-pitched laughter; the sounds coming out seem bigger than her whole body. Aunt Leah smiles and slurps in spaghetti.

"Good question, Maya. Very good question. The answer is, I don't see it, I experience it. I can capture beauty by smelling, touching, feeling, sensing. It really is better than someone seeing something, categorizing it, naming it, analyzing it. I skip all that part and simply feel what there is to feel — a tree, a bird, a meadow, a bowl of bananas, whatever. I snap it and let other people do the analyzing. It's my way of letting people see what I see."

"But how do you work all the technical parts and focusing and stuff?"

"Practice, my dear, lots of practice and memorization. Lord knows I had to work hard to convince York to even let me into the program."

"She took that!" Aunt Leah says this with her mouth still full, pointing to a black and white photo framed on the wall above the sink in the kitchen.

It's a picture of an old man, his eyes hidden under wrinkles, a single tear sitting in a groove on his cheek.

"It's my grandfather. That was taken only a few days before he died of prostate cancer."

"My mother died from cancer too. Of the cervix."

"Cancer gets so many of us. All that guilt and resentment eating us up."

"Maya's mother had no guilt." Aunt Leah says this with way too much emphasis. "Her death almost made her a Canadian celebrity. She had so many people trying to help her."

"She had a baby growing inside when she was dying," I say to Buffy, though I'm not sure why.

Buffy takes off her dark glasses and puts them on the table. She reaches over and grabs my hands.

I look into her dead eyes — unsteady eyes that wobble.

"Maya, I am sending you strength through my fingertips. Wait for it."

We sit in silence. Aunt Leah chewing, Buffy sending, and me waiting.

Aunt Leah leaves at around 10:00 for her job. She wears heels, a blue shirt that rests off her shoulders, and a black skirt that only reaches her thighs. Her hair is down and hair-sprayed and her face is caked in makeup.

"I'm a perfume girl at the Bay," she says when I ask. "You know, spraying people when they walk by or giving them little cards of Poison or Gloria Vanderbilt. I have to get dressed up because the better I look, the more people will like the perfume."

"But isn't the Bay closed at night?" I ask.

"It's a midnight extravaganza," Aunt Leah says like I should have known. "It happens a lot and only the real committed ones get to work. All night, everything is on sale, including perfume, which means I am going to be really busy. Better get my squirting finger ready." She points her index finger and bends it three times like it is doing push-ups. She does it with a solemn face, like her finger is out to get her.

As far as I can tell, Aunt Leah never figured out what she wanted to take in university.

"So make yourself comfortable, Maya. I'll be home before you know it. And tomorrow we can go shopping."

"Whatever," I say, hugging a pillow on the couch. A lamp rattles from the streetcar passing outside.

When she leaves I notice there is no television, and I almost chase her through the hall and down the front steps of the apartment building to tell her but decide that it can wait.

———

When the apartment is dark for the first time, I wake to hear Buffy's voice swelling up through the blackness. The words sound as if they are being spoken from the end of a long copper tunnel, sentences jagged and illogical. Lying still in my couch-bed, I soon realize that the incoherent sounds I hear are not from her mouth, but are her thoughts, her mind, echoing out from inside her head.

They must be the dialogue of her dreams.

I have never heard someone's thoughts when they were sleeping. Maybe it is because the apartment is so small, and Buffy is in her bed just down the hall. Either way, her internal wisdom comforts me.

"Resistance shatters" are the first words I hear. And then,

"Nature lives in silent moments. Touch the ground. Try to feel the sky, because it is you. Eat vegetables whenever you can."

When I focus on them, Buffy's words drown out my own worries regarding my mother's notebook (which is stuffed under the velvet couch until I am ready to read the rest) and the other upsetting things that circulate themselves through my mind: my mother's face when they closed her coffin, my father crying, ladies surrounding a teepee with candles, Elijah scowling at his mother, being sick in an empty house.

Buffy's mind continues to ramble incoherently. "Peace out, peace in, peace everywhere. Always wipe from front to back." Eventually, the rhythm of the strange syllables soothes me into sleep.

———————

Leah comes back at 3 a.m. I can tell by the clock on the bookcase. I close my eyes when she shuts the door and pretend to be sleeping while she slinks across the floor to her bedroom.

I don't smell any perfume.

Chapter Twenty-Two

November 29, 1972

The last two days I have spent in bed. Thinking, crying, swearing. I can't bear to smell myself — primordial rot — I need to take a shower before maggots start growing in my armpits. I'm completely tattered.

He's gone. Amar. He took me and now he's gone.

What an incredible phony he was. But I liked him. Loved him?

I am thinking (as I lie here) about how good it felt when I fell asleep in his arms. On that tacky sofa inside that cabin. It's embarrassing now to think, but I imagined us falling asleep like that forever. Except in a nicer room — a master bedroom. He was so smart. Maybe too smart: he figured out how to trick me into getting close to him, naked in the snow. Into thinking he wasn't just a stripped down, fancy-talking Casanova.

I miss him.

I have spoken to Steven once on the phone. Yesterday. I told him nothing was wrong and that I have merely come down with a flu-type thing that has confined me to my bed. And that no, I do not want any company because I am afraid I may be contagious. And what I have, he doesn't want to catch.

He wants to talk. About the other night when we were supposed to go to Roland's together. About the hours I went missing. About my mother crying when she answered the phone. I told him that talk was overrated. That I'll talk to him when I'm ready.

November 30, 1972

They both showed up in my bedroom last night, Amar in my dream when I was napping, feeding me grapes from his fingertips, and Steven, in the flesh, standing at the end of my bed after walking right into my house and slamming the door to my bedroom open. He has nerve, I tell you.

What's going on? he asked. His eyes were wide and intense, like he was trying to trap me inside them.

Steven, I'm practically buck naked, I said, pulling my comforter up to hide my nightgown.

Oh sorry. He turned around while I slipped a Trent sweatshirt over my matted hair.

So what was it you were saying, Steven?

I said, what's going on? I want to know. All of it.

Nothing's going on, Steven. I told you I have the flu.

Bullshit!

Steven, quiet, my mother is down the hall. I'll tell you if you sit down first. He sat on the corner of the bed. I noticed that he had taken off his shoes before coming in the house and that his socks were bleached white (by his mother, I'm sure).

Tell me, he said again, his voice shaking like a thin branch in the wind.

Steven, I don't have the flu.

What's wrong then?

I'm just stressed out from school.

I don't believe you. Tell me now or I'll leave here and you'll never see me again.

His threat was so dramatic that it scared me. Not that I was scared to be without him, but I think I was just scared to be without anyone. So, before I could stop myself, I started to tell him. The other night, when we were supposed to go out to dinner and . . .

Go on.

The other night, I wasn't there when you came to pick me up because I went out with another man.

What?! He stood up then, with his fingertips on his temples like someone had just screamed fire.

Steven, sit down. (He did.) I'm sorry but I didn't know what else to do.

What do you mean?

There has been this weird sort of distance between us. For the longest time now, it's just not like it was when we first started going out.

You should have talked to me about it. (His voice quivered when he said it.) I don't want to lose you, Marigold.

You haven't lost me, Steven. I'm still here.

I took his hand and looked in his eyes, trying to mean it, and before I knew it, I felt the tears forming a blockage in my throat. Must swallow, I thought.

Oh, Marigold, he said. We'll get through this. (He hugged me. I have to say, he looked decent.)

I grabbed on to him because he was all I had.

Oh, Steven, I'm sorry. (I *am* sorry, in a way.)

Mari, you just have to tell me one thing. I don't care who he is, or why, I just want to know, is it over between you?

Yes, I said. (This I knew for sure.) Yes, it's all over. I started to cry even harder after saying this.

Good, now we can start over.

I'm sorry, Steven.

We rocked back and forth as we held each other, an innocent sort of rock, like two friends greeting each other after being away all summer. Only it's almost December.

And now he's gone home. And I'm alone again, still in bed. I'm starting to think about washing myself — getting rid of the last of Amar living inside me — starting over.

I will do it as soon as I can shove the rest of this guilt down my throat.

December 14, 1972

I've showered and started going to my classes again. I've got a final exam in five days that I need to prepare for, and a paper I need to write on Jane Austen and the complexity of relationships in *Sense and Sensibility*.

I'll show her complex relationships.

Steven held my hand today in the Student Centre. Something about it felt safe and maybe like I could stop worrying about whether Amar was ever going to come back. Like maybe I could just be happy.

All this time pretending to have the flu and I think I have created it for myself. I feel like crap. This morning I had to leave class to go sit on the toilet. Disgusting. I have a cold cloth on my temple right now, but I don't think I have a fever. I'm sure this will pass, like all things.

Steven wants to know where I got the butterfly bracelets I'm wearing. I told him I'd had them forever.

December 19, 1972

The very worst thing that could have happened — has just happened. I came back today from writing my exam, tired, of course, and not wanting to deal with any more shit, and what do I find? Mother. Sitting at the kitchen table with her forehead resting on the palms of her hands.

She had just cooked a plate of chocolate fudge, and the sweetness in the air made it seem insane that she would be upset about anything.

Then I saw it.

My notebook (this one) was sitting on the table in front of her. Closed, but I knew it had not always been. She looked up at me like I had just been given a death sentence, her face red and blotchy from where her hands had been pushing.

Marigold, how could you? She sung the words like a sad song and I freaked.

227

What the hell are you doing?! I reached for my notebook and she grabbed it in her hands. I had to dig my fingernails into the fleshy part beside her thumb to get her to loosen her grip. This is none of your business! I yelled at her.

Marigold, you have brought great shame on your family.

Fuck you.

I am glad your father is not alive to see this.

I took my book and went to my room. Why did she have to bring up Dad? It's not like he chose to get cancer. I'm sure if he had a choice he would have chosen to be here to see this. He would have chosen to be here with me, instead of wherever the hell he is now.

We haven't spoken all night, Mother and I. And we probably never will.

December 22, 1972

I've started throwing up in the mornings. Not a lot, just enough to fill the base of the sink after I brush my teeth. I don't think Mother has heard me, and even if she did, she would probably not ask me why or try to help me. I swear to God she has disowned me. Nothing I could do could make her forgive me. She cries while she dusts the television.

I'm pretty sure I'm pregnant. I feel this vague blob of sickness in me all day long, and it's not just from the heartache of losing the only guy who has every really moved me to my core.

I'm only a week late but I can feel Amar growing inside me, the part of him he left. And I wonder if he can feel it too? Does he know he can never escape it, or me? We will always be tied now, which feels quite nice actually — like he's still here.

December 23, 1972

Christmas depresses me. I don't know why Mother even bothers putting up a tree, it's not like we're going to celebrate anything — not with Dad gone only three years and things the way they are.

I went to the doctor yesterday, the clinic on George Street. I know it's early but I have to know for sure.

I'm twenty, I told the nurse.

No, I'm not married, Doctor Whatever-the-hell-your-name-is.

I winced when they drew the blood, like I was losing pieces of him, or showing him to the world.

I have been thinking a lot about the things he said that night. About life and happiness and all that shit. I think there might be something to it all. I'm going to try reading the *Bhagavad Gita* he gave me. I think if I can figure it out, I can figure him out. And that makes me feel like he is still here. I want to keep searching like he said, make sense of it all. I want to find out how to be happy. I want to be a good person — the kind of person that doesn't sleep with someone she hardly knows.

They are calling me with the results tomorrow. How much you want to bet that Mother is the one to pick up the phone?

December 24, 1972

Christmas is cancelled. I made it to the phone on the first ring yesterday but Mother was standing right there and my face could not hide the shock of the truth.

It's true.

My eyes filled as soon as the nurse told me and I still can't figure out whether they were tears of joy or sadness. Could it be both? It's

strangely comforting to have this little Amar growing inside me —
a better souvenir of him than damn bracelets that's for sure.

So I hung up the phone and Mother asked me right away what
was wrong.

Nothing, I told her. Nothing is wrong.

Why are you crying then? She was wearing yellow rubber
gloves and scrubbing the kitchen sink with Javex.

I just found out some news is all. I felt my knees give out then
and I started to sink towards the ground.

Then she started to lecture me: Marigold, you tell me right
this instance what is going on. Is it that coloured man? Are you still
seeing him? What about Steven, Marigold? Steven is a perfectly
lovely young man and if you ask me (I didn't), he would make you
very, very happy. And happiness is not something that the good Lord
gives to everyone. In fact, I don't think you even deserve it anymore
. . . there was a time, yes, but now, with all the carrying on you
have been doing, why, I think you deserve something much worse.
I don't want to say hell, but maybe something close. Maybe something almost as uncomfortable as hell, maybe some place like that
would suit you —

I'm pregnant, okay.

Her yellow hands froze in the air by her face, like some sort of
screwed-up flower with rubber petals.

Excuse me? She stretched the two words out as long as possible
to delay the time before I had to say it again.

I'm pregnant, and it's the coloured man's baby.

After this, hell truly did break loose. Panting and pacing and
wailing (all from Mother). Things were thrown, pans, a casserole

dish, the kitchen clock, potatoes from a bowl. I got through it all without crying, the only part of me showing my fear was my hands, which were twitching. I left through the back door and went to the only place I could think of. I went to Steven's house.

When I knocked on the front door, Steven's mother and father were sitting in the living room watching *The Mary Tyler Moore Show* in the dark. Through their picture window, I could see their faces reflecting the dancing colour from the television set.

Why, Marigold darling, what a nice surprise, his mother said when she pushed the door open. She flipped on the light to reveal a foyer of cardboard boxes that made me remember — Steven's parents are moving out to PEI next week. Mr. Devine is retiring from the police force and they have bought a house on the ocean. Steven is moving into campus residence.

Is Steven here, Mrs. Devine?

Yes, he's here, upstairs studying. Mrs. Devine's chestnut hair was pulled back off her tired face into a bun. Her blue eyes were calm.

Can I go up?

You go right ahead. Nice to see you, Marigold.

She sat back down beside Mr. Devine in the darkened living room lit up by the flashing colour from their television. I pounded up the stairs. I opened his door and saw him there, at his desk, pen in hand, looking into his wall like he was trying to remember something important.

Steven! I ran to him and put my arms around him from behind. Steven, I said again, softer this time.

Marigold, what happened? he asked. He turned around in his seat and hugged me and that was when I started to cry.

Steven, I love you.

I love you too, Mari. You know that.

How much do you love me, Steven?

As much as there ever was or ever will be.

Steven, I messed up.

Whatever it is, Mari, it's okay. I'm here.

Are you sure? He nodded and I exploded.

I let it go too far with that other man, Steven. I got stoned. And we had sex with each other. He released his hug on me and instead gripped me by the shoulders.

What? he said with his eyebrows scrunching together.

I'm going to have a baby, Steven. I'm having another man's baby and I need your help. I need you to be here for me.

Steven said nothing. In my mind he said, Of course I will be here for you, Mari, we all make mistakes. But out loud he said nothing, only looked down at the floor like a wounded deer.

After three minutes he spoke: I think you should go.

But Steven, I can't go home now. My mother found out and she is furious.

You have to go now, Mari. I can't talk about this yet.

He walked me downstairs and we stood at the door for a second.

Marigold! Steven's younger sister, Leah, ran at me and attached herself around my legs.

Hi Leah. Leah, I have to go now. Leah, you'll have to let me go now.

But I don't want you to go, let's go play, she said, her bottom lip jutting out, her pudgy hands grabbing the backs of my knees.

No, I'm going now, Leah. Sorry.

Bye, Mari, Mrs. Devine said from the living room.

I left them all there. I left them all and walked home.

Mother was curled on the kitchen floor in a mess of broken dishes and slopped food. I know she's alive because I could see her back rising and falling. I went upstairs.

It's amazing to me that one mistake could cause so much upset.

December 28, 1972

I'm engaged to Steven.

Yes, I know it's pretty unbelievable — one, that he would ask, and two, that I would accept. But he did and I did.

On Boxing Day he showed up at my door. Mother was locked in her room and I was flipping through channels, wrapped gifts still laid out around my feet. I was feeling nauseated and had been sucking the salt off saltine crackers for about an hour when he knocked.

I opened the back door right away. He was wet because it had been snowing a sort of slush and apparently he hadn't cared to use an umbrella or cover himself up in any way. He didn't say anything when he saw me, just held one of my hands with his, and put his other one on my belly.

I smiled tentatively, like I didn't know yet what it meant.

Marigold, I love you, he said.

Thanks, Steven.

And my love for you is enough to get over this.

It is? I said.

I want you to marry me, Marigold (he was on his knee by that time). I don't have a ring, but I have something else to show you how serious I am.

He took off his jacket and lifted up his shirt. I started to wonder then if he had been drinking. And there, on his bare chest, over his heart, was my name — Mari — tattooed on his skin.

I reached out to touch it, still bloody and scabbing and gasped, Steven, what did you do?

It's for you. It's all for you. I will help you through this.

I kissed him soft on the lips, but not before I said yes, because well, there really wasn't any other answer to give. I need a father for my baby. I need someone to support me when I drop out of school. I need to find a way to make my mother proud of me again. I guess it doesn't matter that I am sort of in love with someone else. A phantom.

Chapter Twenty-Three

This afternoon, with Buffy out developing photos and Aunt Leah getting the groceries, I sat on Buffy's bed and read the rest of my mother's journal.

And now I know.

It's a lot to learn at one time. My father is not my father. And somewhere, maybe in India, lives the real man who made my mother pregnant the first time.

I get up from Buffy's bed and go back into the living room, stuffing the notebook back into the picnic basket beside my couch. I know I have to get out of here.

Tripping over my boots, I leave the apartment and exit onto St. Clair Avenue. Noise. Cars are blowing smoke into my face. Honking. The sky is criss-crossed with thick black wires, and a streetcar rattles by. I zip up my white parka and pull down my scratchy wool hat over my ears.

I don't know which way to walk. I sit on the front step of Aunt Leah's building, looking west towards Oakwood Avenue. I'm still not sure if I believe that instead of having one missing father, I actually have two. There's a video store across the street with a sign flashing the word "OPEN" in pink. Open, open, open. It's imprinting on my eyeballs. I shift my gaze to watch a family of three walk by in front of me. They are black and dressed in clothes that seem like they were purchased at the Goodwill, but assembled in a fashionable sort of way. The father is tall and broad, walking with arms crossed over his winter jacket. He's wearing some large gold rings on his meaty fingers and doesn't seem to care what his wife and daughter are doing behind him. The woman has an afro and is pulling a little girl in a pink coat down the street, annoyed that she wants to stop and pick up pebbles or look at my suede boots.

"Yoo-hoo, Maya!"

I see Aunt Leah getting out of a brown car across the street. She waves, turns to say goodbye to the person in the car and walks in my direction.

"Hey, Maya darling, what's shaking?" She is wearing a long skirt and platform heels and no jacket. She has huge hoop earrings in her ears.

"Where're the groceries?"

"Changed my mind, I thought maybe it would be best if we went together. I have no idea what you like to eat."

"I know about my father."

"Know what?" She cocks her head like she's got water stuck in her ear.

"That he's not. My father, that is."

"Don't be ridiculous, of course he is." She sits down beside me on the stoop, her legs stretched out and crossed under her long skirt, her arms wrapped around her.

"Why did you lie to me?" I say this quietly to avoid the ugliness in the words.

"What?"

"I know he's not my father. I read my mother's journal. My real father is some dude who walked out on her. I am even more of an orphan than I thought."

"Where did you get it?" She is looking across the street now, into the video store where there is one kid doing nothing behind a counter.

"I found it in Mother's closet. You're not my real aunt."

"You will always be my niece."

"So it's true!" I point at her, my finger almost touching her eyeball.

"Maya, I only wanted to protect you and your family."

"How was that protecting us?"

"It was a web of lies with different layers, and I was not going to be the one to bust them all open."

"Is that supposed to make me feel better?"

"You don't understand. No one ever talked about it . . . what was I supposed to do?"

"How did you find out then?"

"Mom explained it to me after I had returned from visiting you in Saskatoon that first time. I was obsessed with the fact that you didn't look like anyone else in the family. I was jealous, I think. And so to shut me up, she told me what had happened. She said that your Grandma McCann told her and Dad at the hospital when you were born — saying they deserved to know."

"Did Father know who my real father was?"

"Mom and Dad told him. I don't think your parents ever talked about it after that point. They seemed to think that if you don't talk about something, maybe it doesn't really exist."

"You should have told me." I stand up, my voice creating vapour in the cool air. "You are nothing but a big, fat liar."

I start to walk away and Aunt Leah stops me with her inner voice . . . *Maya, please, no, what did I do? For fuck's sake, it's not my fault.*

I turn around and glare at her. And decide to use the best ammunition I have to fight back — what I heard her thinking a couple nights ago when she got home from her "perfume" job.

"And by the way, I know about what you're really doing when you go 'out'! How do you think your parents would feel to hear that you are having sex with men for money?"

I leave Aunt Leah shocked and speech/thought-less on the frozen concrete.

I don't get far down St. Clair. And then like magic, I see him walking towards me.

He looks older. His hair is cut a little shorter and he's wearing a navy blue pea coat, blowing into his bare hands as he steps off the streetcar.

When he looks up and sees me, we both stop. I think my mouth hangs open, because I feel winter in my lungs.

"Elijah," I say.

He smiles. A lopsided sort of smile like always.

"Just the girl I was coming to see."

It turns out that my father called Mrs. Roughen and "suggested" that Elijah come see me at Aunt Leah's — like I can't make my own friends or something. I'm a bit angry with him for pretending to care at this point. But secretly, I'm so, so happy to see Elijah again.

I tell him that I don't want to go home. So instead, we go down to the Retro Café and have breakfast for lunch. I feel extremely grown up sitting with him in the booth. He tells me about how he and his mother have moved in with her new boyfriend, Conrad. He's smoking a cigarette while he talks. The one nasty habit he says he still hasn't been able to give up.

He tells me that he thinks "city life is fucking awesome" and he would never want to go back to living in "a dried up place like Saskatoon."

I'm attracted to the gorgeous turquoise light I catch glimpses of around his head — it seems almost to be mixing with mine over the table. And at one point, I hear him think that I am looking cute, which makes me feel pretty good.

Mostly I nod and smile, scrunching up my toes in my shoes when I don't know what to say. I do remember to thank him for the bees. And to apologize for telling him I hated him after he did it. He says he always knew it wasn't true.

When I get back to the apartment, Aunt Leah is waiting for me.

"Where have you been?" she asks, looking hurt, pulling her fingers through her long hair.

"Just walking around," I say. "I didn't go far."

"Listen, Maya, about what you said . . ."

"Forget it, really. Whatever you want to do."

"It's not what you think. It's just an escort service — I don't have to do anything I don't want to. And I'm getting out of it, really."

"I said — whatever you want to do."

"I want to go back to school, Maya. To university . . . for something big. This will help me do it all on my own."

"Okay." I'm feeling a bit sorry for her now, because I can hear her whimpering from inside. Who am I to tell her how to live?

"But Maya, how did you find out?"

"I just guessed."

I don't tell her about the night when I heard her think it. She was sneaking in, not smelling of perfume, and I heard her think it clear through the dark air: *I've got to stop doing this . . . that guy smelled like garlic. I've got to clean him off me right now.*

"I'm sorry, Maya."

"It has nothing to do with me," I say. I go into Buffy's blue room and hide my face in her pillow, inhaling the smell of her almond face cream.

I wake to hands touching my face.

"Maya, is that you? What are you doing in my bed?"

"Sorry, Buffy," I say. "I needed privacy."

"We all need that, now don't we?" She puts her camera down on her desk with a clunk.

"Did you take some good pictures today?"

"You tell me." She opens an envelope and spreads out photos around me on the bed. Pictures of the spray of a water fountain, a bird warming eggs in a nest, chocolate bars laid out on a table, and one of me.

"That's me!"

"How does it look, describe it to me," Buffy says.

"Well, my eyes are closed."

"I took it when you were sleeping."

"My hair is messed up, and hanging a bit over my face. I have a pillow in a headlock." She laughs and says she figured. "I look old, like a woman almost."

"We are practically women from the moment we come out."

She is sitting on the bed now, and hugs her knees up to her chest so that she looks like one small bony ball. Almost like I could pick her up and roll her down a hill if she would let me.

I can hardly wait for Buffy to fall asleep that night so I can listen to her dream-thoughts. When they start up, I am surprised to hear my name woven within the sentences: *Maya, you are not alone in anything you do.*

It's like someone is talking to me through Buffy's dreams.

Don't resist life. It's what makes you, you.

The words are confusing me. I have to know for sure if it is

241

Buffy talking so I walk into her room and turn on the light in the hall. She is in her bed, without her glasses, and her eyes are closed.

Everything that happens is for your higher good.

Her lips aren't moving.

———————————

Four days later in the middle of the night, Buffy is shaking my shoulders awake. Her fingers are clammy on my skin.

"Maya, get up! We have to go to the hospital."

"Why?"

"It's your Aunt Leah."

"She's not really my aunt."

"Well, she's hurt."

———————————

When we get there, Aunt Leah's face is swollen, black with red bits, so I can hardly recognize her.

"Aunt Leah?"

"She can't hear you, Maya. The doctor said that she's still unconscious. How does she look?"

"She looks terrible." I stare at a quiet Aunt Leah. The only sound coming from her bed is *beep, beep, beep*. Buffy steps up to the bed, which comes almost up to her waist. She lowers her hand on Aunt Leah's face and shudders.

"Ouch, she's banged up pretty good." She reaches around herself for her camera.

"You're taking pictures? Buffy, you can't."

"She may want to see these someday."

"But it's so gruesome."

Buffy holds her arm straight out, fingers touching Aunt Leah's nose and takes three steps backwards. *Click, click, click.*

"Got enough yet?"

"For now."

I hold Aunt Leah's hand in mine. Her nails are painted fuchsia, her skin white; there is blood dried along her cuticles.

"She really is an amazing woman," Buffy says into the dim light of the hospital room.

"They always say that about someone who's sick," I say, my eyes swelling with tears.

"But she really does the best she can. I've known that since I first came to see her about sharing the apartment. She's a good friend to you too." I look at Buffy, her head turned towards the corner of the room.

"I can't lose anyone else, Buffy."

"I know, Maya, no one can."

In two days, Aunt Leah is well enough to come back to the apartment. Aside from the black over her eye socket and a broken rib that hurts when she breathes, she looks the same.

"Really girls, I can do it myself," she says when Buffy and I hold out our arms to lift her out of the bed. But when she steps down, she grimaces and puts her hand to her chest.

"You're going to be just fine, Leah. You just need some rest is all."

Aunt Leah's middle is wrapped in a thick bandage. I see it when she gets undressed, slides herself onto the couch and says, "That's better." She closes her eyes, and Buffy and I sit around her in kitchen chairs pulled into the living room.

"Aunt Leah, what happened?" I say.

"I slipped is all," Aunt Leah says, opening her eyes. "I was coming out of the job centre and someone had puked or something on the sidewalk. If it wasn't puke, it was some sort of chunky ice cream, or mushroom soup. Anyway, I was in such a hurry to get home that I stepped right into it. Stepped right in and my feet came out from under me. I landed on a hot dog cart. The guy had to jump out of the way. I cracked my rib on the corner of it and must have banged my eye into something else. God, I don't remember anything after the slip."

"Leah, you were so lucky."

Buffy and I sit staring at Aunt Leah, me really seeing her and Buffy only pretending that she does.

From her head she tells me the true story, almost like she knows I can hear it: *He beat me up. This is the end of it, really it is.*

"Would you rather be burned or buried after you die?"

Aunt Leah asks Buffy and me this when we're all watching *Another World* in the living room, Aunt Leah on the couch, Buffy and I sprawled out on the floor creating a person arch around the tiny television. Twins Vicki and Marley are cat-fighting on the screen.

"I guess burned," Buffy says. "I think I was buried alive in a past life and the thought of it petrifies me."

"I'd be buried," Aunt Leah says. "Back where I came from, no hot flames involved. What about you, Maya?"

I remember my mother, lying in the box and being lowered into the ground, hiding her down there.

"I want to be cremated too," I say. "Burned."

The phone rings from beside me on the coffee table. I pick it up and say hello. Nothing. Tiny specs of static on the other end.

"Who's there, Maya?" Buffy asks.

"Hello?" I say again. "No one's there." I hang up the receiver. Vicki has just called Marley a witch for stealing Jake away from her. Marley is crying, like it's all too much for her.

"Aunt Leah, did you know that Father sent Elijah to make sure I was okay?"

"Who?"

"Elijah. Mrs. Roughen's son. From Saskatoon."

"No, I didn't know that. Maybe you should call your dad yourself to let him know you're okay."

"I like how things are now."

"She doesn't have to call him," Buffy says. "What he did, well, it was criminal."

"Thank you, Buffy," I say.

"You know, Maya, you really have to go to school soon," Aunt Leah says.

"Where?" I say.

"We'll find you a school around here. You have to finish grade eight." She talks soft and slow so as to not upset her middle.

The next week I start school at Winona Drive Public School, cold cement playground, only a fifteen minute walk from the apartment. I'm the only new girl in grade eight and it's lonely at my desk among the thirty other kids in the class — all different kinds of kids. I feel very inner-city.

The teacher, Mr. Pickle, starts the first class, English. They have been reading Shakespeare, *The Tempest*.

Mr. Pickle adds to how uncomfortable I feel in this sea of new faces by asking me to read out loud to the class. My armpits start to sweat underneath the lime sweater Aunt Leah bought me, while all the little eyes burn gazes through my skull and hundreds of little thoughts express their boredom to themselves.

"We are such stuff/ As dreams are made on; And our little life/ Is rounded with a sleep," I read. My voice cracks when I say it and everyone laughs. I decide then that I have all the friends I need.

———————————

"If you had the choice, would you rather be blind or deaf?" Aunt Leah asks me that night before Buffy gets home. She is lying on the couch again, even though she doesn't need to be there anymore. She's healed.

"Blind," I say on the next beat.

"Yeah, but how can you know what's going on if you can't even see it?" Aunt Leah asks.

"Buffy knows." Her questions are starting to annoy me.

"God, I can't even imagine, Maya. Not being able to see. I would pick deaf for sure, although I'd miss music."

"I want my mother back," I say then, not knowing where it came from, but maybe from realizing that my mother can't see or hear where she is. My face contorts and tears dangle on my eyelashes.

"Aw shucks, Maya. I didn't mean to upset you." Aunt Leah puts her arms around me but I push her away.

"No, I just want things to go back to how they were. I want my parents back. I want my friends back. I want my house back."

"But Steven sold the house," she says seriously. I can tell she is insulted that I pushed her away — red shoots out around her head, burning like electricity in the air, but I don't care.

"Typical," I say.

"You should call him, Maya."

"Nah."

When she gets home, Buffy suggests we hold a séance, to try and contact my mother.

"You'll see then that she's still around you — that you're never alone."

She lights candles and puts them on top of the television set, on the coffee table, on the end table, and over the fridge in the kitchen. Buffy, Aunt Leah, and I each sit cross-legged in a circle. I put my mother's healing stones in the centre. "Yes, that's good," Buffy says when she feels them in her hand. "Things that your mother touched will help invoke her spirit."

We hold hands. We turn out all the lights. We close our eyes and Buffy chants my mother's name: "Marigold, Marigold, Marigold."

After ten minutes, Aunt Leah sighs and says she is going to bed, that this is pointless and that "if Marigold wanted to come back to earth, she certainly wouldn't waste her time in this crappy apartment."

"I'll keep trying with you," Buffy says when Aunt Leah leaves. "She's out there somewhere. We just have to wait for her. You believe, don't you?" I nod, because yes, I do believe in things that others can't see; really I have no choice but to.

"Buffy, sometimes I see and hear weird stuff."

"What kind of stuff?" she asks. We are still holding hands.

"Colour, light — around people's heads."

"Those are their auras, Maya." She says this like it's no big deal at all, like for her all sight is only something she's heard about. "I've heard that everyone has auras around them all the time. There are different levels to the body, you know, more than the physical part, that's for sure."

"Sometimes, I hear stuff too." This makes her take off her square glasses so I can see her foggy eyes. "What kind of stuff?"

"What people are thinking. It comes when it feels like it, I can't control it." Buffy brings her lips together to hide her gaping mouth, and runs her flaky hand over the *I see with my heart* tattoo on her leg.

"Describe it to me."

"It's not an actual sound. But more like a feeling of a sound. I hear what people are thinking, inside my own mind, like it was me thinking it."

"Do you like it?"

"Sometimes it annoys me, but I'm used to it I guess. Sometimes it makes me laugh to hear what people think is important."

"Have you ever heard what I was thinking?"

"Only when you're sleeping. You tell me things."

Buffy says nothing, only holds three fingertips over her lips.

"Who knows, maybe it's not even real. Maybe I'm making it all up in my own imagination."

"It's as real as anything else, Maya," Buffy says. "You can never really be sure, I guess."

"Buffy, my father was not my real father."

"How do you know?"

"I read my mother's journal. My real father lives in India."

"You're kidding?"

And then, like thunder — bang! A smash against glass. I look down, the malachite stone is gone, like my mother had picked it up and thrown it against the window. "She's here," I say to Buffy; she squeezes my hand.

We sit together in the dark for two more hours, and when nothing else happens, we fall asleep on the floor.

Chapter Twenty-Four

After the bees chased my mother's fanfare away (an event that was written up in the *Saskatoon Post* with the headline "Woman's Final Days Marred by Angry Swarm"), it seemed that there was nothing left to do but wait. So I waited. My mother waited. My father paced, and made phone calls, and went to work, and cooked himself hamburgers on the barbeque, and mowed the grass, and filtered out anyone who showed up at our front door.

Until one morning, he let someone in.

An older lady, with a black sweater fastened with a brooch over a tiny white T-shirt, glasses tucked into her palm, delicate folds of skin around her mouth, grey wisps of hair that must have fallen from her bun on the plane — she seemed to extend into the space around her head and torso. Grandmother McCann.

My mother was reading and I was playing solitaire, my kings

and queens laid out on the floor of the teepee. I had helped my mother into the house only once that morning, to use the toilet. The thinness of her body as she squatted on the toilet seat made me feel relieved when she settled back into the padding of her bed. We had all the flaps open, and two fans blowing summer air through the space. I brought her ice chips from the refrigerator, which she traced over the outline of her features to cool off.

"Mother, what are you doing here?" My own mother said this when she saw hers standing at the opening of the teepee, her body framed by the outside world.

"Marigold, I swear, it's absolutely stagnant in here." Grandmother McCann put her small brown suitcase down and immediately started to lift the window and door flaps back further and aim the fans in new directions.

"What do you want?" Mother said, her words written on an imaginary white flag waving in front of her eyes.

"And the décor is completely depressing. You couldn't have dressed it up a bit?" Grandma McCann reached into her bag, took out a Bible and placed it on my mother's small table. "That's better," she said, standing back to examine it.

"Maya, this is your Grandmother McCann," my mother said, and I looked at the old woman standing above me.

"Well, of course she remembers me," Grandma McCann said, reaching down to tap her index finger on my bare shoulder. "I helped look after her the first months of her life."

"We've been here more than ten years, Mother."

It was true. I hadn't seen her since I was a baby and it was hard to be sure about that because I had no memory of it.

"Whether you like it or not, I'm here for you now, Marigold. For both of you." She sat down on the corner of the bed and put her hand on my mother's stomach.

"Who told you?" Mother said, shifting her mother's hand.

"There was an article in the *Toronto Star*, dear. About the people sleeping outside your home trying to help you. About your quest to save your unborn child. I booked my flight as soon as I heard."

"So it wasn't enough to visit because I had cancer?" My mother was sitting up then, not yelling exactly, but speaking louder than she had all week. My father's voice came in from just outside the door.

"Everything all right in there, Marigold?"

"It's fine, Steven."

"Marigold, I never knew you had a sort of . . . what do they call it, sixth sense?"

"I don't, Mother. It was just a misunderstanding."

I turned to the wall and rolled my eyes. *So she admits it*, I thought.

It was quiet then between us. Three generations creating a triangle on the ground — my mother, my grandmother (the woman my own mother would never become), and me (the young girl my little sister would never be able to grow into). I imagined her scratching at the inside of my mother's stomach, trying to get out. Or taking really deep breaths to try to be ready in time. I decided to be the biggest one of us all.

"It's a pleasure to meet you, Grandmother McCann," I said as I shook her warm hand. "I have heard virtually nothing about you."

"She's a cheeky one isn't she, Marigold?"

"Mother please . . . this is not the time."

"It is nice to make your acquaintance as well, Maya Devine."

She took her hand back, folded her arms, and wiped her fingers under her armpit.

The heat turned so intense when my grandmother was visiting that we had to move my mother's bed out of the teepee and into the open yard so she could catch some air. I slept beside her in the bed in my sleeping bag. Grandmother McCann protested for almost half an hour when she learned about mother sleeping outside. "For goodness' sake, just come in the house, Marigold. You're acting like a crazy woman," she said, but my mother insisted and eventually Grandmother McCann settled into my own bed for the night.

"Grandmother McCann doesn't seem to like me very much," I said to my mother when we had settled down for the night.

"It's not about you, really. She just has certain things she can't get past."

"Like the fact that we moved to Saskatoon?"

"We had to move, Maya. We needed a new start."

"But why?"

"It doesn't matter anymore. People do the best they can, Maya. Just remember that. People do the best they can . . ." her voice faded out and I rested my head into the crook of her neck.

While my mother wheezed in her slumber, I stared at the stars coating the sky. One particular star seemed to reach out to me. It wasn't round like the others. No, it had points and was brighter than the rest. When I smiled at it, it swelled up, until it seemed to be sitting in the yard, almost touching me. I opened my eyes wider with excitement as its glow rippled warmth into my whole body, guiding me into sleep.

"There is a young woman at the front door for you, Maya," Grandmother McCann announced the next morning. I was brushing my teeth in the bathroom sink, examining the braids my grandmother had weaved on either side of my head after my shower.

"Who is it?"

"I don't know, but she would like to speak to you."

I pounded down the stairs to see her standing at the front door, leaning onto one hip. Jackie. I hadn't seen her since the day my mother's teepee had been vandalized.

"What are you doing here?" I asked. "Where's your new best friend Diane?"

"Summer camp," Jackie said. She was holding something wrapped in tin foil. "My mother asked me to bring you this. It's a banana loaf." I took the silver brick of cake in my hand and looked at her.

"Why?"

"As some sort of peace offering, I guess. I saw your mom on TV." She was looking at the door frame above my head and fiddling with the jelly bracelets on her wrist. "And she, I mean I, realized that life was too short to be at odds with those whom we once called friends." I stood, baffled by her strange language. I raised the loaf to my nose and took a sniff; it smelled good enough.

"Thank you, Jackie," I said. She continued talking.

"And that you don't need me as your enemy because soon you won't even have a mother or a brother or sister."

That was enough. I swung my arm over me and hurled the

banana loaf at her head. It hit her above her left eyebrow and fell to the ground with a thud.

"I told you before — just go away," I screamed. "I don't want to talk to anyone right now."

She put her hand to her face and slapped me with the other one.

"You are a sucky loser! And your mother's a freak!"

I kicked her between the legs with a bare foot and she charged me, landing on top of me inside the door, swatting at my head.

"What on earth is going on here?" Grandma McCann stood behind us, grabbed Jackie, and attempted to separate us. "Let up there, I'm an old woman." Finally Jackie was on her feet, and Grandma McCann helped me up beside her.

"She deserved it!" Jackie said.

"No one deserves that kind of treatment, young lady. I suggest you run along home now and tell your mother what you have done. And have an extra long chat with Jesus before you go to sleep tonight. You better hope he's going to forgive you for this."

Jackie turned and walked away, her yellow summer top ripped at the collar, her rolled up jean shorts sagging around the bottoms. "What was that about, Maya?" Grandma McCann asked when Jackie was gone.

"She said mean things about Mother."

"Everyone is entitled to an opinion," she said leaning down over the front step, unwrapping the silver package, and bringing it to her nose. "Ah, look, banana loaf."

"I'm not hungry."

"More for me then. Come, let's take this out to your mother."

She put her hand on my shoulder and for some reason, I reached up to hold it. For some other reason, she looked down at me and smiled, making space so I could see her crooked teeth.

Like the many well-wishers who had lit candles on the street in front of our house, Grandmother McCann had come with a miracle cure for my mother's condition too. Prayer. And she forced her into it. Literally put her down on her knees beside her bed, opened the Bible, and asked her to read it out loud for us all to hear. It was just after lunch and the sun was heating up the outside of the teepee like a grey sidewalk.

"Mother, I don't want to pray. I feel too weak to be out of bed right now."

"Marigold, you are never too weak for Jesus. He lifts you up when you need him. Now come on, read, 'The Lord is my Shepherd, I shall not want —'"

"I'm serious, Eleanor. I don't need this."

Grandma McCann closed the book. "What did you call me?"

"Your name, Mother. I called you Eleanor, your name."

"Never call me that again. I will always be Mother to you." She opened the Bible again. "Maybe you would like to pick the passage. Whatever you are drawn to."

"Mother reads the *Bhagavad Gita* instead," I said then.

"The what?"

"Never mind. Never mind what I read. I read the Bible like you."

"Of course you do," Grandma McCann said. She changed the subject by deciding that my mother needed to take a bath. "The water will cleanse her soul and get rid of the guilt that has been building up."

"What guilt might you be referring to?" my mother said in response.

"That is between you and Jesus, Marigold."

We carried her into the bathroom and I started to unbutton her while Grandmother McCann ran the water into the tub. Tumbling water echoed through the hollow room.

"Maya, I can undress myself," she said. But her arms had trembled as she slipped them out from under her shirt and slid her cotton shorts down over her knees and onto the floor.

"I'll add some bubbles," Grandma McCann said, pouring out a dusty pink bottle that had been stashed under the sink (my father had given it to me for Christmas when I was five). Soon, white lavender clouds filled the bathtub and my mother slipped her fragile bones between them and into the water.

While she soaked, my grandmother and I talked.

"So Maya, who was that girl this morning?"

"We used to be friends."

"And you're not anymore?"

"She turned into a bitch."

"Language, Maya!"

"Sorry, she turned into a really not nice person. She keeps intruding with Mother."

"Have you tried everything to make up with her?"

"I don't want us to make up."

"Maya, one thing you will learn in life. It is very important to have friends. People you can confide in."

"But I have Mother." I looked down at the tub, shocked to see only bubbles. My mother's face had slipped underneath.

257

"Marigold!" my grandmother screamed, reaching underneath. My mother came up, gasping for air, slapping the water with her hands so it splashed up around us. We lifted her out of the tub, onto the pink bathmat, and wrapped her in a towel. Grandma McCann rubbed her shoulders while she shook. "There, there, Mari. You are going to be okay. You must have just fallen asleep is all." And then I heard it, from inside my grandmother's head: *My poor baby girl. You have made such a mess of your life.*

I shunned her for the rest of the day.

Death does funny things to people; for my grandmother, it seemed to make her busy. Over the next week (one of my mother's last), she scrubbed the toilet several times a day, almost like she had forgotten it was already done. She did laundry the second the clothes hit the hamper, got groceries, and made my father and me dinner every night. It was after one of those dinners that she bought her ticket home. I was listening from the living room as Grandmother McCann sat with my father at the kitchen table. He was eating roast beef, mashed potatoes, and baby carrots. She had made it all for him. He was still wearing his tie, having just gotten in from work, and it was hanging untied around his neck like a skinny scarf. I noticed that he wasn't wearing his wedding ring — that's when I left the room and heard them talking:

"Eleanor, I have to say this dinner is like nothing I have ever had," my father said.

"Not since your own mother made it for you, I'm sure. How is Frances?"

"Mom and Dad are fine. They retired out to PEI years ago. Well, you know that."

"I have a vague recollection, yes. And your younger sister . . . what was her name?"

"Leah. Leah's doing okay. She's with them. Trying to decide between universities right now."

"Marvellous. I'm sure she'll have a wonderful future."

Then the conversation turned to me. I heard it myself from the floor of the living room, tilting my head towards the kitchen to make sure I didn't miss any (they thought I was with Mother in the backyard).

"And Maya," Grandmother McCann said. "Do you expect that Maya will be able to attend university some day?"

"I don't see why not, Eleanor, if she chooses to. Why?"

"No reason, Steven. It's just that, who knows what kind of genes she's carrying around."

Silence from the kitchen. And then my father: "Eleanor, I would appreciate it if you would never make such a comment about my daughter again. You're lucky we're letting you near her at all." (He spoke in a harsh whisper and she answered back in the same, which may be one of the reasons I was able to block the conversation out in later years. Like if it happens in a whisper, there might be more of a chance that it didn't happen at all.)

"Steven, I can assure you I meant no disrespect. You know I'm sorry for all that, I wasn't in my right mind back then — the heartache I've carried. You certainly didn't have to leave and make it worse."

A pause. My father is thinking that he hates this woman.

"I can assure you, Maya will be fine. We've made sure of it."

"And have her looks posed any sort of problems in school?"

"Excuse me, her looks?"

"Yes, the coloured skin. That's most definitely not from anyone in our family."

"No, Eleanor, her skin colour has not posed any problems. Thank you for your concern." My father's voice was getting louder, and I thought I heard a piece of cutlery drop onto his plate. I took a step back from where I knelt on the carpeting.

"I know it's uncomfortable, but I had to address it. After all, I told you from the beginning it would not be smooth sailing, raising that child."

"She is my child, Eleanor!" This was said very loudly, and was followed by my father's plate crashing to the ground and bits of carrots and gravy flying around the room and into where I was in the living room. My father stormed out to the backyard and my grandmother stayed at the table. I walked in a few minutes later to find her dabbing the corner of her eyes with a Kleenex.

"What's wrong with Father?" I asked her.

"He's haunted by the past is all, Maya. As we all are. As you will be one day." She crossed her thin legs at the ankle and showed her bravery by tucking a grey strand of hair behind her ear. I started to pick up the pieces of carrots that had flown from my father's plate into the living room, placing them one by one into the palm of my hand.

The back door opened and in came my mother, limping in on the arm of her husband.

She walked to where Grandmother Eleanor sat on the couch, lifted and dropped her shoulders in one heavy breath and said: "Mother, I thank you for cutting through all your past misgivings about my family to come and be with me at the final stages of my illness. But I'm afraid I must ask you to leave now. I will no doubt see you in heaven one day."

My grandmother cried real tears then, which she tried to soak up with the side of her hand. Her light was a very murky grey and close to her body. She started to whisper like a mother to her little girl: "But Marigold, I love you. You're my daughter." And when she said it, I saw splotches of pink around her face, which told me that she really meant it. I suppose she was just doing the best she could.

I couldn't get past the two words that had come from my mother's mouth. Those two words that sounded so irreversible: final stages.

The next night, Grandmother McCann took the red-eye flight back to Toronto. She left my father meals for four nights, arranged in Tupperware in the freezer.

Chapter Twenty-Five

Elijah takes me on the St. Clair streetcar down a street with tall trees and to his house. It's a half-house, connected to another, ancient, brick, painted red with a wooden front porch in need of repair. We walk through the front door, and there behind the kitchen counter, is Mrs. Roughen: she's dressed in a purple sweatshirt, her hair hanging limply on her shoulders, no jewellery.

"Hi, Mrs. Roughen." I slip off my worn penny loafers and hold my backpack close in front of my chest for protection.

"Well, I never, in all my life . . . Maya! Let me look at you."

I just smile, trying to forget about how she used my mother in an attempt to become someone important, and trying to remember how sad she really was, and how she tried to listen when Mother needed someone to talk to.

She comes out from behind the counter. Her hands are covered in flour but she puts them on my shoulders anyway. "A little skinny and you need a trim." She holds my split ends up to the light. "But you look good, Maya. It's great to see you." Mrs. Roughen has tears in her eyes. She wraps her arms around me and hugs. "You remind me a lot of your mother," she says from over my shoulder.

"Okay, lay off, Mom. She's not some sort of specimen," Elijah says.

It is the first time I have come to Elijah's house.

It is the seventh time we have met up since that first day at the Retro Café nine months ago.

It is the first time I have seen him since summer ended and he and Mrs. Roughen returned from her boyfriend's cottage in Muskoka.

"We're just going upstairs for a while, Mom," Elijah says.

I follow Elijah up the narrow wooden staircase, stopping at a picture on the wall of a chubby man in a blue tuxedo, holding a white rabbit in the air.

"It's my mother's boyfriend, Conrad," Elijah says. "He's a magician." We reach the top of the stairs, which are covered in green carpeting that's been worn down. "This is his house, so I guess we're lucky to have it. We were living in a crappy basement before — it's all we could afford with my mom's job at the flower shop."

"I like this place," I say, stepping over an empty laundry basket in the middle of the hallway.

"Come into my room."

"Let me guess, you've got something to show me?"

"Not unless you ask nicely," he says, laughing.

Elijah's room is bare except a mattress on the floor with a blue comforter, a small wooden desk without a chair, and a *Joshua Tree* poster on the wall. He sits down on the bed.

"Remember that time we kissed in the shed?" he says.

"Yeah, you kissed me." I stand by the door, pinching my elbows with my fingertips.

"Want to try again? You can kiss me this time."

"I don't think so," I say.

"I'll sit here and you can do it. I won't move." My feet take a step towards him without my permission. "C'mon, do it as a thank-you . . . for the bees that day."

"That really was crazy, Elijah. Someone could have had a reaction or something."

"I like to live dangerously," he says, his mouth curling up just a bit in one corner.

"Still . . . it was nuts."

"Boo!" he springs forward, pushing his hands into the bed.

"Stop it."

"Sorry. Seriously, I won't bite. Not unless you want me to." He bounces his eyebrows up and down.

"Just a small one then." I lean my head forward again, closer to his face so I can smell cherry Chapstick on his lips. I place a small peck on his cheek, and pull away.

"That wasn't so hard was it?" he says smiling.

He puts his arm around my shoulder and strokes my hair, sending flutters down my neck and back. "You're very beautiful, Maya."

I don't know what to say, and luckily, I am saved by a knock at the door.

Thump, thump.

I hear a frenzied voice: *What's going on in there? This is my house. Who is he with? I'll just check. I'll just see. Maybe she'll work in the act?*

"What is that guy talking about?" I exclaim to Elijah.

"Who, me?" Elijah looks confused. "I just said you were beautiful."

"No . . . I meant . . ."

Thump, thump.

Elijah gets up and opens the door.

"Conrad," he says.

I stick out my neck to see a balding, short, slightly pudgy man standing in the hallway with his hands in the pockets of his too-tight acid wash jeans. He's got his lips pursed together in an innocent smile, turquoise streaks shooting from his neck.

"Just checking if everything's a-okay," he says.

"What do you want, Conrad?"

The man steps into Elijah's room.

"So this is the Maya I've heard so much about?" I nod. "You are a beauty, aren't you?" The man rubs his cheek with his palm, around and around.

"This is my mom's boyfriend, Maya. Conrad." Conrad reaches out his hand to me and I shake it. Sweaty. He smiles, though, in a friendly way.

"What act did you mean?" I ask.

"Pardon me?" he says.

"Oh, I meant . . . Elijah says you perform magic?"

"Well, only in my free time," he says, his face swelling red. "It's a hobby really, for the fun of it. Mostly parties and charity functions."

"Conrad works in a toilet paper factory."

265

"Is the manager of a toilet paper making facility, Eli," Conrad says to Elijah, tapping him on the shoulder gently. Elijah rolls his eyes. "Anyway, kids, I just wanted to say hi. Guess I'll go and watch the news with Trudie."

"Bye, Conrad," I say. He has a certain chaotic charm to him, like a father who would be really easy to talk to.

"Nice to meet you, Maya." He trips on the carpet on the way out the door, saying oops out loud and *fuck* in his mind.

"He's a little bit of a freak," Elijah says after he leaves. I laugh and look down at the floor, wondering what comes next.

"So can I kiss you now?" Elijah asks. "For real?"

I make a snort with my nose, like he's made a joke, but I can hear him getting frustrated inside with me.

———————

Later, we have dinner downstairs with Mrs. Roughen and Conrad. She has cooked a roast beef. "Special for your visit," she says to me when I sit down.

We sit. And everyone eyes me for a while. Up and down, around and around while I pick at my carrots with a fork and chew on my bottom lip. Then finally, Mrs. Roughen speaks again: "So Maya, how have you been *doing?*"

"I'm fine," I say and it feels untrue, because I can feel how utterly thrilled Mrs. Roughen is to finally have another boyfriend. Now that is *fine*. And Conrad, he seems to care about what she says, and his thoughts (which are fast-paced and frantic most of the time) seem to calm down when she speaks.

"Is it hard?" she continued. "You know, without your mother."

"God, Mom!" Elijah says. "Give it a rest!"

"Sorry, honey." She tries to change the subject. "And how is your father doing? I heard that he has a new girlfriend as well."

My throat tightens. Pounding in my ears.

"Maya, honey, you're going so red."

"Mom, just leave her alone. She doesn't keep in touch with her dad, okay?"

"Oh gosh, I'm sorry, Maya," Mrs. Roughen says. "I just thought that since he called Elijah . . ."

Pounding, pounding in my ears, from somewhere.

Conrad starts thinking loudly — *Magic rules. Number 1: Perform a trick only after you've perfected it.*

"Don't you think it's important that you keep a good relationship with your father though, Maya? He's all the close family you have left."

Number 2: Never let them see you sweat.

"I've got my Aunt Leah," I manage to squeak out without tearing up.

"You're making her upset," Elijah says. "Her dad left her alone — he's a jerk."

Number 3: Keep your secrets to yourself.

"It's just that I really don't feel like talking about it."

"And why should you?" Conrad says. "You've got other things to concentrate on now." He smiles at me and shows the rot forming along the sides of his bottom teeth. He looks at me with sympathy, almost like a father would. Only this is no family dinner. This family is unreal in every respect.

After dinner, Elijah brings me home.

"I'm sorry," he says again. "You know how my mom can be."

"It's okay." And I mean it.

He kisses me on the doorstep of Aunt Leah's apartment building before I go up. A long, deep kiss that tastes like smoke and leaves us both breathless.

On November 2nd, a Monday, Buffy decides to throw a Day of the Dead party in our apartment. Leah complains that it should be a Halloween party and that no one will show up, but Buffy insists.

"I'm one-quarter Mexican on my Dad's side," Buffy says. "I should be celebrating Day of the Dead and not Halloween."

"Buffy, hate to tell you this, but you're white as a ghost, and you have red hair," Leah says.

"Okay, maybe I'm only a quarter of a quarter Mexican, but still. This is a great way to honour Maya's mother and my aunt Ti-Ti." Buffy's Aunt Tippy had died three years ago in a car accident on the Bloor Street Bridge. They found her car stopped in the middle one morning, the door open, windshield intact and her body on the highway below. They figure she must have lost control, opened the door to escape, and been flung over the railing by another car. At least that's the story that Buffy tells.

"You can throw the party, Buff, but no one's going to come."

"Sure they will, Leah. Maya's boyfriend is coming." Leah looks at me. I sit cross-legged on the living room floor, weaving a thread from the carpet between my bare toes.

"So, he's your boyfriend now, is he?" Aunt Leah says.

"I don't know, maybe. Kind of."

"So it's serious?" Aunt Leah raises her voice when she says this, stretching the "serious" out for what seems like a minute. I shrug my shoulders.

"It's her own business, Leah." Buffy turns towards me. "You'll bring him to the party though, won't you?"

"I guess. If he's not busy."

"Good. So I'll get it all set up. All I need to know is what your mother really liked to do when she was alive."

Aunt Leah and I turn our heads towards one another, our eyebrows raised.

"She liked to read," I say finally. "The *Bhagavad Gita*, she tried to read that millions of times. I have her copy in my bedroom."

"Great. Anything else?" Buffy asks.

"She slept a lot." When Aunt Leah says this, I pinch my lips at her, hiding all of my front teeth underneath. "What? She did sleep a lot, Maya. I'm not lying."

"Fine, I'll use a pillow on the altar," Buffy says.

"She didn't use a pillow much," I say. "Not in the teepee anyway."

"Don't worry, Maya, I'll think of something perfect. It'll be great."

By Monday evening, our apartment has been transformed into something else. Something different. Aunt Leah ends up helping Buffy with the decorations, partly because Buffy can't see how things look and partly because she is too short to reach up over the door and to the upper parts of the wall.

I come home after school to see it for the first time.

The outside of the door is covered in paper skeletons that Buffy got on sale at Kmart, and when I turn the knob and push in, my eyes adjust to the light of white candles burning from little glass jars, some of them with an outline of Jesus on them, along the window-sill. I close the door and in front of my face I see it — a giant cross made of flowers strung up over the living room window that looks out to a brick wall. Buffy comes into the room and grabs my hand to know it's me.

"Marigolds!" Buffy says. "Can you believe how perfect? It's a cross made out of marigold flowers." I don't say anything; she can't see how my mouth is hanging open. "Get it, Maya? Marigolds. Your mother's name was Marigold."

"I get it, Buffy." I drop my backpack to the floor, walk to the cross, and tickle my fingers across the flower petals.

"They do this in Mexico, put marigolds up to honour the dead. Sometimes they make a path from the deceased person's grave to the house, so that the spirit can find her way home for the celebration."

Aunt Leah comes out of the bathroom, leaving a hushed toilet flush behind her. She has just returned from her new job at the CN Tower, where she travels up and down all day telling people that the tower was built in 1975 and is so many meters and so many feet tall. I know she's really there because I've seen her uniform — and they don't give one of those out to just anybody.

"What do you think, kiddo?" she asks me about the display.

"Let me show you the best part, Maya." Buffy takes my hand again and walks me to the corner between the kitchen and the dining room. There, on a small card table covered with a black plastic table cloth, is my mother's journal and, placed beside it, a framed picture of a much younger version of my mother sitting on a pillow with her copy of the *Bhagavad Gita*. There is also another picture of a woman with a broad forehead, looking up to the sky with her arms wrapped around her like she was cold. Beside that picture is a package of cigarettes and a bingo dabber. In front of them both are four small statues, disembodied skeletons, and one of a full-length skeleton dressed in a baggy robe, its teeth parted, its eyes hollow.

"Where did you get this stuff?" I say, referring mostly to my mother's journal. I reach out to grab it, but Aunt Leah holds my hand back.

"From your bag, Maya. Don't worry, no one's going to read it. It's only to remember her by," Aunt Leah says.

"And the picture of her?"

"I had it, Maya. I found it at Mom and Dad's house. In some of Steven's stuff. He must have taken it when they just started going out."

"She looks so young," I say. "And nice."

Mother is standing outside in a summer dress that shows her arms. Her hair is blown over her eyes a bit and she is looking away, like someone has just called her name.

"She must have been just a bit older than you there," Aunt Leah says. "I bought the frame myself."

"Why didn't you ever show me before?" I say, mesmerized by the image of my mother as a teenager, before she met my real father, well before I was born.

"I don't know, I guess I never thought of it."

"Isn't it beautiful, Maya?" Buffy says. "Almost makes me wish

I could see it with my eyes for once." She runs her palms over the dining room table until she holds her camera in her hands. She flops the strap around her neck, raises the camera, and snaps two times towards the altar. Then, she turns to me, strokes her fingers over my nose, and snaps two more times. "That's going to be a great picture."

People start arriving at around 7:00. Some are dressed in their Halloween costumes from a few days ago (fairies, princesses, pumpkins, dirty maids), but most are in their normal clothes, some with leis of marigolds around their necks. They are mostly Buffy's friends from York, from the photography program and some of her other classes.

Buffy leans over to me when the chatter of voices in the room is high enough to block out most of my own thoughts: "I told them they didn't have to dress up. Did they?"

"No, not really," I lied.

"A few of them though?"

"There are some costumes, but most people have marigold leis."

"Good. It's not authentic if they're wearing Halloween costumes."

Aunt Leah puts Michael Jackson's *Thriller* album on the stereo, and I nod my head to the music while people chat and drink red drinks with only a touch of rum. Buffy always seems to have a crowd of people around her, tall people with curly hair and long braids, and confident women who wave their hands in the air when they talk. I can barely see her from behind them, and if it weren't for her voice piping out, I wouldn't know if she was there at all.

Aunt Leah has invited only one friend. A skinny woman with purple eye shadow, teased bangs, and dark circles under her eyes. Her hair seems frazzled somehow, held back with a plastic headband, and she's wearing a red dress with the outline of her underwear showing.

By 9:00 the apartment is full, but Elijah is still not there. When I called him yesterday after school, he said, "I'll be there, little lady." When he said it, it made me think about how young I must appear to him. And I wondered if he just feels sorry for me.

I stand in the corner sipping Kool-Aid and tuning in to various voices around me. These people don't mean what they say. Their voices are too loud and friendly to be real. Their laughs are forced, as if they are trying to convince themselves of something. No one has mentioned my mother's photo in the corner, or the one of Buffy's aunt. Someone is smoking one of the cigarettes from the pack beside Aunt Tippy's photo.

Elijah arrives right after Aunt Leah sets out the food: Mexican taco dip with three layers, cups of coffee, chocolate shaped like tiny skulls and witches. "I'm here," he says when I open the door to see him standing there. He's wet, his hair dark and stuck to his forehead, his black T-shirt sticking to his ribs and showing the roundness of his shoulders. "I had to walk, and it started raining." I close the door, realizing that the trickle I had been hearing was rain on the window, and not in my mind.

"You're not late. We have food. Are you hungry?"

"I guess a little bit," Elijah says, making his way over to the dining room table and dipping four taco chips into the dip. "What's with the shrine?" He points to my mother's picture and shoves the crunchy mess into his mouth.

"This is a Day of the Dead party. It's supposed to invite my mother as the guest of honour."

"Creepy," he says. He pops two chocolate witches into his mouth. "Who's she?"

"That's my roommate Buffy's aunt. She was killed in a car crash."

"Can I have one of those?" He reaches towards the cigarettes.

"No, you can't smoke those." Elijah shrugs and settles himself against the wall.

"Do I smell someone new?" Buffy says, walking over to where Elijah and I stand. "You must be Elijah?" She reaches her hand out to touch his wet hair.

"Are you blind or something?" Elijah says.

"Elijah, stop it," I say.

"More importantly . . . I'm Buffy. I'm Maya's roommate. I'm a photographer and a student." Elijah nods in confusion.

"How do you see what you're taking a picture of?"

"She doesn't have to see, Elijah, she feels it."

"Freaky."

"I guess I'll let you two lovebirds be, then." I'm glad that Buffy can't see me blush. I'm embarrassed that Elijah can.

"And now, you have to meet my Aunt Leah," I say scanning the heads in the room. "Formally."

He had met her one time already. It was when he dropped me off after we had made out for the first time on a bench in some park we were walking by. I was worried that my lips looked red and chapped. Aunt Leah had said hi and he just nodded and snuck off while she was asking me whether I had forgotten my key or not.

"So that's Elijah from Saskatoon," she had said after. "Cute. Must be nice to have something from home." And I had agreed — sometimes I felt like he was all I had.

My eyes stop on Aunt Leah. I think about how no one would ever have guessed what she used to be doing for a living. How she got beat up. How she has become my guardian. I think about how confident she looks as she chats with that skinny guy, in her velvet dress, thumbing the gold beads she's hung around her neck.

"That's her over there," I say to Elijah.

"I know. I've met her before," he says, though he hadn't, not really. We walk over. Aunt Leah shakes his hand and soon they are talking intimately. I go to get Elijah a Coke, and when I return, Aunt Leah has her hand on Elijah's shoulder and is scanning his face with her eyes as they talk.

"Here," I say, handing Elijah the Coke. He nods his chin, his eyes squinted at Aunt Leah.

"Just think about it, Elijah," Aunt Leah says to him, then leaves to refill the chip bowl with Doritos.

"Think about what?" I ask him when she's gone. We are leaning up against the wall side by side, our bodies touching.

"She wants me to try and get you to call your dad. But I'm not supposed to tell you about it."

I am shocked. So shocked that I can see the candy-red blobs jumping off my own mid-section. "Why would she do that to me behind my back?" I ask myself out loud.

"I know," Elijah says. "As far as I'm concerned, your dad deserves what he got. He left you pretty much alone in the house for like, months. You don't owe him anything."

"I've been getting along just fine without him."

"Totally," he says with a grin.

Despite our combined resolve, I struggle with the growing

intensity of my anger, which is still rising within me, quickening my breathing, making my mouth grow dry.

Aunt Leah walks by on her way back to the kitchen. I grab her by the arm.

"Stay out of my business," I say to her. "I don't have to do anything I don't want to." She looks from me to Elijah and back to me. Whitney Houston's "Greatest Love of All" pours out from the stereo.

"Maya, he's my brother," she says, reaching for my arm. "I told him I would try. It's the least I can do. He feels bad about it all."

"I don't care anymore," I say. "He had his chance."

"But he *is* your father."

"He's not my father!" I scream. "Everyone knows my mom fucked some other guy. *He's* the actual keeper of my DNA. *He's* my father."

Unfortunately for me, the song ends just before this last part. Whitney has just told me that learning to love myself is the greatest love of all. The room turns silent. We are all stuck in one tight ship of awkwardness.

Elijah breaks it up. "Yeah, so Maya. I better get going," he says turning towards the door. *This shit is messed up*, I'm surprised to hear him think, though he is surrounded by a wonderfully warm mess of light the colour of green moss.

He opens the door and leaves. I don't say goodbye.

I feel dizzy. Like we are all suddenly on a huge merry-go-round and I'm the only one who wants to get off.

Other people start to leave, to slowly slip out of the room. The next words I hear are from inside Buffy's head: *She's just being honest*, she thinks. *It'll work out.*

Soon the lights are on. All the candles have gone out. Only me, Buffy, and Leah remain. Someone has stolen that package of cigarettes off the altar and the photo of my mother has fallen onto its side. Marigold petals are crushed on the floor.

"You sure know how to clear a room, kid," Aunt Leah says. She walks down the hallway towards her room.

Buffy asks if I want to have a bath.

"Not right now."

"The place must be a mess," she says, trying to change the subject. She holds up her camera from where it hangs between her neck and balances it on top of her thin arms. She clicks randomly around the room, and then at me.

"Maybe you should go to bed now, Buffy." And she does, leaving me alone in the living room, paper skulls torn up around me on the couch.

I wait for Buffy to sleep so I can listen to her thoughts. They aren't about me. She's worried about an upcoming exam and some photo she took that her teacher said is overexposed. But then I hear something that I may be making up within my own mind. It's Buffy's voice, but seems like it's coming from my mother. *Choose your actions carefully*, she says. *Guilt can cripple you.*

I lie down on the futon and close my eyes, but my confusion over all that has happened keeps me awake.

I say sorry to my mother out loud, softly. I say it over and over until I believe that it is how I feel.

I sleep long enough to have one short dream: I'm back at my house in Saskatoon, in the backyard. Only it's different than before. The sky is orange and the evergreens that used to line our fence have morphed into palm trees. I can hear ocean waves lapping up against the other side of our shed. There is no more teepee. And through the kitchen window I can see another family — mom, dad, girl, boy, matching blond hair on all of them, and blue eyes. I notice they are all made of wax, but are moving like normal people despite their stiff, animated faces. They eat spaghetti and laugh as the boy juggles bags of Doritos while smoking a cigarette. The mom is holding the dad's hand across the table. The girl's smile is wide enough to show her plastic teeth.

Chapter Twenty-Six

We are at Elijah's house; it's been two years since I first visited him there. I have my spine pressed out flat on the carpet of his bedroom. Shakespeare's *Twelfth Night* is grasped in my outstretched arms — I'm moving my lips over the words. He is sucking on a cigarette by the window, blowing smoke into the August air.

"So, I was thinking about how we could celebrate your sixteenth birthday," he says between puffs. I drop the book, intrigued.

"How?"

He flicks the cigarette out the window and lands with his knees on either side of my waist.

He leans down and puts his lips on mine. Tiny suns light up in front of my eyes. I kiss him then pull my head away to say thank you. He pushes his pelvis closer to me, pinning me down by the groin.

"Elijah, really, stop."

"What if we didn't?" he says.

We had never not stopped before. It was usually at about this point that I felt my mother in the room with us, pinching her lips and shaking her head from side to side as if to say, *he'll leave you.* As he covers my neck in needle-point kisses, I look for my mother. She isn't there, not that I can see, not that I can feel.

Elijah's head glows pumpkin orange above me.

"Maybe we could?" I say like a question as Elijah starts to take off my flowered summer shirt. Even though he has been my boyfriend for more than two years, there are things I haven't been ready to do. Things I haven't been ready for my mother to see. And now, my shorts are around my ankles and I can feel her *tsk*-ing inside my head.

"She's watching me!" I yelp. Elijah backs up a bit.

"Who's watching you?" He's got a pimple, red with a white point, at the corner of his mouth.

"My mother," I say, embarrassed.

"How many times do I have to tell you, Maya? Dead people can't see things. They have no eyes."

"It's just that I want to wait."

"Okay," he says, rolling off me, a lump in his jean shorts.

"I'm sorry."

"It's fine, Maya. It's up to you. I don't mind getting blue balls again."

"Is that really true?"

"Yes." He stares at the ceiling like he wants it to open up and suck him away. I can hear Mrs. Roughen humming from the kitchen downstairs. Cooking, fixing, fiddling. She's making me a birthday dinner and cake. She's even invited Aunt Leah and Buffy over.

"What if we went in the closet?" Elijah says. "I'm sure that if your mother's spirit was here, she wouldn't be able to fit in the closet with us. It's very small and dark in there." Somehow his logic makes sense.

"All right," I say. "But only for kissing."

"Sure, yeah, only that," he says. He has already opened the closet door and is clearing out a stack of records piled up on the floor. He throws the two feather pillows from his bed into the corner and I follow him in. He clicks the door shut from the inside, leaving us in the hot dark.

"Stuffy in here," I say. The cuffs of Elijah's hanging dress pants tickle my nose as I lie down on my back. His hands move across my front and I jump, with a sharp breath of closet air through my nose.

"Sorry, Maya, I didn't mean to scare you."

We start kissing again. Kissing in the dark. For the first time I feel like we are truly alone. Alone with no one watching.

I put my hand down the front of his jean shorts.

And that's when the accident starts to happen. I start to emerge from myself in the darkness of the closet. I am not me. It's some other girl giving in to the ache inside her that she has tried to keep down.

"Am I hurting you?" I ask him, my hand moving.

"Oh no," he says through a moan.

Like an invisible man, he moves himself on top of me in the dark. I push my shorts down. He stabs me between my legs.

Within five more minutes we have gone too far.

"What happened?" I ask when he is done.

"You know." (Do I?) "We did it. I'm sorry." He breathes quick like he just finished a race.

"Don't be sorry, Elijah," I say, but I can feel my face not smiling.

The doorbell rings from downstairs and echoes through the walls.

"Shit, your aunt and Buffy are here for dinner."

We shuffle around, finding underwear, pulling up shorts and me scooping up what's running down my legs.

"I need to go to the bathroom first."

"I'll go down and see them." Elijah pushes the door of the closet open.

Forgotten light attacks us and in the middle of it, my mother. I can't see her, but I can feel her there, sitting cross-legged on the bed, dressed in the hospital gown she died in. A lamp flickers on the night table. I start to cry.

"Elijah, she knows, she saw." He is brushing his hair into place.

"Maya, she doesn't know. I told you. Dead people, no eyes. And besides, we were in the closet." He pats me on the head and then turns and leaves the room. I hear Buffy talking from downstairs. Will she know too?

I stumble to the bathroom and look at myself in the mirror. Do I look different? Older? Is there a check mark on my forehead? Satisfied that I look pretty much the same, except for some red blotches on my cheeks, I run my fingers through my hair to pull out the tangles and go downstairs.

"Maya, happy birthday!" Aunt Leah says when she sees me.

"You already said that this morning," I say.

"I know, but I wanted to say it again."

"Happy birthday, Maya," Buffy says sweetly, but I can't look at her. Luckily she can't tell.

Soon, we all sit down at the dining room table: me, Elijah, Aunt Leah, Buffy, and Conrad. He has been in the basement all day practising his magic and his forehead is sweaty.

"I swear I could eat a horse," Conrad says, patting his thick hands on his large belly. "Bring it on, Trudie." He rubs his fingertips from his temple to his neck, creating pink lines on his skin. I can see his chest hair poking out from under his T-shirt and the white from his scalp from under the strands sticking up on his head.

"So, Mr. Finn," Buffy says.

"Call me Conrad," he answers.

"Conrad, then. What is it you do?"

"Magic, my dear. I perform magic tricks. Y'know, card tricks, smoke from nowhere, rabbits from hats, ladies in half . . . the classic stuff."

"And where do you do this, Conrad?" Buffy asks. "Where do you perform these, these magic tricks?"

"Festivals, birthday parties, wherever I'm needed. I also do a little busking in the Beaches, juggling and stuff."

I try to imagine Conrad sweating under the summer sun while he juggles balls on the boardwalk by Lake Ontario. Who would watch?

"He works at a toilet paper plant," Elijah says. Conrad fans his words away, trying to erase them.

"Only to make ends meet," he says. "And of course I'm a manager there. Magic, however, is my true vocation. Nothing like showing people something that doesn't exist. That's me, Conrad Finn, Master of Illusion!"

"I'll have to take your word for it, Conrad," Buffy says, smiling.

"In fact, I was hoping to get Maya involved in my act," Conrad says. "She's said no, but my latest assistant has a bad case of the shingles and I've got a festival in Cabbagetown coming up. Maybe you could talk to her?" he says with a grin, trying not to look in my direction.

"I'm right here," I say. "Why don't you just ask me?"

"Oh, okay then, Maya. Will you be my assistant in my magic show next week?"

"Next week?" Elijah says.

"Fine. I'll do it."

"Really?" Conrad's surprised and rubs his elbows in excitement. "Wow, this is going to be really great!"

"I'll be there!" Aunt Leah says. "Wouldn't miss it!"

"Guess you're really in a giving mood today, Maya," Elijah says.

I feel my face get hot. I look down at my fork.

Mrs. Roughen enters with the ham on a plate and places it in the centre of the table. She's got happy little sunbursts jumping around her head, and they are nice to watch. Conrad starts to cut strips of pink meat off and drop them directly into his mouth, licking his meaty fingers as he swallows. "I can't get it into me fast enough," he says.

Elijah stares at me mischievously from across the table. His face so young and smooth compared to Conrad's. His lips are pouty, with a subtle smile, his head cocked to one side at me. I look down at the table again, but smile at our secret.

"Maya, are you okay?" Mrs. Roughen asks after she has put the yams and green beans on the table and filled everyone's glass with apple juice. "Your face is flushed. Do you feel all right?"

"Maybe a bit hot," I say and she turns on the ceiling fan over the table. Then she places her warm hand on my forehead and pushes it in three different spots.

"You don't feel too hot, just red."

"Maybe she's just embarrassed by all the birthday attention," Aunt Leah says. "You know Maya, never wants any of the attention on herself."

"Before we start eating," Mrs. Roughen says, pushing Conrad's raised hand and fork down from his mouth. "I would just like to recognize someone who couldn't be with us today."

My heart dribbles into my toes.

"Marigold Devine was a wonderful woman. And I am honoured to have the opportunity to celebrate the sweet sixteenth birthday of her beautiful daughter, Maya. May Mari rest in peace."

Everyone raises their glasses of apple juice into the centre of the table, except me.

"I really think we should stop talking about my mother. I mean, we should get on with things, right?"

"Maya, Mrs. Roughen was just trying to be thoughtful," Aunt Leah says.

"It's no problem, Leah. I can stop making reference to her, if it suits Maya best," Mrs. Roughen says, fiddling with a large butterfly dangling from a gold chain around her neck.

"Suits me fine," Conrad says as he piles mashed yams into the middle of his plate.

Then, I decide to go for it. To tell everyone what I have been thinking since Elijah and I started dating.

"I have an announcement to make," I say, and Elijah's eyes grow wide. I hear snippets of *What could it be?* and *Is it something bad? Is she knocked-up?* from various minds around the table.

And from Elijah: *Don't tell them what I think you're going to tell them, Maya.* I tell him not to worry, but I'm not sure if he hears me.

"I think that I should move in here." No one says anything. "I mean, it's been almost three years since I left Saskatoon. I don't need my father anymore. In fact, I don't want to ever see him again."

"Don't say that, Maya," Aunt Leah says.

"I should be able to live my own life now."

"But Maya," Buffy says. "I thought you liked living with Leah and I?"

I do like living with Aunt Leah and Buffy, but can't shake from my mind the thought of being part of a real family and having a new mother in Mrs. Roughen.

"I don't want to impose on you guys anymore, you're busy. Aunt Leah, you can't keep paying to support me. And it would be nice to have my own bedroom."

"So, you would like Conrad and I to support you?" Mrs. Roughen says and I wonder if I have made a huge mistake. Have I ruined everything?

"My parents and her dad send cheques for her," Aunt Leah says. "That helps a lot."

Silence again. Elijah is smiling at me from the other side of the table.

"I say let the girl stay," Conrad says, using his tongue to lick something from the corner of his mouth. "She and Eli seem to be getting along. She makes the kid smile, so why not?"

Mrs. Roughen erupts. "If it's all right with Leah, I would be delighted!" She stands up and hugs me from behind. "It's like I finally have the daughter I always wanted."

After dinner, I blow out my sixteen candles while everyone watches. For presents, Mrs. Roughen gives me a silver chain with a heart pendant that she fastens around my neck. Elijah gives me a Wonder Woman comic. Not because I like comics but because he says I remind him of her.

Aunt Leah and Buffy give me a framed picture of the three of us with our arms around each other last Christmas Eve — Buffy had set the timer. Into the wooden frame are inscribed the words "The Three Musketeers," which stirs up the icing in my stomach, leaving me with a sick feeling.

Back at the apartment, Buffy tells me they will miss me but that they are glad to see me making some of my own choices.

"Why would you want to hang around some old blind chick anyway?" Buffy says.

"I did. I mean, I do. I will still see you, Buffy."

"I know. Thanks, kid." She puts her tiny arms around my neck and hugs me. When she pulls away, there is a tear dripping down from under her glasses.

Buffy goes to bed and leaves me and Aunt Leah alone. Aunt Leah starts the conversation we have been having for years: "Maya, I still don't think you should give up on your father."

"He's not my father."

"He raised you, Maya. That's something. He does want to be a part of your life still."

"He gave up on that a few years ago."

"He was just confused about what to do."

"I've got to go to sleep now, Aunt Leah."

And with that, our conversation ends. Again.

That night when the apartment is silent, I listen for Buffy's sleeping thoughts, and for the first time in a while, I hear nothing.

Two days later I gather my stuff in one box to take over to Elijah's. My clothes, my mother's books and journal, her stones, the aromatherapy bottles, my high school textbooks. I find my Corey Hart tape hidden inside a box of tampons. *Don't masquerade with the guy in shades, oh no*. I toss the tape in the trash bin almost filled to the top.

I open my mother's picnic basket to stuff in a few more things, and that's when I see something bumpy in the top lining. I swipe my hand across the rough cotton and discover that there is a little slit along the side and something has been stuffed up underneath. Almost three years and I've never noticed it there.

I soon see that it's a letter from my Grandmother McCann. To my mother. I take the small yellowing envelope in my hands and slide out the papers, four of them folded together into one. And I allow myself to read what my grandmother had written:

February 14, 1974

Dear Marigold:

I trust you had a safe journey and have settled in fine. I'm sorry that things have become strained between us and that you felt you had to leave your home.

I thought I could deal with what you have done, with the mistake you made with the coloured man. I thought now that you were married to Steven, things would feel right for me. But I know that what you have done may send you to hell and I can't get over that. I can't stop the guilt I have that my daughter has borne an illegitimate child. That fact will never seem right to me and I don't think that our Heavenly Father would fault me for that.

I'm sorry also for telling Steven that your affair was with that strange man in the broken-down van. I'm sorry for that, but again, I thought it would help make things right. He needed to know and if you didn't want him to know, well, then you should not have allowed yourself to do what you did. You should not have made yourself impure by giving in to the sins of the flesh. This I know for sure.

Mostly though, I would like to apologize for what I did to Maya. I can't say for sure what happened that day. I'm not certain why I left her there. You know how my memory is. But that park was full of people, other parents, kids, and she was never in any danger. I knew someone would look out for her. And it was only a matter of minutes until you came looking for us and found her asleep in her little stroller. No harm done.

She's a perfectly lovely child, but there are some things I just can't get past. You can't tell me that Steven is not reminded of what you did every time he looks at the child. I hoped that with time I wouldn't be reminded of your sin, but Maya is its embodiment.

The words you screamed before you left were so harsh. They were words that no mother should have to hear — you brought me to my knees later, and not just in prayer. Ever since losing your father, I have worn myself down and down, and now I feel like I am one raw nerve. It's hard to function. I just wanted the best for you. I am sorry that you and Steven have felt it necessary to move all the way to the Prairies.

I think that is all I need to say. I hope to hear from you soon. I will await an invitation when and if you ever feel ready. I will end by saying goodbye and good luck.

Your Mother.

I unload my belongings on the floor of Conrad Finn's guest bedroom with a thump. Grandmother McCann's letter has been torn into seventy-two small pieces and deposited in the trash bin on the corner of St. Clair and Winona. I left the bits behind as I boarded the streetcar that would take me to the subway and then out to Elijah's house on the Danforth.

"All settled in?" Elijah asks me. I am slumped against the side of the bed, my butt on the floor. "I have to say, it's pretty damn cool that you asked to stay here." He reaches over and puts his hand on my boob. I slap him away.

"Stop it, Elijah, seriously. It's not about that."

"Sorry. I just thought . . ."

"You thought wrong. I need a place to stay is all." We both stare out the window, not touching, not moving. "My own grandmother tried to get rid of me," I say then.

"What?"

"My mother's mother. She didn't like me so she left me in a park when I was a baby."

Elijah runs his fingers through his shaggy hair and shakes his head. "Maya, I tell ya. There is no end to your baggage."

"Why don't you break up with me then?" I say, terrified that he will. He stands up and walks towards the door.

"You'd like that, wouldn't you?"

"No, I wouldn't," I say after he disappears around the corner.

Chapter Twenty-Seven

In the end, we dragged my mother from the teepee. If she had had the energy, she would have left screaming. Instead, she hung limply in my father's arms, letting go of the weight of her body.

After August 1st, she had stopped eating, stopped using the bathroom much, and simply stared and slept a lot. The skin around her mouth shrivelled into her bones and her face glowed yellow, especially around sunset. I could feel my baby sister curling up tighter and tighter inside her body. And one morning, with the sun hidden behind a cloud morphing everything from happy to sad, both my father and I knew it was time to go.

"Maya, I'm taking your mother to the hospital today," he said to me while I slurped corn puffs from a white bowl.

"She doesn't want to go there," I said.

"The decision is final." My father left the room and returned with a pair of my mother's shoes dangling off each of his fingertips. "I'm going to get her now."

We both knew what this meant.

My mother had run out of time to be brave or depressed or angry. The girl she used to be — naïve, passionate, curious, dramatic — had slipped away long ago, maybe right when Amar had left her. Despite what people thought, she was not mystical or heroic (I see that especially now). She was just a sick lady who regretted her life.

My father tried to put my mother's shoes on, but she pushed him away. I stood near the doorway flap, wrapping my arms around the teepee so it wouldn't fly away in the morning wind.

"We're going to the hospital now, and that's that," he said to her.

She licked her lips, swallowed hard, put her hand on her stomach and closed her eyes.

"Don't worry, Mother, the doctors can help you." My father turned and gave me a look that spoke like a twelve-page apology letter. His own eyes were only half open.

"C'mon, Mari, you don't have to wear the shoes but please put your housecoat on." She did. But when he tried to lift her, her body hung heavy like her limbs had already started to harden. "Maya, help me lift her. Take a hold of her feet."

We carried her to my father's car, her body stretched out like a sagging starfish. We settled her into the back seat like an infant, and I heard this weird chanting from inside Mother's mind: *All things must end. All things must start again. All things must end. All things must start again.*

"Marigold, for fuck's sake, lift your feet onto the goddamn seat." My father had started cursing, something he did when he was under stress or put in a situation that seemed to have no logical or satisfying solution.

I tucked her legs into the car and sat down with them across my lap. Light legs, like two straws trying to suck up life from the air.

Father revved up the gas before we went, as if trying to wind us all up and spring us to the hospital in an instant. Mother popped her lips and moaned as we drove, rubbing her cheek against the leather of the seat. The window was down, and air was blowing in barbeque from outdoor picnics. Picnics full of happy families. My hair flew up in the breeze like it was trying to escape and my mother, who now had a short mane of auburn grass sticking up on her head, moved her head back and forth as the wind tickled her scalp. Every so often she mumbled, and because I couldn't see her mouth I couldn't tell if it came from outside or inside. *Don't worry, Maya*, she said. *You'll be better off without me.*

Within minutes of getting to the hospital, Father and I were standing at the wall of a green room while nurses hooked my mother up to feeding tubes, took her blood pressure, and drew blood. One nurse with a broad frown and a clipboard approached my father as he leaned against a gurney with a bedpan sticking in his back.

"Mr. Devine, can you please tell me exactly what drugs your wife has been taking and what sort of treatment she has been undergoing?"

"No drugs, no treatment," my father said with a straight face and stern voice that filled the room.

"I see," the nurse said, looking towards my mother on the bed.

"She didn't want it," I said. "She wanted to do this on her own." The nurse put her chubby hand on my bare shoulder.

"Mr. Devine, can I talk to you alone for a moment?" My father looked down at me, his eyes dead like they had surrendered.

"Maya, go get me a Coke," he told me then, holding out a palm full of quarters he had been jiggling in his pocket. I took the coins and left the room, turning once the door shut to see the nurse's solemn face through the rectangle glass in the door. She was thinking that my mother was a selfish idiot.

I fed quarters into the machine, pressed the square Coke button and waited as the can fell down with a clunk.

That's when I felt it, heat, wet, between my legs and dripping down my thigh.

I grabbed the can and squatted on the ground, putting my hand underneath myself to stop whatever it was from dripping out onto the floor. The thought of standing up terrified me so I stayed down, squatting, waiting for an idea of what to do.

"Can I help you with anything?" A voice from above me, a woman's voice. I looked up to see her standing there, a nurse dressed in pink hospital scrubs, a stethoscope around her neck, her blond hair pulled back in a ponytail. The hallway lights created a halo around her face.

"I'm okay," I said to her, lifting my body up but keeping my legs squeezed together.

"You're bleeding!" she said, pointing at my legs. I looked down to scc two red streaks weaving their way from my shorts to my ankles. I burst out into sobs.

"I don't know what's happening to me," I said. "My father is going to be angry." The Coke can dropped to the ground and rolled under a gurney. The nurse took a tissue from her pocket and wiped up the blood from my legs.

"It looks like you just have your period is all," she said, her voice calm like a smooth lake. "Is it your first time?" I nodded. She held my hand and told me to follow her into an empty room. I limped beside her, afraid that something would pop out. Inside the room she helped me change out of my shorts and underwear, which were bloody, and into a new pair of cotton underwear and hospital pants. She also gave me a pad and told me to go into the bathroom and fasten it into my underwear.

"What's your name?" she asked when I came out of the washroom.

"Maya."

"This is not a bad thing, Maya. It just means you have become a woman. This is a really momentous day for you!"

When the nurse stood up, I reached up to grab her hand.

"Thank you for helping me."

"My pleasure, Maya." Her smile was warm and normal. Her cheeks plumped up at just the right spots. "Now take some more of these pads and put them in your purse for later." I stuffed the two plastic packages into the tiny purse that hung by a string on my shoulder. Inside were two extra quarters and the piece of paper my mother had given me to read out loud when it was time.

"Can I ask you a question?"

"Of course, ask away." She was still smiling, but without showing her teeth, her lips curling up towards her ears.

"Do you know of any way to keep a baby alive outside a woman's body when it's not done growing?"

The nurse looked at me seriously and bit her bottom lip. "Well, it all depends on how far along the baby is. The doctors can do a lot to help premature babies these days."

"Three months," I said.

"Three months is too early," she said. "A baby wouldn't be able to survive on its own that early." She had told me what I already knew.

"Thanks anyway," I said. "Can I stay here for a while?" I did, but when someone else needed the room, the nurse came in and led me back out into the hallway.

When I returned to my mother's room, my father was sitting by the bed holding her hand. She was dressed in a hospital gown and sleeping, a tube growing out of her arm and attached to a metal pole like string hanging down from a tree. There was a plant behind my father on the windowsill, dark forest pot, green leaves and yellow flowers. They were marigolds.

"What took you so long? I was looking for you all over the hospital." I put my hand on my purse. I couldn't look him in the eyes so instead I looked out the window when I spoke.

"Sorry."

"Come over here and hold your mother's hand."

When I traded places with my father, he got up and paced from one end of the room to the other.

"I met a nice nurse," I said. But when he didn't respond, I looked down at my mother's sleeping face.

For the next four days we went back and forth between our house and the hospital. Sometime during the second day, people started gathering in the lobby of the hospital — ladies with flabby hips, old men reading the paper, a news lady with a cameraman. They were waiting for word about my mother. They wanted to know what would happen to the woman they saw on TV: would they save her and her unborn child? Would she save herself? Would she offer some sort of prediction about when the end of the world was due? Lottery numbers for tonight's draw perhaps? Would she magically rise up off the bed as she died?

Eventually, the hospital staff pushed these people into the parking lot.

"She's stable but medicated," my father told them on our way in one morning. "We would appreciate our privacy." And me, walking beside him with a pad stuck to my underwear (I had found some old Kotex of my mother's under the sink in the bathroom), would smile at their faces shooting out pity glares, feeling my face go red with embarrassment.

On the fourth day, my father decided to go back to work.

"Just for the afternoon, Maya," he said. "I have a new actress coming in that I need to interview. I've been trying to set this up for a while. She could be the next big thing." I was sitting on a blue chair that leaned back in the corner of the room. "I'll be back before three. Call me if there are any problems." He handed me a piece of paper with his work phone number on it, tucked his dress shirt into his pants, and walked towards the door. My mother's nurse stopped him before he got there.

"Where are you going, Mr. Devine?"

"I need to go to the office for a few hours, that's all."

"And the girl?"

"She's staying her with her mother."

"That's not really allowed," my mother's nurse said.

"It's only for a couple hours," he said and pushed past the nurse and out of the room.

"Looks like you've been abandoned," she said when he was gone and I wondered if it was true.

One hour later, after the doctor looked over the chart hanging at the end of my mother's bed, he told me to call my father and tell him to come back. He said it in a way that pretended like I didn't know why, and his colours were all gritty and black when he spoke.

"Maya, it really is best that your father be here. You're too young to look after your mother all by yourself. Call him and tell him to come back now."

When the doctor left, I picked up the phone beside the bed and dialed the numbers from the paper my father gave me. A woman's voice answered, giggling before she spoke. "Steven Devine's office," she said, like she was announcing a surprise.

"Can I speak to my father, please?" I said to her in the deepest voice I could make.

"Oh, yeah, of course. Just a moment, please." There was shuffling around, no more giggles, and then my father's voice.

"Maya, what's wrong?"

"The doctor says you need to come back now."

"I'm on my way."

I hung up the phone. I knew something was coming. The bones around my mother's eyes seemed to have grown harder. Her eyelids were shut, her lips were dry and bitten. I leaned my lips down near her ear: "Mother, I became a woman," I said. Her lips opened a bit and she spoke like dust was caught in her throat.

"Be careful how you use that," she said and smiled a little bit, like a skeleton looking for candy on Halloween. Then she touched my hand, stroked it, and a tiny tear dropped from her eye.

When my father arrived, he had sweat on his temples, in his hair, and in the armpits of his white dress shirt.

"Let me sit there," he said to me.

I scowled at him with my eyes, as if to say "this is my spot," but when I heard him thinking that this was his last chance, I moved from the chair beside my mother's bed, to the window. I looked out at the sun heating up the afternoon. There were people in the parking lot of the hospital. They were standing in a circle, praying, and a cameraman was filming them.

"Steven," my mother said then. "I'm sorry."

"You just rest now, Mari."

"I didn't deserve you."

Outside, the people were swaying with their arms up in the air and hugging each other. One woman seemed like she was crying and another woman was rubbing her back. They had all sorts of beautiful colours melting into the air above them: turquoise, grape, sparkling mauve — the colours of goodness and caring.

"I wasn't a very good husband," my father said then, inhaling the words with his nose after they came out. "I tried, but I just . . . you sleep for a while now."

"You were as good as you could be," she told him. From the corner of my eye I saw him stand up over her. "Live for you now," she said in a whisper. "Like you should have in the first place." My father leaned down, kissed her on her nose, and walked out of the room. This left only my mother and me.

I will never forget the peaceful sort of stillness that descended into the room when the end came. It was like a thick fog that no longer let me see out. For a moment, I remember thinking that something that feels like *that* must be all right. But of course, I couldn't tell anyone — they would never believe me.

And that is the complete story of how my mother died.

This may be exactly how things happened, or maybe not quite. I promise everything is how I remember it, but perspective is a strange beast — totally shaping what we think we know. Either way, I had to write it all in here. To remember my mother for what she was, what she tried to be, and what everyone else hoped she could be. To say goodbye to her. To move on.

And now, after so much writing, and so little eating, drinking, or sleeping, I will put my pen down and rest. It's done. And it hardly hurts anymore.

Chapter Twenty-Eight

I wait in Conrad's musty-smelling Buick on the side of the road — just behind the street in Cabbagetown where we will be performing. I'm pretty sure that Mrs. Roughen has put too much makeup on my face. The blue eye shadow, black mascara, and ruby lips must be what are making me feel so pathetic. Pathetic and repulsive — and only because this whole thing is so unlike myself. Who would believe that I, Maya Devine, at sixteen and only having had sex that one time, could be some sort of a magic vixen. There is nothing magic or vixen-like about me.

I can't believe I've agreed to do this. And as the minutes tick on since Conrad left, I feel increasingly more upset about going onstage. Aunt Leah will be here, I tell myself. And Buffy. And maybe Elijah if he's got around to it — although after the fight we had last time I saw him, I sincerely doubt it.

He said I was spending too much time practising the trick with Conrad down in the basement. He accused me of "blowing him off" now that we live in the same house. Complained that we see each other less than we used to. I ignored him. Said I didn't have time to think about it until after the festival. And if you ask me, it's him blowing me off now that we've done it. Even Mrs. Roughen says he can be difficult sometimes. Whatever. I don't need him, really.

My practice sessions with Conrad always went the same: I got into the box, he did up the buckles, he sawed, he separated, I saw the red-heeled feet that weren't mine, he said "ta-da," spun me around, and then put me back together. Then we did it again.

"I think it's so great that you're helping me out," he told me. "And I can assure you, once you get in front of the crowd, it will all be worth it."

He smiled a sort of lopsided smile when he said it — like my father sometimes did — and for a second, made me think that grey hair can actually look quite distinguished on an older man.

I look into the rearview mirror, wiping off a black line of mascara that has smeared onto my eyelid. I see a red halo around my head. A protective red barrier of fear and ego. I smooth my hands over it, hoping it will just go away and that no one else will see it — see into me.

"It's a go!" Conrad screams out suddenly, appearing on the other side of the windshield glass in his black cape and tall hat. "First act went great, and your bit is up next!"

He helps me out of the car and I nearly trip on the long aqua gown with the slit that he has made me wear. It's a cloudy end of summer day. Muggy. And it feels like it might start raining at any moment.

Conrad takes my hand and leads me through a small alley, under a black curtain, up a short flight of stairs, and onto the stage.

There are people out there — lots of them. But I don't look at anyone directly. At this point, I still prefer to watch the mingling of light above their heads and to listen to their mildly annoying inner voices. *Get this show moving! Gosh, I hope the second half is not as bad as the first. Who does this guy think he is? Why are we even having a break? What's coming on next? I wonder if they are any hot dogs left down the street?*

It's a street festival, so there is a lot of competition for people's attention, and I can tell they might not be around long. To appease them once onstage, I throw my hands up in the hair and put on a huge fake smile like I'm important.

"And this," Conrad announces into his microphone. "Is the marvelous Maya!" There is a small round of applause and a familiar voice that seems to be thinking nice thoughts about me — I choose to ignore it.

My stomach buzzes with butterflies as I limp on red heels to Conrad's black body box where I am supposed to lie down. He helps me in. He buckles up the box as planned. The audience gasps — I can tell they are getting more interested.

"And now, I will perform the impossible. I will cut this girl, my own daughter, in half, in front of your very eyes."

His daughter? I think.

Conrad lifts his blade into the air and starts sawing into the box.

Since I know how this next part will go, I allow myself to turn my head and look into the eyes of those watching me. Many of them are sitting on little fold-up chairs like the ones parents use for card games in their basements. The chairs — about twenty of them — have been arranged into neat rows and are filled with men, women, and young children in shorts and baseball hats.

I quickly spot Aunt Leah. She's in the third row with Buffy on the chair to her left. It's a comfort to see them. But then I see who they've brought with them.

He's there to their right. He's smiling tentatively. And beside him, is her. Her long, raven-black hair, her red lips are like I remember. They're holding hands.

It's then that I feel the warmth flowing up over my shins, soaking into my satin dress. It's then that I know that magic is not always foolproof. Not if someone does not lie still enough.

"Father?" I say before everything turns black.

————

When I wake up, there are two people around me on the Emergency room stretcher: Mrs. Roughen and my mother. My mother's face is white and translucent, while Mrs. Roughen's is harsh and real. My mother smiles from a few inches higher, but Mrs. Roughen has a crinkled forehead and her lips are inside her mouth.

"Maya, how do you feel?" She asks me. My mother says nothing.

"Where am I?"

"You're in the hospital, dear. There was an accident at the magic show. The doctor says the blade only grazed your leg, but the shock of it combined with the heat in the box must have caused you to lose consciousness."

"My mother's here," I say. Mrs. Roughen raises her eyebrows and pats me on the hand.

"Yes, Maya, I'm sure your mother is always with you. There's nothing to be afraid of."

"And my father, I saw my father, when I was trapped in the box."

"We'll talk about that later, Maya. Now, you just need to rest."

When I wake up again, Aunt Leah stands over me.

"I'm sorry," she says. "I shouldn't have invited him."

I choose instead to look down at the floor tile, aqua like my dress, cracked and stained.

"It's just that he really wanted to see you — it's been so long, Maya."

I scowl at her, but not really because of what she's saying, mostly because of what she's thinking: *I should have never listened to Elijah.*

"Let him have his new family," I say with a straight sort of seriousness.

"But he still wants to see you." Aunt Leah's brown hair is messed up like she's been pulling at it. "He's waiting downstairs."

"Don't you get it? He left me alone for months, Leah. A little kid, alone!"

She doesn't say anything, just looks down at me with shocked, sad eyes. I turn towards the wall — which is how I stay until Mrs. Roughen and Conrad arrive to take me home.

————————

They set me up on the couch. I have a bandage wrapped around my calf, with padding on my shin. I still feel light-headed. Conrad sits his large bottom on the corner of the couch, rubbing his chin.

"I don't know whether the blade caught the incorrect grove, or if it slipped or what. You know that it was never meant to cut you, they aim to the sides, not down."

"It's not your fault. I was wiggling around too much. I freaked out."

"But we were so well practised." He looks away towards the window, brushing the hair from his forehead and rocking his pear-shaped body.

Mrs. Roughen makes me hot dogs and green Kool-Aid for dinner. She puts the plate and cup on the coffee table in front of me even though I tell her I'm fine to eat at the kitchen table.

"I'm feeling a lot better now actually," I say.

"You take all the time you need," Mrs. Roughen says. "You will need your energy for tomorrow."

"What's tomorrow?"

"We're taking you to visit with your father, Maya." I sit up on the couch.

"I already told Aunt Leah I don't want to see him."

"Aunt Leah explained to me all that happened after your mother died, and while I know what he's done is horrendous, Maya, you need to see him, for closure's sake."

"I have enough closure, thank you."

"I'm sorry, but you have no say in the matter. Tomorrow morning we are taking you to your father's hotel room. It's what your mother would have wanted."

"You have no idea what she would have wanted!" I scream at her.

I stand up, throw my comforter to the floor, and limp up to my bedroom.

Elijah is in his room, sitting on his bed leafing through a music magazine with MC Hammer on the cover. He looks over when he hears me.

"You okay?"

"I'm fine," I say. "You?"

"Doing just great," he says and looks back at the magazine, thumbing through its pages.

Screw him.

I go into my makeshift room — with my pyjamas spread out on the guest comforter, my bags still in the corner.

I take my mother's copy of the *Bhagavad Gita* off the bookshelf and open it to any page, like we used to do to try and pretend we were different than we were. "The sovereign soul of him who lives self-governed and at peace is centered in itself, taking alike pleasure and pain; heat, cold; glory and shame."

And then, I know what I'm going to do.

I pack my things back up during the night while everyone sleeps. I put crystals, clothes, bottles, letters, journal back into paper bags and the picnic basket.

In the morning I make it official. "I'm going back to live with Aunt Leah and Buffy because I do not want to see my father."

Mrs. Roughen stares at me. She's got old eye shadow crusting in the corners of her eyelids.

"Well, Maya. I had no idea that this was the kind of person you were. Shirking responsibility, giving up when the going gets tough."

"I guess I'm just the kind of person who knows what she wants."

Like mother, like daughter, I hear her think, and she leaves me on the front step. Conrad comes out and sits beside me. He says nothing but puts his hand on my knee. Luckily, I'm wearing jeans.

"Maya, don't listen to her, she's just upset that it didn't work out." His hand starts moving back and forth across my knee cap. "Don't worry. I have met the true Maya. You are sweet and kind and always willing to help out."

My eyes sweat with tears at his words. I turn my head towards him. "Thank you for saying that, Conrad, it really means a lot to—"

His lips land on mine — dry and prickly. He sticks me with his tongue.

"Stop!" I scream at him, pushing him off at the shoulders.

He winks at me and does a little salute. I go out to the sidewalk to wait for Aunt Leah. Soon, Elijah joins me.

"You're taking this all a bit far, aren't you? You just moved in, for fuck's sake."

"Nice language," I say.

"Listen, I'm sorry. I shouldn't have told Leah to invite him. I wasn't being what you would call a big person. I guess I wanted to hurt you the way you are hurting me."

"Whatever."

"But Maya, I really do, you know . . . love you." His dark hair is flat on his forehead. He's got something white in the corner of his mouth. Despite how macho I find him, he reminds me of a little boy. A little boy drowning in a black lake, begging me to help him.

"Sorry" is all I say as I gather my stuff and bring it down to the curb. I look back at him like he is a collection of molecules that have separated, leaving only empty space. I already miss where he used to be.

Aunt Leah arrives in a cab like she said she would after I called in the morning. I told her then that I refused to see him because he's not my real father anyway, and that he should have told me the truth about who I was. I told her that I wanted to come home.

She smiles when I open the car door and calmly helps me load my baggage in the trunk. She puts her arm around me in the back seat when we drive.

Chapter Twenty-Nine

My last two years of high school pass like a frantic dream. I interest myself in nothing but textbooks, English homework, 7 a.m. wake-up alarms, and pencils with the eraser ends rubbed down to nothing. I take classes all through the summers. I work harder than I've ever worked at anything to finish all my OACs, and soon, it's 1991 and I'm seventeen and about to graduate early.

"So Maya, do you think you'll go to university?" Buffy asks one night after dinner. Our apartment has filled with smoke from the fish sticks I fried up in a pan. Although Buffy can't see how smoky the air looks, I'm sure she can smell the smoke better than anyone. I wave my hands in front of my face before answering her.

"Don't know."

"You really should think about it."

Buffy has finished her degree but is having a difficult time getting work as a photographer. "I'll just have to let my portfolio speak for itself" is what she has been saying, and luckily she has a father who will support her until the world can accept a blind girl taking pictures. Ever since Buffy finished university last year, she has been mind-talking less and less at night. It's as if with school done her mind is finally quieting down.

I miss the things I used to hear throughout the apartment. Three weeks before her final exam, I heard her going on for almost an hour about how we need to be courageous almost more than anything. And that even though life seems to suck you down to the bottom sometimes, you should simply observe what is happening and go on. *Go on, feel depressed. Just don't resist it*, she had said. *What you resist goes on and on.*

So when Buffy asks me about university, I'm anxious to hear what she thinks.

"I think I might take some time off first," I say to Buffy.

"Interesting idea," she says, removing her glasses and rubbing her fingertips over her eyes and then through her red hair. "But it's hard to go back afterwards."

"I'll do what I need to do." My voice emerges like a slow-moving snake, thick, close to the earth, in no big hurry.

"I just want you to be happy, Maya," Buffy says.

"Thank you."

"Do you ever think about Elijah?"

I'm surprised when her question stings. "No, he's got some new girl."

"Sorry that whole thing didn't work out. I know you really liked him."

This is one of the first conversations Buffy and I have had alone for a while. Mainly because I haven't felt much like talking to anyone and Aunt Leah is usually around to pick up my slack. Tonight she's working late at the Tower and I agreed to cook.

"You seem like you've been so down," Buffy says, but I don't respond. Instead, I chomp fish sticks off the end of my fork and exhale all the air from my lungs. "I just wish I could make you see that life is meant to be lived."

"I'm still living," I say, getting up from the table and going to the kitchen to put my dish in the sink. I comb my fingers through my hair and look back at the table. Buffy looks so small sitting there; her feet barely touch the ground. I am amazed by what wisdom can come in small packages.

They tell me after my last day of high school.

"Maya, Buffy and I want to give you your graduation gift." Aunt Leah pushes me down onto the living room chair. She's still in her polyester work vest that barely buttons down over her breasts.

"But I just got back from school. Can't I even take my shoes off first?"

"This is too big," Aunt Leah says. Buffy smiles at us from the other corner of the room, where she leans against the wall. "We found your father."

"What do you mean? I already know, he's got a new family, he wants me to go visit him, but I told you —"

"No, your real father."

"What?"

"Amar Ghosh. Your real father. We found him."

"But how . . . when . . . how did you even know his name?"

"I read your mother's journal. Don't be mad, Maya. This could be really good." Aunt Leah stands over me with her hands hugging her chest, as if protecting herself from my reaction. "Buffy was the one who had the idea. She thought it would be good for you to meet him. So we made phone calls, put pieces together. We looked through records of changes of address by men with the last name Ghosh who used to live in Toronto but moved to India around 1972. We called them all, and we found him."

"You talked to my real father?" The bite of this news feels like a full set of teeth digging into my throat.

"Leah talked to your grandfather in India," Buffy says. "He knows where your father is and if you go there, he can take you to him." My throat lets barely any air through when I try to speak.

"But I can't go to India. I have no money."

That's when Aunt Leah pulls out the ticket from her back pocket. In a thin white folder with the words "Air India" written on the front. "That's what our gift is. We bought you a plane ticket." She hands me the folder and I take it; there are bills of money sticking up from the top.

"And we saved up so that you would have spending money." A block has formed at the bottom of my throat, maybe a lump of fish, or a lump of coal.

"Thank you. But I can't go to India," I say again. "If I wanted to go, I would have gone by now."

"Don't you see, Maya?" Buffy says, feeling her way along the back of the couch and over to me. "This is the perfect thing to do now. You said you wanted to take time off. Why not use the time to figure out these things about your past?"

"I'm not sure I want to see my father, though." My blood starts to bubble from my feet up over my calves and into my stomach.

"I know you don't want to see Steven," Aunt Leah says. "And I understand that . . . what he did, well, I see now that it was awful. I've told him you don't want him in your life. But I thought this would be different."

"Why is it different?" I say. "He abandoned me too, didn't he?"

"But he didn't even know you existed! You should hear how excited your grandfather was when I told him."

"I'm not sure I can accept this," I say. I put the ticket back on the table without opening it. After sitting with them quietly for a few minutes, I stand up and take a step towards the door.

"Maya, stop!" Buffy says to the wall. "Don't leave like this." I turn towards them, pick up the ticket again, take out the bills, and put them in my pocket.

"I'm sorry, I just need to think," I say. I shut the door behind me and stand alone in the hallway. Someone's cooking curry and onions, which makes my eyes water as I look down at the money in my hands.

I decide then to go get drunk.

I pay some scruffy guy five bucks to buy me a mickey of vodka from the LCBO. I take the subway to Nathan Phillips Square — where the homeless people hang out. Because it's June, the air has warmed up and the rains have almost stopped. I push my back up against a window of a building. All the lights are out on the inside and a man wearing a grey toque is slumped beside me over a grate. The sun has just gone down and the voices of the homeless people are growing louder and more frantic.

I take my first sip of vodka. It burns a path into my body and immediately gets picked up by my blood stream. My feet buzz with warmth and I laugh to myself, waking up the sleeping guy.

"Keep it down," he says. "I'm trying to get a little shut-eye." His words are slurred, and I see then that his eyes are red and his face a mess of grey stubble.

"Sorry," I whisper, hugging the bottle closer to my chest.

"Do I know you?" the man asks then, rubbing his greasy hands over the front of his sweatshirt and adjusting the garbage bag at his feet.

"I don't think so." I look in the other direction.

"I think we've met before." I take another look at him — he's mistaken. I have never seen him before in my life.

"Maybe I'm your daughter," I say. The vodka soaks into all my cells, lighting me up.

"That's it," he says. "You're my daughter. Nice to see you again, daughter." He holds out his hand, cuticles chewed up to his knuckles, black stuff shoved under the nails. I shake it.

"Nice to meet you, too, Dad," I say.

"You sure have turned into a beautiful girl," the man says. "So exotic looking, with the black hair and all. And your eyes like glowing sunflowers."

"Thanks, Dad. I guess I take after you." We laugh together, me and the homeless man who doesn't even seem to have a name. I raise my bottle to him. "It's my first time getting drunk."

"Congratulations!" he shouts, and we laugh again, our backs bouncing against the office windows behind us.

"Got to start some time." I take another swing and feel my eyebrows start to droop down towards my eyes.

"What's your name?"

"Maya."

"I've been meaning to ask you, Maya. How's your mother?"

"My mother?" I'm stunned by the question and choke a bit on the vodka going down. "My mother is just fine. Beautiful, happy, successful, like you always remembered her."

"Ah, yes, I remember her." The homeless man pulls his toque back over his eyes and slumps his body to the side, resting his head on his garbage bag. I take off my green sweater and drape it over his shoulders. Then I stand up, throw my half-empty bottle into the garbage can and start walking. So far, I have been homeless for two hours.

I start walking up Yonge Street. Flashing lights that make my head spin, loud voices that crash their way into my thoughts, men who look like ladies. I look to the left and think I see an older Corey Hart wearing a black leather jacket and slumped against the wall in an alley. Something contracts in my head behind my eyes. The man turns his head to show me he's not Corey Hart at all, just some middle-aged man with spiked hair and a hopeless frown. He starts to walk towards me, shouting, "Young lady, young lady!" I pick up my pace away from him — past sex stores, Chinese restaurants, meat shops with naked chickens slapping against windows. Then, I stop. I stop right where I am supposed to.

The sign above the store says "Yonge Street Tattoo," and a

smaller sign reads, "We make your dreams a reality." White lights flash from all corners of the window, making me wonder if it's there at all. Is it just a mirage? I open the heavy door and go inside, my fingers numb to everything I touch.

"I want a tattoo," I tell the man sitting behind a small desk smoking a cigarette. He's got fifteen earrings in each ear and even more in his nose, lip, and the little piece of skin between his eyebrows. A tattooed lion raises a claw at me from the top of his shaved head; colourful vines peek out from under his sleeves.

"How much 'ya got?" he asks. I pull the bills out of my pocket and lay them on the desk so he can count them. "Twenty, forty, hundred, two hundred bucks. That'll do." He points to the diagrams of eagles, crosses, and skulls taped to the wall behind his head. "What do you want?"

"What do you recommend?"

"Depends. If you're religious, you could get Jesus on the cross. If you like animals, why not get a snake wrapped around your arm or curled up on the small of your back. Barbed wire is always attractive as well." He takes a deep drag of his cigarette and puts it out into an ashtray filled with butts.

"I want to get someone's name. On my chest, here."

"So, on your tit you mean?"

"No, here. Over my heart." I lay my hand on the left side.

"Get on the table then." I lie down on the cold silver table, which seems to be spinning in place.

"Does it matter that I'm a little drunk?"

"Nah, as long as you can stay still. Now, whose name do you want? A boyfriend's?"

"No, I want the name 'Mari' — M-A-R-I — as pretty as you can make it."

"Take off your shirt then." I remove my blouse and pull my bra strap down off my shoulder. My nipples protrude through white cotton, but I'm not embarrassed. I'm feeling too much to feel anything. He uses a cotton swab to disinfect my skin and pulls out an electric needle from his drawer. "Black ink okay? It's all you can afford."

"Aren't you going to draw an outline or anything?"

"I prefer to go freehand. Now, just relax and it won't hurt too much." The man leans over me on the table, red light sticking to his body, breathing the smell of nicotine smoke in my face. I close my eyes as the needle pricks me in and out. My ears feel like they are vibrating up and down, my whole body is swimming in invisible waves.

I think about my father with the straight pin and ink . . . pushing it in and out by his own hand.

"It hurts," I tell him, even though my skin feels mostly numb.

"Just hold still."

When he has finished the M and A, my guts start to churn. I put my hand on my stomach, roll to the side and throw up orange chunks onto the man's lap.

"Ah, Christ, why'd you have to do that?" he says, reaching for some paper towel. "I'm only halfway finished."

"I just need to get a drink of water and splash my face."

"Feel free." He points to the sink at the back of the room. I slide off the table and walk until my mouth hangs open over the running tap. Rusty water slides down my throat. I look up at myself in the mirror. I'm in my bra, my eyes are puffy slits, my hair has matted around my face, and my lips are dry and cracked.

This is not me.

On the left side of my chest, two black letters have formed in the middle of red blotches. "M" and "A." MA. Two black letters that weren't there when I woke up this morning, or when I went to my final English class, when Mr. Henry wished us "all the best for the future and a million bright tomorrows," or when Alicia Silver wrote "Wish I had gotten to know you better" in my yearbook. No, these letters, this drunk girl in the mirror, this is not me. I splash my face with water but I don't go away.

"You ready, girl?" the tattoo man asks me, and at that moment I know that I am. Something is different. I walk back to the table.

"I changed my mind. I want the last two letters to be Y and A, not R and I."

"So you want me to finish it with 'YA'?"

"Yeah, finish it with 'YA.'"

"All right, lie back on the table."

Buffy and Aunt Leah are still awake when I put my key in the lock of the apartment door. It's 2 a.m. They are sitting in the living room, across from each other.

"Maya, you're back!" Aunt Leah says when I push open the door. "Look, I'm sorry, kid. I should have been way more sensitive to you." I sit on the floor between them.

"Maya, have you been drinking?" Buffy says first. "You smell like booze."

"Yes," I say. "Yes, I have been drinking."

"Oh gosh," Aunt Leah says, her voice high and screechy. "I drove you to drink! This is all my fault."

"I got my name tattooed on my chest." I pull my collar down and peel the gauze to show her.

"So you did . . ." Aunt Leah says, for lack of anything else.

"Did it hurt?" Buffy asks.

"Not really, I was drunk." We sit in a triangle, in silence. Until I decide to speak again. "I want to go to India." Aunt Leah picks up the ticket and hands it to me.

"We want you to go to India," she says.

"But I spent my spending money on this tattoo. I'm sorry."

"We'll get you some more, Maya," Buffy says. "I'll get you some more."

That night Buffy's voice comes back. Her nighttime voice. Her voice that speaks from her mind and doesn't even need an open mouth. Before I hear the words, the blackness above my head starts to fill with colour: pinks and oranges, greens and blues, zipping around when I close my eyes and when I open them too. And in the middle, Buffy's thoughts. *Find your family*, she says.

Chapter Thirty

My plane slips between the clouds, down, down, and onto the parched beige land below. Ten minutes on the tarmac makes my eyeballs ache and the inside of my mouth start to sweat. Entire families scurry up and down the aisles, pushing small children towards the washroom, while old women in leather sandals limp behind. Beside me, a fat man in a business suit snores with his hands crossed on his large belly, the smell of onion blowing out from between his parted lips. The air inside the cabin grows thicker with every minute, curry lingers in the air from the in-flight meal, the plastic door from the bathroom continues to slam shut after use.

If they don't let us out soon, I may not make it out at all.

As I slip my arm out of my zip-up sweatshirt (useful when the air conditioning was on), I hear the door slide back at the front of the plane. The people in the aisles move towards the front, all of them murmuring frantically in words I can't understand. A man puts his fingers flat on another man's back and pushes him forward. This causes the man to throw his body backwards, pushing the first man to the ground. They argue. The man's wife helps him up, then adjusts her pink sari and looks towards the floor. Where have I sent myself? I rub my fingertips over the flat stones in my hand and imagine my mother holding my other hand.

I'm sure she would have quoted something from the *Gita* at this point, and tried to change the subject when I asked her what it meant.

"It just means you can get through anything," she may have said if I persisted.

Buffy would say the same thing.

I make it into the Delhi airport, which is like a large warehouse packed solid with people: people yelling, people hurrying, people throwing bags and boxes around with no apparent system. I clutch the backpack Aunt Leah helped me pick out at Mountain Equipment Co-op. She made me sew a Canadian flag to the outside as well, as if that hasn't been done before.

"People respect Canadians," she had told me. "You'll get treated better."

But this isn't a sightseeing trip. I do not care how others perceive me, or if I get a discounted fare somewhere. I am here for one reason only: to meet my real father.

I find the place where I think my bag will be spit out and wait. Men stare at me — tall men, short men, dirty men, men with beards, men with long noses and greasy hands. Their eyes run up and down my body as I try to create a protective ball of light around myself. Their thoughts are loud, in other languages, and not coated with respect of any kind.

Where have I sent myself?

I think back to Buffy's directions spoken at a coffee shop in Pearson Airport. "Get to New Delhi. Take a taxi to the address on the paper. Find your grandfather, Raj Ghosh — he will take you to where your father is."

I look at the paper in my hand. A scrap pulled from the junk mail pile, there's an advertisement for steam cleaning on the other side. An address: 1 3 Brahma Road.

After picking up my duffle bag, I push myself through the crowd and out towards the curb outside the airport. A huge crowd waits for taxis on the street. Families, children, the staring men. Babies cry out in frustration and are hushed by stern voices. I feel hands slide down my shoulder, on my back, and across my breasts as I walk. Though their thoughts are in a different language, I still get a clear sense of what they're thinking — dirty things about my breasts and ass. I slap them away like I'm swatting hungry mosquitoes.

A young English couple takes pity on me and invites me to share their airport limo into town. I only smile while they chat about their impending yoga retreat and the peace it will bring them. I don't talk, because I don't think I am able to at this point. They stop and drop me on a busy street in New Delhi. I thank them with a nod and emerge into the outside air.

The smell hits me first. Armpits, burning garbage, incense floating in dust, one combined smell like nothing that has entered my nose before. It chokes itself down and churns up my stomach.

I cover my face with my hand, trying to avoid the smoky air and breathe in only that which is on my palm. I feel small and insignificant against the many faded signs above me for travel companies and sandwich meat, the dark boys pedalling rickshaws, the thin men without helmets on motorcycles and the tiny half-yellow, half-green vehicles with no doors screeching by in furious streaks.

Men touch their hands to the heads of emaciated cows as they pass, kiss their fingers and then touch their own heads. Women squat in the dirt while their urine creates yellow rivers that intersect on the ground. I look down at my sandals to see my toes already covered with grime from the street.

There's a monkey looking at me now. Sitting on a curb, silky grey, with a black face and sagging nipples. I smile at the way he crosses his feet in front of him like a person.

"Hello, little monkey." These are the first real words I have managed to say since I got off the plane. They stumble out of the dryness in my throat. I take a step towards the beast, which is watching me. He holds out his palm for a handout. I reach out to grab his hand when I hear a voice: "Don't touch him!" It's a cab driver, and he's laughing. "Those monkeys will bite you if you don't watch it."

"Oh, sorry," I say to him. His face is hidden inside the dark cab.

"Don't be sorry to me. You want a ride?"

"Oh, yes. Yes, please." I walk towards the car, which is dirty, old, no bumper, paint chipping. I sit in the back seat; the cracks in the upholstery cut at my legs. I can see the man's face in the rearview window: shiny skin, dark eyebrows, white teeth under brown lips. A strong face. A calm face. "I'm going to this address." I hand the piece of paper over the seat and the man looks at it and nods. Then he revs the engine and we jerk to a start. He plows the car through the crowd of people, who scatter like ants on a sidewalk.

"Where you from?" the driver asks without turning his head. His words are thick and even.

"Canada," I say.

"Ahh, Canada. I have a brother living in Brampton. Canada took him and I haven't seen him for over ten years."

"Too bad," I say, my hand still covering my nose. The man nods again and turns up the radio. A hectic melody of sitars and flutes scratches out of the speaker. That's all I hear until we arrive.

"It's that one there," he says pointing and I hand him the money. "Welcome to the mystical land of India." He laughs again and is still laughing when I shut the door and step out onto the street.

The house spreads out flat in front of me, beige and red brick, all one level and surrounded by a black gate that I push in and walk through. A path leads me to the front door. For once, I can't even hear my own thoughts. I have been dropped into India, into a moment with no end and no beginning. I knock on the door. It seems to open instantly.

What I notice first is the colour around his body, clean and bright, yellows and purples. Then, it's his white beard, long and fluffed up into a smile over his neck. He's mostly bald on top and his wrinkled forehead creates arrows that point down to his wide nose. He wears rectangular-framed glasses and his eyes are dark like deep Ontario lakes. His body, draped in white, hunches over a cane that he clutches with bony knuckles.

"Maya, I presume." His voice wraps round me like a blanket

and before I can say anything I start to cry, then sob, then moan, my hands rubbing my eyes, tears streaming down my cheeks. He stands in front of me on the doorstep, watching me and smiling, and reaches one hand up and places it on my shoulder. "Come in, my dear." He points into the house and I follow him.

Though the rooms inside are quite large, there is not much furniture. Only a table when it might be needed and a chair for resting by a window. I think, what a large house for one old man, if indeed he does live alone. There is no kitchen like I'm used to, just an open area in the centre of the house with no roof and a small area for cooking. By the time he has seated me in a wooden armchair in a sitting room, I have not seen evidence of anyone else in the house.

"It is only the stress of your long journey that is making this reaction in you." He coughs into his hand. "Once you sleep through the night you will feel much better." He hands me a green cup filled with water, which I take and sip down.

"It was a long time flying." He nods and smiles, lowering himself to a pillow on the floor. "Do you live here all alone?"

"Yes, all alone, just me."

"No wife?"

"No, no, my wife and I were divorced many, many years ago."

"Oh, yeah. I forgot. And she died from a brain aneurism."

"That's right." The old man coughs again and rubs his thin fingers on his chest. "I guess she had nothing to live for once we were not together." I look at him. He smiles, with teeth this time, and laughs so that the phlegm dances around in his lungs, creating crackles. "I'm kidding with you," he says, and I'm glad for it.

"And is it true that you are my grandfather?"

"You tell me that. Are you my granddaughter?"

"I think so."

"Then yes, let's make it so. You are my long-lost granddaughter, Maya Devine, and I am your grandfather, Raj." He pulls an orange from a hidden pocket and digs his thumb into its skin, pulling pieces and piling them beside him on the floor. When the orange is naked he holds it up to offer it to me.

"No, thank you. I am not hungry yet."

"Suit yourself." He breaks the orange apart and feeds the slices between his lips, swallowing them down with only a few chomps of his wrinkled jaw.

"I do need to use the washroom though." My grandfather's face lights up.

"Ahh, you will be happy to know that when I retired from the university ten years ago, I did myself the privilege of installing a flush toilet in my home. This will make it much more comfortable for you." He grasps my arm and walks me down a hall. I stop to look into a small room decorated with shiny paintings of Hindu gods; they sit on lotus flowers and have trunks for noses and many arms reaching out to the side. Around the room are unlit candles and plants clinging to the walls.

"C'mon, Maya," Grandfather says from further down the hall. "I'm an old man. I don't have all day." He chuckles in his throat and I follow him to the toilet.

After the sun sets we eat dinner together at a wooden table. I help him cook rice and curried chickpeas on the stove, even though he told me to relax and recuperate from the jet lag.

"So you lived in Canada then?" I ask him when we are eating.

"Yes, in Toronto, for twenty years. I taught courses in Indian History and Sanskrit at the University of Toronto."

"Have you ever read the *Bhagavad Gita*?" His eyes widen at my question and his cheeks puff up in glee.

"My dear, I do not mean to be immodest, but I studied the *Gita* when I went to university in Calcutta and taught on the subject later on at Jawaharlal Nehru University. I think you will find me to be one of Delhi's premier experts on the study of the *Bhagavad Gita* and the *Mahabharata* in general. In my younger days, before being invited to Canada, I even wrote a book on the subject. A collection of essays on the *Gita*."

"What about?"

"Oh, fascinating topics like whether Mahatma Gandhi was correct in his view that the *Gita* was an allegorical demonstration of the conflict between knowledge and ignorance." I stick out my lip and nod my head like I know what he's talking about. "And the idea that an individual life is part of a grander reality which lies beyond human perception."

"So you've read it then."

"Many times."

"My mother used to read it too."

He puts his fork down on his empty plate, weaves his fingers like he is praying and settles his dark eyes on mine. "From what your aunt told me on the phone, your mother had much strength, strength to live with secrets, to deal with a serious illness."

"I guess. Will you tell me about my father?" I correct myself: "About the man that I have heard is my father?"

"Ah, yes — my son, Amar, a sweet gift from his mother. He has a soul unattached to the mundane expectations of earthly life."

"What is he like?"

"The day my son was born, everything else stopped in my world. It was only about him from then on. I was extremely lucky, you know, because even though his mother had graduated from the University of Toronto with an English degree, she still agreed to stay home and raise my son. Even though this was a big deal, for a woman in the thirties to graduate with a degree, she gave it all up to be a mother to Amar, and I am thankful for that."

"Did you have other children?" I say. Grandfather Raj takes off his glasses and places them on the table.

"No other children, no. We tried though. Ivy wanted them desperately, but Amar was our one and only miracle. She never really accepted that, however. I think she resented me for it, to her death even."

"Her name was Ivy?"

"Yes, Ivy — like the veins that covered the brick of the building where we met. I was much older than she — ten years — so that started out as a bit of an issue."

"And what was my real father like when he was growing up?" My long-lost grandfather stands and walks to a cabinet, where he removes a stack of photos, square and in colour. He lays them out in front of me on the table.

"This is Amar." He points to a crying baby with dark hair, naked in a bathtub. "And this was his mother." A woman, long hair and wide eyes, leans over the baby, scrubbing him with a white wash-cloth. She smiles in a tired sort of way. I pick up the photo and look closer, amazed.

"She has my eyes! I mean, I have her eyes."

"I noticed as soon as you walked in. In fact, I said to myself, 'What do you know, there are my dead wife's eyes.'"

The rest of the photos show the same dark-haired boy at various points in his childhood and young adulthood: climbing a tree in the backyard, holding a cricket stick in a park, graduating from high school with one of those flat hats, alone on a bed in an empty apartment with red, blurry eyes.

"Amar put off university a little too long. He got mixed up with the wrong group of friends, I'm afraid, and although the strong light of his soul never dimmed, he never stayed in one place or one job for any length of time."

"I'm putting off university right now too."

"But you'll attend, I hope?"

"We'll see what life throws at me."

"Anyway, enough of this talk about your father. I thought you came here to find out for yourself?" I nod several times fast. "Tomorrow we will board a bus and travel to Varanasi. There, I will introduce you to your father."

In the morning we walk to the bus station. I know Grandfather Raj must be tired because I heard him pacing all night long. Up and down the halls, in and out of the toilet, back and forth from room to room of the empty house. When we woke up and I asked him about it, he said he was restless. "At eighty-three years old, I have not much left to sleep for" were his exact words.

Colour coats the street, red and orange powder sprinkled on the ground we walk over.

"Festival last night," Grandfather Raj tells me. "This powder was used as a way to honour the gods." I walk slow to keep in line with his hunched-over limp. Simple sandals are strapped onto his dry feet, his skin already coated in red dust. Dirt settles on our legs as we walk, and the smell seems a bit better in this part of town. That, or I have gotten used to it already.

He pays for my ticket and allows me to sit by the window in the rickety old bus. When the men turn around in their seats to stare at me, he shoos them away with his hand, saying words in Hindi that I imagine mean something like, "That's my granddaughter you're ogling."

The journey to Varanasi is slow. The packed bus hits every bump in the road. Speakers at the front blare out high-pitched voices that remind me of chipmunks crying out in pain. I have only my backpack with me, with an extra sweatshirt and underwear, my money, and some things that belonged to my mother.

"When we get there, don't tell him you are his daughter right away, it will be too much of a shock," Grandfather Raj says. "I will tell him you are a student at the university interested in learning more about his lifestyle."

"And what kind of lifestyle is that?"

"We're almost there now."

Soon, the bus stops and the men push their way out onto the

streets of Varanasi. Narrow passageways are filled with bicycles and rickshaws coming from all directions. Young women balance fruit on their head while boys push carts piled with vegetables. Stray dogs brush their prickly fur against my bare legs as they pass. I follow Grandfather Raj to a river, where men and women bathe and dry their clothes on dusty steps.

"The river Ganges," he tells me and then points ahead of us and to the left. "And on that small hill, we will find your father."

We hike another ten minutes to the top. A man with a yellow turban and long black hair greets us outside what looks like a make-shift house made out of old logs, tree branches and mud. He's not wearing a shirt and his eyes are only half open.

"Bom Shiva!" The man says to Grandfather Raj as he reaches down and sucks smoke from a clay pipe. Grandfather Raj scrunches his lips and looks to the sky in annoyance.

"Amar Ghosh?" he says, and the man lifts his thin arm to direct us behind him.

"Stay close to me," Grandfather Raj instructs as we maneuver our way around fire pits and rusty cooking pots.

There are two old logs holding up a piece of striped fabric like a lean-to, and underneath this teepee sits a man. Grandfather Raj moves towards him in recognition. The man lifts his grey beard, looks up at Grandfather Raj, and says with composure, "Ah, Father, what an old man you have become."

Also shirtless, he is wearing ochre-coloured pants and his thin knees press into his chest. He supports himself by bare feet in the dirt and I can see the shape of every muscle holding his skeleton together. Beads hang around his neck, his hair white and frizzy on top of his head. He has two white lines drawn on his forehead, leading between his eyes. Oily skin and lighter eyes than the other men I have seen. Eyes that shine in the midday sun.

"Have you been keeping well?" Grandfather Raj has tears growing under his thick eyelashes. He strokes his hand through his beard.

"Ah yes, well as Shiva," Amar answers back with a complacent smile. Then he looks at me and reaches out his hand towards my arm. "Where did you get those bracelets, girl?"

My hand falls on my wrist. I am wearing the bangles. The ones my mother left in the picnic basket in her closet. The ones that Amar gave to her after they spent the night together. The bangles with the butterfly charms hanging down, flying around my arm when I walk.

"They were my mother's," I say to him, and a crease forms between his eyebrows.

"Amar, this is Maya," Grandfather Raj says. "She is a student from the university, studying the life of the Indian sadhus."

Amar's eyes grow wide with surprise. He nods and points to a log beside him, where we both lean down to sit.

"Tell me, Maya, where are you from?"

"Canada," I say. "Saskatoon, Saskatchewan."

"And you are interested in the life of the holy sadhus?" I nod. "Well, let me tell you then. The sadhus know that by letting go of all material possessions and attachments you become truly free." Grandfather Raj studies my face, eager for some sort of reaction. I give him none.

"We accept change as a constant in life, and through this transcend the ultimate fear, the fear of death." Amar points around him to the other men milling about, some with matted hair, turbans, and long orange robes wrapped around their bodies. "Here, we live for the god Shiva, the destroyer and rejuvenator." His eyes are locked onto mine like he is trying to get into my head, and at that moment, I am able to get into his. I hear his inside words like I'm listening to a Walkman. *Tell me why you are really here*, he says.

"Are you one of them?" I ask.

"Yes."

Grandfather Raj rocks back and forth on the log, taking deep breathes, coughing, wringing his hands in his lap.

"How did you become like this?"

"A calling," Amar says with a solemn certainty. "And then, many years following my guru."

"Can I stay with you?" I surprise myself with this question.

"As I tell all visitors, you are welcome." He spreads his arms wide, running his long fingers through the warm air.

"All right then." I take off my backpack and put it on the ground. Grandfather Raj turns his head towards me.

"Are you sure, Maya? Are you sure you want to stay?" I nod. "Very well then, but an empty hill is no place for an old man. You can take the bus back to my home when you are ready." He stands up, places his warm hand on the top of my head, and shuffles away through the dirt.

Amar and I speak very little throughout the afternoon. Above us, the clouds churn in the sky, threatening rain. The wind increases and blows Amar's grey hair about his head. His eyes are closed most of the time, like he is dancing inside himself. I sit on my feet and watch boats floating in muddy water in the distance. Smoke rises from arched domes along the riverbed. When the sun begins to

335

descend into the ground, and the air grows cool enough that I need a jacket, I open my mouth to speak.

"I'm hungry. Is there something I can eat?"

He opens his eyes halfway and smiles with only his lips.

"Of course," he says and stands up. He enters into the makeshift shelter and returns with a small plastic plate of vegetables and rice, which he places on my lap.

"Thank you," I say and he nods, raising a black cup to his lips. The carrots and peas are cold, but the rice seems to have retained some heat since it was cooked. I eat the food with my hands and when I'm done, place the plate on the ground beside me. "What happens in the evening here?" I ask him.

He sighs before he speaks. "We pray to Shiva and then we sleep on the ground." From the other side of the shelter, someone plays a guitar. Strummed notes dance from strings and through the air. "Celebrations are beginning," he says. "Let's go round."

He stands up and I follow him around to the other side of the shelter, leaving my bag on the ground where we had been sitting all afternoon. The man we met with the pipe is there, as well as some other men wearing orange robes, wooden beads, and yellow turbans. Though they are sitting around with each other, they all smile to themselves.

"Bom Shiva!" the man with the pipe says each time he takes a puff. Then, he passes the pipe along.

The guitar has three strings, and the man playing wears a headband to hold back his thick black hair. He sings quietly, something in Hindi. I sit near him to listen closer.

"Hare Om Nama Shiva," he says over and over, each time with a new melody.

"What does that mean?" I ask him, but he keeps singing without looking at me.

"He is praising Shiva," Amar says, sitting on a log beside me. "Praising Shiva in his own way."

The pipe has reached Amar and he wraps his lips around and inhales the smoke, which slips out from his lips and wraps around us both. "Hash?" he says, offering the pipe to me. I take it in my hands and suck a small amount of smoke from the head of the pipe, coughing it back out into the air. "Maybe not yet," he says, laughing, and takes the pipe and hands it to another man with thick eyebrows and the same white lines on his face as Amar. Then, he sits with his legs crossed on the ground, each of his palms laid flat on his knees. He drags his breath in and out, his eyes closed.

I'm getting frustrated by his lack of communication, so in my head I start to talk to him: *I'm your daughter, you dope! Don't you even remember? Don't you remember my mother and what you did? Don't you remember getting her pregnant and leaving her?*

Amar's state remains the same, and so I continue to yell at him from inside my head: *She's dead! She died, you idiot. Don't you even care?*

And then I hear it, my first response to what I always thought would be my little secret. Amar's lips stay closed, but I hear his voice from inside his mind: *I did not know she had passed. Please forgive me.*

I look at him. He's unchanged, and as an experiment, I respond to him with my mind: *Why did you leave?*

Amar opens his eyes and looks at me like he can see through my clothes and my skin and all my insides. He smiles warmly. He looks at me like he has found a piece of himself. Light jumps from the fire now burning and reflects in a tear in the corner of his eye. He opens his mouth to speak. "I had to follow the path that was laid out for me. That's why I had to leave."

I stare at him. My chin drops open, my eyes wide so that smoke burns them.

"You answered my thoughts," I say.

"Were they really only thoughts? How do we know for sure?"

"I was saying something in my head and you responded." Amar sticks out his bottom lip and shrugs his shoulders. "You know who I am?" I say and he nods. "You remember my mother?" He nods again.

"I am sorry you lost your mother."

"Thank you" is all I can think to say. "It was a long time ago now though, six years."

"You know, time can only help a little in getting us free from the past that is always present."

"Did you love her?"

He shifts himself on the ground. "Perhaps I could have."

"What does that mean?"

"I was foolish. I let myself be lead by something other than my head." He coughs. "My life is meant for Shiva, for celibacy, for the removal of all material things. That is how I will transcend. I know that now."

"But you were cruel to leave her like you did. You changed the course of her life."

"I wasn't myself because of the death of my own mother. Death can cause a person to fall asleep. I met your mother, with her flowing auburn hair and her green eyes and skin so soft all over her body. Your mother's innocence and nervousness almost made me forget about it all. But I couldn't in the end."

"So you left?"

"I didn't know there was a baby after. I didn't know there was you. Maybe it was better that way?"

"You hurt her very much."

"I'm sorry. To you and your mother."

People are shouting out from around the fire. The man that Grandfather Raj and I first met with the pipe shakes and convulses on the ground, rocks and sticks creating lines of blood on his bare back.

"Is he all right?" I ask Amar. "Is he having a seizure?" Amar points to his own hairy stomach.

"God is inside him," he says and from inside his head he tells me again: *I'm sorry for not being there for you.*

When the man, whose name turns out to be Gaur, is revived, he lies flat on the ground while others tend to him by putting a cloth on his head and feeding rice through his lips.

"He'll be all right," Amar assures me and we lie down together on the ground beside the fire.

"But why do any of us have to be here at all?" I shiver under my fleece sweatshirt.

"You are surrounded in the purple light of your crown chakra right now," Amar says. "And that is a good place to be." He stands up and soon I feel a blanket fall over me. I am the warmest I have ever been, even when the rain starts, when water pounds on my back through cloth and into my skin. Even when I wake up freezing cold at 4 a.m., I have never felt more at home.

Two years pass before I think about returning to Grandfather Raj in New Delhi.

Chapter Thirty-One

"Maya, gorgeous, your breakfast is ready." My mother's voice wakes me from sleep, her warm hand on my arm. "Your father is already eating, so come out whenever you feel ready."

I open my eyes into cool inside air. Logs stacked beside each other make the walls around me, a small wrought iron bed in the corner of an empty room. A blanket hangs over the doorway instead of a door, a yellow and red wool blanket, still swinging from when my mother left the room. My toes slip out from under the dense comforter and onto the wood floor. I push the door blanket aside and see them sitting at a table — smiling, touching hands, memorizing one another's eyes. My mother, Marigold McCann, and the man she has told me is my father, Amar Ghosh.

Amar eats chickpea curry and rice, his dark hair pulled back into a silky ponytail. He's laughing at a joke I must have missed. His face dances without wrinkles, his shoulders bounce themselves into stillness.

"Well, hello, sleepyhead," he says when he sees me, his long fingers clasped in front of him like he's praying for something. "We thought you would never wake up. It's almost noon." Their smiles join into one long grin. I rub my knuckles over my eyes and pinch the skin on my arm, squeezing only numbness.

"Look at that!" my mother yells, tripping on her fuzzy house-coat as she runs towards the window. "A hummingbird! Finally there is a hummingbird using the feeder I put out." Her face glows and rainbow light dances around her pink skin. Locks of hair drop down her back like an auburn waterfall. She looks to be about twenty, same age as me.

Amar stands up and hugs my mom from behind, pulling her to him and stroking her hair. "I told you, Marigold, I told you they would come if we were patient."

The sun coats the skin on their faces, making them both the colour of gold.

And then the light goes away. Something is wrong. I see it first in his hair. Amar's ponytail starts to drip black spots onto the floor, and then the rest of his body grows smaller, spreading onto the ground, fading.

He's melting.

My mother turns from the hummingbird when she no longer feels him touching her. When she sees him, now a puddle on the kitchen floor, she screams. My blood stops from the pitch of it. She falls to the floor and hugs her knees into her chest.

"Why, why, why," she chants like a monk and I join her.

"Why, why, why," we moan together.

And then a voice from my bedroom, familiar, distant, formal: "Maya, don't drink it."

"Drink what?" I say over my mother's whining.

"Mari, you can't let her drink it." It's my father's voice. My father as I knew him: Steven Devine.

"Stop it, stop it!" I yell to him. "I said I didn't want to see you!"

"But I only want to help you," he says in a monotone and then steps out from behind the doorframe. He looks young, like I have never seen him, his hair shaved close to his scalp, body lean, his blue eyes wide like a child's. "I only wanted to tell you not to drink that." He points to the table, to a large baby bottle filled with milk. "Mari's mother put something in it, Maya. She wants to get rid of you. Please don't drink it."

"I wasn't planning to," I say and he lifts one corner of his mouth into a half smile.

Mother still moans and cries on the floor. She turns her head to look at us standing over her and then closes her mouth, creating silence in the room. Then she stands and walks towards the counter. She takes a knife from the drawer and looks me in the eyes. I feel her hopelessness sink into my core.

Before I can stop her, she plunges the knife into her belly, doubling over, spilling two kinds of blood onto the floor.

My own screams are what wake me.

I don't remember where I am until I smell it. India. Dirt and rain mingle with curry in the smoky air around our open fire. Amar is beside me, leaning his bare back against a rotten log.

"What?" he says. His hair is messy and he has bags under his eyes. He's been smoking hash most of the night, and it often makes him snarly in the morning.

I choke on dirt that my nose has vacuumed in from the ground. My eyelids are crusty from choppy sleep.

"I had a nightmare, I guess," I say. He looks away. He's not in the mood for it today. One thing I have learned about my father, Amar, is that he has good days and bad days. Sometimes he can look at you with all-encompassing joy, and sometimes he doesn't care if you're there at all.

"Was it about your mother?" he finally asks me. I nod with pinched lips. "Have these years with me not taught you anything?" he says, almost annoyed. "Your mother is still alive, only in different form. She is still around you, with you." Then he sighs and looks back towards the crackling fire at his feet.

All the days of the last two years have melted into one. One long day of meditating, collecting money from passing strangers, sleeping in filth, smoking the channel pipe, and sitting silently with my real father, while he protects me from wandering hands and eyes and dozes in and out of drug-induced sleep.

Today, he's got a sort of greyness around his head that is hard to look at.

"Sometimes I feel like maybe she didn't exist at all." I look at Amar and wish he would open his eyes.

"There she is now," he says mockingly. "Hello, Marigold, nice to see you again." He nods his head to the sky and opens one hand in from of him as if saying, "Why, come in."

"You're crazy, I think," I tell him but he only smiles, creating a curvature in his grey beard.

Allison Baggio

"Crazy is as we perceive it," he says.

I pull a string of my matted hair out in front of my face. The hair is oily and sticky and puffed up in dreads. "Can you believe I was once in a shampoo commercial?" I say to Amar, hoping to change the subject.

"Shampoo. I can barely remember such a thing," he says placing the flats of his hands over his face.

Bathing in the Ganges River made me sick for the first six months. The remnants of dead things in the muddy water made me hurl up everything I ate for hundreds of meals.

"You will get used to it," the sadhu men told me, patting me on my head when they passed me doubled over in the dirt out behind the shelter. And they were right. My mouth tasted like spicy vomit so many times that it must have grown tired. After six months, not only could I bathe in the Ganges, I could drink the water from the tap by the road, I could eat whatever Indian food Amar found for me, and most importantly I had the strength to become more aware of my biological father.

He hardly ate. I'm not sure if this started with my arrival, or if he hadn't been eating for a while. From the look of him I would say he gave up on food years ago. He would put food down in front of me — rice, curry, vegetables — and keep back only a few handfuls for himself. A few handfuls that he would chew slowly with his mouth closed, transfixed by no exact point ahead of him. When his chewing finished, he would return to his meditation, which continued throughout much of the day. Sometimes I would join him, trying to find that centre within myself, that place where all my thoughts are silenced. Other times I would look around, at people passing, dragging cows through the streets. I would look at the people who looked at me, at my body, wrapped in bright-coloured cloth, and my light face and eyes. Sometimes I would just study him, pretend I was lounging in his grey beard sliding down his brown shoulders.

When he looked at me, he did it like he was taking me apart, piece by piece, and trying to find out what I was made of. Sometimes it seemed like he was trying to see my mother, like she was still living in my eyeballs or stretched out across my skin. He looked at me like I was a novelty from a Niagara Falls gift shop, like he was wondering if he should bother reaching into his pocket to find the four bucks that would let him keep me.

The other sadhus in the area seemed to respect Amar well enough. They gave him smoke from their pipes (and me too, occasionally), they put their dirty hands on his back, practised yoga with him, and bowed their heads when he passed. He got many handouts from random people, but he only ever took what he needed. He told me that the less he had, the more he had, period. And that's why he was here. That's why he had left my mother.

We are standing over a dead body. The man in orange robes. The man whom Amar said was originally from Rishikesh. His name was Ananta, and this morning he chose to start a new life.

"'Tis nothing but Mahasamadhi, the yogi's final conscious exit from his body," Amar tells me as we look down on him, his eyes closed like he is resting, even through the rain that has started. I feel tears in my eyes.

To me, it all smacks of tragedy. Just yesterday, this man, now dead with his back against a tree, had given me an extra blanket during the first monsoon rain at night.

"Find warmth, girl," Ananta had said to me, and I took his blanket, huddling with the others under the makeshift shelter.

"Don't cry for him, Maya," Amar says now. "As a yogi, he created a soul free from resistance. He made all amends with this earthly life. And now he has kicked the frame, as they say."

I raise my arms, almost like I'm trying to touch the calm expressions on their faces as they pass by. One by one they bow their prayer hands towards him. From their minds I hear steady Hindu chants, solemn goodbyes, and complacent humming. "But how can no one be sad?" I ask Amar.

"They are not happy. They are not sad. They are beyond these types of feelings."

"What will happen to his body?"

"He'll be cremated in one of the burning ghats by the river. Come, let's go inside now. It's time for afternoon prayers." I don't move, feeling stuck in calm, grounded, away from all thoughts.

"But I never thought that death could not be a sad thing," I say.

"You learn something every day," he says, stroking his oily beard.

That night we sleep inside an old monastery that has been offered to us. The rain pounds on the plaster roof like it's intent on getting through. We lie on thin cots laid out along the floor and I am use my backpack, filled with my only possessions, as a pillow. Our bodies are wrapped in hash smoke that went up before dusk. Amar speaks to me through the dark.

"Tomorrow, we are to go on pilgrimage to Agra. We must find a permanent place to sleep during the monsoons."

"What if I don't want to go?" I whisper into black air.

"This temple is only temporary. The weather is too dangerous, food is scarce. We must travel and seek the assistance of strangers and tourists."

I don't respond to him, not yet. Instead I flip my fingers through the butterfly bracelets still on my wrists, bracelets that tinkle against each other, creating breaks in the silence.

"What if I don't go with you?" I say.

"Then you don't."

"What if I went back to New Delhi, and back to Canada?"

"Only you know that."

"Will you be mad?" He says nothing. I wait. I want him to hug me, like a father. Like I'm daddy's little girl. I want him to plead from his core that he can't bear to see me go.

It will be different without you, I finally hear him think.

Is that all? Different?

Not good or bad. Less bright though, I'll admit.

We fall asleep after that.

The next morning, I say goodbye to Amar at the Varanasi bus station. He walked me there to make sure I got on the right bus, and accepted money along the way to have enough for my ticket. "Shiva blesses you," he said each time someone handed him a coin.

We stand in front of each other in awkward silence, his head wrapped in a white turban for the journey, his knuckles clutching a walking stick. Around his head are the most beautiful purple swirls of light.

You have this purple light, too, Amar thinks. I nod and smile without speaking.

I reach in and pull out the soft-covered book, tattered with dog-ears, my *Bhagavad Gita*. I'd never shown it to him before, kept it stuffed at the bottom of my backpack these last couple of years.

"It was my mother's," I say, holding it out to him. He turns it over in his hand.

"I gave it to her," he says and smiles. "I had this last when I was at my mother's cabin outside Peterborough, before she died. I remember the cabin well — behind the big rock, off the road, on the Indian River." He tucks the book under his arm. "And so it has made the long journey back to the hands it came from."

"Like me," I say, wiping my dreads off my face and securing my backpack on my shoulders. He leans in and kisses me on the forehead. Then he turns and limps away from me. Just like that. Like an old man looking for a shady place to sit.

"Wait — will I ever see you again?" I yell after him.

He turns towards me briefly, shrugs his bare shoulders and raises his palms towards the sky. Then, he leaves, clipping his sandals away through the sand.

———

Once off the bus in New Delhi, I find my way back to Grandfather Raj's guided only by the dim memory of my first visit there. I knock, three times, and finally let myself into the dimly lit house, learning soon that he's sick in bed and hasn't the strength to show enthusiasm at my return.

I'm happy to find that my return plane ticket has been waiting for me while I have been living with Amar in Varanasi. And all it takes to arrange my flight back to Toronto is for me to bring Grandfather Raj his rotary dial in bed and prop his head up with my stained arm. Canada has been fading like a childhood dream: the people I knew there — Aunt Leah, Buffy, Elijah, Corey Hart. The things — school desks, streetcars, shopping malls, television, cleanliness. My last night in India progresses slowly, my body laid out on the floor of Grandfather Raj's guest room (after growing discomfort from the softness of the bed), while he snores from his bedroom, sending rumbles through the stale air of the house.

Aunt Leah is waiting for me when my plane lands in Toronto. When I called her to tell her I was coming home, her voice came back raspy and breathy, like she was a ghost on the other end. We hadn't spoken since I left, but I had sent her letters and found a pile from her waiting for me at Grandfather Raj's. She was back in school, studying theatre. She wanted to know when I was coming back.

The first thing she does, after she hugs me, is tell me I stink and that I'm too skinny. Just like a mother would.

"And what have you done to your hair?" she says, holding a

dreadlock up in the air like she just peeled a leech off her foot. Her own hair is cut short, neat and tidy around her scalp and dyed a kind of plum colour. She looks like she's lost weight.

"They're called dreadlocks," I say. "They are all the Indian rage among those who don't wash."

I squint my eyes. The shiny chrome and speckled carpet of the terminal is making me dizzy. Advertising boards assault me with their beautiful people and catchy slogans.

"You told me you looked different, but I never would have imagined this!" She scans me up and down, scraping her lips with her teeth and shaking her head.

"Can we go now?" I say, tired of being gawked at.

"Maya, what happened to you over there?" She asks this with all seriousness and so I answer her with the same.

"I threw up a lot, I slept outside, I smoked a hash pipe, and I met my real father." Her eyes blink wide.

"What's he like?"

"He's not really a fatherly type. He's a sadhu — y'know, one of India's wandering holy men — which means he doesn't have a lot, nor does he want a lot, but that's fine."

"Maya, you're so *different*!"

"It has been two years, Leah."

People stare at me as I walk with Aunt Leah through the airport. I guess it's my crusty pink top that gapes open in the front, allowing the black letters of "Maya" to peek out from the skin on my chest. Maybe it's the rings on my toes, or my hair, or maybe there's something else different about me, something more important.

Chapter Thirty-Two

The apartment feels hollow without Buffy in it. Aunt Leah tells me that she's married a deaf man and they have been away honeymooning in Africa for the last three weeks.

"God, I wish you could have been at the wedding, Maya. It was so gorgeous." Aunt Leah scrapes scrambled eggs onto my plate. It's my third morning home — August 5, 1993.

"Don't they find it hard to communicate with each other?" I push the eggs to the corner of my plate, my stomach still a bit queasy.

"Buffy holds his hands when he does sign language and she does it back to him. She's getting quite good." Aunt Leah twitters her fingers in front of her face. "And he knows how to speak to a certain extent, so that helps."

"Good for them."

"As she said during her wedding speech, with her ears and his eyes, they're a complete set!"

"Makes sense, I guess."

"Ben is such a sweet guy — you'd like him."

"Don't tell me he's a musician or something."

"No, he's a photographer too. That's why they're in Africa, you know, photographing the world's most powerful beasts. She finally has someone to give her some valid critiques of her work."

"I'm happy for her. How's school going?"

Aunt Leah stands and crosses her hands on her chest. "Maya, I love it. I have finally found my calling. The lights, the crowd." She raises her hands towards the fixture over the dining room table. "I have found what makes me passionate. I am living my most authentic life." She drops her head and swings her arms out behind her in a bow.

Aunt Leah wants to become an actress. Last year, she enrolled herself in the dramatic arts program at Ryerson. She said the pretending she did in her previous jobs was what inspired her to get into acting. "Real world experience" is what she called it.

I hold my hand out towards her, my mother's healing stones in my palm.

"Aunt Leah, I want you to have these." She looks down at my hand.

"But they were your mother's," she says.

"I know. I don't need them anymore." She picks them up. "Keep them in your pocket for luck." She closes her fingers around them and looks up at me.

"What are you going to do now?" she asks, and I shrug. "He's

been calling. Steven. He still wants to see you, if you're interested."
I shrug again. "Not to rush you or anything."

"I've got a good idea of the forgiveness I need to make. And to
who."

"Elijah Roughen called too, looking for you."

"What did you tell him?"

"I told him you went to see your father and he wanted me to tell
you he was sorry." *I can't tell her he's engaged*, she thinks.

"I don't care if he's engaged," I say, and she looks up with her
eyebrows kissing her hairline. "I'm never getting married."

"Never say never," Aunt Leah says, standing up to dump my
uneaten eggs into the garbage bin.

———

It takes me two weeks — a few days after the eighth anniversary of
my mother's death, and my own twentieth birthday — to ask Aunt
Leah to call him. He's in Toronto two days later.

I've got the address of his hotel — the Comfort something —
written on a little piece of paper she gave me, his room number
scrawled underneath.

Room 309. It all comes down to Room 309.

I have no idea what I'm going to say when he opens the door.
Years of pretending things didn't exist have left me with a distinct
fear of confrontation. And perhaps that's why it's taken me so long
to agree to see him. Why I travelled to India to try and escape the
memory of him.

After taking the subway to Yonge Station — forced to stand

amid the rush hour commuters, stuck under some guy's sweaty armpit — I finally make it into the late afternoon sunlight and walk down Charles Street. Everyone around me seems to be going about their business — sweeping sidewalks, drinking coffee, arguing with each other. I see the mosaic of colours above their heads and absorb their collective inner complaints about the weather and the long work hours, and the pinch of their high heeled shoes. I want to tell them all to shut up, to toughen up because it could always be worse than this — it is worse than this, somewhere.

The hallway outside his room smells like cigarette smoke has been slowly seeping out from under the doors for decades. To prepare mentally, I try to focus on all that my father went through: losing a wife, a daughter. And I think for a moment about the things he sacrificed to be there for Mother — and how he never told anyone her secret.

I knock on the door. I lean over and fiddle with my toe ring while I wait for it to open.

"Maya?"

I look up, and for a tiny second, I almost believe that this female voice could belong to my father. But it's not him, of course.

"Maya, you're here. Come in."

This voice and this face I remember distinctly from the time shortly after I lost my mother. Her skin is still soft and olive like an exotic porcelain doll's. She's got red, red lips and hoop earrings with diamonds on them. She's wearing a black sundress that shows her cleavage. She's more beautiful than I remember.

"Connie, I told you I wanted to get the door." This voice is my father's. It echoes and is coming from what I assume is the bathroom.

Then he comes to stand in front of me. Beside Connie.

"Maya," he says. "You're all grown up now."

"Yup, seven years will do that. Just had my twentieth birthday — Aunt Leah made cupcakes."

"Leah's been the best, hasn't she?" he says, but he's interrupted.

"Well, I think you're just gorgeous, my dear," Connie says in her crisp Spanish accent. "Your eyes are beautiful. All you need to do is blow out that hair and you'd be all set."

"It doesn't blow out," I tell her. "These are knots."

"Well, boy cuts are really in right now."

"Connie, go get Hailey ready," my father says, and she goes back into the bathroom. He has tears in his eyes. He's got way more wrinkles than the last time I saw him and the grey has taken over all his hair. He's wearing an aqua striped Ralph Lauren golf shirt and khaki pants that fall under his heels. His face is clean-shaven. His "Mari" tattoo is well covered — if it's still there at all.

"Who's Hailey?" I say. I'm standing just inside the door now, and he has his arm reaching out as if he's going to shut it behind me.

"My daughter, Maya. Connie is my wife now, and three years ago we had a daughter."

"Hmmm, and you didn't think to invite me to the wedding?" I say jokingly, but by the grey blobs showing up around my father's face, I know that he is in no mood for jokes.

"I would have," he says seriously. "I would have invited you if we were, you know, in touch." He coughs uncomfortably.

"No matter."

Then I smile. And that, that tiny lifting of lip corners, is the extent of my own apology.

He starts in on his.

"Maya, I don't know how to begin to say sorry for what I did. For so long I've wanted to make things right again between us, but I didn't want to push you."

"Thank you," I say.

"I was just so shaken up back then, about everything that had happened, it was like I wasn't myself anymore. I was walking around the world in a daze, and I had no idea what to do next."

"I think I felt the same way," I say.

"To leave you alone like that, it was unacceptable, but as foolish as it sounds now, I thought it was the best thing. I never felt like I was a proper father to you. I had so much hidden bitterness towards your mother."

I raise my eyebrows at him, but he doesn't stop.

"And when I saw you . . . I thought of him. Your biological father. It reminded me over and over what had happened, and after she died, I just couldn't stand it anymore. I just didn't know what to do or say to make it all better."

"There was nothing you could have said—"

"Quite honestly, I was selfish. Totally selfish."

I don't disagree with him.

"I also want you to know that I never stopped worrying about you. You probably didn't know, but I checked on you most nights when you were sleeping, just stood at your doorway like an idiot half the time watching your little chest rise and fall and feeling more lost with each breath. I sat in my car and watched you go into school some mornings. I talked to your teacher to make sure you were doing okay."

"I felt you around me sometimes."

"It really was hard for me to lose our family."

"You've got a pretty nice family now," I say. "You didn't need me or Mother for that."

"Please don't blame Connie for this, Maya." He's sweating at the temples. "She didn't even know you were still around. She still thinks you were gone to live with your grandparents. Of course, she wouldn't have let this stupidity go on."

"I don't blame anyone," I say. "I've learned one important thing in the last two years: it feels a lot lighter to just let go of everything."

"It's just that when I lost your mother—"

"When *we* lost her," I say. "When *we* both lost her."

"Yes, when we lost her, it was a huge blow. All those years of waiting for things to get better with her, and then, well they got worse. They got as bad as they could be."

"Death doesn't have to be sad," I say, surprising myself and wondering about my own sincerity.

"You're brave, just like your mother was," he says. "The truth is that I think I realized that your mother was never mine to lose." His hair is slicked back off his face with some sort of gel. I smell citrus when he leans in to hug me.

It is an awkward sort of hug — stiff and distant — but one that seems appropriate and long-awaited.

Connie comes back into the room with a young child squirming in her arms. She has golden brown pigtails and wears an OshKosh jumper. A halo of purple light around her entire body seems to reach to the ceiling. She has my father's eyes — serious blue eyes that question and consider.

"Hailey, this is Maya," Connie says. "Your big sister. She just returned from a long vacation to India. You know where the Taj Mahal is, don't you, Hailey?" Connie turns to me. "She's very smart."

Hailey runs from her mother and wraps herself around my father's leg. He picks her up and nuzzles her hair, kisses her softly on the cheek. *Now that's a father.*

I take a step towards them. "Hello, Hailey," I say in a whisper, feeling like I've entered some sort of time warp. That, or all the years are happening at once; maybe Hailey is actually me. Maybe Steven Devine is actually my father.

He puts the little girl down and Connie grabs her by the hand.

"We'll wait for you in the lobby," she says, leading Hailey out the door.

"Bye, Maya," Hailey says. *I wonder where we're going now*, I hear her think.

And from Connie's head, just a little bit of humming that matches the apple-green streaks bouncing off her forehead. Warm green, like a real mother.

"Does she know?" I ask him when the door has clicked behind them and we have sat together on the couch by the window.

"Know what?"

"That I'm not really your daughter."

"You are."

"Well, not really."

He rubs the flats of his fingers over his forehead and then scratches his head near his temple. "No, Maya, I haven't gone into that with her." His expression hangs limp like he has no strength to lift it. He studies my eyes for a reaction. He looks into me so hard that I have to look away. Then, I find myself smiling at how surreal the situation feels.

"Pretty big secret to keep," I say.

"I guess I've gotten good at it."

I smile again and he grins and looks at his feet. There is a long pause between us. "I think I'm going to go home now," I say to break it.

"Maya, you're welcome to stay longer."

"But Connie and Hailey are waiting."

"I don't feel like I've apologized enough."

"It's not bad, it's not good. It's just how it is," I say. I stand up from the green acrylic loveseat and take a step towards the door. "And I accept your apology."

He leans over and hugs me again, a bit softer than the first time. "What are you going to do now, Maya?"

I shrug my shoulders and bottom lip together. "Find my own home," I guess.

"Take care of yourself," he says. *Don't forget about me.*

"How could I?" I say, and he smiles.

I turn and walk down the hall, the word "forgiveness" bouncing around in my brain. When I get home I tell Aunt Leah everything and she holds me in her arms. She doesn't notice I'm not actually crying.

The next day, I tell her I'm leaving.

"But you just got back," Aunt Leah says, her mouth open in shock.

"I can't be here. Not in the city with all these people around me. I feel suffocated, like the buildings are going to fall on me."

"Where will you go?"

"I'm going out to Peterborough. I'll buy a tent, find some campground." I don't tell her about the cabin — it seems almost too intimate to mention aloud.

"I don't think you should do that. Winter's coming . . . you can't be out there on your own."

"I'll be fine. I'll find a job, lodging, whatever. I'll figure it out just like I did in India. If there is one thing I learned out there, it's that I don't really need anyone but myself to get by."

She looked at me for a long time, like she was taking a mental picture of each curve of my face, each strand of my hair. "You'd better call and let me know what you're doing. Otherwise, I'm coming out there for you."

"I will."

"And take warm socks and food and all that. Don't be foolish."

She hugs me and I whisper "thank you" into the heat of her hair.

———————

I don't fit in on the Greyhound to Peterborough. Everyone has baseball hats and T-shirts with beer logos on them. They say "fuck" a lot and talk loudly to each other over the seats. They munch on Doritos and throw the wrappers on the ground. The guy in front of me turns around and asks me if I want to get laid.

"No, thank you" is my response. I clutch an empty notebook, a thick one that would fit notes for five courses. Everything I own is in a duffle bag at my feet: two pairs of pants, three pairs of underwear, a grey sweater Aunt Leah gave me for the trip, my mother's journal,

and a small Ziploc bag of almonds and cashews. The butterfly bracelets, now tarnished, are still on my wrists. I have a brand new blue-
ink Bic pen tucked in the bag's front pocket.

"Your loss, ho-bag," I hear the guy ahead of me say. The guys
are drinking beer on the bus without the driver noticing. I knew I
should have sat closer to the front.

"That girl is a freak," one guy says and his friend across the aisle
turns around to see me.

"Cool dreads," the guy wearing a Labatt Blue hat and T-shirt
says to me.

"Thank you."

He turns around again towards the front. They are students
going back to Trent for school. I am left wondering what they could
possibly be learning.

Someone's playing music out of a portable player. My heart
sticks in my esophagus. Corey Hart — he's still following me.
They're playing his song and calling it retro.

> *I am by your side*
> *In this truth I will confide*
> *You can always count on me*
> *I will never hide you see, oh no*
> *'Cause I will never disappear*
> *Turn the darkest corner I'll be there*

"Turn that shit off," someone yells, and Soul Asylum's "Runaway
Train" comes on.

It's early September, Labour Day weekend, and hot, almost
thirty degrees Celsius, but nothing compared to the dry heat in
India. Nothing I can't handle. The bus ushers me into Peterborough

for the first time. We drive through town, up hills, down one-way streets, into awkward intersections before pulling in at the downtown Greyhound terminal. I let the drunk students pile out ahead of me. One of them folds over the curb and pukes on the sidewalk before getting up to join his buddies.

I have an address and nothing else. *Forgiveness, forgiveness, forgiveness*, I think as I get in a taxi.

"I need to go to 235 King Street," I tell the dark-haired man behind the steering wheel. He sucks on his cigarette.

"Any chance you could put that out?" I ask him.

"You would like me to put out the cigarette?"

"You got it." To my surprise, he does, tossing the butt onto the wet pavement — the rain has just started.

He drops me off in front of a six-floor apartment building. I pay the cabbie with the money Aunt Leah gave me, adding a little extra for putting out the cigarette. He has another one lit before he pulls out of the parking lot.

She's in apartment 311. Third floor, eleventh apartment. I take the steps slowly, stumbling under the weight of my duffle bag and brand new rolled-up sleeping bag. I step up onto the top step like I'm stepping up to receive an award. A woman with a hooked nose in a green velour housecoat meets me in the hall.

"Yes," she says with a crooked smile.

"I'm looking for Eleanor McCann," I say.

"Well, she's in number 311, but who knows if she'll open the door or not." The woman holds her fingers up straight beside her mouth. "She's not very social."

"She's my grandmother," I tell the woman matter-of-factly, and she apologizes and goes back into 304.

I knock four times before I realize it's open. Open so that you just have to push, not even turn the knob.

"Grandmother," I say as I walk in, noticing how strange the word feels. "Grandmother," I say again, just to prove it.

A tiny voice from the living room: "Hello, there."

"Grandmother McCann, it's me, Maya."

She's sitting in a blue La-Z-Boy facing the TV. There's a man on the screen trying to sell her a new sofa.

"Sylvia?" She turns her head to look at me with her shrivelled face, deep-set eyes, and flesh puckered at the mouth.

"Grandmother McCann, is it okay that I'm here?"

"You sit right down here," she says pointing to a folding chair beside her. She's trapped behind a TV tray with a bag of WonderBread and some cheese slices still in the plastic. "I started to worry when I didn't see you yesterday at Mass. You are always up there in the first pew."

"No, I think you're mistaken. I'm not . . ." She raises her hand and drops it to her heart, hidden under a floral muumuu and what smells like a thin layer of Vicks VapoRub.

"Of course you aren't. I cannot believe I didn't recognize you when you came in."

"Grandmother McCann . . ." I open my eyes wide and wait for her to say my name.

"Marigold!" she says. "My beautiful daughter, Marigold. You finally came back to see me."

She doesn't remember me. I've come two hours by bus, and she doesn't even know who I am. I think about how she reacted when she found out I was going to be born, how she left me in the park, poisoned my baby bottle — or was that just a dream?

"Marigold dear, I've waited all these years to tell you how sorry I am for what happened. My life without you has been a shadow of what it should have been. First I lose your father, and then you and the baby . . . I should have been much more careful with that baby."

I take a deep breath, look to the ceiling and sigh, rolling back the tears with my hot breath.

"Tell me, Marigold, how long will you be staying?" She is reaching out to me with her crooked old fingers. I let her stroke my bare arm.

"I'm sorry, I can't stay long." How long does forgiveness take when the person doesn't know who you are? "I'll stay for dinner, but then I have to go."

"But I have nothing prepared."

"I'll get takeout. You just stay here."

I leave my stuff on the floor of her apartment, and by the time I return with a paper bag filled with Chinese food, Grandmother McCann has fallen asleep in her chair. Still tucked behind the TV table, she's wet herself and it's dripped down and created circles on the carpet.

I move the table aside, pick her up and carry her to the bedroom, amazed by how light she is.

"Thank you, Marigold," she says after I have changed her clothes and laid her into her bed. "Did I tell you I'm sorry about the baby?"

"I know, Mother," I whisper. "I forgive you."

As I leave, the light around her face glows blue to opal white, heating the space between us.

The cab driver hasn't heard of it, but I get him to take me out there anyway.

"Near Douro, you say?"

"Yes, an old cabin with a huge rock in front of it. It's on the Indian River."

"A rock? That'll be easy to find."

"I'll pay you to help me find it."

"All right, lady, but we're losing our light here."

We drive to the outskirts of town, past open fields with greasy tractors, past new highways being laid, past roadside stands selling autumn corn. He slows down just past Douro and goes south. Then, he turns down the first gravel road with no signs, our tires slowly crunching pebbles, me bouncing in the back seat. The sun has almost set completely. Soon, we use our headlights as probes, combing up and down dusty roads with only trees as scenery, occasionally coming across a house lit by a single light bulb, or a cottage boarded up for fall. *That's not it, that's not it.* With nothing from the front seat, not even from inside the cab driver's mind, I start to consider that maybe I am searching for something that doesn't want to be found.

And then something taps me on the shoulder.

"What about that!" I say.

"It's a boulder, yes, I'll give you that, but there isn't no cottage 'round here."

"Let me out of the car."

"I can't leave you here, lady. It's dangerous at night. There are black bears."

"I don't care, let me out." I open the door the second the car stops, and reach back in to give him the last of my money.

"I can't leave you here, lady," he says again, not taking the twenty-dollar bill.

"Look, there was a driveway," I say pointing to a dirt road, covered up by brush. "A driveway must lead somewhere."

"You're taking a chance."

"So I am." I slam the car door, throw the money in the open window and steer my feet in the direction of the bush.

"I'll come back in an hour just in case you need a ride back!" I hear the man yell out the window. I ignore his offer.

The car speeds away, leaving me in the intimacy of the near-black night. A moon fades in, stars pop out.

I push through tree branches with my bare arms, stamp on leaves with my sandals, and work myself deeper into the bush.

I don't have to go far. I find it. The cabin where I was conceived — now broken down and covered with vines and rot. It looks like part of it might even have caught on fire at some point.

The cabin where Amar took my mother.

The door pushes open with my hand. "There is nothing valuable in here," people must say when they find it. Nothing valuable to them. A bunch of crappy boards, cracked windows, mice droppings, broken bottles.

The perfect spot to be alone with myself, and to try to make my mother real again.

Chapter Thirty-Three

The inside of the cabin is filled with dust, dirt, and stagnant air. It reminds me of the space inside my mother's teepee — lonely, like it's waiting for something. I throw my backpack of food and clothes into the corner and unroll my sleeping bag onto the ripped, out-dated couch. Was it here they sat?

It starts to get dark so I reach into my bag and get a candle and match. I light it, and as I did in India, sit quietly in the glow from the flame, dancing, flickering just for me.

This place is dripping with parts of my mother. And of Amar. It is filled with all that they both were, and all that they never became: together or apart. A tree branch hits the window outside, shaking in the wind, alerting me over and over. Tap, tap, tap — is it my mother welcoming me back?

The memories of this room are suffocating.

I eat some banana chips from my pocket, and then close my eyes and try to meditate. I go into myself and it feels familiar — nothing can get me in here. But soon, like a burning instinct, my eyes spring open and I know what I have to do. I dig into my bag for the notebook I brought, *my* notebook. It's thick, and its empty pages seem to call me by name: *Maya, Maya, it's time.* Yellow and green flashes spring from my body like jumping grasshoppers in the dark.

I start writing as soon as I screw the legs back on a single chair and clear some old newspaper and ash off the table in the kitchen. I start the story of my mother's death from the beginning. The story of when my mother kicked her frame.

My pen scratches on the paper like I am carving history. I push so hard that I make indents on the next page, and the next, and the next. I write about the teepee, about when my mother refused treatment, shaved her head. I tell the story of when the people came to try to help her, when they waited outside our house to see her, how they prayed in a circle for her to live. I also write about how, maybe, she didn't deserve all the attention she received.

I write about my father, his moodiness, his longing to help, his frustration, the way he used to pace the hallway when he felt sad.

I write about the baby, my little sister who never got a chance because she was dying before she could even see the world.

I write about the day we dragged my mother to the hospital, the day I got my period for the first time. How she seemed to see something that I couldn't near the end. How brave she was through it all.

I think about the people who've hurt me, and whether it was even about me at all. I think about the people I may have hurt, like Mrs. Roughen, Elijah, Connie, and Jackie — was she really so awful? Was there in fact something within me that was hurting all along?

Outside the cabin, the rain has started again. Water dribbles on the broken windows and rotten wood, churning up the musty odour of memory and the whispering sound of secrets that were never spoken.

I keep writing, page after page, line after line, filling the notebook with the story of my mother and her exit from this earth. I scribble tiny words until my hand aches, until my fingers seize, until my head spins, until my eyes can hardly focus on the page in front of me. I steady myself and finish the story of my mother's death, as I remember it. My perspective, my truth. I reach into myself, and what I discover is that my mother never really went anywhere. And that it's all real — all of it. Even the illusions are part of the truth.

When I'm finished, I close the notebook on the table. No more empty pages. No more lines. I close the notebook and push it away from me. A shiver slithers up my spine. The sun has set for the second time since I started writing. Sleep pulls at me. I'm weak with hunger and thirst.

Instead of lying down to sleep, I open the cabin door and go outside, walking ten paces over moss and cracked dirt. I hear the swish of water through the black on the other side of the overgrown trees. Was it here? Was it here they made snow angels? Was it here that I was conceived? I drop to the ground. It calls me. I put my back against a tree.

Above me the stars greet me like they have been waiting, pricking points of light all through my body, relaxing me. "All is forgiven," I say but no one hears. No one but the wind, and a little red cardinal on a branch.

Fly away if you decide, the bird says without opening its beak. *You're still here when you go!* He flaps his wings through pine and disappears.

And then it all comes down to me. Me and this night. Me and this story. Buried in a thousand shades of green, by an old cabin where I started to be. That which has been blocking my vision has dissolved. Could it be that I know all I need to know?

I close my eyes and see nothing but white light, and then flashes of memories that send warmth through my body.

I'm in Aunt Leah and Buffy's hot apartment hugging them both at the same time. Aunt Leah is round and cozy under my right arm, and Buffy is fragile and familiar under my left. I can feel hot breath on my face from each of their mouths.

I'm sitting in the Retro Café with Elijah shortly after I came to Toronto. He's smoking a cigarette and holding my hand across the table. We're laughing in a hushed way, about how strange it feels to be looking at each other again.

I'm in India. Amar and I are meditating together in the dirt. A huge flock of black birds unfurls above us, flapping their wings frantically across the blue sky. We turn at the same time and beam at each other.

With that, I see a tunnel. The same old tunnel I have heard about, with shining lights trying to suck me in. In my peripheral vision: moving shapes, people, spirits, walking towards the end. In my body: calm, centeredness, a sense that I am one with all these other figures, that nothing can stop us if we all walk together. So I follow.

And then she appears, out of nowhere, or out of the only

somewhere that really is. My mother. Young, strong, not scary like when I saw her in the closet, and she's holding a baby — a healthy, pink, wiggling baby that smiles and laughs when my mother tickles her feet. My sister that never was. I stop to watch them. Mother looks up at me and smiles.

I reach out and she puts the baby in my arms. My sister is surrounded by amber light that keeps her warm and comforts her. She has no tears, only grins that ripple like waves over her face.

We sink into one another, but soon the baby pulls away and looks towards her mother — we both do — and I hand her back. Mother smiles again and takes a step backwards. I stretch my arms out towards them in urgency. Grasping at what was, what is.

Then, like warm water pouring down over my head, I can feel their peace, their happiness. Mother begins to walk away until I can barely distinguish the shape of her body from the dark shapes beside her. Away, until they are all one with the white light. I'm alone, but not. There is a giant magnet pulling me back to where I came from.

And with a thought I'm back, over the cabin, hovering in the air. Is that me down below? I'm laid out on the ground, flat on my back. Not me but the shell of me. I see that the sun is coming up, and I know it's not over. With a long sucking breath, I plunge down and land back in my body.

I'm awake and looking up at the sky, brilliant with pink and orange from the approaching day. It's warm and the rising sun heats my face just like it did in India. *There is so much more for me than this,* I think, *so many more.*

I stand up and stumble back into the cabin through the door that doesn't close all the way. I'm dizzy and weak and longing to get out of here. All my things are laid out where I left them, and my notebook with my mother's story is closed and lying on the table.

I start to frantically sweep piles of old newspapers and twigs into one corner of the room with my foot, trying to make things more orderly than when I arrived. I push open the mildewed curtains so the sun shines in. I rub the sleeve of my shirt over the old kitchen countertop and across the windowsills, leaving dark smudges on my arm.

Next, I pack up my belongings into my bag, pick up the notebook and hold it lovingly against my chest. *This was you, Mother. Good or bad, this was it.*

I put the notebook under my arm and grab my things, leaving my sleeping bag unrolled on the couch. I stand in the doorway of the run-down cabin, looking into the empty room one more time. I hear a car pass by on the road and I wonder if another one will be by soon. The door creaks as I try my best to shut it. I turn then, looking towards the overgrown path that will lead me away from here.

Chapter Thirty–Four

My father takes my mother and me into the backyard. He wears his work suit and holds a paper bag in his hand. It's summertime. I am nine years old. My father clutches the top of the bag with white fingertips and then, pulls something out, like a rabbit from a hat, long and thin and wrapped in plastic.

"A bubble maker!" he tells us.

"But it looks like just a stick with some strings hanging down," I say.

"That's why we need this!" He takes out a pink bottle from his pocket, unscrews the white cap, and pours liquid into a bucket at his feet. "We can make bubbles, big ones, beautiful ones," he says while the bucket fills with water from the hose, spitting droplets on his pants.

My mother, impressed to the point of a small smile, pushes me forward, towards him.

"Go help your father," she says. "Go see what he wants to show you." Her smile shrivels back into ambivalence.

I take two steps towards him. He uses his index finger to loosen his tie. His other hand holds the hose.

"Take that out of the plastic," he instructs me, pointing to the string and stick leaning up against his pant leg. I do. "Now, dip it into this water." He puts the hose away. Dunking my arm up to my elbow in the soapy water, I soak the string. "Now, pull that out, separate the string and run around," he tells me. "You're going to love this!"

I look at my mother, my hand still hidden under suds. She nods, so I pull the sloppy string from the bucket and run towards the back fence.

Head-sized bubbles slip from the holes in the string, colours dancing on their skin. They dangle in the air before bursting on needles of emerald grass.

"I like it!" I tell him, and he laughs. My mother does too, giggles that hardly leave her mouth.

"Run faster, Maya!" she says waving her hands by her ears. "See how many you can keep in the air at one time."

I dip the rope again and take another dash around the yard, tripping my feet on the grass, skipping, looking towards the sky.

"Looks like your father brought you a nice present," my mother says, and I stop and look at her while bubbles break open on my body. Her cheeks are rosy like they have just been pinched, her eyes glow, and yellow and green buzz around her reddish hair.

I wonder: when a bubble disappears, what is the proof that it ever existed at all? Mist in the air, a lingering soapy smell, moisture on your face?

"I want to try it again!" I yell to my parents. I dunk the string again, pushing strands of sticky hair behind my ear. My father moves towards my mother, putting his hand on her hip. She rests her palm on the small part of his back and steps closer to him. I smile. The sun lights our bodies. We glow from the inside.

My arm swoops from the bucket in one grand motion, revealing the biggest bubble so far. As big as my entire body, it floats up in the air, bobbing, while rainbows dance all over its surface. I can see the shape of my mother laughing through the other side, full-out, so that her head flies back and her mouth opens wide.

My father pokes his finger into the bubble, creating only a dent in its side. Could it be that he is not pushing hard enough? Could it be that this bubble will never pop?

"Don't break it," I say. "Not yet."

ACKNOWLEDGEMENTS

Thank you to everyone who has ever encouraged my writing, especially during the inevitable times of self-doubt. To Elizabeth Ruth for speaking the words that helped me decide that yes, I too could get there if I just stuck with it. To the Humber School for Writers, and to Shaena Lambert for offering the first thoughtful and very lengthy critique of this book (it took me three years to get through your notes, but boy were they appreciated!).

Thanks also to the Humber School for Writers Literary Agency, and especially to Natalie St. Pierre for believing in Maya and in me as a writer — I am so lucky to have your enthusiasm on my side. To the wonderful team at ECW Press and especially Jen Hale for understanding this story in the exact same way as I do (we share a brain, don't you know?), and helping me bring it to its very best place. You truly were my midwife in the birthing of this novel.

Thank you to Corey and Julie Hart for being so gracious and supportive about the use of Corey's lyrics in this book. To all my friends and family who have shown their excitement about this novel and to Connie Yarkie, Lori Kerr, Lara McInnis, and Jeanette Simon for early reads and comments; also to Bianca Fera for taking my photo.

Warm thanks as well to my brother Andrew Exworth, my grandparents Ray and Janine Beaulieu, and my parents-in-law, Ron and Judy Baggio, for their encouragement. And of course, to my parents, Nancy and Terry Exworth, for always being there for me no matter what — love you, kiss, kiss. Thanks also to the Universe (or however you prefer to refer to it), for giving me yet another example of how thoughts can become things — mine created this book!

Finally, to my husband, Tom Baggio, and to my two beautiful little sweeties, Noah and Lily. Thank you for putting up with me while I write. Without even trying, you have given me everything.

LYRICS PERMISSIONS